Your favourite authors love to curl up with Cathy Bramley's feel-good fiction . . .

'Filled with warmth and laughter'
Carole Matthews

'Delightfully warm with plenty of twists and turns'
Trisha Ashley

'Warm, cosy and deliciously romantic'
Holly Martin

'A ray of sunshine'
Phillipa Ashley

'A real treat. No one does friendship
better than Cathy'
Karen Swan

'Magical, heart-felt and uplifting'
Carmel Harrington

'The perfect romantic tale'
Ali McNamara

'A heartwarming tale of self-discovery'
Woman & Home

'Charming, cosy, candlelit romance, all wrapped up
in a gorgeous setting'
Veronica Henry

Cathy Bramley is the *Sunday Times* Top Ten best-selling author of *The Summer That Changed Us*, *A Patchwork Family*, *My Kind of Happy*, *The Merry Christmas Project* and *The Lemon Tree Café*. Her other romantic comedies include *Ivy Lane*, *Appleby Farm*, *Wickham Hall*, *Conditional Love*, *The Plumberry School of Comfort Food* and *White Lies and Wishes*. She lives in a Nottinghamshire village with her family and a dog.

Cathy turned to writing after spending eighteen years running her own marketing agency. She has always been an avid reader, never without a book on the go, and now thinks she may have found her dream job!

Cathy loves to hear from her readers. You can get in touch via her website www.CathyBramley.co.uk, on Facebook @CathyBramleyAuthor, on Twitter @CathyBramley or on Instagram @CathyBramley

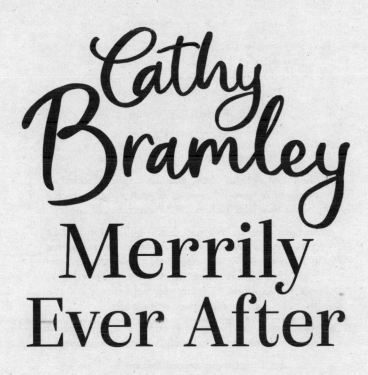

Cathy Bramley

Merrily Ever After

ORION

An Orion paperback

First published in Great Britain in 2022 by Orion Fiction
an imprint of The Orion Publishing Group Ltd
Carmelite House, 50 Victoria Embankment
London EC4Y 0DZ

An Hachette UK company

1 3 5 7 9 10 8 6 4 2

A CIP catalogue record for this book is
available from the British Library.

ISBN (Mass Market Paperback) 978 1 3987 0141 0
ISBN (eBook) 978 1 3987 0142 7

Typeset by Born Group
Printed and bound in Great Britain by Clays Ltd, Elcograf S.p.A.

MIX
Paper from
responsible sources
FSC® C104740

www.orionbooks.co.uk

This book is dedicated to Isabelle Broom,
founding member of the Omlit and
Juggared Society,
my forever friend, kumquat may

Prologue

Dear Mum,

I don't normally write you imaginary letters, do I? But it's been such a crazy year that I really want to share it with you, even if only like this — a letter in a notebook that you'll never read. Crazy in a good way, I'm happy to report, but I'd love to be able to tell you my secrets face to face and have you here to experience life alongside me.

No matter how happy I am, there will always be a piece of my heart aching with sadness, because even after all these years, I still miss you, Mum. I wish you'd been here to help me grow up, to launch me into adulthood, to be 'my person'.

What were you like, Sam Shaw, who were you? I wish I knew more about you. I wish I knew whether we're alike. I wish I'd known about my father too. If you were here now, I wouldn't let you dodge my questions and distract me like you did when I was a little girl. I'd make you tell me the story of how you two met and what happened to your relationship. I wonder whether he's still alive and where he lives, I don't even know if you told him he was my father. But if you did, maybe he thinks about me occasionally.

Most of the time, I'm sad that you're not here, but occasionally I'm angry. Angry that you left me alone in the world, that you didn't love me enough to stay alive, angry that no one helped you when you were ill. If only you'd been able to get the support you needed, maybe you'd still be here now. You were twenty-eight when you took your own life, much younger than I am now. Too young.

I've got people in my life who love me. Astrid, my old teacher, has always been there for me. Nell is the best friend I could wish for and as close to me as a sister. And, of course, now I'm slowly becoming part of Cole's family too. I'm not alone, but no one will ever take your place.

That's all I wanted to say really. That life is good and I'm happy. Another Christmas is upon us. It's going to be a special one this year, I can feel it in the air. But I'll miss you, Mum, I always will.

Love,
Merry xxx

Chapter One

Merry

There was no mistaking that autumn was making way for winter, I thought, as Cole and I, plus his children, set off for a walk after our Sunday lunch. Mornings were frosty, sometimes even *inside* the old-fashioned windows in Holly Cottage. Our double bed was piled high with cosy blankets, and hot chocolate with whipped cream had become my daily winter warmer after work – a treat which Harley and Freya had particularly enjoyed this week while they'd been staying with us during the school holidays.

Outside, most of the trees were bare now, except the holly bush in the front garden, which was rosy with berries, and like ours, the other homes along World's End Lane had daily twists of smoke spiralling from their chimneys. In the small Derbyshire town of Wetherley, where we lived, the council had erected the lights which would be officially switched on next week and this morning I'd heard my first Christmas song on the radio: Michael Bublé's velvety voice singing about a white Christmas.

It was a bit early to be thinking of Christmas, even for me, an avid festive fan. But the temperature was hovering above freezing and only my thick layers were preventing *me* from hovering just above freezing too.

I shivered and Cole squeezed my gloved hand.

'Chilly,' he asked, and then added with a grin, 'or was that a shiver of relief that the kids are going back to Lydia's tonight?'

Cole and I had only been living together since September, and this was the longest time they'd spent with us at the cottage. Yesterday, we'd carved pumpkins and then taken Freya trick or treating, while Harley met up with his friends. It was all very new to me, and I was loving every minute.

'Absolutely not!' I retorted. 'It has been great fun and I've enjoyed spending time with them. It has felt like . . .' I faltered, not sure whether to say what was on my mind.

'Go on,' he said, his eyes bright with encouragement.

'Like we're a family,' I admitted. 'It has been really fun.'

'Good.' He brought my hand to his lips and kissed it, smiling to himself. 'That's great.'

After leaving home via the gate Cole had installed in the back fence, we'd tramped through the woods separating Holly Cottage from the new houses, which his company had finished building in the spring. They were all occupied now and looking more lived-in as each season passed by.

Now, we'd emerged from the trees and the four of us were following the footpath along the river into town: nine-year-old Freya was skipping ahead, in a world of her own, and Harley was behind her, his gaze fixed on his phone. At thirteen, he was almost as tall as me; he'd had a growth spurt since the summer, when he'd relocated back to the UK from Canada with his mum and sister.

The plan for the afternoon was to burn off some energy and make room for a slice of freshly baked *apfel strudel*, which, according to my friend Astrid, would be out of the oven and cooling by the time we arrived at her flat in the Rosebridge retirement village.

Astrid was my old art teacher from school, she had always been like family to me, but now our bond was even stronger because she and Cole's dad, Fred, were 'courting', as Fred put it. He lived at Rosebridge too, but although they spent most of their time together, each had their own flats for a bit of space now and then.

'Merry?' Freya stopped in her tracks and whirled around, causing Harley to tut and elbow past her. Her cheeks were pink with cold, and the ends of her plaits were sticking out from under her woolly hat. She couldn't have looked more adorable if she tried.

'Yes, sweetheart?' I said, catching hold of her hand.

'Did you have a pet when you were growing up?' she asked.

I shook my head. 'My mum and I didn't have room because we lived in a very small flat.'

'Astrid lives in a flat,' Freya replied, 'and she has Otto the dog.'

'She does, but it's bigger than our flat was,' I said, not adding that, regardless of space, my mum didn't have the spare money to spend on a pet. 'Mind you, there was a snake at one of my foster homes,' I added, pulling a face at the memory. 'They used to feed it whole frozen chicks and mice.'

'Cool.' Harley looked at me over his shoulder. 'Maybe I'll ask for a snake. The boys at school would like that.'

'I don't think your mother would,' said Cole dryly.

I winced, imagining the look on Lydia's face when Harley suggested they got a snake, particularly when he told her where he'd got the idea from.

'They grow very big,' I said hurriedly. 'And live for years.'

'Even better,' replied Harley, nodding enthusiastically. He tapped his screen, mumbling under his breath as he typed, 'UK, pet snakes . . .'

'Daddy, did you have a pet?' Freya asked innocently.

Cole caught my eye before answering and we both suppressed a smile; this was well-trodden ground and all part of his daughter's campaign to get an animal of some description.

'I did,' he replied. 'Your granny had chickens, until the fox got them. And we had an old cat called Fergus, who only lost all his front fangs so we—'

'Changed his name to Fangless!' Freya finished for him. 'Poor Fergus. So could I . . .?'

'It's snowing!' Harley yelled suddenly. 'I just felt a snowflake on my face. YES!'

I looked up to the sky. A few tiny specks floated in the air. It was certainly cold enough, but it was a bit early in the season for Derbyshire to get its first snowfall.

'Hello, snow, I've missed you!' Freya squealed, instantly forgetting about her mission to get a pet.

She stretched her arms out, attempting to catch the snowflakes on her tongue.

'Me too,' said Harley heavily.

'Just sleet, I think,' Cole commented, examining the dots on the sleeve of his coat.

'Typical,' Harley muttered.

'You never know,' I said, noting Harley's disappointment. 'It might snow properly before the day is out.'

'I hope so, because then school will close, and I won't have to go. Not like in Whistler. The weather doesn't stop anything there,' Harley commented, his voice managing to combine hope with nostalgia.

I felt for him; while Freya had slipped back seamlessly into the life she'd had before their year in Canada, Harley was still missing what he'd left behind. It didn't sound as if he was too keen on school either.

I glanced at Cole to see if he'd picked up on his son's tone, but it didn't look like it. Instead, he scooped up his daughter and pretended to dance with her.

'Oh, the weather outside is frightful,' he started to croon. 'But Freya is so delightful.'

The little girl laughed and wriggled free. 'If it snows lots, I'm going to build a snowman. And sledging!' Her face lit up at the prospect. 'Can we go sledging?'

'But it won't snow lots, will it?' Harley said flatly. 'Because this is England. Anyway, we left our sledges in Whistler.'

I put a tentative arm around his shoulder. 'Then we should get new ones, so that when it does snow properly – which it will at some point – we'll be ready. You'll have to show me how it's done; I've never been on a sledge in my life.'

'No way!' Harley looked at me in disbelief and then grinned. 'It's easy, I can teach you.'

'You're on,' I said, pleased to have made him smile. I was still working on my role in their lives; as their dad's girlfriend, I wasn't always sure what I should or shouldn't say or do. This time, it looked as if I'd got it right. I felt something on my face and looked up. 'I think it might be snow, you know.'

Harley and Freya scampered ahead, chatting about where the best place to go sledging would be, and Cole wrapped his arm around my waist, drawing me close.

'Thank you,' he murmured, leaning in to kiss me.

'For what?' I asked, checking that the kids weren't looking.

I wasn't yet comfortable with public displays of affection with their father. My best friend Nell once told me that it had taken two years before she felt able to even hold hands with Olek in front of his son, Max. I'd scoffed at her at the time, but now I knew exactly how she'd felt.

'For being a wonderful woman.' He kissed me again. 'For being brilliant with my kids and making co-parenting so much more fun than when I was doing it alone.'

'You're welcome.' My voice was casual, but inside my heart soared. Sometimes I felt like pinching myself; I loved this man and I knew he loved me.

Ahead of us, the children were laughing as Freya got stuck climbing over the stile. Once on the other side, we'd almost be in town. Another five minutes or so and we'd be at Astrid's, where, no doubt, Fred would be waiting for his slice of *apfel strudel* too.

Cole and I picked up our pace and I snuggled against him. 'Is there anything more exciting than the first snow in winter?' I mused happily.

He pretended to think about it. 'Actually, yes, I think there is.'

He was very handsome, my man, I thought, taking in his rugged features, the healthy glow from a working life spent outdoors and deep brown eyes which were sparkling with mischief.

'It was a rhetorical question,' I said with a laugh. 'I'm sure if I really thought about it my brain would come up with something. But look how much fun your kids are having. And imagine if we were to get snowed in and had to spend the day cosied up in front of the fire or digging our way out of Holly Cottage to fetch supplies.'

'Hmm. True, but even more exciting than snow is waiting to get a word in edgeways, to ask a wonderful woman the most important question a man can ask.' He stopped walking and, taking hold of my scarf, tugged me gently towards him.

I raised an eyebrow, intrigued. 'Ask away.'

His eyes were on mine, my hands in his, and suddenly I realised what was happening. 'Merry, I'm in love with you, you make my every day magical. And I wondered . . . will you do me the honour of becoming my wife?'

My heart stuttered in my chest, and I stared at him, for once completely speechless. The rest of the world faded away until there was just him and me, snowflakes fluttering like confetti; a tiny perfect moment stretching between us, one I'd remember for the rest of my days.

Finally, I gasped, incredulous and elated. 'Cole, is this . . . Are you proposing?'

He nodded. 'If you'll have me. This year has been one of the best of my life and it's all because of you,' he said, his expression soft and earnest and full of love. 'You said yourself it feels like we are a family and seeing you with the kids this week has made me love you even more. The only way next year could top this one is if we were married. So, what do you say?'

A bubble of laughter escaped from me. 'I say yes!' I threw my arms around his neck and kissed him, for once not caring that the children might see. *Married*. I was going to be Mrs Cole Robinson. 'Absolutely! Thank you.'

Cole's face relaxed into a smile of relief. 'No, thank *you*, darling, you've made me a very happy man.'

'I love you,' I said, kissing him again. 'So much.'

'Dad? We're going on ahead,' Harley shouted, interrupting. 'See you at Astrid's.'

I stepped away from Cole automatically, but he held onto me.

'Wait there, please!' he called to them and then lowered his voice. 'I want to tell them now before we tell anyone else, is that OK with you?'

A wave of nerves wiped the smile from my face. 'Do you think they'll mind?'

'Not at all, they'll be pleased! They've had a great week staying with us and they'll be excited about the wedding.'

'Hurry up then!' Freya yelled.

My stomach lurched as we ran to catch up with them, wishing I could share his optimism. What if they were completely against the idea? I thought they liked me, but that was as their dad's girlfriend, maybe they didn't want a stepmum? What if Harley stormed off? What if Freya burst into tears?

'I'm thirteen,' Harley protested when we reached them. 'I walk home from school by myself, I don't need to walk with you.'

'I know, son,' said Cole, reaching for my hand. 'But that wasn't why we asked you to wait. We've got something to tell you. I've just asked Merry to marry me and she said yes.'

I held my breath as I watched the expressions on their faces, hoping that this would be good news.

'Oh right.' Harley frowned and shoved his hands in his pockets. He was impossible to read. Maybe he wasn't sure himself how he felt about it. After all, it had come as a surprise to me so it would certainly be a shock to the children. 'Erm, congratulations, I guess.'

'Thank you,' I murmured.

Cole ruffled his son's hair. 'Thanks, mate, I appreciate that.'

'When?' Freya asked. 'Because this tooth is wobbly and I don't want a gappy smile on the photographs.' She peeled off her glove and gave one of her top teeth a good wiggle to demonstrate.

'We haven't set a date yet,' I told her, taking heart from the fact that she saw our wedding as something to be happy about. 'But your smile will be beautiful no matter what.

Would you like to be my bridesmaid?'

'Yes!' Freya launched herself at me, wrapping her arms around my hips. I hugged her back, grateful for her simple approval. 'Do I get a long dress and flowers, and can I wear make-up?'

'We can sort all that out,' said Cole fondly. 'And you'll be an usher on the day, I hope, Harley?'

'If you like,' he replied with a shrug. 'Can we go to Astrid's now?'

Cole nodded. 'Make sure you hold hands across the road.'

'Can we tell Grandad and Astrid?' Freya demanded.

Cole looked at me for guidance and I nodded.

'Yes!' She jumped on the spot, punching the air with both fists. 'Come on, Harley, let's run.'

Once they'd gone, I sagged against Cole with relief. 'At least Freya is excited, although Harley didn't show much enthusiasm.'

Cole didn't seem perturbed. 'Don't worry about him, it's not cool to show your emotions at thirteen, that's all. Oh, by the way, I've got something for you.'

He pulled out a small blue velvet box from his jacket pocket and lifted the lid. Inside was a ring with a square-cut diamond in the centre, three smaller diamonds set at each side of it.

'Oh, Cole, that's beautiful!' My eyes filled with tears, and I wiped them away, laughing. 'What I can see of it.'

My hand was shaking as he slid the ring onto my finger. 'There. Now we're officially engaged. Does it fit OK?'

'As if it was made to measure,' I said, holding up my hand and examining my finger.

He looked very pleased with himself. 'I measured your finger with a piece of cotton while you were asleep. I didn't want to waste any time getting it altered.'

I laughed. 'You think of everything, my clever husband-to-be.'

'I think of you,' he replied, drawing me in for another kiss. 'Almost all of the time.'

'Come on then.' I climbed up onto the stile, swung my leg over and jumped down. 'I can't wait to tell Nell, she'll be amazed, maybe I'll phone her from Astrid's or go round later tonight and flash my beautiful ring at her. Do you want to come, we could—'

'Just hold on a second,' Cole said, laughing, as he hopped over the stile effortlessly and landed beside me. 'Before you get carried away with who you need to tell first, I have one more surprise, or rather a question.'

I stopped admiring my ring finger for a second to look at him. 'Ooh, intriguing.'

'The thing is . . .' He paused and bit his lip sheepishly. 'I've already called the registry office to get a rough idea of when they'd be able to fit us in . . . And they'd had a cancellation on Christmas Eve. So we could actually be married by Christmas.'

I could see he was holding his breath, waiting for my reaction.

'*This* Christmas Eve?' We stared at each other, our breath forming icy clouds in front of our faces as my brain processed what he'd said. 'As in just a few weeks from now?'

Cole nodded. 'Seven weeks and five days to be exact.'

'Wow. But . . .' I blinked at him. 'That's not long to organise a wedding. You're a man who likes to plan everything properly.'

'And you're a woman who likes to fly by the seat of her pants. Pants that I very much approve of by the way.' He kissed my neck, making my legs go weak. 'Let's face it, if we had a year to plan a wedding, you'd leave most of it until the last minute and then race around like a whirlwind, with me tearing my hair out.'

I laughed. 'I love that you know me so well and despite that still want to marry me.'

'So, I thought it might be fun to compromise,' he continued. 'We organise a last-minute wedding. What do you think: crazy idea or brilliant plan?'

My mind whirred. There'd be a lot to do, decisions to make, things to organise, but . . . I could feel anticipation bubbling inside me.

'I'm up for it.' I smiled at him, my eyes sparkling with the prospect of the challenge. 'One hundred per cent. It's crazy *and* brilliant. I mean, what are we waiting for? Let's do it.'

'Thank goodness for that.' He pretended to wipe his brow. 'Because it's already booked.'

'I can't believe this is happening,' I said, laughing. 'You were right: getting married on Christmas Eve is far more exciting than the first snow in winter.'

And then I kissed my new fiancé with a passion that earned us a toot from the horn of a car.

Chapter Two

Emily

The corridors of the Darley Academy secondary school in Derbyshire were still quiet at seven thirty, but it wouldn't be long before the feet of over a thousand young people would be scuffing their way along them, filling the air with laughter, noise and the strong smell of body spray.

Emily, shivering slightly from the change in temperature from her warm car, made her way to the staffroom, in search of coffee.

The room was empty and while she waited for the kettle to boil, her mind wandered to her dad. She hoped he was keeping warm; when she'd been round to his flat last night, he hadn't had the fire on, and his hands and feet had been like blocks of ice.

At least he wouldn't be on his own for long. His carer, Diane, was due to call in at eight o'clock. She'd make him a hot drink and some breakfast, leave him something for lunch and get him comfortable for the day.

Coffee made, Emily slung her bag over her shoulder and set off for the head teacher's office.

'Morning, Alison.' Emily put the drinks down on her boss's desk and sat down in the visitor's chair opposite her.

'Good morning.' Alison looked up from her laptop. 'You look adorable. Thanks for the coffee.'

'You're welcome,' Emily replied, wondering if *adorable* was a compliment or not.

She smoothed down the skirt of her green corduroy pinafore dress: a chance find in her favourite vintage shop in Bakewell. She'd customised the outfit by adding new buttons and contrast stitching to the hem and styled it with a Peter Pan-collared shirt. It had looked quirky in the mirror this morning. Now she was wondering if she looked more like a kid on her first day at primary school.

Emily unzipped her bag and took out a stack of papers and her laptop, while Alison drank her coffee. The job was only a year contract, and the way things were, she'd gladly accept a permanent position if she was offered one, so it was important to make a good impression and she knew Alison appreciated her getting in early. It wasn't always possible. Sometimes her dad refused to let the carer into his flat, and Emily's number was listed as the emergency contact. The only contact come to that.

Not that being a school secretary was Emily's dream (she was still working out what was), but it had been the perfect solution to her problem. She'd left her old job as a PA to an international recruitment consultant for this one in September when it became obvious that the only way she was going to be able to combine looking after her dad and earning a living was to have early finishes, weekends without any extra overtime and long holidays. Her old position had been exciting but had demanded more of her than she could give at the moment.

Emily sipped her coffee and slid a pile of letters across the desk for her boss to sign.

'You're seeing Robbie Evans's parents at nine thirty,' she said, checking the diary. 'Shall I sit in and take notes?'

'Not again.' Alison pulled a face. 'No need, thanks. There's no way they can deflect the blame from their darling son this time.' She opened her drawer and pulled out a long plait of hair which Robbie had liberated from the head of Bethany James during an art lesson yesterday afternoon. 'Exhibit A. That child is treading a thin line. One more stunt like this and goodbye Robbie. He is out of this academy and will be someone else's problem.'

Emily didn't fancy being in the Evans's shoes. Alison was tall and lean and cut a forbidding figure as she patrolled the corridors. She could silence a crowd of kids simply by standing still and looking down at the pupils from the balcony, arms folded.

A complete contrast to Emily, who was short, blonde and blessed with a mischievous sense of fun and a bulging wardrobe of kooky clothes. All of which made her a hit with the kids but didn't necessarily garner their respect.

'What else have we got?' Alison passed the signed letters across the desk.

'Mr Rendall wants to see you at eight a.m. tomorrow,' Emily said, scanning her emails.

'What nuggets of wisdom is he planning to impart this time, I wonder?' Alison gave a long-suffering sigh.

'Something about the parent parking situation, I think.'

The chair of governors was a lovely man in his seventies and loved to talk about his army days and how the world would be a better place if only youngsters had to do a stint in the forces. Unfortunately, for Mr Rendall, Alison liked meetings to be brief and stick to the point.

'If he's got a solution to that, I'm all ears,' Alison said dryly.

'I could organise a tray of coffee and biscuits and chat to him for a few minutes, let him get his latest anecdote out of the way before you join us?' Emily suggested. 'Year nine were doing Christmas baking on Friday, there are still some cinnamon cookies left, I'll rescue them from the staffroom.'

Alison gave her a look of gratitude. 'Perfect. You're a marvel. Christmas baking already? This term is flying, the holidays will be here before we know it.'

'Indeed.' Emily's throat went dry; she didn't want to think about Christmas just yet. That was the deadline she'd given herself to take action. She intended to use those two weeks away from school to do some proper research and decide what to do about her father. Incidents were happening increasingly often now. She'd get a call from a neighbour or from her father himself. Although, last night, she'd found the phone in the freezer on top of his newspaper. Would it even work properly after that? She should have checked. What if something were to happen? A shudder of fear ran through her.

'Emily?' Alison's concerned voice broke into her thoughts.

'Sorry,' she stuttered, refreshing her laptop screen. 'Talking of Christmas, Wetherley Primary school has invited you to their Festive Concert on—' Emily stopped mid-sentence at the sound of a polite cough. She turned to see Olivia, the school receptionist, hovering in the open doorway.

'Sorry to interrupt,' said Olivia. 'But there's a phone call for Emily.'

'Could you take a message for me please?' Emily asked, glancing at the time; it was only seven forty-five. She didn't officially start until eight thirty. 'I'll call whoever it is back as soon as I can.'

'Thanks, Olivia,' Alison repeated, dismissing her with a smile. 'You were saying, Emily, the concert?'

Olivia coughed again. 'Emily, I really think you should take it. It's the police.'

The drive to her dad's flat in Bakewell usually took half an hour, but the heavy morning traffic slowed her down. Emily drove as fast as she could, her stomach tied in knots and guilt weighing heavy on her shoulders. Dad must be terrified. Why hadn't she acted sooner? The signs had been there for a while; something like this had been inevitable.

At the word 'police', Emily had raced to the phone to take the call. The pounding in her ears had made it difficult to concentrate on what the police officer was telling her. But she heard the main points: her dad had turned up at the station, confused and with a nasty gash to his arm.

Thank heavens he'd been wearing that little capsule around his neck that she'd bought him. Inside was a slip of paper with his name on it, in case, like today, he forgot it, and her phone number because he had no chance of remembering that. She hadn't included his address. That could lead to all sorts of issues if someone unscrupulous came across him when he was in one of his less lucid states. She'd furnished the officer with the address of her father's ground-floor maison-ette, which was a good half an hour's walk from the station, and the police were meeting her there. She'd already warned Julia, his landlady, who lived upstairs. If they arrived before her, Julia had offered to let them in with her spare key. She'd called Diane too, who would have arrived to an empty flat.

Alison had told her to leave immediately and take as long as she needed. But Emily wasn't daft, she'd detected the undertone, the same 'not again' face Alison had used for Robbie Evans. So much for her early start to the day.

With a pang of anxiety, Emily banished thoughts of work from her head, her father was the priority. She pulled up behind the police car and dashed to his flat.

'Hello, Dad? It's me, Emily,' she called, letting herself in.

'That's my daughter,' she heard him say from the living room. 'She'll soon get to the bottom of this nonsense.'

Her dad, Ray Meadows, was sitting in his armchair – a threadbare thing he'd hauled out of a skip. Skips were his obsession, he was forever putting things in or taking things out. She'd found an old birdcage covered in dried droppings in the kitchen last week.

Two police officers were with him: a man who was crouched down, turning on the electric fire, and a woman on the sofa, a notebook in her hand.

She hurried over to her dad and hugged him tightly. His face was cold to the touch and despite the blanket tucked over his shoulders, he was trembling. Hardly surprising, given that he was still in his pyjamas.

'Dad! You gave me such a fright. Are you all right?'

Ray frowned. 'Why wouldn't I be?'

It struck her how much weight he'd lost recently. He'd always been lean, but now he was wafer thin, his wrists bony, his jaw and cheekbones sharp. She did her best to make sure he ate, but was it enough?

The male officer straightened up and smiled at her. 'I'm PC James and this is PC Bright. I take it you're Emily, Mr Meadows's daughter?'

She nodded. 'Correct. Thank you for bringing him home, I'm so sorry to have troubled you.'

'The only thing wrong with me is these two,' Ray continued and lowered his voice to a whisper. 'I can't get rid of them. I think they must be from some sort of religion. The woman with the big nose keeps asking questions. If they're after my money, they're going to be disappointed.'

'They're police officers, Dad. No one is after your money.' Emily could hardly look poor PC Bright in the eye; her nose was certainly her strongest feature. 'Sorry. He gets confused sometimes. Your nose is perfectly in proportion.'

'For an aardvark,' muttered her father.

'I'll put the kettle on,' said PC James, muffling a laugh as he sidled out of the room.

'You get called all sorts in this job,' noted PC Bright, tugging her fringe down over her face.

'Glad you're here, love,' said her father, grasping Emily's hand.

'Of course, I'm here.' She swallowed. 'I always will be, I promise.'

She shouldn't make promises she couldn't keep, but what else could she say?

'What were you doing going out without getting dressed?' she asked. 'You could have called me if you had a problem.'

'The car was gone,' he replied, blinking at her. 'I went outside this morning to get something out of it. I forget what, now. But there was no sign of it.'

'You don't own a car, Dad.' Emily's heart sank.

PC Bright took out her notebook. 'So, there isn't a missing car?'

Emily shook her head. 'I'm sorry for the mix-up. But no.'

Ray frowned. 'A blue Escort van. I sleep in it sometimes.'

A memory of a day trip to the seaside flooded back to her. They'd gone off in his van, just the two of them, and spent the whole day at the beach. Fish and chips, bottles of fizzy orange and free rides on the funfair because Dad had known one of the staff. Mum had been furious when they'd got home. Emily wracked her brains to remember why . . . Oh yes, Dad had taken her to the dentist early in the morning to have a tooth out. Afterwards, he was supposed to take her back to school but decided to cheer her up with an adventure instead.

'You did have a blue van a long time ago.' Emily squeezed his hand, remembering the man he'd been: irreverent, fun and completely unpredictable. 'But you haven't been driving since you moved back to Bakewell.'

'But I'm sure I . . .' Ray drifted off, scratching his chin.

'That's probably a good thing in the circumstances. Your father came to the station on foot to report the car missing, wearing only pyjamas and slippers,' said PC Bright. 'We gave him some thick socks and wrapped him up. He had a hot drink while we were getting in touch with you.'

'Thank you. Again. He's never done anything like this before.' As far as she knew at least. Apprehension fluttered in her chest; how long could he carry on living alone? He was safe this time, but what about the next?

'Here you are, Mr Meadows.' PC James placed a mug of tea at her dad's side. 'Not sure how you like it, but this is warm and wet.'

Ray jumped. 'Where the bloody hell have you just sprung from?'

'This is PC James,' Emily explained patiently. 'He brought you home.'

'He did no such thing?' Ray spluttered.

'I made one for you too, Emily,' the officer said kindly. 'You look like you need it.'

'Thanks. I do. I don't know if I'm shivering with the cold or shock.' Emily stood up to accept the mug from him.

'A call from the police station does that to a person,' remarked PC Bright. 'Thankfully, there was no harm done.'

'We'll leave you in peace in a moment,' said PC James, resuming his spot in front of the fire. He hadn't made tea for himself, or his colleague, Emily noticed, so hopefully, this wasn't going to take too long. 'Mr Meadows wasn't too happy about getting in the patrol car. Put up quite a bit of resistance. He knocked his right arm on the car door. He'll probably have quite a bruise.'

'Oh Dad.' Emily could have wept. She knew exactly how that would have gone. He had never hurt her, but she'd witnessed him panic when he didn't understand what was happening to him. 'I'm so sorry.'

'It's OK. He didn't strike anyone.' PC Bright held Emily's gaze. 'Has he been violent before?'

Emily shook her head, tears filling her eyes. 'He's an old hippy at heart. Soft as butter. He'd be mortified if he realised . . .' She broke off before she said too much.

Her greatest fear was that social services would intervene and he'd be deemed too vulnerable to be living independently. What if he was put in a home without her being able to do anything about it?

She took a deep breath. Not long until Christmas. Then she'd put a plan together. She just needed to get him safely to the holidays.

'And I'd already told you about the wound to his left arm,' PC James continued. 'We've cleaned it up, but you might want to let his GP know, so they can send a nurse round to change his dressing.'

'Will do,' Emily promised.

'This lad makes a pretty decent cuppa.' Ray Meadows slurped his tea and grinned at PC James. 'You should give my Emily some tips. Hers are always like tar. I just like to show the water the teabag, get two or three uses out of it.'

Emily felt the tension drain from her body. Just like that, he was himself again, thank goodness.

'Cheeky!' she said. 'You can make your own next time then.'

'Thank you, Mr, er . . .?' PC James prompted, clearly testing him.

'Meadows, Ray Meadows.' Her dad extended a hand. 'Look at me, still in my pyjamas. If you don't mind, I'm going to have a bath and then get my breakfast.'

The officers exchanged glances, clearly amazed at the transformation in the man who less than an hour ago couldn't remember his own name.

'We'll get out of your way,' said PC Bright, putting her notebook back in the pocket of her overcoat. 'Look after that arm.'

'Arm?' Ray stared at his forearm as if noticing the plaster for the first time. 'Oh yes, caught it on the back gate. Just a scratch.'

'I'm sorry to have taken up your day.' Emily showed the officers to the door.

'Our duty is to keep the public safe. That includes Ray,' said PC James. 'Do social services know that your father has dementia?'

Emily hesitated. 'They do, but he's deteriorated a lot in the last couple of months.'

'I'm sorry, it must be tough.' He nodded and stepped out from the flat into the corridor.

PC Bright followed him and then turned back. 'And you? Are you getting some support?'

Emily blinked back tears; she was OK until someone was kind to her. 'I'm fine. We're both fine. Thanks again.'

The officer held eye contact for a moment, as if weighing up whether to say more or not. Emily took a step back to close the door.

'Glad to hear it.' The officer raised her hand to say goodbye and left. 'Good luck.'

Chapter Three

Emily

At the end of the school day, as soon as she could get away, Emily tidied her desk, put her coat on and, after reminding Alison about tomorrow's early meeting with the chair of governors, she headed out to the staff car park.

The sky was grey and the daylight all but gone. She shivered in the cold and slipped her gloves on. Snow was forecast again later in the week, and it wouldn't be long before the Derbyshire peaks were covered in white for the winter.

'Everything OK?' a voice called to her.

She looked over her shoulder to see Olivia, scurrying to catch her up.

'After this morning's phone call, I mean. You rushed past when you got back to school looking like you had the world on your shoulders, and I didn't like to pry.'

'Thank you for asking, but not really,' Emily admitted. 'My dad has dementia. He needs more and more of my time and I—' She stopped short of admitting that she couldn't cope. Olivia was a sweet girl, similar age, and the closest thing she had to a friend at the school. But she couldn't risk it getting back to Alison.

'I'm so sorry.' Olivia laid a hand on her arm. 'That must be terrible for you all.'

'Thanks. It is hard.' Except that her dad didn't have anyone except her. There was no *all*. Even her mum hadn't seen her ex for over a decade. So, the reason Emily looked as if she had the world on her shoulders, was because she did.

Olivia zapped her car to unlock it. 'If I can do anything, let me know. My great-aunt had Alzheimer's; it crept up stealthily. She'd always had a good sense of humour, but one year she came down to breakfast on Christmas Day in nothing but a Santa hat. We laughed about it at the time, but it was heartbreaking to watch her fade away. I'm here if you ever need to talk. See you tomorrow.'

Emily could only nod and smile as she climbed into her car. It had been a stressful day and the little stone cottage she rented with its thick walls, open fire and pink décor was calling her. She was going to treat herself to a long soak in her claw-footed bath. But not before she'd been to check on her dad. She hadn't felt comfortable about leaving him on his own this morning, but she hadn't had much choice.

While she waited for the car to warm up, she sent her best friend, Izzy, a text.

Not been the best day. Dad went walkabout this morning in his pjs and ended up at the police station.

Oh mate!! Poor Ray and POOR YOU! Is he OK?

No harm done, luckily, but he's getting worse, Izzy, and I don't know how much longer he'll be able to live on his own. I'm worried to death.

I'm sorry you're going through this on your own. You need a break too. Could you get Gavin to look after him for a weekend and you come over here?

25

A few days pootling about by the sea with her best friend would be heaven. Emily missed her dreadfully since Izzy had moved to Jersey with her boyfriend. She'd wanted to live by the sea for as long as Emily had known her, so when Andrew was offered a job in finance over there, she left her own job to go with him. Now she was running a successful Airbnb business, looking to buy another property and loving life. Emily had only managed to visit her a few times but had always come away determined to do something more rewarding with her own life. But with Dad needing her more and more, that seemed like an impossible dream.

And as for the idea of Gavin, her boyfriend of eight months, stepping in to help . . . nope, not going to happen.

She sighed and sent back as optimistic a reply as she could muster.

I would love that. Maybe over Christmas when he's not so busy. Love you xxx

Love you too xxx

She put the car into reverse, but before she had chance to move, her phone pinged with another message. This time it was from Gavin. Her stomach fluttered; things had been a bit tense between them recently. It was almost as if he was jealous of the time she was spending with her dad. She tried to involve him as much as she could, like when she'd taken Dad for a walk after lunch last Sunday and invited Gavin to come, but Gavin had declined her offer, saying there was no point joining them because Ray took all of Emily's attention and he felt ignored.

She held her breath as she opened the text message.

We're going for a curry after five-a-side football later.
Fancy joining us this time? You won't be the only girl x

She smiled, pleasantly surprised; this sounded much more
like the old Gavin. She'd have preferred a night out with
just him, or even better, a night in, but she knew better
than to suggest it. Plus, her favourite food in the entire
world was curry. There was a jibe with the 'this time'
comment, but fair play; she usually turned down his after-
football invites. The bath could wait, she decided, her
thumbs flying over the screen to reply. Maybe tonight they
could put the past behind them and move on.

Curry?!?! Just try to stop me! Thanks for inviting me,
sounds great, text me the details. I've got to drop in on
Dad first, he wasn't well earlier, but I'll see you there xx

Emily watched the screen. *Gavin is typing*, it said at the top.
He was probably going to ask what was wrong with him.

Cool x

Was that it? Never mind; he would still be at work. Plenty
of time to catch up later.

She replaced the phone in her handbag and set off to
her dad's.

Emily sat across the kitchen table from her dad watching
him eat the plate of sausages and mashed potato she'd made
for him. No vegetables. He flatly refused to eat anything
healthy. She should have left by now, but there'd been so
much to do when she got here, and he'd been so grateful
for her help. He'd lost his watch and had emptied every

27

cupboard and drawer to try to find it. Together they had tidied everything away, but the watch hadn't turned up. Next, she'd made him help her change his bed sheets and towels and she'd filled the washing machine and emptied it twice over. By which time he declared he was feeling a bit peckish and fancied sausage and mash. She hadn't found sausages or potatoes in his kitchen, but she had found his watch hidden behind a tin of baked beans. After that, she'd taken him shopping to the little supermarket nearby.

'What day is it?' Ray asked her, slurping from his mug of tea.

'Monday, remember?' He'd asked her several times.

'We always have chops for dinner on Monday. Never mind.' Ray smiled blankly at his daughter. 'Mum makes me eat the fat, even though I don't like it. Aren't you having any dinner?'

'No, Dad, I'm going out with Gavin.' She'd told him that already too.

Or at least she was supposed to be, but she'd been here much longer than planned. She could still just about make it to the Indian restaurant. There'd be no time to go home and get changed out of her pinafore dress and flat shoes now. Pity, Gavin liked her to make an effort when she was with his friends. Her phone was about to die too, which was a bit of a blow. Dad only had an ancient Nokia so she couldn't borrow his charger. His phone was working after its spell in the freezer, though, so that was something.

'New chap?' Ray looked over at her.

'No, you've met Gavin,' she said. 'Tall, dark hair, supports Manchester United?'

He looked down at his plate and squirted a mountain of ketchup onto his mashed potato. 'Oh yeah.'

Emily swallowed a sigh at the obvious lie. He clearly had no recollection of Gavin at all. How long before he stopped recognising her when she came round? How long before his lucid moments became a thing of the past altogether? The thought made her feel sick. The incident with the police this morning was a wake-up call. She'd thought that having a carer to visit him every morning was enough. But trying to report his non-existent car as stolen had changed things.

'Are you eating properly, Dad?' Emily asked, watching him devour his dinner.

He looked shifty. 'Not much of a cook, but I can open a tin. Don't worry, I never go hungry. What day is it?'

She took a deep breath and reached for his hand across the table. 'Monday.'

He thought about it for a moment and gave a curt nod. 'We have chops on Monday.'

Maybe so, she thought, but she couldn't imagine him being able to cook meat safely anymore. She'd selected some ready meals for him earlier, easy stuff he could microwave. Maybe it was time to investigate a meals delivery service. Another job for the list.

As soon as he'd finished eating, he put his plate in the sink and went back into the living room. She quickly washed the dishes, slipped on her coat and headed back to kiss him goodbye and collect her handbag. A glance at her phone told her that the battery was on one per cent now, but she could give it a quick blast on the car charger when she left.

'I'll see you soon, Dad,' she said. 'What are you looking at?'

He wasn't in his armchair, as she'd expected. Instead, he'd opened the curtains and he was gazing out into the darkness, his hands cupped around his forehead so he could see through the window better. 'She's normally back by now.'

She touched his arm. 'Who is?'

He flinched and turned to stare at her as if she was a stranger. 'Mum.' His eyes filled with tears. 'She went to the butcher's for some chops for Dad's dinner. She's been gone for ages.'

'I'm sure she'll be back soon,' she soothed, trying to keep her own emotions in check.

She'd never known her grandmother, but she did understand her dad's mounting unease. Because there was a time when she'd been the one at the window waiting for *him*. Even before they'd officially parted ways, her parents had spent as much time apart as they had together. A lot of water had passed under the bridge, since her mum, Tina, had called time on the relationship for good, and Emily no longer resented him for his frequent absences. But she remembered vividly those times as a little girl, unable to drag herself from the window, waiting for him to come home.

'But what if she doesn't come back? I don't like it on my own.' Ray started to cry quietly, his chest heaving and shoulders shaking.

It broke Emily's heart to see him so upset about something that wasn't even real.

'Come and sit by the fire, Dad.' She took his hand and led him to his chair. 'Don't worry, you aren't on your own, I'll stay with you.'

She felt a prickle of guilt for standing Gavin up at such short notice. But she couldn't leave her dad. She'd send Gavin a message as soon as her dad was calmer, she decided. He wouldn't like it, but it was the best she could do.

★

A noise woke her; the crashing of crockery and splash of a tap turned on too forcefully. Emily sat up in the dark, startled and disorientated and her heart thumping. Not at home, or at Gavin's. Oh yes, she'd stayed the night on Dad's lumpy sofa. She reached for her phone to check the time, but it was dead.

'Dad?' Her voice was croaky, still laced with sleep.

'Kettle's on, Tina,' he called back brightly. 'Won't be long.'

'I'm Emily, Tina's daughter,' she replied. '*Your* daughter.'

'Here we are. Stewed tea, just as you like it.' He shuffled in, dripping liquid from two overfilled mugs.

Outside the window, she could hear cars, a bus, the sound of a child crying. What the hell?

She fought her way off the saggy cushions, heart racing, and yanked back the curtains. It was light outside. Which meant it must be at least eight o'clock. It was always still dark when she drove to school. She tried to read the time on the DVD player under the TV, but it was flashing a row of zeros.

A feeling of dread crept over her. 'What's the time?'

'Lost my watch, haven't I,' he said, turning in a circle looking for somewhere to put the mugs.

Emily didn't bother reminding him that they'd found it last night. Instead she switched on the TV, found the breakfast programme, and groaned. It was just after eight. 'I don't believe it, I'm usually at work by now. Thanks for the tea, Dad, but I need to go.'

She couldn't go to work wearing clothes that she'd slept in all night, which meant a trip back home to Wysedale before continuing to school. She'd never been this late before, never. She shoved her feet in her shoes, scooping up her belongings and her bag.

'Oh, OK.' Her dad's face fell.

'Sorry, but I'm really, really late. I'll ring you in my lunch hour.' She kissed his cheek and moved around him to get to the door. 'Remember the nurse is coming to look at your arm today. You mustn't go out; you must be here when she comes. Promise me?'

'Not got anywhere to go anyway.'

His face was so forlorn that Emily hesitated in the doorway, reluctant to abandon him and yet desperate to get going. Since he'd moved back, she hadn't heard him speak of any friends, but there must be someone, somewhere. 'Have you got anyone I could call, ask them to pop in and see you?'

He sat down in his armchair and fumbled with the remote control before setting it down again. 'Never been one for friends. I had itchy feet when I was a young man. Moved around too much, chasing rainbows and greener grass. I regret some of that. I wasn't good to your mum, and you suffered too and . . . everyone else. I wasn't good to anyone really. I'm just a nuisance. My father even told me that once, that I was a waste of space.'

She shook her head in despair. Whatever her dad's faults, she'd never say anything as unkind as that. Her mum had once told her that there had been a rift between him and his parents. They hadn't had patience with his black moods, as she'd put it, so he'd been asked to leave at seventeen and he'd never gone back. 'You're not a waste of space. You're my dad. And I love you.'

She turned away swiftly before he saw the tears in her eyes. She was almost at the door when a key rattled in the lock and Diane walked in; Emily could have kissed her. Diane was short and stocky with steely grey curls and had the sunniest personality Emily had ever encountered.

She reminded her of Cinderella's fairy godmother in the Disney film. Nothing was ever too much trouble, and nothing fazed her.

'Oh hello, love,' Diane beamed. 'I didn't know you'd be here, does that mean you don't need me this morning?'

'We do need you,' said Emily, with a sniff, pressing her hand to Diane's shoulder. 'Very much.'

As soon as she'd cleared the ice from the car windscreen and plugged her phone into the charger, Emily set off. She'd have to pull over at some point and call the school, send her apologies. The meeting with Mr Rendall would be under way by now. She wondered if anyone had been around to sort out the coffee or whether Alison would have had to do it herself. She cringed. How many times had Alison thanked her for making sure all her meetings ran smoothly, for ensuring visitors were looked after and all the small details were miraculously taken care of without Alison herself having to remember? But not today . . .

The traffic was appalling; there was so much more of it now than at her usual earlier time. She sat at a junction waiting to turn right for what seemed like ages, her knuckles white on the steering wheel. A tiny gap appeared, and she accelerated recklessly out into the stream of cars and was immediately tooted at by a woman in a big four-wheel drive.

'Sorry, lady,' Emily said aloud, raising her hand to apologise. 'Desperate times.'

Her phone came to life, automatically connecting to the car via Bluetooth. It began to beep and ding with an assortment of messages and notifications. The line of cars in front of her slowed to a standstill on the approach to a roundabout and she took the opportunity to glance across at her phone. Several from eBay and Vinted and other places she kept an eye on for clothing bargains. Voicemail from Gavin.

Shit. Emily groaned.

She didn't want to call him now, not when she was late for work and already stressed, because if he had a go at her she'd probably burst into tears. She'd send him a message to apologise as soon as she was home, she decided. Another apology – it was all she seemed to be doing these days.

As she reached the front of the queue, her phone rang, and Alison's direct line flashed up on the screen. *Oh hell.*

Emily answered the call hands-free, before nosing the car out into the stream of cars. 'Hello, Alison, I'm so, so sorry. I've had an absolute nightmare of a night with my father,' she blurted out before her boss could speak. 'I'm on my way home now and should be with you in half an hour, forty-five minutes, max. Did the meeting with the chair of governors go OK?'

'Oh dear, you poor thing,' Alison said kindly. 'I sympathise, I really do, but I just wish you'd let me know that you were going to be absent this morning. Especially given the early meeting that you'd set up.'

Emily's throat felt so constricted that the words stuck in her throat. 'I . . . I . . .'

'Olivia is standing in for you this morning,' Alison continued. 'Come to my office when you eventually arrive. See you soon.'

The line went dead.

Emily swallowed in horror. She wouldn't get the sack over this, but she had just reduced the chances of her contract being made permanent. She drove the rest of the way home in a daze, wondering how to redeem herself.

As soon as she pulled up, she dashed from the car and fumbled with her door key, determined to be as quick as possible getting changed. Once upstairs in her bedroom, she plugged her phone in to charge and she stripped off yesterday's clothes. She felt as if someone had hollowed her out with a spoon, she was trembly and overwhelmed and desperate for a cup of coffee. Dealing with Dad was becoming harder and harder. Izzy was right, she could do with a break.

She quickly chose a dress from her wardrobe, clean underwear and tights from her drawer and decided to call Gavin on speaker phone while she got dressed. She needed to hear a friendly voice, talk to someone who loved her. Besides which, she owed him an apology for last night.

She scrolled to his number and called it. The phone rang out for so long that she was ready to leave a voicemail when suddenly his voice came on the line.

'Emily? Look, sorry, I can't talk, I'm at work.' His voice was low and curt.

'I know, I'm sorry if this is a bad time.' She picked up the phone and pressed it to her ear as if that somehow would bring him closer. 'I just needed to hear your voice. I've had such a crap time, I ended up having to stay with Dad—'

'*You've* had a crap time?' He let out a harsh laugh. 'Try being stood up by your girlfriend with all your mates taking the piss out of you.'

'Oh, darling, I'm so sorry,' she pleaded. 'But did you still have a good night, how was football?'

There was a cold silence on the other end of the line and her stomach tightened.

'Do you actually even care?' he said finally. 'Look, I get it, your dad needs you, et cetera, et cetera. Anyway, I've said my piece in my message. Let's leave it there, shall we? I've got to go.'

Emily froze. 'What do you mean? What message? I haven't had a chance to listen to your voicemail yet.'

'You haven't had time. Classic,' he muttered. 'Sorry, Emily, but this isn't working. I'm calling it a day. We're finished.'

'What? You're dumping me? Gavin?' For the second time that morning, the line went dead and she stared at the phone in shock.

Could today get any worse?

She regretted the thought immediately and swallowed the lump in her throat. The way Emily's life was going, it was dangerous to tempt fate.

Chapter Four

Merry

The day after Cole's surprise proposal, I opened Merry and Bright as usual. The handmade candle shop was my pride and joy. In prime position in the centre of Wetherley overlooking the market square, it had once been the town's bank and still had mullioned windows and black beams, features which I adored. Cole, his sister Hester, and brother-in-law Paul owned the building. I rented the ground floor after Cole had built a workroom at the back where Fred and I made our candles, and a retail space at the front lined with lovely reclaimed oak shelves and decorated simply with fairy lights. The upper floors consisted of a three-bedroomed duplex, where Cole had lived until moving in with me.

I'd become a bit of a workaholic over the last eighteen months since running the business full-time. Today, however, I'd have happily taken the day off to get my head around how I was going to fit in planning a wedding during retail's busiest time of the year. Unfortunately, there was always a mountain of emails, messages and orders to process which accumulated over the weekend and it took Fred and me all morning to clear the backlog.

Not that I was getting stressed, more that I couldn't concentrate on anything. Cole was just as bad. He was supposed to be working on a muddy building site and usually didn't get in touch unless it was important. Yet today we'd been sending each other gooey text messages and I had a permanent dreamy smile on my face.

'Merry? Ahem . . .'

Fred's voice startled me. I was sitting at my desk, supposedly dealing with enquiries from Instagram and Etsy, but when I looked down at the paper, it was covered with doodles of hearts and flowers and lots of Mrs Robinson signatures.

I flipped the pad over quickly. 'Sorry, miles away.'

'I noticed.' He chuckled, heading for the kettle. 'I've replied to all the emails and packed up the online orders. Do you want me to get started on a batch of lemon, lime and rosemary? We're running low.'

'Oh Fred,' I sighed, 'what would I do without you?'

Fred had asked if he could help me out last December because he was interested in seeing how candles were made. We'd jokingly referred to him as the work experience boy, even though he'd retired from his profession as a chemistry teacher years earlier. Now he was my right-hand man. I'd trialled other staff over the course of the year, but none of them could hold a candle to Fred − literally. He had an amazing nose; his favourite thing was to experiment with essential oils and he had helped me grow the product range considerably since coming on board.

'You'd manage fine,' he said, patting my shoulder. 'Just like you did before I came along and got under your feet.'

I watched him make us both coffee, aware of an uneasy sensation deep inside. I knew I was over-reliant on him; Astrid had hinted more than once that she'd like them to spend more time together, spread their wings a little and, for that to happen, I needed to take on an extra member of staff. But winter was setting in now, I was sure I could put off doing anything about it until spring.

We took our mugs into the front of the shop and were stuffing parcels into a postal sack ready for collection when the door opened and in came Nell. She was hidden behind an enormous bouquet of flowers.

'Congratulations, my darling girl!' she cried, enveloping me in a tight hug and waving to Fred over my shoulder.

Nell and I held on to each other for a long moment and I felt close to tears. We'd been best friends for twenty years, at each other's sides through good and bad times, and she was closer to me than anyone else in the world.

'I am so pleased to see you.' I pressed my check to hers.

We'd spoken on the phone last night after Cole had taken the children back to Lydia, but it was no substitute for seeing each other face to face.

'Me too. Sorry I couldn't come earlier. But you know what Mondays are like.'

It was the day of her weekly visit to the wholesaler to stock up on the nuts and dried fruit for her market stall Nell's Nuts.

'I do.' I pulled a guilty face. 'It's busy here too, not that I've achieved much today.'

'Of course, you haven't,' she scoffed. 'How are you feeling today, has it sunk in yet?'

'She's been floating around the shop humming to herself all morning,' Fred piped up. 'So I'd say she's pretty happy. Quite happy about it myself, I must admit.'

'Awww,' said Nell and I together.

'I can't help it,' I admitted. 'I feel like I'm on cloud nine. It's all so sudden and exciting. I'm almost too happy.'

'No such thing,' Nell said firmly. 'Oh, I forgot. These are for you.'

She handed me the flowers and produced a bottle from her bag. 'And I insist you open the bubbly when you get home tonight and celebrate with Cole.'

'Champagne? Wow.' I glanced at the label. 'Not sure about having it on a Monday. Isn't that a bit extravagant?'

'It's not just any old Monday,' she pointed out. 'My best friend is getting married to someone I actually approve of and if that isn't a good reason to celebrate, then I'm Tinkerbell the fairy.'

'I'm so glad you approve of him. His dad's not too bad either.' I slid my eyes to Fred, who flapped a hand in embarrassment. 'I promise I'll open it. The flowers are gorgeous too.' The red of the roses and hypericum berries were vivid amongst glossy evergreens, feathery ferns and snowy white gypsophila. 'Perfect flowers for a winter wedding.'

'That did cross my mind,' Nell said. 'Depending on your colour scheme.'

My colour scheme. A small sigh escaped me; I was excited to get married, but it was slowly dawning on me just how much there was to do between now and Christmas Eve.

Nell narrowed her eyes, sensitive as always to my every mood. 'By your own admission you aren't doing anything, so you won't put up a fight if I drag you out for a coffee and a celebratory cake, will you?'

'Are you not supposed to be on your stall?'

She shook her head. 'I'm not opening today, I thought we might have a wedding to plan.'

The chance to share the load with my best mate over coffee and cake was too good to miss. I looked at Fred.

'Is that all right with you?'

'Of course! I'll put these in water for you.' He picked up the flowers and shooed me off. 'Leave everything to me.'

Nell jerked her head towards Fred. 'He's a keeper.'

'I hope so,' I replied, pulling on my coat. 'Now, come on, let's go and talk weddings.'

Fifteen minutes later, we were ensconced at a window table in the café across the market square from Merry and Bright waiting for our lattes and cinnamon buns. Outside, the market was full of colour and noise, people buying and selling everything, from fabric to falafel, books to baby clothes, and a thousand other things besides. Before having the shop, I'd worked from home, but I thrived having people around me and feeling part of Wetherley's town centre. Growing up in care had always made me feel different, as if I didn't belong anywhere. I still had flashes of self-doubt, but this last year had changed my outlook and I was beginning to accept that I had a valuable part to play in the community.

'So? Let's have a proper look at the rock then,' said Nell once the waiter had delivered our order.

'Ta-dah!' I held up my hand to show her the ring. 'He chose it himself. I love it.'

'I'm not surprised, it's perfect for you. He's pushed the boat out, hasn't he?' She pulled an impressed face. 'No Granny's old cast-offs for you.'

I stroked the diamond with the pad of my right thumb. It still felt odd having a ring on my actual ring finger. The sparkle surprised me every time it caught the light. 'I think Hester's already claimed all the family heirlooms, which is absolutely fine by me. I haven't got anything of my mum's, so hopefully this will become an heirloom one day to pass on to my own children.'

I was all for family traditions, always enjoying listening to tales of Nell's family rituals and learning and joining in with the things Cole and his family did, and I was eager to have traditions of my own – *our* own.

Nell raised her cup. 'To you and Cole, may you be blissfully happy. Cheers!'

I chinked my coffee against hers and we both took a sip and while we tucked into our buns, I took her through the highlights of Cole's surprise proposal again.

'I spent most of the afternoon in tears – happy ones, obviously. Cole had already told his dad that he was planning to propose and had organised for Hester and Paul to be there too. Astrid had also been in on the secret; she was beside herself with excitement and confessed that she'd almost given it away several times. Fred made a speech saying how happy he was that I was joining the family and I felt surrounded by love,' I said.

Nell gave a dreamy sigh. 'Such a happy day. And the kids? How did they take the news?'

I pondered that as I popped the last piece of cake into my mouth. 'Good question. At first, Freya seemed happy that I'd asked her to be a bridesmaid. Although then I worried that I should have checked with Cole and Lydia first.'

Nell tutted softly. 'You don't always have to put other people first, you know, especially when it comes to your own wedding.'

'It's a minefield, though, trying not to overstep the mark and tread on other people's toes.' I smiled ruefully. 'Anyway, then Freya started to worry that Lydia might be sad that Daddy's having a wedding without her, and she said she wants us to invite Lydia.'

'I'd leave that one for Cole to sort out.' Nell winced. 'Try not to worry. And Harley?'

I thought back to his demeanour yesterday. He had changed since coming back from Canada and not just physically. He had been gregarious and outgoing when Cole and I had gone out at Easter to visit, bristling with more energy than he knew what to do with. Now he was quieter and glued to his phone. Cole put it down to hormones and being a teenager and he was probably right. I'd loved seeing Harley come alive when it had started to snow, but once at Astrid's he'd retreated into his shell again.

'He didn't say much about us getting married,' I admitted. 'He was more bothered about who he was going to be spending Christmas Day with. They were in Canada with Lydia last year, but then Cole flew out to join them. I don't know what's happening this year.'

'Maybe you'll be otherwise engaged on Christmas Day.' Nell raised her eyebrows suggestively. 'Seeing as it'll be your honeymoon.'

I shook my head. 'Christmas is a special time for the kids; Freya still believes in Santa. Cole and I have the rest of our lives together. If we get the opportunity to spend the day with them, we will.'

Family was the best gift of all. By marrying me, Cole was giving me the one thing I'd been searching for my whole life. Honeymoon or not, I didn't want to miss spending Christmas Day with my new family, and I was sure he'd feel the same.

'As long as you're happy, I'm happy.' Nell knew how important family was to me. 'Cole came to see me you know, before he proposed.'

'Bloody hell!' I stared at her. 'You knew too? I think I must have been the only person on the planet in the dark about it.'

She laughed at my indignant expression. 'You know what he's like. He wanted to make sure he got everything right.'

Love for him swelled inside me. That was Cole to a tee; he liked to think things through. It was my role in the relationship to throw spur-of-the-moment suggestions into the mix and his to consider the pros and cons before agreeing.

My face softened into a smile. 'That's my Cole. What did he say?'

'He phoned and said he had something to talk to me about and could he come over. I spent the day worrying that you were ill and hadn't told me. Then he turned up and said he intended to propose to you and wanted to know if I had any objections. I can't tell you how relieved I was.'

'Sounds very Victorian,' I replied, bemused. 'As if he was asking permission for my hand.'

Nell giggled. 'It was a bit like that. But I think he knew I'd give it to him straight and tell him if you were unlikely to say yes, or whether I had any concerns.'

'And did you have concerns?'

'Not at all. If you remember, I was the one who encouraged you to live together.'

'True.'

Nell had always been brutal when it came to telling me what she thought about my boyfriends, but she'd liked Cole from the beginning. I'd been hesitant to move in with him – although technically he'd moved into Holly Cottage with me – because living together had sounded the death knell for my last relationship. I didn't want the same thing happening with Cole and me; I was too in love with him to take the risk. But in the end it hadn't been a risk, the opposite in fact.

'True,' I conceded. 'I'm glad I listened to you.'

'I do give good advice,' she said with a grin. 'I gave Cole some too. You've got me to thank for the wedding being in the not-too-distant future.'

I frowned. 'What did you say?'

'That Christmas hasn't always held the best of memories for you,' she said with a gentle smile. 'Let's make this the year that changes all that. I suggested he phoned the registry office and see if they could squeeze you in.'

'Oh Nell.' I felt tears well in my eyes. 'You're right. This will change how I think about Christmas forever.'

Christmas had lost its magic for me when I was eleven. I'd spent a few weeks staying with foster carers, which was something I'd had to do every so often because my mum had had a history of mental health issues. But she'd promised me that I'd be home in time for us to spend Christmas together. I'd never forget the day I was called into the headteacher's office, where a social worker was waiting to tell me that Mum had passed away. I later learned that she'd taken her own life. I think about her all the time but especially at Christmas.

'Besides, I look better in winter colours than spring, so I wasn't being entirely selfless,' she confessed, making me laugh. 'Look, I'm just glad you said yes. Now we can get started on the fun bits, like your wedding dress.'

I beamed at her. 'My wedding dress – I still can't believe I'm getting married. I did have a quick look online last night and I've seen a couple I might order.'

'Oh no, no, no.' Nell looked appalled. She opened the diary on her phone. 'This is the most important shopping experience of your life! You need to try on dozens of dresses and twirl around to see how they feel, and I need to watch you come out of the changing rooms and cry at how beautiful you look. We're going to make a special occasion of it. How about one afternoon next week? I'll close the stall and you can close the shop early.'

'Are you sure?' She'd normally have to be bedridden with illness not to go to work because she had no one else to run it for her. And she wasn't open today either. Very odd.

'Absolutely sure,' she confirmed. 'Please indulge me. We'll make some appointments and go from shop to shop like royalty. They give you champagne, you know. Probably not the good stuff, but even so.' She paused, registering the expression on my face. 'What is it?'

'Nothing.' I swallowed the lump in my throat and did my best to smile. 'Or at least nothing new. I miss my mum, that's all. I wish she could be part of it. Mothers love this sort of thing, don't they? Organising their daughter's wedding? We could have had such fun together.'

'Oh love.' She placed her hand on top of mine. 'I know I'm a poor substitute, but *we'll* still have fun and if you want someone older with us to get all emotional and take a million photos of you wearing a hideous meringue dress, we could always bring *my* mum along. Remember how well that worked out for me?'

We both laughed. Mrs Thornbury had somehow managed to make wedding dress shopping all about her and when Nell had stepped out of the changing room wearing *the* dress, she'd fainted and given herself a nosebleed. Nell had been left without an audience and ordered not to get blood on her dress, while her mother had lapped up all the attention — and the champagne, I seemed to remember.

'Just you and me will be enough,' I said softly. 'And I know I'm lucky to have so many lovely friends, but there are times in your life when family means the world.'

'Soon you'll be Mrs Robinson and officially part of Cole's family with more relations than you can shake a

46

stick at. You'll have a father-in-law. Stepchildren. You'll even have a sister-in-law! And, of course, though we're not real family, you'll always, always have me.'

'You're better than real family,' I said, giving her a hug. 'And on that note, you will be my maid of honour, won't you?'

Nell tilted her head to one side, considering my offer. 'I was thinking more along the lines of best woman. How does that sound?'

'Perfect.' I grinned at her. 'Best friend, best woman. Consider yourself hired.'

Chapter Five

Merry

'The problem with you,' said Nell, as we entered Wedding Belles bridal boutique in Bakewell, 'is that you look good in everything.'

'Thanks,' I replied, 'I think.'

'It's true.' She leaned on the marble counter and massaged her aching calf muscles. 'You haven't looked bad in a single dress you've tried on. And you've tried on *a lot* of dresses.'

I did think she was being a bit daft wearing high-heeled boots for an afternoon of traipsing around shops. But she had insisted, claiming that we needed to look the part if we were to get the VIP treatment. This was our fourth shop, and we were beginning to flag.

'What your friend means,' said the proprietor, who introduced herself as Abigail, 'is that you're blessed with a wonderful figure with perfect proportions and that you have the pick of the store: style, length, fabric . . . the choice is yours. I'm sure you'll find your dream dress amongst our designs.'

'Gosh.' I puffed my cheeks out, taking in the rails and rails of bridal gowns. 'I don't know where to start, there's even more choice here than in the last place.'

'Do you have a budget?' Abigail asked, guiding us to a silver velvet sofa in the middle of the floor.

Nell flopped down gratefully, while I hovered at a display of tulle veils and tiaras.

'No,' I said, realising that I should have given this some thought. I didn't want to skimp, but on the other hand I wasn't about to blow a fortune on a dress I'd only wear once.

Her eyes lit up. 'Then you must look at our Signature collection, exclusive to us and designed in Paris.'

'OK.' I suppressed a tiny burp. Each shop we'd been in had offered us a complimentary glass of Prosecco. Nell had declined as she was driving. I hadn't. I'd probably had enough now, however, or I might succumb to a dress from Paris, which sounded like it might be expensive.

Luckily, Nell intervened. 'Maybe we could browse first, get a feel for what Merry likes?'

'Absolutely.' Abigail's smile didn't quite manage to hide her dismay. 'Take as long as you need. Anything which catches your eye, hang on the empty rail and when you've made your selections, I'll show you to the changing room.'

For the next twenty minutes, we had great fun pulling out dresses from the rack, swirling them around and holding them up to ourselves. We looked at everything, from glamourous, strapless, taffeta numbers to slinky satin bias-cut sheaths, to dresses fit for a Disney princess. We narrowed it down to six dresses and Abigail wheeled the rail to the changing room for me.

'Here you are, ladies,' she said, whisking a heavy damask curtain open on a large changing room with mirrors on three sides. 'Do let me know if you need help. Can I get you a glass of fizz?'

We declined and she left us to it.

I glanced at the rail of dresses and sighed.

'They're all nice,' I hissed to Nell, slipping off my jeans and hoodie, while she undid the buttons on a cream lace dress with a voluminous skirt. 'But nothing has leapt out at me. I want something feminine but not too girly. I want a bit of glamour but not too blingy.'

'And this is only for you, you've got the bridesmaids to sort out next.' Nell held out the dress for me and I stepped gingerly into it.

My heart skipped at the prospect of taking Freya dress shopping; our first stepmum and daughter expedition. Perhaps I could persuade Harley to come along too to buy a new suit.

'Just so you know, I'm not going to be a diva about what you wear,' I promised, looking at her in the mirror as she fastened me up. 'I want you to love it.' I had a sudden thought and groaned. 'I should have asked Hester to be a bridesmaid. Do you think she'll be hurt that I didn't?'

Cole's sister had been an amazing friend. She was a presenter on a TV shopping channel and had secured me a regular slot on *The Retail Therapy Show*. Without that national boost, the Merry and Bright brand of candles wouldn't have grown as big or as quickly as it had, and I would probably still have been operating from the kitchen table. I owed her a lot, and I could have shown my thanks by giving her a part to play at the wedding. The time to have asked her was when we announced our engagement. The opportunity had gone.

Nell shrugged. 'She'll probably be relieved. Weddings are more enjoyable when you haven't got a role to play. Not that I mind being your best woman, of course. Why didn't you ask her?'

'I'm keeping it small. There won't be many of us at the ceremony and if I start adding loads of bridesmaids, there'll be more people in the bridal party than the congregation. I'm inviting your parents and Max, of course, I hope that's OK?'

Nell grinned. 'Mum will be thrilled. Any excuse for a new hat. Unfortunately, Max won't be around, much to Olek's disappointment. He'll be with his mum and her family for a week. He was with us last year, so it's only fair, but Olek loves to see him open his presents. Christmas won't be the same without him, but at least we'll have your wedding to look forward to.'

'You have a great relationship with Max,' I said wistfully. 'You make it look so easy. I'm constantly walking on eggshells, worried about saying the wrong thing.'

There were some white court shoes in the changing room, and she bent down to put them on for me.

'Don't stress about it, it takes time to build up trust with kids. Let them lead the way, try to be the adult that they need in their lives, maybe a role which isn't covered already. Freya and Harley have got two parents, those roles are filled.'

I mulled that over. 'But what about when you see them misbehave or do something they shouldn't? Freya wrote "Harley is a poo" on their bedroom wall. When I told Cole, he just laughed and told me a similar story from when he was little.'

Nell snorted. 'Not your job to sort. Nobody likes other people disciplining their kids. I just try to be a good friend to Max. Be a friend and you can't go far wrong.'

I nodded. 'Good advice.'

'So, ladies, how are you getting on?' Abigail pulled back the curtain to check on us. 'Oh, now that one fits you perfectly.'

I stared at my back view in the mirror. 'You think? I feel a bit exposed.' Although it had long sleeves, and was quite high at the neck, the back had a deep V and a lot of my pasty flesh was on show.

'You'd have to think about some sort of backless bra,' said Nell.

'And a bit of fake tan perhaps?' Abigail stepped closer and tugged at the skirt to display it to its full potential.

I had very pale skin and blonde hair. The idea of sporting an orangey glow was the very opposite of the look I was going for.

'I don't really get on with fake tan.' I caught Nell's eye and we both sniggered.

We'd once caught a train to London for a party and had used the journey to get ready. Hair and make-up had been no problem. Unfortunately, Nell had persuaded me to use fake tan wipes, which she promised were fool-proof. By the time we reached London St Pancras, we were sporting deep brown stripes down our arms and shins and no amount of scrubbing with make-up remover would shift it. We spent the party sweltering in cardigans, hiding behind chairs with our handbags dangling in front of our legs. I'd been cautious around fake tan ever since; the last thing I wanted at my wedding was to look like a satsuma in a dress.

'I'll leave you to it,' said Abigail coolly.

I clambered out of the lace dress and into a fitted velvet dress and matching coat.

Once again, Abigail came to have a look.

'This one's nice,' I said, giving her a twirl. 'I feel a bit like Mary Poppins, I could wear some little button-up boots to match.'

Abigail clasped her hands together. 'That would look fabulous. You have good taste. This dress is one of my particular favourites, it's very sought after.'

'Of course it is,' Nell murmured under her breath.

I pondered my reflection. It was a lovely outfit and fitted the bill. If I bought it now, that would be a big weight off my mind.

'Thank you, we'll think about it,' said Nell to Abigail, tugging the curtain closed.

'I think this one is fine,' I commented, giving myself one last look before unbuttoning the coat.

'Exactly,' she said briskly, putting the coat back on its hanger. 'Which is why you're not buying it. Fine is adequate, it's like saying this one will do and that's not enough. This is your wedding dress, it has to be perfect. You'll know when you see it. It'll stop you in your tracks. You'll get all emotional and goosepimply. Trust me. This dress will not be coming with you up the aisle.'

'OK,' I said meekly.

Ten minutes later I was dressed, and we were back out in the street. It was almost five o'clock, darkness had fallen while we'd been in the bridal boutique, and it was bitterly cold. Both of us were wrapped in hats, gloves and scarves, but we still huddled together, arm in arm, for warmth. This week, the temperature had plunged so low that it was probably even too cold to snow.

'Where next?' Nell asked, as we wandered through the streets of Bakewell. 'More shopping, more fizz, or home?'

'Home, I think,' I replied, picturing a roaring fire and an evening snuggling up with Cole. 'Thanks for today. I had fun.'

'Me too. Sorry you didn't find a dress,' said Nell. 'But I'm glad you didn't make any rash decisions to buy the first one which fitted you nicely.'

'You know, maybe I will order a few dresses online just to— Oh!' My feet came to an abrupt halt as something in a shop window caught my eye. 'Look!'

'What's the matter?' Nell looked at me sharply to see why I'd yanked on her arm. She followed my gaze to the window. 'Wow.'

We were directly in front of a vintage clothing store which I'd been in several times before. It hadn't crossed my mind to try here for a wedding dress. But in the window was a mannequin dressed in the most beautiful gown I'd ever seen. It was a soft cream with hints of gold thread running through it, there was a beaded lace bodice which tapered to a point at the front, long sleeves, slightly puffed at the shoulder and a long floor-length silk skirt edged in lace.

I stood there, frozen to the spot, unable to drag my eyes away from the dress as the door opened, and a woman came out. Her face was obscured by her hat and scarf, and she was holding a large cardboard box in front of her. She noticed us looking in the window.

'It's a beauty, isn't it?' she said. 'You can't beat vintage for elegance.'

'It's perfect,' I replied, a lump forming in my throat. 'It's exactly what I was looking for.'

'The original bride it was made for was married for over sixty years; you'd never tell it was that old though.' The woman's phone began to ring from the depths of her shoulder bag, and she moved away to answer it.

'If you believe in omens, staying married for that long has got to be a good one,' said Nell, peering to read the price tag. 'Are you going to see if it fits?'

'It'll fit.' I rubbed at my arms, shivering despite my thick coat. 'I've got goosepimples.'

She raised an eyebrow. 'And you know what that means.'

I grinned. 'It means I'm about to say yes to the dress.'

Chapter Six

Emily

'Ooh, I've got something for you,' Violet said, raising her finger as if a thought had just struck her. Violet was a larger-than-life lady with an eye for colour, which explained the fact that her name matched her hair, and she was currently wearing a fuchsia floor-length Afghan coat over her jeans and jumper. 'Now, where did I put it? Bear with me, I'll nip in the back and look. Won't be a jiffy.'

'Take as long as you like,' Emily said happily, watching the shopkeeper disappear into the stockroom. 'You know me, you'll have to kick me out at closing time. Although I've already stayed longer than planned.'

'Only because you've helped me,' Violet shouted from the stockroom. 'I'd still be fumbling with those buttons with my fat fingers.'

Emily's eyes slid to the mannequin in the window which she'd helped style. The 1950s wedding dress had a long row of tiny buttons down the back which her small fingers had made quick work of. The two women had marvelled over the dress's heritage and the neat stitching. Emily could sew very basic stuff, she'd learned from her mum, but the level of detail on this bridal gown was exquisite.

Popping into Vintage by Violet after school had been a brilliant idea. She loved nothing more than mooching amongst the rails, spotting potential in other people's cast-offs. And because she was a regular, Violet sometimes put items to one side for Emily, knowing she might like them. Today's find was a classic Victoriana cotton and lace blouse. There were a couple of tears in it, and a missing button, but she could fix those easily. She hadn't decided whether to sell it on or keep it. She smiled to herself, who was she kidding. This one would be a keeper.

She deserved a treat; the last week had been the most stressful she could ever remember. Going back into school after Gavin had dumped her, knowing that she'd let Alison down, had been miserable. She hadn't had much sleep and anxiety had given her a headache. Alison had been sympathetic, but Emily had spent the day struggling to concentrate. They were back to normal now, but Emily felt pressure to keep a lid on her personal life and try not to let it impact her working day. Easier said than done.

'OK, here you go.' Violet made a space on the glass-topped counter by sweeping vintage hair accessories to one side with her arm. She then dropped a large cardboard box down in front of Emily. 'These any good to you?'

Emily peered inside the flap and saw a large quantity of red hats with white trims. She hadn't known what to expect, but it certainly hadn't been this. 'Santa hats?'

Violet nodded. 'Someone donated them this morning and wouldn't take no for an answer. I thought they might be useful for school, Christmas jumper day maybe. You can have them, free of charge, if you like.'

'Are you sure?' The music teacher was after something festive for the school choir to wear at the Christmas concert; these would be perfect.

'Absolutely. You'd be doing me a favour,' Violet chuckled. 'Three dozen acrylic Santa hats don't really go with my aesthetic.'

Emily grinned. 'Point taken. In that case, I'm happy to take them off your hands.'

'Ooh, look!' Violet nodded to the window. 'That dress has caught someone's eye already!'

Outside the shop, two women were staring at the vintage wedding dress.

'I was just about to close, but I'll hang on, just in case,' Violet decided.

'I'll leave you to it,' said Emily. She tightened her scarf and picked up the box, which thankfully didn't weigh much. 'Thanks for the hats and the blouse.'

Violet opened the door for her, and Emily stepped out into the dark. The two women were still looking at the dress and Emily winked at Violet, sending her silent good luck vibes.

'It's a beauty, isn't it?' she said. 'You can't beat vintage for elegance.'

One of the women turned round and smiled at her, clearly besotted. 'It's perfect.'

They exchanged a few words until Emily's phone began to ring. She walked away to answer it.

'Is that Miss Meadows?' The female voice on the end of the line sounded harassed. 'I'm the community nurse due to be visiting your father.'

Emily's heart thumped. 'Please tell me he hasn't gone missing?'

'He's here,' she said, 'but he thinks I'm from the police and I've come to take him away.'

She started to run towards the street where she'd parked her car; she could be there in ten minutes. 'I'm sorry, he gets confused, and the police *have* been recently. Not because he was in any trouble,' she added swiftly, in case the nurse was worried he might be dangerous.

'I'm going to have to reschedule,' said the nurse. 'I've got other patients; I can't hang around.'

'I understand, but if you could just wait a few minutes.' Emily unlocked her car, threw her bag and the box on the back seat and jumped in. 'I'll be there as quick as I can.'

By the time Emily made it to her dad's flat, the nurse had persuaded Ray to let her in. Emily apologised to her, thanked her for waiting and tried to make amends with cups of tea and the mince pies which she had bought to take into school tomorrow.

The nurse had pulled up a chair beside Ray and put on some disposable gloves. She was peeling off the old dressing when Emily brought in the tea tray and set it down on the table.

'How's the arm doing?' she asked, not wanting to look at the wound herself.

'Not too bad now,' said the nurse, rummaging in her bag. 'But any bigger and it would have needed stitches.'

'You were lucky, Dad.'

Everything had stepped up a gear with her dad's care since that call from the police station. Emily realised that day had been a pivotal moment. Having her dad's condition witnessed by those two officers had made it all very real. She'd explained to his doctor that his bouts of confusion were getting worse, social services had increased the carer's daily visits from one to two, and various nurses had been visiting every couple of days to change his dressing.

'Clumsy old fool, I am. Caught it on a gate,' Ray said cheerfully, marvelling at the size of the cut on his arm. 'I was doing a bit of gardening for a chap I met in the shop.'

Emily exchanged a look with the nurse, who knew all about Ray's dawn raid on the police station in his pyjamas.

'However you did it, Dad, if you'd been wearing a coat, it wouldn't have happened.'

'I thought we had global warming now and we're all getting too hot, that's what you told me,' Ray grumbled. 'Gave me earache about it all the way to London.'

'You remember that?' Emily couldn't help but laugh. How could he forget his name one minute and then dredge up a memory from years ago the next?

'Course I do.' He winced as the nurse cleaned his arm with antiseptic.

There'd been a protest in London about climate change which she and Izzy had wanted to join. They must have been about sixteen, full of outrage and passion, and angry at the adult world for ruining the planet. They'd hitchhike to London, she declared earnestly, because it was a green form of transport and cheap. Her mum hadn't wanted her to go, saying it would be dangerous amongst a big crowd and she hadn't been keen on them hitchhiking either, but Emily had been adamant. In the end, her parents had relented, but only after she'd written down exactly what their intended route was.

They'd set off, early one Saturday morning, carrying a cardboard sign with London painted on it. For fifteen minutes, they'd stood at the side of the main road, thumbs out, their optimism waning with every passing car. Until a blue van had pulled up.

'Dad?' Emily had exclaimed as the side window rolled down.

'You won't believe this.' Ray's green eyes were wide with innocence. 'As luck would have it, turns out I've got to go to London today, so I can give you a lift. Hop in then.'

Emily didn't believe it, not for one minute, but Izzy had cheered and thrown herself into the van straight away. Emily had followed her, a bit peeved that Dad had diluted their adventure. Real protesters didn't get lifts from their parents, it just wasn't cool.

'I couldn't do it, love,' he'd said softly, squeezing her hand when they made it back home late that night. 'I couldn't let you be picked up by any Tom, Dick or Harry. You're too precious to me.'

Emily looked at her dad now and felt a rush of love for him. It was these special memories which kept them bound together, reminding her why she was happy to be here for him, even though in the past he hadn't always been there for her.

'Your daughter is right, Ray,' the nurse said. 'You were lucky that you only sustained a graze. I see this all too often, I'm afraid. The patient, and sometimes their loved ones too, often dismiss incidents like this as a one-off. And then things escalate, and care needs to be sorted out fast.'

'Care?' Emily said. 'As in a care home?'

'Most of the time, I'm fine,' Ray grumbled. 'I just have the odd funny turn.'

Emily took his hand. 'You are getting more and more of these episodes, Dad. It worries me.'

'I know, love,' he said in a quiet voice. 'I wish I could do something about it. I don't know what I'd do without you.'

The nurse gave Emily a sympathetic smile. 'It's not an easy decision to make, but it's something you need to consider. Better to have a plan of action and be in control than for the matter to be taken out of your hands in an emergency.'

She was right, Emily knew, but it was such a big irreversible decision.

'Do you hear that, Dad?' Emily said. 'The nurse is right. Anything could happen when I'm not here to look after you.'

'I'm a bloody liability,' her dad sighed. 'I should do what our old tom cat did when he was past it; wander off and let nature take its course.'

'Don't say that.' Emily shuddered. 'Please. No more wanderings. You need to stay safe.'

Ray looked at her, defeated. 'I can't promise, Emily.' He rapped his knuckles on his skull. 'It's this stupid thing, playing tricks on me. I don't want to be a burden.'

They held each other's gaze for a long moment. He seemed to be waiting for her to say something, giving her responsibility that she didn't want. A care home; was that really the answer? She gave herself a shake and broke eye contact. She didn't want to think about it. Not yet.

'I'll feed back to the occupational health team,' the nurse said, jotting down some notes and packing up. 'You'll get a letter through the post.'

'I don't know what to do,' Emily told her as she showed her out. 'He and my mum separated a long time ago and I'm an only child. It feels wrong to be making decisions on behalf of a parent. What if it's the wrong decision? Or what if I choose the wrong place?'

'I haven't been through this myself,' the nurse said kindly. 'But in my line of work, I hear all sorts of tales of good and bad care providers. Take a look at Springwood House. You might be pleasantly surprised.'

Emily thanked her, closed the door and returned to the living room. Ray had turned the television on and was staring at what appeared to be a crime drama. He was agitated, rubbing his forehead repeatedly, his eyes darting left and right.

'Quick,' he said urgently, without looking at her. 'Sit down and watch *Morse*.'

'No thanks, Dad. Are you hungry? I can make you something.'

'Just sit down,' he said irritably. He perched on the edge of his armchair, his eyes not leaving the TV. 'I can't believe it.'

Emily did as she was told. On the screen, a woman walked along a narrow street at night, on the phone to a friend. She ended the call and slipped her phone back in her coat pocket. There was a flash of movement in the shadows, followed by a scream.

'There!' her dad shouted, pointing at the screen. 'There he is, he's been hiding.'

'It's OK, Dad. He's the villain,' said Emily. 'There's always a baddie in these things. Turn it off if it's bothering you.'

Her dad shook his head. 'I can't. I need to know if it's me.'

Emily stared at him, confused. 'I don't understand. If what's you?'

He jabbed a finger at the television again, his face tense with worry. 'Is that me doing those terrible things? Am I a bad man?'

'You're asking if that tall man with blonde hair in *Morse* is you?' She shook her head slowly in disbelief.

'Is it?' he repeated.

She dropped her face in her hands and tried to hold it together. She was way out of her depth. What on earth did you say to a man who believed he was somehow starring as a criminal in an episode of *Morse*?

A wave of loneliness hit her. If only she had someone to help her deal with this. It wouldn't be fair to ask her mum, not after they'd been separated for so long, and anyway, her stepdad wouldn't be happy about it. Talking to Izzy was great, but it was no substitute for having her here. And Gavin . . . he might not have been much practical help, or in fact a sympathetic ear, but she missed him. The solid presence of him, the hug at the end of the day to make her feel that everything would be OK.

But no, she was in this on her own.

She took a deep breath, got to her feet and put her arms around his shoulders. 'No, Dad, it isn't. That's another man. I'll show you.'

She pulled him to his feet and took him to the mirror over the fireplace.

'That's you.' She pointed to his reflection. 'And that's me standing beside you. You have grey hair and a stubbly beard.'

Her dad put a hand up to his face, feeling along his jaw. 'Are you sure?'

She nodded. 'I promise. The man on the TV is an actor. He's not you.'

Her dad's face crumpled. 'Thank God. I thought . . . I'm no angel, but if I'd killed someone I'd have to turn myself in.'

'You haven't done anything wrong,' she said, trying to lead him back to his armchair. 'You're just confused. It's OK.'

She'd be leaving him soon. The carer would pop in later, but then he'd be on his own again. What would the next incident be? she wondered. And the next? She thought about what the nurse had said about having a plan of action. Maybe the time had come to make that plan after all, rather than leave it until Christmas. It wouldn't hurt to get organised, do some research. Yes, she thought, pleased to have finally come to a decision: tomorrow she would make an appointment to visit Springwood House.

Chapter Seven

Merry

It was evening and Merry and Bright, like all the shops around the market square, was closed for the day. I was in the workroom preparing for tomorrow.

The big stainless-steel wax melter I'd imported from America was clean and ready to be switched on in the morning and I was working my way along three long rows of empty glass jars, fixing wicks to the inside with my glue gun. We'd come a long way from the days when I could only melt a litre or two of wax at a time on my little hob at Holly Cottage. Then a batch would make between ten and twenty candles at a time. Now we had the capacity to make two hundred of my small-sized candles in one go. Perfectly melted wax, every time, in just under two hours – it had been a pricey investment, but it had revolutionised Merry and Bright.

This was my favourite time to work. As much as I loved the bustle of customers coming and going during the day and chatting to people about our different products and explaining how they were made, I relished the peace and quiet of an empty space at the end of the working day. Being creative for me was like therapy, while my hands were busy stirring and pouring and sticking labels to the jars, my mind would still, my breathing steady and solutions to problems which had been niggling me all day would ease their way to the surface.

Tonight I was thinking about how best to grow the business. We'd had a good year and now the pressure was on to ensure that next year would be equally as successful. The monthly sales slots on *The Retail Therapy Show* had opened my eyes to the possibilities of selling to other retailers, but how should I go about that, and when? And how could I increase production to keep up with demand? Questions, questions . . .

From the doorway came the sound of a gentle cough, and I smiled, loving the way Cole announced his presence softly, knowing I'd jump out of my skin if he didn't. He was leaning on the door frame, watching me, a faraway look in his eyes.

'Hey you.' I was still holding the glue gun and he held his hands up in mock surrender.

'Don't shoot.'

I laughed. 'Don't worry, I'd hate for you to come to a sticky end.' I switched off the gun at the wall, set it down to cool and washed my hands. 'You look deep in thought.'

'I am. Very deep.' He crossed the room in three long strides, wrapping his arms around me from behind while I dried my hands. He bent down, his lips finding the hollow of my collarbone.

'Should I be worried?' I said huskily, leaning back into him. 'Mind you, kiss me like that again and you could literally say anything, and my brain wouldn't even be able to process it.'

'I was just looking at you, thinking how such a beautiful woman could possibly be my fiancée. And that I'd do anything for you.'

'Just love me forever. That'll do.' I turned around to face him and kissed him back.

Mushy or not, I felt the same about him. Although I'd had boyfriends before, Cole was the first man who'd taught me not only how to love but how to be loved. There was no doubt in my heart that he was the one I wanted to spend the rest of my life with.

'That's easy.' He pulled back from our kiss and traced his fingertips down my spine. 'I was also thinking that I used to be the workaholic in this relationship and now here you are and it's after seven o'clock. I was driving past on my way home and saw the lights still on.'

'Sorry. It was like this last year just before Christmas, if your dad hadn't joined me at Merry and Bright, I'd never have got through the orders.'

'And now the business has grown, and you've still only got my dad on the payroll.' He laughed softly. 'I don't know how you manage.'

'I need to employ more staff, but . . .' I shrugged. 'It's not easy finding the right people.'

Just after we'd opened the shop in spring, I'd hired a guy who'd previously managed a sports shop to work alongside Fred, but he had insisted on stacking the shelves so high with candles that customers couldn't reach them. Then he started arriving late and phoning in sick on Monday mornings and I'd had to let him go. Next there'd been the woman with marketing experience who I'd employed to help grow the brand while manning the shop. She quickly got too big for her boots and tried delegating her work to me. The final straw was when she told me off for experimenting with new scents when I was scheduled to be doing something else. She didn't last long after that.

Cole gave me a cynical look. 'You mean you don't believe anyone else can do the job as well as you.'

My shoulders sagged. 'I know I've got to let go a bit more, but Merry and Bright is my baby, my brand. Letting anyone in is a big deal for me.'

He kissed my forehead. 'Merry, I've been there. Hiring a site foreman was a big step for me. I took Josh on before I really needed him. But now I couldn't manage without him; not only have I got someone to share problems with, but if I'm not there, I know the building site is in safe hands.'

I nodded, acknowledging he was right. 'I'll give it some serious thought in the New Year, I promise. I'll have to,' I said. 'I went in to check on Fred earlier and found him dozing behind the counter. It made me feel terribly guilty, he should be winding down at his age, not working in my shop. We were fairly quiet, so I sent him home early.'

Cole chuckled. 'Good old Dad. I know how he feels though,' he said, stifling a yawn. 'I've had a crazy busy week too.'

As soon as Orchard Gardens, his last construction project, had been finished earlier this year, he had bought another plot of land nearby. This time, he was building three luxury homes. It had been this opportunity that had put his plans to buy a house for himself on hold in the spring. I preferred older properties, but I had to admit, he did build beautiful homes; I was friends with two sisters, Cesca and Fliss, who'd bought houses next door to each other in Orchard Gardens, so I got to go inside regularly.

'Let's go home,' I said, turning the computer off, 'get the fire on and think about where to hold the wedding reception.'

'Aha!' he exclaimed smugly. 'A bit of good news on that score. Drumroll please?'

I groaned as he picked up two pens and tapped them on the desk.

Come on, little drummer boy, the suspense is killing me.' He was drumming mad. Fred once told me that one summer he'd spent hours in the garden with an upturned bucket and two sticks, perfecting the drum solo from Phil Collins's 'In the Air Tonight' until the neighbours had complained.

'What do you think of this place for the wedding reception?' He took out a glossy brochure from inside his coat and handed it to me. The front cover depicted a grand-looking hotel set in acres of Derbyshire countryside.

'The Claybourne Hotel?' I read, flicking through it. 'It's beautiful, very fancy.'

If I was honest, it was too fancy for my tastes. My ideal venue for the reception would have been Holly Cottage: relaxed, cosy, familiar. But it wasn't big enough, and I didn't want the responsibility of getting the house ready for wedding guests before leaving for the actual ceremony.

'I hoped you'd say that.' He took my coat from the hook on the back of the door and held it out for me. 'It's got a lovely garden room we could use. I've made an appointment for us to view this Saturday afternoon. If you can close early, we can drive over, perhaps have dinner in the restaurant while we're there, test out the menu. What do you think?'

I slipped my arms into the sleeves and turned around to face him. 'Oh Cole, I'm sorry, but I can't this weekend.' I felt awful seeing his face fall in disappointment. 'We've got to make the candles for our next TV appearance. It's a Black Friday special and we're expecting mammoth sales. I'll be working late.'

'I understand,' he said with a sad smile. 'No worries. I'll call them back, rearrange.'

'You could always go by yourself?' I suggested. 'If you like it, I'm sure I will too.'

As soon as the words left my mouth, I regretted them. His brow furrowed and he looked at me with dismay. 'You don't want to see the venue for our wedding reception for yourself?'

'No! I mean, yes, of course I do,' I said, backtracking. 'But you could check it out and if you approve, we can nip back together.'

He gave me a weak smile. 'Sure. We haven't got the kids this weekend, so I'll be at a loose end; I might as well do something useful.'

'I really am sorry,' I said. 'I'll advertise for another part-time member of staff, even if it's just to help out over Christmas.'

'Hey, it's fine, I'm proud of you,' he replied, wrapping his arms around me. 'I'm marrying a successful, ambitious businesswoman; I wouldn't dream of standing in your way. I just don't want you to take on too much, that's all.'

I rested my cheek on his chest, grateful to feel his strength, his support. 'Thank you. Sometimes it does feel a bit overwhelming.'

'Have I put too much on your plate, springing this wedding on you?' he asked, concerned.

I shook my head. 'The wedding is exciting, I'm loving it. And my dress is gorgeous. But Christmas is coming, I've got Merry and Bright to run, and then there's our family to think about. Holly Cottage isn't big enough for all of us. Harley and Freya need their own rooms, it's not fair to make them share. And maybe there'll be another addition to the crew next year too.'

I'd told Cole that I wanted a family on our first night together. It had been one of the reasons my last relationship fell apart and I'd wanted him to know how I felt from the start. It hadn't made him run for the hills, thank goodness, and it was still true. But there'd been so much change this year, as we gradually knitted our lives together, that we'd actively put off discussing a family, allowing ourselves the time to get to know each other and enjoying our own company before adding a baby into the mix.

'Let's just try to take it one day at a time and deal with what needs dealing with. We can put finding a new home for our extended family on January's agenda.' He tightened his arms around my waist, bringing me close. 'But if we're saying we're ready to have a baby, that's an even bigger reason to get your team sorted out. Agreed?'

'Agreed,' I said, pretending to salute.

He grinned. 'And there is something I'd like to take care of without you getting involved.'

'Oh?'

'The honeymoon. Will you leave it with me, no questions?'

'We're having a honeymoon?' I was surprised. I'd assumed we wouldn't have one, given the short notice. And there was the small matter of what to do about the shop. Not that I'd dream of ruining the moment by mentioning that right now.

He pressed his lips together and pretended to zip his mouth shut, making me laugh.

'Not one single question?' I pressed.

'Just trust me.' He kissed me, a smile hovering at his lips.

'I do. A new husband, mystery honeymoon and a baby to look forward to,' I said, shaking my head in wonder. 'Now please can we go home? All this excitement has made me hungry.'

Chapter Eight

Emily

'It's much more homely than I anticipated,' Emily remarked, as Gail, the manager of Springwood House care home, showed her around. She was so glad that she'd taken the nurse's advice. Seeing the facilities, the staff and some of the other residents was already giving her hope.

'That's the best compliment you could pay us,' said the manager, ushering her towards the large glass doors which formed almost one whole wall of the room. 'Because everyone deserves to feel at home.'

'Absolutely,' Emily agreed.

They were almost through the tour of the facilities. Gail had shown her a little flat that was available now – a clean and bright living space with a view over the gardens and a kitchenette to one side with a fridge, sink and space for a kettle. There was a separate bedroom and a sparkling new en suite bathroom. She had tried to envisage it with her dad's shabby belongings in it but decided to cross that bridge if they came to it.

Christmas was already in full swing here at the home, despite it still being November. The communal areas had garlands of tinsel and strings of fairy lights hanging from every possible point. So far, she had counted three huge Christmas trees.

'Guilty as charged. We get into the Christmas spirit earlier and earlier each year,' Gail laughed when Emily commented on it. 'The decorations add colour and sparkle and who doesn't feel jolly when there's a Christmas tree lighting up a room?'

'Very true,' said Emily, warming to Gail more and more.

Emily had been allowed into the main kitchen, which was spotlessly clean, as well as the dining room, which could easily have belonged to a small hotel. She'd seen a lady having her hair styled in the on-site salon and now they were entering the living room, which, despite its size, managed to feel cosy and comfortable.

An old lady wearing the most amazing 1970s maxi dress was doing a jigsaw puzzle and chatting away to herself, two others were laughing over a magazine and an elderly man was tapping on an iPad. One old chap had a young visitor, a granddaughter perhaps, and together with a member of staff they were hanging striped candy canes on yet another Christmas tree in the corner. Another lady about Ray's age was having coffee with a woman who looked so like her that she had to be her daughter. A member of staff with a tea trolley passed amongst them. It was all very civilised.

'Hello, Will!' Gail waved as an attractive man arrived carrying a portable speaker. 'How's it going?'

'Great!' He began arranging chairs into a semicircle. 'Six people booked in for today.'

'Armchair athletics,' Gail explained as they left the room. 'It's proving quite popular.'

'I'm quite jealous,' Emily replied, taking a last look at the man before she left. If the staff all looked like that, she'd be tempted into an armchair herself. 'Do you run many activities?'

'You'd be surprised just how many,' she said. 'We focus on what people can do rather than what they can't. We have a garden which is maintained by residents, we have craft groups for those who enjoy knitting and sewing, card games, cooking, you name it. What are your father's hobbies?'

Emily hesitated. The weird thing was that even though she had taken on the job of looking after him over the last eighteen months or so, prior to that, she had only seen him once or twice a year. Since he'd left Bakewell for good after he and Tina split up. It had been an awful time; Tina had been miserable, and Emily had missed her dad terribly. He'd turn up now and again with belated gifts for her birthday, but he hadn't been great at keeping in touch. She knew he'd lived in Edinburgh for a few years, but he'd never encouraged her to visit. All in all, he was a bit of a mystery to her. She wracked her brains to remember the things which used to interest him, and her mind flitted to the box of dusty old vinyl records in his flat.

'Music,' she said, aware that Gail was waiting for an answer. 'He used to have music on in the car all the time and play records at home. He struggles with buttons and knobs now and he forgets how to turn things on. He loved music festivals when he was younger, too.'

He'd taken her to Glastonbury once. Only for the day, but it had been magical. Mum hadn't wanted him to take her, convinced he'd forget about her, and she'd get lost. That was exactly what had happened; it had been one of the best days of her life. Emily smirked to herself remembering the fun she had had in a tent with a boy called Nevin. Happy days.

73

'No problem,' said Gail, bringing Emily back to the present. 'We can help him play music in his own room and there are lots of group musical opportunities too. We bring people in from the community to lead us for various sessions. We also have dancing lessons and even aerobics and yoga. And, of course, there are plenty of comfy chairs if anyone fancies a nap and several TV sets for those who don't want to miss their favourite shows.'

'It certainly sounds as if Dad won't get bored.'

'Definitely not, but also there's no pressure to do anything. Our residents can do as much or as little as they like.'

'And what about Christmas?'

They were back in the foyer and Gail waved a hand over a noticeboard. 'Activities galore. And there's a Christmas fair coming up. That's always fun; relatives and friends of our residents are encouraged to come to support the stallholders. And we have a local school coming in to sing carols.'

That rang a bell now Gail mentioned it, and a closer look at the poster confirmed it.

'The Darley Academy is where I work,' Emily said. 'The choir are fab.'

'Then you must come along.'

Emily nodded. If her father was here by then, she would.

'Do people have to stay here at Christmas or are they allowed out?'

Gail smiled warmly. 'This would be your father's home, it's not prison. Some residents go to stay with their families, and some families choose to spend part of Christmas Day here. I must say our cook does a fabulous three-bird roast.'

'That does sound tempting.'

Emily hadn't made plans for Christmas, or rather she had but they'd included Gavin, so now she'd have to rethink. She and Izzy had had a long FaceTime call the other night about everything. Izzy had declared Emily well rid of Gavin and said that him dumping Emily had saved her flying over and staging an intervention. Gavin, as far as Izzy was concerned, wasn't worth another thought and although it was still early days, her heart was beginning to heal and Emily was inclined to agree with her.

She had already gone through several stages of emotion since Gavin ended their relationship. Shock that technically he'd dumped her over voicemail, even if she hadn't listened to it before she'd spoken to him. Next, upset that he didn't want her anymore, that effectively he'd broken up with her because she was spending too much time looking after her dad. Sad, too, because she was going to miss him, he made her laugh, brought fun into her life – OK, he hadn't been perfect, but then neither was she. But last night, she had come home, put on her pyjamas and eaten a plate of buttered toast while bingeing on a Netflix series Izzy had told her about and she felt . . . relieved. It was a relief to be able to focus on Springwood House without Gavin complaining that he was being sidelined again. Her own company, she decided was better than the company of someone who wasn't interested in giving her the support she needed.

As far as Christmas was concerned, she always had an open invitation to join her mum and stepdad, Ian. They liked to have Christmas lunch at the local pub and spend the rest of the day watching TV with a bottle of sherry and a family-sized tub of chocolates and she always felt like a gooseberry. But, it was either that, or spend it on her own, or possibly with a plate of three-bird roast at a dementia care home. None of the options were how she'd thought she'd be spending the festive season at her age.

Next year, she promised herself, she was going to make sure she did something which filled her with joy.

'I can see this is a lot for you to take in,' Gail said, studying her face. 'Is there anyone else in the family you'd like to bring for a tour?'

'I don't think so,' she replied, wishing with all her heart that there was someone she could bring. 'I was worried that everyone would be really old, but that's not the case. I'm glad, Dad's only sixty-five.'

'Early-onset dementia is a lot more common that you'd think,' said Gail. 'Many of the people you see here today had full-time careers not too long ago. We have a variety of levels of care. The self-contained flat I showed you is for those who can look after themselves and want their independence. But we also have rooms designed for people who need more help bathing and dressing, for example.'

Emily nodded. 'And you can move from one room to another if necessary? I imagine that makes the transition easier when the time comes.'

'Exactly. Anything that makes life smoother is a good thing for everyone,' Gail acknowledged, showing Emily to the door and handing her a brochure. 'Nice to meet you. I don't want to put any pressure on you, but vacancies don't hang around for long.'

Emily could believe that. She took one last look at Springwood House before heading back to her car. She placed the brochure on the passenger seat and plugged her phone in to charge. There was such a lot to think about, she mused, as she turned on the engine and waited for the condensation to clear on the inside of the windscreen. But her gut feeling was that moving her dad in would be the right thing to do. He would be safe at night if he decided to go for a wander and there would be someone on hand twenty-four hours a day to make sure he was eating properly. And he'd have company too.

She bit her lip. Maybe she should accept the vacancy immediately. What if someone else took the flat? But what was Ray going to think? She hoped he'd see it as a positive move and not a punishment.

Emily wouldn't be able to manage the move by herself. His landlady, Julia, would probably help if she asked her. But her dad had his pride, he wouldn't want to involve Julia, a relative stranger, in such personal matters.

Which only left one other person. Someone who had every right to not want to get roped in.

Emily steeled herself, imagining how well this was going to go down. But, unfortunately, she didn't have other options. Might as well get it over with and go there now.

'Hey, Siri,' she said, using the car's hands-free system. 'Call Mum.'

'Calling Mum,' the robotic voice replied politely.

'Hello, love!' said Tina seconds later.

'Hi, Mum,' said Emily. 'I don't suppose you're free this afternoon?'

Chapter Nine

Emily

'This is nice, isn't it?' said Tina, sampling an olive on the end of a cocktail stick from a delicatessen stall. 'They know how to do Christmas in places like this. We could be on a film set. What was that TV series we used to like?' She paused, thinking. '*Cranford*, that was it.'

Her mum had been about to set off on a solo jaunt to Wetherley market while her partner Ian spent the afternoon with his golf buddies. The golf course itself was closed at this time of year, but the clubhouse bar was always open. Tina teased him about it, called it a youth club for the over sixties, but secretly she was relieved he had a hobby that got him out of the house while she got on with her sewing. An hour after phoning her, Emily and her mum were browsing the market stalls in the town centre.

'It's lovely, I can't believe I've never been here before.' Emily picked up a jar of lime pickle from the stall and paid for it. She'd got a very average ready-made curry for tonight's dinner. A spoonful of this might elevate it a little. 'This was a great idea. Thanks for suggesting it, Mum.'

Tina's face lit up and she linked arms with Emily. 'I'm glad you were free to come. It's nice to have a catch-up, hear all your news. We don't get much time on our own these days like we used to, do we?'

'No, we don't.' Emily was hit by a rush of guilt that she was probably going to ruin the mood by bringing up her dad. Particularly as she needed to ask her mum a favour. It wasn't that there was any animosity between her parents, more that Ray was part of Tina's past and she preferred to keep it that way.

Emily looked around at the cobbled streets and the lovely old Tudor buildings, their windows sparkling with Christmas displays. At the edge of the marketplace was a giant Christmas tree decked out with thousands of coloured baubles, and the old-fashioned lamp posts surrounding the edge of the market were strung with fairy lights.

'Told you,' Tina replied. 'Who needs foreign Christmas markets when you've got this on your doorstep. Mind you, I've only started coming since the fabric stall opened. That haberdashery place on the high street is a café now. I ask you,' she tutted. 'How many coffee shops do we need?'

'Just one,' Emily said, 'and preferably soon. I could murder a coffee and cake stop right now.'

'Let me get my fabric first. Here we are.' Tina stopped beside a stall piled high with rolls of fabric arranged in a rainbow of colours. 'Oh goodness, look at these prints!'

Emily smiled at her mum fondly as she ran her hands over the fabric. Tina was a whizz with a sewing machine, there was nothing she couldn't turn her hand to. She'd even made a three-piece suit for a friend's husband once, when he'd brought a bolt of linen back from his travels. Prom dresses, christening gowns, curtains and even loose sofa covers, Tina wasn't fazed by any dressmaking project. Emily knew her way around a sewing machine too; her mum had taught her well. But for her it was all about second-hand clothing, repairing, repurposing and breathing new life into clothes which were far too good for landfill. Sustainable fashion might be a buzz word these days, but she'd been winkling out treasures from charity shops for as long as she could remember. In fact, there was bound to be a charity shop in Wetherley, perhaps they could go there later.

'So, what have you got to tell me?' asked Tina, rooting a shopping list out of her handbag. 'Come on, out with it. You haven't stopped chewing your lip since you picked me up.'

'It's about Dad,' Emily began with a sigh.

Tina rolled her eyes. 'Now there's a surprise.'

And while her mum sifted through the display of taffetas and satins to find something to make a party dress for the daughter of a friend, Emily brought her up to date with Ray's antics.

'Part of me thinks that moving him into Springwood House is the best thing for him. But the other part is telling me that I'm being selfish and that I'd be doing it because it's a neat solution for me. What do you think?' she concluded.

'Three and a half metres of this please,' said Tina to the woman behind the counter, tapping a silver stretchy fabric before turning to Emily. Two pink spots had appeared on her mum's cheeks and Emily hoped she didn't live to regret asking for her advice. 'I'll tell you what I think. I think Ray Meadows realised he wasn't getting any younger and suspected something might be wrong health-wise, so he slunk back to Bakewell with his tail between his legs and decided to set up home close to you in case he needed looking after. I think this is the longest he's ever stuck around. What does that tell you? He's not as daft as he looks, that man.'

'Need any silver thread?' asked the woman, putting down her knitting. She was wearing fingerless gloves and the end of her nose was red with cold.

'No thanks, love.' Tina shook her head. 'But I will take a four-inch zip please.'

'Maybe he just feels more at home in Bakewell.' Emily shrugged, not wanting to admit that she had asked herself the same question but had decided not to probe too deeply.

'He moved away for good when you were eighteen. Even before that, he was away as much as he was here,' Tina muttered, fingering a red cotton calico printed with gingerbread men. 'So I don't know why he'd class Bakewell as home.'

Maybe so, but he'd been here when Emily had needed him most and she'd never forget that. The time when Tina hadn't gone to the doctors despite having terrible stomach pains and had ended up with peritonitis and septicaemia the night before Emily's first GCSE exam. After watching her mum being driven away to the emergency department, ambulance lights flashing, sirens blaring, Emily had called her dad. There was loud music playing in the background wherever he was, and it had taken a lot of repeating herself to get the message across. But he'd told her to sit tight, and he'd get to her as soon as he could. By the time she woke up the following day and got herself ready to go into school to sit her French exam, there he was in the kitchen making her some toast. He'd driven her to school, reassured her that he'd take care of everything and held her when she cried frightened tears. It wasn't something Mum liked to talk about and Emily had no intention of bringing it up now. She knew he hadn't been perfect, but she'd always remember that he'd showed up for her when it mattered. And that was why she was showing up for him now.

'I don't know either,' Emily replied diplomatically, 'but he's here and if I don't move him into a home, the only other solution is that I find somewhere for me and Dad to live together.' And bang would go her chances of ever having a boyfriend again, she thought glumly.

'Caring for your errant father at thirty-five?' Her mother looked appalled. 'That's too much of a sacrifice. It was bad enough when you gave up that lovely job you had.'

Emily sighed; this was well-trodden ground, and she couldn't defend it, because Tina was right. 'My job at the school is fine. Good even.'

The stallholder held out a paper bag and Tina counted out the exact money in cash, then stowed her purchases away. The two women continued past the next stalls.

'Ray doesn't deserve you,' said Tina hotly. 'Swanning back here, expecting you to be an unpaid nursemaid.'

'He's not expecting anything of the sort,' Emily replied. 'And he's very grateful.'

Tina harrumphed. 'He's not expecting you to pay for it, I hope?'

'No, don't worry about that.' Social services had been really helpful in this department, as had Gail. It seemed almost certain that her dad would receive funding for his care.

'That's something, I suppose,' her mum muttered.

Emily couldn't blame her for her lack of sympathy. Ray had never been a fixed presence in their life. When she was growing up, he would be there one day, happy and settled, and the next he would be off, telling them he had a job somewhere, a chance to make some real money. If it worked out, then she and Tina could join him, he'd say. But that had never happened.

'Almonds!' Tina exclaimed, pointing to a stall called Nell's Nuts. 'I'll get some for the top of the Christmas cake.'

There was always a Dundee cake at Christmas, decorated with whole almonds because Ian didn't like icing. Which was a shame, because marzipan was Emily's favourite bit.

There were two women about her age behind the counter of Nell's Nuts. One was holding her phone and both were absorbed in whatever was on the screen, bent towards each other, their woolly hats touching. They were obviously good friends and Emily felt a pang of longing for Izzy.

'He thinks he's managing most of the time,' Emily said, casting her eye over the array of dried fruits and nuts. Weren't some nuts good for the brain? She was sure she'd read it somewhere. Maybe she'd get some too. 'And when he's not . . . confused, he hates being a burden.'

'You are an angel, you know that.' Tina sighed and gave her a look so loaded with love, that it made Emily's heart melt. Emily could see she was torn. She and Ian had been together for over a decade and seemed happy enough. But once, after a couple of sherries, Tina had confided, in a rare conversation, that she had been besotted with Ray and that he had broken her heart not once but several times.

'Mum, I owe everything to you,' Emily said fondly. 'You did a great job of bringing me up virtually by yourself. And, in a way, I've got Dad to thank for the fact you and I have such a close relationship. You were a great mum; all my friends wanted an invitation after school for your home-made pizza and they were jealous of the dresses you made for my dolls.'

'I *was* a great mum?' Tina teased.

Emily gave her a hug. 'You still are. You've brought me up to be a kind person and do the right thing. I want to do the right thing by Dad, but I need your help.'

In front of her, behind the counter of the nut stall, Emily became aware of a lull in the two women's conversation. She glanced up to see them watching her and her mum.

'Excuse us for overhearing,' said a woman with big green eyes and wisps of blonde hair escaping from her woolly hat. 'But that's such a sweet thing to say about your mum.'

'Oh goodness.' Tina blushed. 'She's a good girl. I couldn't wish for a lovelier daughter.'

Emily put an arm around her mum's waist. 'Back atcha, Mum.'

'You two obviously have a good relationship.' The other woman, wearing an apron with Nell's Nut's emblazoned across the front, flicked her thick copper plait over her shoulder. 'Anything my mum says to me comes with a side order of constructive criticism.'

'I was just thinking the same about your relationship.' Emily smiled at the two women. 'My best friend moved to Jersey and girlie chats aren't the same over FaceTime.'

The blonde woman gave her a sympathetic look. 'I can imagine. Don't get any ideas about moving away, Nell, unless you plan on taking me with you.'

'Does that mean I get to come on the honeymoon with you?' her friend replied, waggling her eyebrows, making the other one laugh.

Tina tutted. 'That's another thing your father has put the kibosh on: holidays or doing anything that matters. When was the last time you saw Izzy?'

Emily nodded towards the women and grinned. 'Don't let's start bickering, Mum, not after we made such a good impression.'

Tina leaned forward conspiratorially. 'And her boyfriend finished with her because she was paying her father far more attention than him. Honestly, that man has got a lot to answer for.'

Emily gave a hoot of laughter and nudged her. 'Mum! If you've quite finished publicly dissecting my love life!'

The woman in the apron leaned her elbows on the counter, looking interested. 'That boyfriend sounds like a charmer. Narrow escape there. We all have to kiss a few frogs before finding our prince, isn't that right?' She jerked her head at her friend. 'This one is getting married to an absolute gem. And don't apologise for having a lively debate, we were just doing the same. I mean, what sort of bride doesn't want a hen party?'

'You're getting married? Congratulations!' said Emily. A fleeting memory popped into her mind: two women's heads together, at the window of Vintage by Violet, gazing up at that 1950s wedding dress. Could it have been these two?

The woman nodded. 'On Christmas Eve. Because Christmas Eve isn't busy enough, right?'

'Oh, quite soon! How exciting.' Emily brushed the image aside. Christmas Eve wasn't far away; this bride-to-be would have bought her dress months ago.

Emily did love a good wedding. The last one she'd been to was the wedding of a colleague and the look on the groom's face as he'd turned to see his bride walk up the aisle towards him had Emily reaching for the tissues. Hopefully she'd get her turn, but romance wasn't on the cards just now. What the whole Gavin episode had shown her was that until she could put more effort into a rela tionship, there was no point getting involved with anyone.

'Thank you,' said the blonde woman. 'It's all a bit of a whirlwind, very exciting of course, but lots to do. I just don't think I can squeeze in a hen party on top of every-thing else, but Nell here won't take no for an answer.'

'You enjoyed my hen party,' said Nell. The friends exchanged looks and giggled. 'Don't deprive me of a repeat performance.'

'Oh, have a party,' encouraged Tina, earning herself a small cheer from Nell. 'Besides, it's a good chance for your mum and your mother-in-law to bond over a few drinks, sort out any friction before the big day.'

The blonde one blinked. 'Um . . .'

She looked so awkward that Emily leapt to her rescue. 'I'm a firm believer in celebrating every special moment, big or small,' she said. Although now she thought about it, she hadn't had such a moment for quite a while. 'If the universe sends an opportunity to celebrate, take it. Anyway, people who say they're too busy for a party definitely need one!'

'Truth!' said Nell.

'Maybe you're right,' the other woman agreed. 'Perhaps I'd regret it in the future if I didn't have any embarrassing photos to look back on.'

'Yes! Well done!' Nell high-fived Emily. 'I'll organise the whole thing. And no condoms or L plates, Scout's honour.'

'Fine, a hen party it is,' she conceded. 'Now, are you going to make these poor ladies wait until Christmas to get served or what?'

'What can I get you?' Nell asked brightly. 'I've got a special offer on mixed nuts.'

Tina hesitated. 'Oh, go on then, I can never resist a bargain, give me three pounds worth. And 500 grams of whole almonds as well, please.'

'Going back to Dad,' Emily began again, keeping her voice low. 'If I move him into Springwood House, I'll feel comfortable leaving him and going travelling again. And the way it's going, if I don't do something, I'm not sure I'll keep the job I've got for much longer.'

Nell weighed mixed nuts into a paper bag and put them on the counter.

'And you're sure this is the right thing?' Tina got her purse out. 'Moving him into a care home? He's only sixty-five.'

'I don't know if I'll ever be sure,' Emily admitted. 'All I know is that I'm doing my best and it would really help if I had your support.'

The blonde woman looked up. 'I'm sorry, that sounds like a hard decision to make. Oops, sorry, I'm eavesdropping again.'

'It's fine,' said Emily. 'It's a relief to talk about it, to be honest. He's got dementia and it's becoming dangerous to leave him on his own.'

'I'm so sorry to hear that,' consoled Nell. 'That's quite a responsibility.'

Emily nodded. 'I know. I've never wanted siblings more.'

'Take some walnuts for your dad,' she said, scooping some into a paper bag. 'Free of charge. Omega three is meant to be good for the brain. Every little helps.'

'That's so kind, thank you.' Emily was touched; people could be so generous.

The blonde woman gave her a sympathetic smile. 'I said something similar to Nell recently. Although, in my case, it was to do with choosing a wedding dress. I don't have parents, or siblings.'

Emily cringed inwardly, remembering Tina's suggestion of getting the mothers-in-law together.

'But, luckily, she's got me, and her wedding dress is to die for.' Nell smiled. 'That'll be five pounds twenty pence please.'

'And *you've* got me,' said Tina, handing over the money and flashing Emily a loving smile. 'And, of course, I'll help you. Let me know what you need me to do.'

She let out a sigh of relief. 'Thanks, Mum, I will.'

That was one parent on board with the plan, now all she had to do was work out how to get the other one to cooperate.

Chapter Ten

Merry

'OK, so one last update from me, ladies and gentlemen,' said Simone, one of Hester's colleagues, as she flashed her pearly veneers at the camera. 'Get your orders in for the cosy fleece blankets before they all go. The cougar is sold out, there are very limited numbers of the snow leopard and the new tiger fleece in pink and white is proving very popular!'

Simone held her smile for five more seconds before breathing a sigh of relief. She dropped the thick blanket she'd been holding onto the velvet chair which served as a prop and walked off set.

'All yours, Hester,' she said, removing her earpiece. 'Ooh, Merry, save me a set of those Christmas candles, darling. Just the thing to give the nanny.'

I gave her a thumbs up and stood still while one of the studio staff fiddled with my microphone pack. I checked that I didn't have lipstick on my teeth and took a couple of deep breaths.

'All good?' Hester asked, leading me away from the blankets to the other half of the brightly lit studio. It had been set up with a shelf unit stacked with candles and two armchairs and a coffee table.

'Raring to go,' I told her and the two of us positioned ourselves beside the shelves of product.

Hester was such a pro; she never displayed a hint of nerves. I, on the other hand, had legs like jelly despite this being my eleventh appearance on her show, the penultimate slot for Merry and Bright before Christmas.

The studio manager counted us down and then we were live. Hester did her welcome spiel and I smiled and nodded, never entirely sure if I was in shot or not.

Today we were selling my Christmas gift sets and I was giving viewers an exclusive offer on a brand-new product for next year, a large candle with three wicks with a scent that I was excited about.

'So.' Hester beamed into the camera and picked up one of my gift boxes. 'I've got something very special for you and I know you're going to love it, but before I hand over to Merry, just a quick update on the lion-print blanket in chestnut . . .'

I tried to pay attention and not fidget while she whipped the audience up into a state of panic about the imminent extinction of big-cat-themed fleeces. I always forgot how hot it was in the studio under the lights. I was wearing a maxi dress and boots and could already feel a prickle of heat under my arms, I'd have a sweaty upper lip before long. Hester, in a silk shirt and leather trousers, seemed impervious to the temperature.

Finally, she turned her smile to me. 'And now, Merry, tell us about the candles . . .'

Before long I was in the swing of things and able to chat naturally to Hester about our Christmas candles, at least as naturally as could be expected with a cameraman almost in my face.

'These are perfect if you're having a quiet night in with a loved one. Or a great way of adding a touch of luxury to a dinner table. You can even incorporate them into your Christmas decorations,' I said. 'The more, the merrier.'

Hester laughed. 'Absolutely! Merry and Bright candles are all handmade by you, in Derbyshire, aren't they?'

'Yes, that's correct.' I nodded to Hester, making sure I ignored the camera as instructed. 'We make everything in our workroom in Wetherley in small batches using only the best ingredients. Our shop is there too, it's easy to find, opposite the market.'

'And all your packaging is recyclable?'

I told her it was and then gave a few statistics – not too many, viewers were easily bored, I'd learned.

'So, what have you got new and exclusive for *Retail Therapy* viewers?'

'Something very special.' I picked up a packaged candle from the display on the table in front of us and removed the box. 'We've developed a new scent called Home. It's a blend of vanilla and cocoa beans, with soft undertones of cedarwood and musk.'

'Mmm, that smells delicious even before you've lit it.' Hester enthused. 'Let's light some, shall we?'

'Sure.' I lit each of the three wicks.

'Mmm, this is definitely an aroma I'd like to come home to,' Hester said to the camera and gave a quick run-through of the prices and reminded her audience just how lucky they were to be getting a sneak preview.

'Isn't it lovely?' I said, picking up my cue. 'It conjures up a feeling of warmth and cosiness. Our homes are our sanctuaries, a place to retreat and relax, a safe space. This is as close as I could get to creating a perfume which feels like a hug.'

'Wow. Hugs are something we can never have too much of.'

'At Merry and Bright, we think so.' I smiled at my soon-to-be sister-in-law, who gave great hugs.

'Oh, my goodness.' Hester bent down to inhale the new candle again. 'That really is a comforting smell.'

'Thank you. Home is part of our new range for spring. So, it won't be available anywhere else except on this show, today.'

'You heard Merry!' Hester beamed at the camera. 'The number is on your screens now. Make sure you don't miss out on this incredible exclusive deal. Can you tell us about how Home came about?'

Although the show was largely unscripted, I always practised what I was going to say, including little details which would appeal to the show's audience. Way back in the spring, when I'd first been allocated the slot, the show's producer, Conan, had spent the morning giving me some instructions on what to say and not to say. About finding the balance between selling the product and not boring viewers to tears. If I forgot anything important, Hester had a hot sheet on each product to hand and the voice of the producer in her ear too.

'Of course,' I began. 'Next year at Merry and Bright we're focusing on self-care. We want to encourage our customers to make time for themselves, to be as good to themselves as they would be to others. Kindness begins at home. Even if just for fifteen minutes a day.'

'That is so true!' Hester agreed. 'We should be our own best friends! And you've picked vanilla and cocoa beans. Why is that?'

'I think they evoke—' My voice stopped suddenly as the strangest thing happened. From nowhere, a wave of emotion hit me so strongly that the words died on my tongue. I tried again. 'They make me feel—'

'Yes, Merry?' Hester prompted, tilting her head to one side.

Suddenly, my carefully prepared bullet points about comfort and the sweet smells associated with childhood refused to come. Instead, all I could think about were the real reasons I'd chosen these oils, the real memories these aromas brought back to me. They did remind me of home, but more specifically of my mum and the few short years we spent together. I missed her. After all these years, there still wasn't a day that passed by without me thinking about her.

I swallowed and looked at Hester, who gave a sign of encouragement.

'The truth is,' I began again in a faltering voice, 'that for a long time after my mum died, I hankered after the home we'd shared. We used to have hot chocolate in bed on cold nights, and when she collected me from school, we'd bake fairy cakes and decorate them with vanilla buttercream. Those are the smells of home for me.'

'That's a wonderful memory,' Hester enthused. 'What could be more comforting than the smell of home baking! Now tell us about the woody aromas you've included. What says "home" to you about them?'

'The notes of cedarwood and musk are in there because . . .' The bright studio lights were hot on my face and, I felt thirsty, my mouth dry. The other half of the studio was in darkness and over by the scruffy sofa were a stack of bottles of water. It was all I could do not to dash off-set out of the brightness and grab a drink. 'Because—' I tried swallowing, hoping it would help appropriate words to emerge from my mouth.

Don't go there, do not go there, Merry, chanted a voice inside my head. But I couldn't help it. I knew what I wanted to say, what I had to say.

'What do they evoke for you?' Hester prompted.

'My mum,' I said simply. 'Her name was Sam. Sammy to her friends. She represented home.'

Hester nodded sympathetically. She knew all about my childhood, that after Mum died, I'd been alone in the world, sent from foster parents to foster parents before moving to the children's home where I spent my teenage years.

But Hester's eyes were also wary. Her show was all about selling an aspirational lifestyle; becoming an orphan at eleven years old was not what her producer wanted.

'Home can be a person just as much as a place,' said Hester brightly. 'I know I'd be happy to come home to a house smelling like this.'

'She always wore the same perfume. Every day,' I told her. 'And that desire to feel at home for me comes from missing her, from missing the home we'd shared.'

'What a lovely tribute to your mum,' said Hester, her eyes shining. 'My mum passed away a couple of years ago and I can never go through the perfume department without stopping at the Givenchy counter and spraying her favourite scent on my wrist.'

'I can't remember what my mum's perfume was called, but it had cedarwood and musk in it, I'm sure of that.'

Hester's eyes had the slightly glazed look which I recognised as having the voice of her producer gabbling instructions in her ear. I felt a stab of alarm; I'd veered too far off topic.

'And that's the lovely thing about scented candles,' I said, rallying quickly. 'You can use them to create any atmosphere you want. I always put one in the hallway, to make everyone feel at home when they arrive.'

'That's a fabulous idea!' Hester gushed with relief. 'I've got friends coming over this weekend. I think a trio of

Home candles will make a lovely centrepiece to decorate the table. OK, ladies and gentlemen, the number is on your screens. The calls are coming in thick and fast now, so don't miss out on this exclusive handmade candle offer from Merry and Bright . . .'

Fifteen minutes later, our slot was over, and we were back in the green room.

Hester's producer, Conan, stomped in to find me holding a cup of tea in shaky hands and Hester squashed beside me on the sofa.

'What the hell happened there?' He looked from Hester to me in disbelief. 'I thought you were going to cry at one point.'

So did I, I thought.

'I'm really sorry,' I said sheepishly. 'It won't happen again.'

'We're supposed to be selling dreams, not nightmares,' he commented gruffly.

'Chillax, dude,' Hester teased. 'The candles are selling, aren't they?'

Conan apparently couldn't think of anything to say to that, so after stopping in front of the mirror to smooth down a tuft of his wiry hair, he stalked off.

'That really got to you, didn't it?' Hester said.

'The memories just hit me from nowhere.'

'I don't think you ever get over losing a parent. I still burst into tears about Mum at the most random moments.' She handed me a tissue from a box on the table in front of us.

I gave her a wan smile and blew my nose. 'Sorry I dragged up difficult memories for you. I don't know what's wrong with me.'

'You're running a successful business, it's almost Christmas and suddenly, you're getting married,' Hester pointed out. 'It's not surprising that you're a bit emotional.'

'But all those things are good things,' I said. 'I can hardly complain about them.'

'Merry . . .' She hesitated, tucking her hair behind her ear. 'Oh, nothing, ignore me.'

'Go on,' I said, sensing her discomfort.

'OK, I'll say it.' Her words came out in a rush. 'I think you're taking on a lot and spreading yourself too thin. And not just yourself, Dad too.'

I blinked at her, taken aback by her tone. 'We all have busy lives, I'm no different. And Fred seems perfectly happy.'

'I'm glad the business has grown, but I remember how busy you were last Christmas, and that was before you were selling nationwide. Plus, now there's the wedding to organise and only Dad in the shop.' Hester's smile was still in place, but there was no mistaking the reprimand. 'Cole told me he fell asleep at the counter the other day. It's not fair on him, and I don't think Astrid is happy that he's working so hard. I think you rely on him too much.'

My cheeks were blazing; it sounded as if they'd been talking about me behind my back. Did Cole's family think I was taking advantage of Fred's good nature? With less than six weeks until I became a Robinson, the last thing I wanted was to upset anyone.

I pressed my hands to my hot face. 'I hear what you're saying. I'd already decided to take on more staff just as soon as I get around to it.'

Hester raised a sceptical eyebrow. 'And when will that be?'

Just then, the door opened, and Conan bounced back in. 'I stand corrected, ladies, the story behind Merry's Home candle is proving irresistible to viewers, we're exceeding our normal figures.'

'Thank goodness for that,' I said. 'I thought I'd blown it with *Retail Therapy* forever.'

'See you next time for a final Christmas blast, eh?' He winked at me and disappeared.

'Can you cope with the extra demand?' Hester pursed her lips.

'Of course,' I said, with more confidence than I felt. I'd work twenty-four-hour shifts if I had to. There was no way I was going to miss an opportunity this big. 'Now, can we please stop being Debbie Downers and change the subject?'

'Sorry, I just worry about everyone.' Hester gave a sheepish smile. 'But yes, let us talk weddings. What can I do to help?'

I pulled a bridal magazine out from my handbag and flicked to a page I'd marked previously. 'For starters, I'd like your opinion on wedding flowers. What do you think of this?'

'Wow.' Her eyes widened. 'It's Christmas, it's a wedding and you're the bride. I say you can get away with anything you want.'

'Right answer,' I said, giving her a hug, glad that the awkwardness between us had vanished. 'So that's one decision made, only ninety-nine to go.'

Chapter Eleven

Emily

28 NOVEMBER

'Morning, Dad!' Emily called when she let herself in.

'Who's there?' Ray Meadows appeared from the living room, bleary-eyed and still wearing his pyjamas and dressing gown.

'Your daughter, Emily,' she said, kissing his cheek. 'Who else is going to call you Dad, eh?'

He blinked several times and nodded. 'Didn't know you were coming.'

He meant that he'd forgotten. She'd spent hours here last night and had told him multiple times to expect her this morning. She felt a pang of sadness; he'd declined rapidly over the last few weeks. It was hard to keep a smile on her face sometimes and not let him see how upset she was.

'Well, it's a nice surprise then, isn't it. I've brought you a fresh sausage roll from the bakery.' She held out the paper bag. The pastry was still warm and smelled delicious and she hoped that the aroma might help tickle his taste buds into action. She was sure he'd got thinner in the last couple of weeks, and he didn't have any weight to lose. Still, from now on, he'd have all his food cooked for him and wouldn't have to rely on memory to eat regularly.

Springwood House was expecting him at lunchtime. All she had to do was get him and his belongings there.

Emily felt like she'd been living in the eye of a tornado for the last week. Once she'd contacted Gail to confirm her dad's place at the home, everything had moved very quickly. But not a moment too soon; he'd got himself into trouble this week for walking out of a shop without paying. The security officer was very understanding about it and the supermarket manager had agreed not to press charges, but it had meant dashing out of work again to the rescue. She'd stayed late at school to make up for lost time, but it wasn't ideal. Alison needed her there when school was open.

Ray took the bag from her and peered inside. 'Not hungry. You woke me up. I've not been asleep long.'

He seemed to sleep whenever and wherever he liked these days. The other evening when she'd called round after school, she'd found him asleep on the bathroom floor on a pile of towels.

'Save it for later then,' she said, leading him into the kitchen and putting the kettle on.

He pulled out a chair and sat at the table. Immediately contradicting himself, he tucked into the sausage roll. She watched him fondly while he demolished it in four bites.

'I thought we'd go for a walk, Dad,' she said, brushing the crumbs off the lapel of his dressing gown. 'Perhaps go to the park and get a coffee from the café? It's chilly, but the sun is out and if we wrap up—'

'I can't leave the flat.' He looked hopefully into the bag. She regretted not buying more than one sausage roll. 'I'm waiting for Emily.'

He didn't recognise her, she thought with a pang, as she put a cup of tea in front of him.

'OK, well, after you've drunk this, why don't you go and get washed and shaved ready for when she arrives?'

It took some negotiation, but finally Ray was persuaded into the bathroom. She left him to it and went into the living room and waved to her mum, who was waiting in her car outside.

Two minutes later, Tina was at the front door. Emily put a finger to her lips and indicated the bathroom, from where the sound of running water was accompanied by a low tuneless hum.

Tina looked around her, taking in her ex's living arrangements. She wrinkled her nose and sniffed. 'Let's get some windows open, let some fresh air in. Does he know what's happening?'

'No. I don't think he'd take it in,' Emily replied with a sigh. 'We talked about it in the week, when his mind was clear, but he's not with it today. My plan is to take him out of the house while you pack the car for me. Then, when we get back, I'll tell him he's got a doctor's appointment or something and hopefully he'll go along with it and get into the car. I feel bad about deceiving him, but I don't want to cause him too much distress either.'

Tina nodded. 'OK. You'd better give me the tour then before he gets to the end of whatever song he's warbling.'

Emily quickly showed her where everything was. 'The big furniture stays with the flat, but that's OK because his new place is furnished. It's smaller things to make him feel at home that we need. His footstool, cushions, pictures. Oh, and his records. The manager of Springwood House has said he'll be able to play them there. And anything else you can think of.'

'Pillows?' Tina suggested. 'I know I sleep much better on my own pillows.'

Emily nodded. 'Good idea. All his bedding. I managed to pack a couple of bags of his clothes while he was dozing last night. But if you could pack the last few bits, like the stuff on his bed that he was wearing yesterday please, and his slippers. Oh, and another jacket.' He didn't own a lot. In fact, going through her dad's meagre things had made her feel quite sad.

'What about all his personal stuff, papers and whatnot?' Tina asked, pointing to a small chest of drawers. 'Do you want any of that?'

Emily hesitated. Would he want anything other than his wallet today? she wondered. She decided against it. The main priority was to make the transition from this home to the next as painless as possible. 'Leave them, once I've got him settled, I'll come back and have a proper sort-out.'

'Understood.' Tina nodded. 'I'm proud of you, love.'

'Thanks, Mum.' Emily hugged her. 'And thanks for agreeing to help. Just having someone with me so I'm not in this alone means a lot. Especially when I know it can't be easy for you.'

'It does feel odd. But a lot of water has gone under the bridge since your father and I were together.' Tina smiled sadly and glanced at the saggy old armchair in front of Ray's ancient TV. 'I've found happiness with Ian, I'm not sure your father has been so lucky.'

The bathroom door opened, making both women jump.

'Quick,' Emily hissed. 'Hide behind the door!'

She bundled her mother out of sight and quickly shepherded her dad into his bedroom, where she'd already laid out some clothes for him. He stood in the middle of the floor looking dishevelled and disorientated. The front of his pyjama shirt was wet, so at least she knew he'd had a wash.

'What's going on?' he said, narrowing his eyes.

Her heart thumped with nerves and for an awful moment she wondered if he'd overheard something. 'Nothing,' she replied smoothly, 'you're going to get dressed, that's all.'

'You remind me of my daughter,' he grumbled. 'She's bossy too.'

'Cheeky monkey,' she said, slipping his dressing gown off his shoulders. She peered at his face, his jaw was still peppered with white bristles, some of them in long tufts. 'Did you have a shave?'

He rubbed a hand over his chin. 'I've had half a shave. Goodnight then.' He pulled back the duvet on his bed.

'It's morning time, Dad, you've just had a wash and now we're going for a walk.'

'It'll have to be a quick one,' he grumbled, sitting down on the bed and taking off his slippers. 'I'm going to work later.'

Outside the bedroom door, Emily heard a snort of laughter and prayed her dad hadn't heard it too.

'Can you manage getting dressed or shall I help?' she said uneasily as he began to unbutton his pyjama shirt. She'd rather not see her dad's dangly bits if she could help it.

'Of course, I can, goodnight.'

'Actually, Dad . . .'

It was another half an hour before Ray was ready to leave the house and Emily was exhausted.

'Why don't you pop upstairs to tell Julia where we're going,' she suggested.

Amazingly, he did so without question, which was a huge relief. Julia, of course, knew exactly what was going on. She had been an absolute trooper and had agreed to release Ray from the rest of his lease without a murmur. She was probably glad to see the back of him, Emily mused.

It must have been a worry for her recently, having Ray as a neighbour.

Emily nipped back to check on her mum.

'It's been a long time since I've been inside your father's drawers,' she said, pulling out a pair of boxer shorts. 'Mind you, I think I remember these.'

Emily winced. 'Spare me the details. I've left a key to the flat and my car keys in the kitchen. Text me when it's safe to come back.'

'Will do. Good luck.'

'I'm going to need it,' said Emily with a sigh. 'At the moment, he's torn between going to work and heading back to bed.'

'I had to laugh when he said he was going to work,' Tina replied, rolling her eyes. 'He was never very keen on earning a living when he and I were together.'

There was a clunking noise from the hallway.

'Hello?' Ray shouted. 'Is someone in here? Come out or I'm calling the police.'

'No need, it's just me, Dad!' Emily dashed back out to find him peering suspiciously into the hall from the doorway. 'Right, come on, I want to show you all the Christmas trees at the bottom of the road. Would you like to see those?'

'I can't go out; I'm waiting for my daughter.'

'And here I am! I've just arrived.' Emily plastered on a smile and looped her arm through her father's. It was going to be a very long morning. 'Let's go.'

Three hours later, Emily and Ray were standing side by side looking out of the window of his new one-bedroomed flat at Springwood House.

'This is nice,' he said. 'I like a room with a view.'

'It is nice, I'm glad you like it,' Emily smiled with relief. 'And we'll have it looking like home in no time.'

'It's a long time since I've been to London,' Ray continued. 'I don't remember it being as green as this.'

'Which part of London do you like best?' she asked, not commenting on the fact that the view from the window was in fact Springwood House's gardens.

'Camden,' Ray replied. 'I met John Lennon there. He'd had a row with Yoko, so I bought him a beer.'

Emily grinned; she had to hand it to her dad, he had a brilliant imagination. 'You'd have thought with all his money, he'd have got the drinks in.'

She unpacked the teabags, mugs and milk from the bag that Tina had marked as 'emergency' and made them both a drink. Once Ray was sitting down with a mug in his hand, she hung some of his clothes in the wardrobe.

Springwood House was a good few degrees warmer than her dad's old flat and after all the fetching and carrying, she was hot.

'OK if I leave you here while I unload more from the car?' Emily said, pushing her hair back from her face and stripping off her coat and sweatshirt until she was just in her dungarees and T-shirt.

Ray slurped his tea and chuckled. 'Of course you can, I'm sure I'll be safe on my own for a few minutes.'

Safe. The power of that tiny word was almost enough to make her cry. For so long, she had worried that he wasn't safe living by himself and now, hopefully, that worry had vanished.

The manager, Gail, had been here to check them in and introduce them to some of the staff and a man called Peter had shown them up to the flat. 'There are pull cords in all the rooms,' he'd said, demonstrating. 'And we pop in regularly. No one is on their own for long.'

'Yes, Dad,' she said, swallowing the lump in her throat. 'I think you will. I'll be as quick as I can.'

She headed out of the room and along the corridor to the staircase. She ran lightly down the stairs and turned left. Or should she have turned right? She looked both ways, undecided, there were signs saying Fire Exit in both directions, but which way was the car park?

A man appeared from around the corner and walked towards her. He was dressed in jeans and scruffy trainers and had his hands in the front pouch of his hoodie, his blonde hair was tousled and if she didn't know better, she'd have thought he'd just walked off a beach. All he needed was a surfboard tucked under his arm to complete the look.

'Hey.' He slowed to a halt, and she was struck by the intense blue of his eyes. 'You look a bit lost. Can I help?'

She blinked at him, surprised; he seemed out of place in a residential home.

'Yes please. I haven't got my bearings yet,' she replied gratefully. 'I'm looking for the car park.'

'It's a bit of a rabbit warren at first.' He inclined his head to the left and grinned. 'That way. Not trying to escape already, are you?'

'Not quite.' She smiled. 'My dad's moving in today, I'm still unloading the car.'

'Ah, tough day then.' He nodded, his face kind and full of understanding. 'Well, I've got a few minutes to spare before my exercise class, I'll help. Lead on.'

'Oh,' she said, suddenly recognising him. 'You're the bedroom athletics guy! I think I saw you when I came to look around.'

He burst out laughing. 'I think you mean armchair athletics.'

She pressed her hands to her hot face. 'I meant that. Ugh. Can you forget I said that please?'

He shook his head and pretended to look apologetic. 'Unlikely, I'm afraid, I might even put it on my CV. So, would you like some help?'

'It's very kind of you.' Her stomach gave a little flip, he had an instant charm about him. If she hadn't been so preoccupied with getting her dad settled, she would be quite happy to stand here for a bit longer and chat. 'But you were obviously going somewhere yourself, I don't want to hold you up.'

'You're not.' He held out a hand for her to shake. 'I'm Will, pleased to meet you. Occupational therapist by day and a mean cards player by night.'

'Emily,' she said, shaking his hand. 'I've never met an occupational therapist before, but I can imagine playing cards would make you very popular here.'

'Yep,' he replied, ruffling his hair until it stuck out in all directions. 'Snap, pairs, rummy . . . I was a whizz at cribbage in my teenage years, but I'm a bit rusty now. And as for dominoes, I don't like to boast but—'

He paused as a door opened very slowly and an elderly woman wearing an elegant gold brocade coat peered out crossly.

'Hello, Maude, looking gorgeous as ever,' said Will. 'Everything OK?'

'I ordered a taxi hours ago,' she replied imperiously. 'At this rate, I'm going to miss my flight.'

'We can't have that. Leave it with me.' Will smiled. 'You go back inside and put the kettle on, I'll phone them again.'

'Very well.' Maude harrumphed indignantly and shut the door.

'Sorry about that,' said Will with a lopsided grin. 'Maude used to be a fabric buyer for Liberty and travelled all over the world. I think that must have been her happiest time because she still wants to be there. Now, where were we?'

'You were boasting about your dominoes prowess,' Emily replied, 'but I see you also have concierge skills too.'

He bowed deeply. 'What can I say, I'm a man of many talents.'

Emily didn't doubt it; he'd already managed to cheer her up with his sunny attitude. But although the move so far had gone smoothly, her chest still felt buzzy with anxiety. Her dad seemed OK for now, but what was going to happen when she left? How would he cope tonight alone in a strange place? Or was it enough to be grateful that he was going to be safe, warm and fed?

'You're frowning.' Will studied her face. 'What's up? Sorry, forget I said that. None of my business. Come on, let's find your car.' He gestured along the corridor towards the exit and Emily fell into step beside him.

I feel like I'm abandoning him. That was what she wanted to say, but couldn't, not to a stranger. Because what if he agreed?

'It's been a stressful few days,' she said instead. Stressful was an understatement. It had been a nightmare trying to sort out all the arrangements without impacting on her job: getting power of attorney, speaking to her dad's bank, his doctor, social services . . . But after today, hopefully things would ease off. The plan for this evening was pyjamas on, phone off, a Netflix binge-watch and a takeaway. She couldn't wait.

Will nodded. 'I bet. It's hard to watch someone you love deteriorating.'

'Yep.' She quickly blinked away tears before he noticed.

The young woman on duty at reception released the doors for them with a button behind the desk. The cold air came as a welcome relief after the stifling temperature of Springwood House. Emily pointed out her car and together they managed to empty it in one go.

'You're a star,' said Emily, breathlessly when they got as far as the door of her dad's flat. She dropped the suitcases she was carrying by her feet and shook out her aching arms.

'No worries.' Will lowered a stack of boxes to the carpet. 'Want me to bring them in?'

Emily was about to say that she did when the sound of her dad's raised voice reached them from inside.

'It was here!' Ray shouted. 'I saw it myself. Now it's gone. I've been burgled. I'm calling the police!'

'Oh dear. Someone's not happy,' she said, wincing as she slid the cases inside the door. 'I was going to introduce you, but perhaps we'll leave it for now. Thanks for your help.'

'Any time.' He touched her arm briefly. 'I'll leave you to it. Hope to catch you again soon.'

'Me too,' said Emily, her bare skin tingling where his hand had been.

She watched him for a second and then closed the door behind her, turning to see what was going on with her dad. All the clothes she had hung in the wardrobe were now strewn across the floor. Ray was on his knees rummaging through another bag and throwing things over his shoulder.

'Dad! What's the matter?' she asked, horrified at the state of the room.

'I need my tin! It's private. And now it's gone!' he cried furiously.

There was a knock at the door and Gail appeared.

'Just popping in to see how . . . Oh, gosh, someone's been busy.' She gave Emily a reassuring smile and led her father to one of the armchairs. The fight seemed to go out of him, and he slumped against the cushions, unshed tears shining in his eyes.

'He says his tin is missing and that he's been burgled,' Emily replied, bewildered. 'But I've never seen a tin.'

Of course, this could be a figment of his imagination, she realised, like the stolen car, or his mum not returning from the butcher's.

'Tell me about the tin, Ray,' Gail's voice was calming as she took a seat opposite him.

'It's always in the wardrobe,' he mumbled. 'At the back under my spare towels.'

'I'm sure it'll turn up,' said Gail, patting his knee.

'What colour is it, Dad?' Emily scoured the floor, trying to remember if she'd seen a tin when unpacking. She sat beside him, perched on the arm of his chair, and took his hand in hers.

'Red, I think, and black. Scottish. It's the only thing I've got.' Her dad heaved a sigh and closed his eyes. 'I need it with me, or I'll forget.'

'Forget what?' Emily asked. But his breathing was slowing, and his hand twitched in hers. She laid it down gently on his stomach and reached for a blanket to cover him. He'd dropped off to sleep. 'Poor thing,' she murmured, brushing his hair from his face. 'He's exhausted.'

Gail got to her feet. 'A nap is the best thing for him.'

'Do you know the weird thing?' Emily frowned. 'He only seemed bothered by the missing tin, which I've never even seen before, and not by the fact he's in a new place.'

'Brains are complex things,' she said wisely. 'The contents of the tin may have links to his past that he remembers more clearly. Dementia attacks the short-term memory first. What he did this morning might have already vanished from his memory banks.'

Emily thought back to the lovely walk they'd had this morning while her mum had packed up the car for her. Despite his reluctance to go out, Ray had enjoyed looking at all the Christmas decorations along the little run of shops in the next street to his and it had unlocked stories that she'd never heard before. He'd told her about his best Christmas present — a chemistry set which he'd spent the whole of Boxing Day playing with and confided in her that he'd always wanted to be an inventor but wasn't clever at school.

'I'd better go back to his old flat,' she said, getting to her feet gently so as not to wake her dad. 'I don't know what's special about this tin, but I ought to find it for him. I'll be as quick as I can.'

Gail glanced at the time. 'No rush. It's time for lunch soon anyway. When he wakes up, someone will bring him down. And afterwards, he might like to sit in the lounge to meet some of the others. Everyone loves a new resident; he'll have no end of invitations to this, that and the other by the time you come back. Does he play cards?'

'He used to,' she answered. She had a sudden recollection of sitting at the dining table playing cards and using buttons from her mum's old button tin for money. She'd completely forgotten about that. It had been a Sunday evening thing: a game of cards and cheese and biscuits for supper. The memory cheered her.

'Good.' Gail gave her an efficient smile. 'Now do you need any help? Anything heavy in the car to bring up?'

'All done, thank you' she replied. 'I had help from Will.'

'Ah, lovely Will,' said Gail with a wide smile. 'He's our community occupational therapist and one of our volunteers, and very popular with our residents.'

'I can imagine,' remarked Emily.

Gail raised an eyebrow and she felt herself flush.

'I'd better go and hunt down the elusive red, black and Scottish tin,' she muttered, and after kissing Ray's cheek, fled from the room.

Emily called her mum to update her as she unlocked her car.

'He's in,' she said when Tina picked up the call. 'And it went surprisingly well.'

'Good,' Tina replied. 'And now at least you can relax, knowing he won't be able to go wandering off in the middle of the night. You must be exhausted.'

'It was fine, I had help actually.' She smiled to herself thinking of Will. Would he be there when she got back, playing cards, she wondered, or doing his armchair exercises? 'But you're right, I'm ready for a rest. First, though, I've got to go and look for a red and black tin. He got a bit worked up when he couldn't find it. You didn't see anything, did you?'

No,' said Tina warily, 'but knowing what your dad was like when he was younger, I hope it's not full of whacky baccy.'

Emily winced. 'Me too. The manager assures me the residents can do whatever they like, but presumably she draws the line at rolling spliffs at the breakfast table.'

Tina laughed. 'I don't know, it could certainly make the place very cheerful. Anyway, good luck, love, keep me posted.'

Emily ended the call and headed off back to Ray's flat. As soon as she pulled up, Julia flew out to greet her. She was an attractive woman in her sixties, all curves and curls and never without mascara and lipstick.

'How is he?' she asked, her hands clasped together under her chin. 'I haven't been able to settle to anything since he left.'

Emily filled her in as the two of them entered the communal hallway.

'I think I've done the right thing,' she told the older woman. 'It wasn't fair to let things continue as they were.'

'I suppose so,' she said, looking regretful. 'And he did have a terrible habit of coming up to see me without any clothes on.'

Emily's eyebrows shot up. 'Oh dear. You didn't tell me!'

Julia looked coy. 'I've been single for eight years, dear, at my age you don't look a gift horse in the mouth.'

'I see.' Emily cleared her throat; that was an image she'd struggle to erase. 'Well, as long as he didn't bother you.'

'My friends were quite envious when a tall handsome man moved in below me,' Julia continued, fingering her necklace girlishly. 'And I must admit I had thought at one time that he and I . . . Well, too late for that now.'

Emily squeezed Julia's arm. 'I know he's very fond of you in his way.'

Julia smiled sadly. 'At first I thought he was being enigmatic and mysterious, but then I realised he was being vague because he couldn't remember things. Never mind.' She clapped her hands together as if bringing that chapter to a close. 'I'll missing him banging around down here. And no rush to clear his things. I won't be advertising for a new tenant until the new year.'

'Thank you.' Emily felt a wave of relief. That meant she could leave the clearing of the flat until the school Christmas holidays. 'You haven't seen a red and black tin, have you?' she asked.

Julia nodded. 'Just now as it happens. I wasn't expecting you back today and came for a little look around to check the heating was off and so on. I found the tin inside the boiler cupboard and thought it might be important.'

So much for it having been always kept in his wardrobe.

'It is important apparently,' said Emily. 'Thank you, I probably wouldn't have even looked in there.'

'Full of memories, I'd guess. I've put it in the kitchen.'

Emily followed her inside, finding a battered old Scottish shortbread tin on the kitchen table. So, this was it, she marvelled, the one thing that her dad had wanted with him. She shook her head and smiled.

'You've been such a help,' she said, tucking the tin under her arm. 'In so many ways. Thank you, Julia.'

The two women hugged, and Emily locked the door as they left.

'There's a lovely photo of you and Ray in there,' Julia said, nodding towards the tin, and then turned crimson. 'I wasn't snooping. The lid fell off.'

'Of course you weren't,' said Emily, keen to get away and look for herself. She had hardly got any photos of the two of them. 'Goodbye.'

Once in the car, she sat the tin on her knee, desperate to look inside. Did she have the right to go through her dad's personal items or was it an invasion of his privacy? She was sure her dad would show her the contents of the tin as soon as she took it to Springwood House anyway. But . . . she drummed her fingers on the lid indecisively . . . surely looking at a photograph of herself and her dad wouldn't be wrong, would it, providing she didn't look at anything else?

It wouldn't, she decided, prising open the tin, especially as Julia had already had a look.

The lid was very stiff, which rather contradicted Julia's claims. However, the photograph Julia mentioned was still on the top of the rest of the contents. She didn't recognise the setting, but it had obviously been taken at

Christmastime: there was a little tree in the background covered in fairy lights and tinsel which caught the light.

The man in the photograph was unmistakably her dad. And there was Emily, no more than a baby, being held in his arms. She stared at it, taking in the details, her fuzz of blonde hair, her little red dress and white tights. And Ray, slim and wiry with dark blonde hair, wearing jeans, as he always did, and a checked shirt. It was such a happy photograph, he was grinning at her, and she was laughing at him, reaching towards his face with chubby fingers. It was lovely to see him so healthy and full of life. The contrast between Ray now and then was hard to look at and she felt a lump begin to form in her throat. But she did look, because she had so few memories of Christmas spent as a family, and even fewer photographs of her with her dad. She'd treasure this one, she'd make a copy for herself and, if he wanted her to, she could put the original in a frame in his room.

She set off to Springwood House for the second time that day, her heart full of joy. There was no doubt from this picture that her dad loved her. Loved her enough to hold onto this old photograph all these years. He might be unreliable, and he might not be able to express himself in words, but this was proof that she mattered to him, and she didn't think she'd ever felt as close to him in her life.

Chapter Twelve

Emily

It was early afternoon when Emily made it back to Springwood House with Ray's shortbread tin. Already, the winter sky had started to darken, and every window glowed with light. She buzzed the door and the young woman behind the reception desk let her in.

'You'll be popular,' she said, nodding to the tin. She had dark shiny hair pinned up into a bun and big hoop earrings. 'Biscuits are hard currency around here.'

'It's empty, I'm afraid.' Emily shook it to demonstrate. 'Well, empty of shortbread anyway. Is lunch over, do you know?'

'Peckish, are we?' the receptionist teased. 'Mind you, the food is good here; the staff all fight for leftovers when fish pie is on the menu. And yes, lunch is over. Who are you looking for?'

'Ray Meadows. I'm his daughter, Emily, he moved in today.'

'I'm Kylie,' she said, pointing to the name badge on her blouse. 'I've met Ray, he got a bit lost, bless him. He came to reception, carrying a Fleetwood Mac album.'

'That sounds like him.' Emily smiled, pleased that he'd recovered enough from mislaying the tin to go exploring. 'He's got more records than clothes. Unlike me, who's got more clothes than anything else.'

Kylie looked approvingly at Emily's dungarees which she'd had for so long that they'd come back in style again. 'I knew it: you work in fashion, don't you? Your outfit is so cool.'

'Hardly, I'm a school secretary,' Emily replied, flattered. 'Collecting clothes is a hobby, that's all.'

'Wow, I bet the kids love you.' Kylie still looked impressed. 'Our school secretary was terrifying. She had a hairy chin and wore her glasses right on the end of her nose like the scary one in *Monsters, Inc.*'

Emily laughed. 'I'm not sure they love me, but I don't think I scare them.'

'Anyway, the album cover is over there if you want to collect it.' Kylie pointed.

Emily followed Kylie's finger. As well as a multitude of twinkling fairy lights and baubles, a Fleetwood Mac album was wedged into the tree. 'Whoops, sorry about that.'

'No harm done; it already had a few bent branches.' Kylie waved a hand dismissively. 'Bernard hung his damp pyjama bottoms on it to dry yesterday. We see it all here. Try the communal lounge, for your dad. They serve coffee in there after lunch, he was watching telly last time I looked. Just don't stir up trouble with your non-existent biscuits.' She smiled warmly.

'I'll do my best.' Emily plucked the album from the tree, stacked it on top of the tin and headed off in search of her dad, bumping into Gail on the way.

'You found the famous tin then,' said Gail.

'Yes. Thank goodness. Hopefully, he'll feel happier when he's got it back. Was he OK at lunch?'

'Absolutely fine,' replied the manager. She cleared her throat and looked at the ground.

After almost a term working in a school and having to

get to the bottom of numerous teenage dramas, Emily was attuned to someone hiding something.

'If there's something you're not telling me, I would rather know,' Emily said. 'Please.'

'Ray got a bit agitated at the TV at one point when Lavinia used the remote to switch programmes, that's all,' replied Gail, effusively, putting her hand on Emily's shoulder. 'Nothing we're not used to.'

Emily winced. 'Poor Lavinia, I hope he wasn't too rude.'

She chuckled. 'No harm done – she gives as good as she gets, does our Lavinia. And Ray is obviously very fond of the shopping channel.'

Emily frowned. 'That's news to me. I think the TV in his flat was so ancient that he could only get a few channels. And I do know he hates shopping.'

Gail shrugged. 'Ours is not to reason why . . . Anyway, there was a truce when I left them, and they seemed quite friendly.'

A friend already, thought Emily, going into the lounge to find him. She remembered what he'd said about not having anyone to call because he'd never been one for friends. Perhaps being at Springwood House would open a new chapter for him, a chance to build relationships.

Emily found Ray in front of the TV at the end of a sofa, feet up on a pouffe, looking very comfortable. Sitting at the opposite end was a lady with lovely long silver hair. She was regal in her posture, straight-backed and hands clasped in her lap, her fingers glittered with emerald and ruby rings. If this was Lavinia, her name suited her perfectly.

The coffee table between them contained two empty mugs and a plate with just a few crumbs. Emily's stomach rumbled; it had been a long day and she hadn't managed to eat lunch yet. She set the tin down on the table along with the Fleetwood Mac album.

'Hi, Dad,' Emily said, touching his shoulder softly, so as not to make him jump. 'You look like you've made yourself at home already.'

Ray blinked a couple of times before he recognised her. 'Hello, love.'

The old lady's head swivelled towards her immediately. 'Who's this?

'I'm Emily,' she replied, taking a seat. 'And you?'

'Lavinia,' the old lady informed her. 'What a lovely face you have. You must be the same age as me, twenty-five?'

'You flatter me,' said Emily, deciding to go along with it. 'I'm thirty-five.'

'You must give me the name of your facialist,' Lavinia replied. 'Your skin is remarkable. We were watching a lovely programme on television, where they sell all sorts of face creams. I was going to order some, I'm starting to get a few wrinkles,' she whispered, stroking her beautiful, if a little crinkly, skin. 'But this gentleman started shouting at the television set, so we turned it off, and since then we've been having a lovely chat, haven't we?' She turned to Ray.

'You mean you have,' he grumbled. 'You've been nattering on for ages.'

'I apologise for my father's rudeness, Lavinia.' Emily was mortified, although Lavinia didn't seem to mind.

'Oh, you're his daughter, the famous one!' Lavinia's eyes widened. 'From the television!'

Emily smiled. 'I wish. No, I work in a school.'

'Who is this woman?' Ray asked Emily in a loud whisper.

'Lavinia, dear,' said his companion. 'And who are you?'

'Ray,' he replied. 'Pleased to meet you.'

The two of them reached across the sofa to shake hands formally. They'd probably been through this introduction a handful of times already, Emily thought sadly.

A woman in uniform approached just then with a tea trolley and collected their used crockery.

'Hello, dear, are you new?' asked Lavinia, beaming at the woman.

'I'm Yaz,' she replied, pointing to her name badge. 'I made your coffee earlier.'

'Of course, will you let Carlos know I'm here for my blow-dry,' Lavinia said, patting her hair. 'I'm due at a party at six and have yet to change into my gown.'

'Will do.' Yaz nodded meekly and smiled at Emily. 'Would you like a tea or coffee?'

Emily accepted a cup of coffee; it was lukewarm and she drank it down in one go.

'How do you cope?' she marvelled, putting the cup back on the trolley.

Yaz laughed. 'I just roll with it. Having short-term memory problems can have advantages. People are always making new friends. Even if they're the same ones they met the day before. Top-up?' She nodded at the empty cup.

'Please. Doesn't that get confusing?' Emily looked at Lavinia and Ray, eyeing each other up like strangers again. 'And do they ever make lasting friendships?'

'Confusion comes with the territory here. We remind them, of course, as long as it doesn't cause anyone stress. And yes, people do develop friendships.' Yaz poured more coffee in Emily's cup. 'Sometimes our residents forget to come down for meals, or, like Lavinia, they prefer to survive on biscuits served while they're waiting for their hair appointment.'

'Or shout at the TV in my dad's case.' Emily winced, imagining poor Lavinia getting the brunt of it.

'That's a classic one, but we're always on hand to help out.' She picked up a cloth and wiped up crumbs from a table. 'Sometimes people confuse a TV programme with reality. Especially if something gruesome happens.'

'Yep, we've had that one.' Emily grimaced, remembering how her dad had thought he was the villain in *Morse*.

As Yaz moved on to some other residents, she looked at Ray now. He and Lavinia had fallen asleep, and Emily decided to leave them in peace. She drank her coffee, picked up her things and set off for Ray's flat, intending to finish the unpacking.

As she got to the bottom of the staircase, she saw Will again, running down the stairs towards her.

'Still here?' Will said with a grin. 'You must have had a long day.'

'I was going to say the same to you,' she remarked, unable to keep the smile from her face. 'Gail says you volunteer when you're not doing your actual job here.'

If he noticed her blush at the admission that she'd been talking about him, he was polite enough not to mention it. He nodded. 'Been doing it for a couple of years. It's my way of giving back. Not everyone has visitors and that's where the volunteers can step in. If I can bring a bit of entertainment, a fresh face to bring a smile, why not do it?' he said lightly, as if every person in their thirties would volunteer their time if they had a chance.

What a generous heart, thought Emily. He couldn't be more opposite in character to Gavin, who had once rolled his eyes at Ray when he hadn't been able to remember Gavin's name. 'I'm sure your presence is much appreciated.'

He waved away her compliment. 'Care homes get a bad rap, but the truth is that the staff are doing their best. Caring for the forgotten ones, the ones who don't fit neatly into society anymore. And, honestly, being with these guys is such an education.'

She nodded. 'I can imagine. I've just met Lavinia, who's apparently off to a party tonight as soon as she's had her hair done.'

'Ah, the lovely Lavinia,' Will laughed. 'She was a model for *Vogue* in the 1940s. Can you imagine the stories she has to tell about London back then? They often can't remember what they had for lunch, but then come out with these amazing memories.'

That reminded Emily of the photo she'd seen of her and her dad. 'I'm hoping that this tin of Dad's unlocks some memories for him. I'd like to know more about *his* life.' She took the lid off the tin and handed Will the photograph. 'Obviously I was too young to remember it, but I'm sure he will.'

'Cute baby,' he said, turning the photograph over to read the words on the back. 'Merry first Christmas. So this was your first Christmas, then?'

Emily shrugged; she hadn't thought to look at the reverse. 'I guess so.'

She had a sudden feeling of unease at showing her dad's things to a stranger without his permission so took the photograph back and replaced the lid.

'So, you were saying,' she said, changing the subject. 'About the exciting moments provided by the residents. Any good ones today?'

'The best bit was helping a very nice person unload her car. Other than that it's been a pretty standard Saturday. I've played dominoes with a couple of the old boys and then popped in to see Bernard, who has been struggling since he had a knee replacement.' He glanced at her and pulled a face. 'Makes me sound like a right party animal, doesn't it?'

'Welcome to my world,' Emily said, flattered to be listed as a highlight. 'A hot date for me means chicken korma for one in front of an episode of *Friends*.'

'I refuse to believe that.' He grinned. 'Although, if it's true, you've just made me feel tons better.'

She laughed. 'Sad but true, I'm afraid. I'd better get on, or I'll never get home to eat it. Nice to see you. Bye.'

He raised a hand. 'See you soon, I hope.'

Me too, she thought, conscious of his gaze on her as she trotted up the stairs.

For the next half an hour, Emily occupied herself making up Ray's bed and finding homes for all his bits and pieces. She'd put the kettle on to make a drink when in walked Ray, accompanied as far as the door by Yaz.

'There you go, Ray,' she said, waving to me. 'Looks like your daughter heard you coming; the kettle's already on.'

He walked slowly inside, studying the room as if he hadn't seen it before, and lowered himself into his old chair with a sigh.

'Hi, Dad.' She pressed a kiss to the top of his head. 'Did you have a nice nap?'

He blinked at her. 'Me? No. Just had lunch. I'm ready for a nap now though.'

She lifted his feet and set them on the footstool. 'I'll make you one last cuppa, then I'll get off home, leave you in peace.'

'There's the tin!' Ray cried, spotting it on the counter in the little kitchenette. He struggled up from the chair and almost knocked over the carton of milk in his haste. He hugged it to himself. 'They stole my tin. They're after my money.'

'I don't think they are, Dad. And we've got it back now,

that's the main thing,' she said softly. 'Shall we look inside?'

He tugged the lid off as he sank back down. The photograph of the two of them was still on the top of everything else.

'What a lovely photo,' she commented, taking the picture out. 'Do you remember it being taken?'

Ray nodded. 'Handsome bugger, wasn't I?'

'Oi.' She gave him a playful nudge. 'You're supposed to say what a beautiful baby, I was!'

'Very bonny.' He sighed and relaxed back into his chair, muttering something under his breath that she couldn't quite catch. She thought she heard him say *sunny*, but that didn't make any sense.

'What did you say?' Emily prompted.

'Sorry, love,' he said, turning his head to one side. His eyelids drooped. 'I'm going to have a nap before lunch.'

'You've already had your—' She groaned with disappointment. She'd lost him again; now she wouldn't learn anything else about the Christmas when it was taken.

She looked at the photograph one last time before putting it away. She'd wanted to take it with her to have a copy made, but she couldn't risk Ray kicking up a fuss and accusing the staff of stealing it.

She made him his tea as promised, even though it would probably be cold when he woke up and kissed him goodbye.

'See you tomorrow, Dad,' she said softly, laying a blanket across him. 'And thank you for keeping that picture all these years. It means a lot.'

She made her way out to the car park again.

A takeaway for one and an episode of something comforting was in her immediate future and she couldn't wait. What a party animal, she mused, recalling her chat with Will. She felt shattered; it had been a rollercoaster

of a day as far as her emotions were concerned. The end of
independent living for her dad, but hopefully, the start of
a new phase of life – for both of them.

Chapter Thirteen

Merry

'I think this tree might even be more gorgeous than last year's.' Hester cuddled up to her husband, Paul, and tucked her hand in his pocket.

Tonight was the annual Christmas lights switch-on and, as per tradition, Wetherley market square was packed with people in celebratory mood. Frost sparkled on pavements and stars dazzled in a velvet sky. Lights were strung from lamp post to lamp post, zigzagging across the cobbled streets which surrounded the square. Most of the shops, mine included, had added fairy lights to their window displays and the whole of the town centre looked impossibly charming. The assembled crowd was singing along to the Christmas music blasting out from the stage which had been erected beside a ginormous Norwegian spruce. All we needed now was for the tree's lights to be turned on by this year's celebrity, and the festive season would be officially under way in Wetherley.

'It is certainly well hung,' said Astrid, in her clipped German accent, glancing up at the tree's decorations. She bent down to pick up her little dog, Otto, who was pawing at her legs and missed Nell and me smothering our giggles at her turn of phrase.

'We've brought flasks of mulled wine and hot chocolate with us,' said Fred, doing his best not to react. He unzipped the bag at his feet. 'What would everyone like?'

'Hot chocolate please,' I replied.

'Me too,' said Cole, slipping an arm around my waist. 'Christmas or not, red wine and cinnamon should never share a glass in my opinion.'

'Bah humbug,' said Hester, poking her tongue out at her brother as she accepted a cup of mulled wine from her dad.

Nell and her husband Olek opted for mulled wine too and Astrid handed round some of her *lebkuchen*, delicious, chewy biscuits, full of Christmas spices. I bit into one and as I did, I caught the eye of the DJ on stage. It was Nigel, who ran the hardware store and who'd overseen last year's music too. We waved to each other, and he shouted down to me to save him one of Astrid's biscuits. Just then, the rest of the Christmas committee joined him on stage and Nigel lowered the volume of the music.

'I feel quite nostalgic,' remarked Hester. 'Last year, it was us up there in the spotlight.'

'A grand job you made of it too,' said Fred, smiling proudly.'And you, Merry.'

Last year, I had overseen the committee, and although not without its challenges, the project had been great fun. Cole had been my landlord at the time, and when I'd admitted that I couldn't find a celebrity to switch on the lights, he'd persuaded Hester to do it. Everyone had agreed it had been a great event and a successful start to Wetherley's festivities.

The main celebration was traditionally held in the market square on Christmas Eve after all the traders had finished work. I'd had the idea of filling the whole area with Christmas trees, each one individually decorated by a different community group. All had gone swimmingly until we'd had a power cut. While I'd distributed Merry and Bright candles to everyone, Cole had fetched a generator to provide us with an emergency electricity supply. I couldn't have managed without him, and it had marked the start of our love story.

The Christmas Project last year had been on a much grander scale in order to pay tribute to an elderly man who'd passed away and who'd been a popular member of the community. This year, apart from tonight's switch-on, there'd just be a few mince pies and carols in the market square on Christmas Eve and so Nell and I weren't needed on the committee.

It was just as well; as Hester had pointed out during my last visit to the TV studio, I had enough on my plate. I'd been extra-vigilant with Fred since then, looking for signs that he had had enough of working for me. I hadn't brought up the subject with him, or Astrid for that matter. I knew it was a bit cowardly of me, but I feared his answer. I'd decided to put my head in the sand for now and tackle the staffing issues just as soon as I'd got the wedding out of the way. Until then, we'd just have to manage; I didn't have time to train up new staff.

'Merry, you look miles away.' Paul waved a hand in front of my face. 'I was just saying that this year's switch-on has got its work cut out to beat your success last year.'

'Oh, I don't know.' I inclined my head towards Tasha Sandean, the head teacher of Wetherley Primary school, who was posing on the stage beside a tall muscular man in a leather biker jacket while a photographer took their picture. 'Our leader looks pretty on it to me.'

'Wow, *scharf*!' said Astrid with wide eyes, feeding Otto a small piece of biscuit. 'I have never heard of this celebrity boy, but he is very handsome.'

'His name is Jaden Hall, he is a footballer,' pointed out Olek. 'Plays for a second division side. I'm surprised to see him in Wetherley.'

'I heard Tasha was at university with his brother,' I said. 'And she can be very persuasive when she wants something.'

Tasha had turned Wetherley school around by all accounts. If I ever had children, I'd want them under her care. She had also swept my ex-boyfriend, Daniel, off his feet this time last year. Which, although I'd found hard to swallow at the time, was a blessing in disguise because our breakup led to me falling in love with Cole.

'As are you, darling, seeing as your idea was voted the winner last year,' Cole reminded me.

'We did the right thing, standing down, Merry,' said Nell. 'If you don't step back and let others take a turn, you get taken for granted.'

'Besides,' added Cole, sipping his hot chocolate, 'Christmas Eve is going to be the start of our married life. My fiancée will be too busy to organise Wetherley's celebrations.'

Everyone whooped and cheered at the mention of 'my fiancée'.

'Ahhh,' said Hester. 'I'm so excited for this wedding. Do we have a venue yet?'

Cole and I exchanged glances. We'd just come from the Claybourne Hotel, where the wedding organiser had shown us the garden room. Cole had been impressed with it when he'd been by himself, and so, as agreed, we'd gone back together. He'd wanted to book it there and then. I knew we didn't have a lot of time, but I wanted a bit longer to mull it over. The atmosphere in the car driving back hadn't exactly been frosty, but it wasn't relaxed either.

'Possibly,' I said diplomatically. 'We've seen one, but I think we should see some others before we decide.'

'Have we got time to do that?' asked Cole, not unreasonably. 'It's taken ages to find a moment when we were both free to visit this one.'

'If you have found one still available, I would book it quickly in case someone else does,' Olek advised.

I heaved a sigh. I loved Nell's husband dearly, he was solid and dependable and the perfect foil to Nell's feisty personality. As usual, he was talking perfect sense.

'But only if they love it,' said Nell, looping her arm through his. 'It has to be right.'

Nell was making perfect sense too.

'*Genau,*' said Astrid, agreeing.

'Do you love it,' Fred asked, putting me on the spot, 'enough to have your reception there?'

'It's lovely,' I began, 'but it's just so grand. I'd be happy with a small room at a pub.'

Cole frowned. 'Small?'

I nodded. 'Somewhere homely.'

'I know!' Hester held her arms out. 'Have it at our house! We wanted to host a party on Christmas Eve anyway. There we go, sorted.'

Paul nodded. 'Great idea.'

'Oh Hester, Paul, thank you!' My heart lifted. After our uncomfortable discussion the other day, I'd felt a bit unsure of my place in Hester's affections, but this generous offer felt like an olive branch. Plus, this was exactly the sort of thing I wanted for my wedding, somewhere small and intimate.'That would be perfect, and so kind of you.'

I felt the weight of Cole's hand on my shoulder. 'Thanks, sis. It's a lovely offer, but I think we'll book a venue. Thanks all the same.'

His sister shrugged amicably. 'Fair enough If you change your mind, let us know.'

'I think—' I started to argue the point, but Paul interrupted me.

'Who's going to be your best man?' he asked, straightening his shoulders as if auditioning for the part.

Cole rubbed a hand across his jaw. 'I haven't asked anyone yet; I've only just got around to ask Merry to be my bride. All the other members of the wedding party are TBC.'

'Not all,' countered Nell, raising her cup of mulled wine. 'Ta-dah! You're looking at the best woman.'

'The very best,' I agreed. 'And I'll have to think about who's going to give me away.'

In films, the moment when the groom turned around to see his bride for the first time on the arm of her father was always emotionally charged. It wasn't going to be half as romantic if I had to stride up there on my own and it might be nice to have the comforting presence of someone who cared about me to hang on to.

Olek gave a small bow. 'I'm sure you'll have many offers, but we have been friends for a long time, and you are like a sister to Nell. So, I would be proud to have you on my arm.'

'Oh darling!' Nell stood on her tiptoes and kissed his cheek. 'That is so sweet.'

'Thank you, Olek,' I said, touched by his offer.

'Same here,' added Paul, raising a hand. 'Happy to play any part. I love weddings.'

'That's true,' Hester remarked, holding her cup out for a refill from Fred. 'The vicar kept having to stop during our vows because Paul was so choked up.'

'He'd probably seen the invoice for the reception,' Cole teased.

'It was worth every penny,' said Fred gallantly. 'And, Merry dear, I know I'm technically on the groom's side, but I'd be delighted to do the honours.'

'You're a sweetheart, Fred.' I squeezed his arm. 'Thank you for always making me feel part of the family, even though I'm not yet.'

'Bit weird though.' Hester wrinkled her nose. 'Your father-in-law-to-be giving you away.'

'Prince Charles gave Meghan Markle away,' Fred pointed out. 'If Charlie can do it, don't see why I can't.'

'I bet he'd give her back if he could,' Paul remarked with a grin.

I said nothing. I'd had a crush on Prince Harry since I was a teenager. I'd been ridiculously jealous when he and Meghan had announced their engagement.

'*Meine gute*,' Astrid cried, shaking her head. 'Merry isn't some chattel to be transferred from the possession of one man to another. She is an independent woman, choosing to spend her life with the person she loves. Why does she need anyone to give her away, especially a man?'

'Go, Astrid!' Hester said admiringly. 'You're so right. Down with everyday sexism.'

'Thanks, everyone,' I said, laughing. 'I don't know whether to be insulted or flattered that all the men in my life appear to be eager to give me away.'

Unexpectedly, my thoughts flew to one particular man and my smile fell. My father. The one man whose official job it should be to give me away had never been in my life at all. I didn't even know his name.

Cole squeezed my hand. 'It's just because everyone around you loves you.'

'Just a thought,' said Nell, 'but you could go down the aisle with me behind you doing our best Beyoncé dancing, and singing about putting a ring on it?'

A suggestion which resulted in Nell, Hester and I blasting out the chorus badly until the music died down, Tasha stepped up to the microphone on stage and the light switch-on began in earnest.

'Three, two, one . . . Merry Christmas, Wetherley!' shouted the footballer a few minutes later as he pressed down on the plunger.

To the side of the stage, the magnificent tree sparkled into life, casting a colourful glow on the faces of the children who were gathered in front. We all clapped and cheered and as Jaden Hall scribbled his name onto a football and threw it out into the crowd, Nigel whacked up the music again. Soon we were all singing along to the old Wizzard favourite and wishing it could be Christmas every day.

Half an hour later, Cole and I said our goodbyes and strolled back towards where he'd parked the car. I glanced at the Merry and Bright sign above the window of the old bank, remembering vividly the makeshift workshop on the first floor Cole had kitted out for me when my cottage had been flooded last year. I'd brought Hester and Fred here before the light switch-on and Fred had started working for me the very next day. As if reading my mind, Cole slowed to a halt.

'You know what tonight is?' he said, pulling me close. 'It's a year since we had our first kiss. It was over there in the doorway of the old bank under the mistletoe.'

'How could I forget?' I snuggled into him, my hands finding their way inside his jacket and around his waist. 'I think that was the night I fell in love with you.'

He smiled at me, brushing away a strand of my hair. 'I remember going home that night not believing my luck.'

'And now here we are, about to get married.'

'And now here we are,' he repeated. 'And I still can't believe my luck.'

'Me neither, it's been such an exciting year, the best year of my life. I honestly wouldn't change a thing.' I stamped my feet. 'Although, right now, this hanging around is making my feet cold. I wouldn't mind changing that.'

'We'll head off in a second.' He took in a breath, looking hesitant. 'Merry, talking of cold feet, I've had a few weeks to get used to the idea of getting married, but you've had it sprung on you. So, if you have any doubts about rushing into it, I want you to know that it's perfectly fine, you only have to say.'

I smiled up at him. It was such a thoughtful thing to say, so typical of Cole. He always seemed to tune in to my feelings, and it was one of the reasons I loved him so much. 'I can't wait to be Mrs Robinson,' I assured him, 'but I must admit I am nervous. It's not just about the wedding, but about being married too. I have no experience of what it's like to be part of a normal family. What if I'm rubbish at it? I'd hate to let you down.'

'You couldn't possibly let me down.' Cole kissed me tenderly. 'All it takes is a capacity to love and to let yourself be loved, and you can do both of those things. If anyone should be nervous, it's me. I had the happy childhood, the stable home life, and yet I'm the one with a failed marriage behind me.'

'Hold on there, mister,' I said sternly. 'Did it fail, or did it just end? There's a difference. You and Lydia seem unscarred by it, and you've got two lovely children. I don't see failure; I see a new chapter. One with me in it.'

'Well, when you put it like that, it doesn't seem so bad,' he said, laughing. 'I can't wait to marry you.'

'Then we're on the same page.' I smiled back. 'Except for one thing: why did you say no to Hester's offer?'

'I'm not using my little sister's house for our wedding reception,' Cole replied firmly. 'There's no need for us to do this cheaply.'

'I wasn't thinking of the cost,' I protested. 'But we don't need anywhere fancy and their house is lovely and homely. Plus, you know she enjoys hosting.'

Cole's expression softened, he placed a hand behind my neck and brushed my lips with his. 'I'm not hiding my beautiful new wife under a bushel. The wedding is about us demonstrating to the world that we're going to spend our lives together. And with a big party to celebrate.'

'I'm not really bothered what the world thinks, I just want you.' I gave him a cheeky grin. 'I'd be happy to run away to Gretna Green if I didn't know how much Freya wants to be a bridesmaid.'

He shook his head fondly. 'That's so typical of you to be thinking of my kids. Do you really want to have the wedding reception at Paul and Hester's house?'

'Yes, I really do. It will be perfect.'

'Fine, if that's what the lady wants, then that's what the lady shall have,' he said, laughing. 'I'd better let Hester know we've changed our mind.'

'Fantastic! Thank you, you won't regret it,' I said and then kissed him to seal the deal. 'And just think, now the venue is sorted, you'll be able to cross something off that secret spreadsheet you think I don't know about.'

He blinked at me in surprise and we both laughed.

'Do you know one of my favourite things about you?' he said, tracing his fingertips along the curve of my face.

'You always make me feel better about myself. I don't deserve you.'

'Of course, you do, you silly goose,' I argued. 'Actually, I've changed my mind: I do have cold feet. Can we go home now? My toes are like ice cubes. Let's go and get warm.'

'In a minute,' he said and then pulled me into the doorway of the old bank and slid a hand inside my coat. 'First, we have to snog inappropriately in the doorway like teenagers. It's tradition.'

'Our first tradition,' I murmured, shivering as his warm fingers found my bare skin. 'But maybe not one to share with the grandkids.'

Chapter Fourteen

Merry

'There he is, I can see his hair!' Freya bounced on her toes beside me and waved, reaching her arm up as high as she could. 'HARLEY!'

This was a new experience for me, collecting the kids from school. It was intimidating, standing on the corner just outside the school gates as a tidal wave of teenagers poured out of the Darley Academy.

Eventually, I spotted Harley walking alone behind a group of jostling boys, thumping each other with their rucksacks and howling with laughter, their voices loud in celebration at being set free.

'Hey, Robbo,' one of the boys yelled over his shoulder to Harley. 'Looks like Mummy's here to pick you up.'

My heart ached for him. Vague memories of my own schooldays flooded back. Was there anything more excruciating than being singled out by your peers?

'Shut up,' Harley grunted, his pace slowing as he approached. 'And she's not my mum.'

One of the others whistled suggestively. 'Bit old for you, isn't she?'

'Gosh.' Freya crept closer to me, her eyes wide. 'They think you're his girlfriend. Shall I tell them?'

'No,' I said quickly, resting my hand on her shoulder. 'Let's start walking to the car. Harley can follow us.'

'That's quite enough!' came an authoritative voice. A woman, dwarfed by a huge pink puffa coat marched into the middle of the group. 'This lady is my visitor,' she barked.

Harley glanced at me with alarm, and I pulled a face, which I hoped conveyed that this was news to me too.

'Those comments were completely inappropriate,' the woman continued sternly. 'One more word and you'll all be in detention until Christmas.' She jammed her hands on her hips and glared at the boys until they sloped off. 'Sorry about that.' She had her hood up, but I could just make out green eyes beneath a blunt blonde fringe as she came towards us. 'And I know you haven't come to see me really, but it seemed like a good thing to say.'

'I appreciate it.' I smiled gratefully. 'I've not done school pick-up before, I didn't know the rules.'

'No harm done.' She gave me a sympathetic look and then turned to Harley. 'OK, mate?'

'Yes, miss,' he muttered, his cheeks which had begun to sprout a few spots, turned pink. 'I'm getting in the car.' Harley held his hand out for the key, which I gave willingly.

'I don't miss being that age,' the woman whispered as we shared a look of sympathy. As our eyes met, I had a fleeting sensation of déjà vu, as if we'd met before.

'Me neither,' I said, wracking my brains as to where I knew her from.

'I like your pink coat,' said Freya to the teacher.

The woman grinned and shoved her hands inside deep pockets. 'Thanks. Got it in a charity shop for ten quid. It's supposed to be for wearing after you've been surfing, to warm you up, but it's brilliant for standing out in the cold on playground duty.'

Her voice was familiar now that she'd stopped yelling; she looked at me and blinked as if she was trying to place me too.

'Have we . . .?' I started to ask her if we'd met, but I was interrupted by a girl yelling at the top of her voice that she was going to kill somebody or other if they didn't delete that picture.

'Excuse me, more drama,' said the woman with a sigh. 'Nice to meet you!' She darted off and jumped into the middle of another argument, this time, a group of girls, and Freya and I went back to the car.

Harley was in the front passenger seat, arms folded, and his hood pulled low over his face. His expression was thunderous as I climbed in beside him. 'You're supposed to stay in the car.'

'I know that now, I'm sorry,' I said, doing up my seat belt. 'But Freya really wanted to watch you come out.'

'She knows that's not allowed. Only weirdos get met by someone. She did it on purpose. They'll never let me forget that now.' He turned to the back of the car to give his sister a death stare.

It would have petrified me, but she shrugged it off. 'I wanted to see that girl you were talking to last night. Which one was it?'

That was the final straw for Harley. He reached into the back of the car and grabbed hold of Freya's coat, making her squeal with indignation. 'Never listen outside my room again, you little rat,' he roared.

I squeezed my eyes shut for a second and took a breath. Cole had offered to come with me today to help pick wedding outfits for the kids, but I'd declined. It'll be a chance for us to bond, I'd said. It'll be fun, I'd said with all the positivity of someone who didn't have a clue. I reached into my bag and took out my emergency weapon. 'OK, guys. Who wants chocolate?'

The rest of the journey passed without incident and soon I found us a parking spot on a side street outside a pet shop. I left them looking at the hamster run in the window while I paid for a ticket at the meter. In my head, I had a fantasy that they'd always remember the time I took them shopping for clothes for the wedding, and how much fun it had been. We hadn't got off to a great start, but I was remaining optimistic.

'This one's fur is the same colour as my hair!' Freya exclaimed, tapping the window. 'I'd have that one. I'd call it Chewy.'

'Look at all their poos.' Harley wrinkled his nose. 'I bet they stink. I'd call it Pooey.'

'So immature,' said Freya with a scathing sigh.

I stuck the parking ticket on my car windscreen and gazed at their russet-brown heads bent together. I wasn't going to try to mother them, but I was about to be part of their family and I loved them already. It was unlikely that they felt the same way about me, especially after my faux pas at school just now, but hopefully it would come in time. For now, I was aiming to be someone they could entrust with their secrets, someone to talk to. A friend, as Nell had advised me to be.

'Let's go,' I said. 'I thought we could do the shopping first and then get something to eat. What do you think?'

'Or,' Harley suggested slyly, 'skip the shopping and head straight for food. I'm starving.'

'The shop shuts soon, so unfortunately not.' I knew Harley's tricks, and his voracious appetite. I produced more snacks from my bag, this time two bags of crisps. 'This will keep you going.'

Freya declined, but Harley tore into a bag straight away.

'Santa's Grotto!' Freya gasped, pointing to the fake snow-covered wooden hut which had been erected in the town centre. It was surrounded by Christmas trees, and two people dressed in elf outfits were trying to control a queue of overexcited children by singing songs and doing silly dances with each other. 'Can we go and visit Santa?' She looked up at me, hope glistening in her eyes.

My heart lurched as a memory hit me from years ago. Of seeing other kids going to visit Santa, sit on his knee and tell them what they wanted for Christmas. Of Mum not being able to afford it and pretending the tickets had all gone.

'I'm sorry, I would love to,' I said, hating the disappointment on her face, 'but I don't think we have time to stand in that queue. Another time though, I promise.'

'Lucky escape,' Harley muttered, shovelling a handful of crisps into his mouth.

'Can I have a fur jacket to wear around my shoulders. Except not proper fur because it's not fair to monks?' Freya slipped her hand into mine as she said it. It was such a natural gesture that it couldn't possibly be a ploy to get her own way, but in that second, I'd have given her anything she asked for.

'Mink not monks, you idiot.' Harley caught my eye and let out a splutter of laughter, which melted my heart. He was so like his father. His face seemed to hold a lot of tension these days, but when he smiled, it was like the sun coming out.

'Let's see what they've got,' I said diplomatically. 'A faux fur jacket might be nice on a wintry day.'

'Mummy says when she and Daddy got married, he told her she looked like a princess,' Freya remarked, seemingly without guile.

'I'm sure she did,' I said as warmly as I could. The image of Cole declaring his eternal love to another woman wasn't high on my list of mood-boosting thoughts.

To be fair to Lydia, it must be weird seeing your ex marry someone new. Presumably, she'd been just as much in love with Cole back then as I was now. She was always nice to me, but I wondered what she really thought. I'd spoken to Nell about it, and she said I didn't know how lucky I was that Lydia seemed fairly laid-back about my existence in her children's life. Apparently, Olek's ex-wife made no attempt to hide the fact that she hated Nell, even though she and Olek had separated by the time Nell had met him.

Lydia, on the other hand, had written down their shoe sizes for me, informed me that Freya had an inappropriate penchant for strapless sequinned corsets, which, unfortunately, at her tender age of nine had no way of staying in place, and that getting Harley to wear anything other than a hoodie, joggers and trainers would be a triumph. Challenge accepted, I thought, herding them both towards Molly's Wedding Emporium. I'd been here with Nell, and although I hadn't fallen in love with any of their bridal dresses, there was plenty of children's wear which might do.

As if on cue, Harley fell back so that he was walking beside me. 'I'll just get some new trainers. No point wasting money on getting me smart shoes. I've got shoes for school, and I hate them. I only agreed to wear them on school days. Shoes are so lame.'

'That's kind of you to try to save us money, Harley,' I replied, pointing to the rubbish bin for his empty crisp packet, 'but the dress code is smart for all of us. You can always sell them on eBay afterwards if you don't want to keep them.'

Harley's face brightened. 'I'll think about it.'

'If there's a yellow dress, can I have it?' Freya asked.

'Hmm, I'm not sure about that,' I said, feeling bad when her face crumpled. The colour theme for the wedding was a muted palette of green and white with a hint of pink. I'd been planning on steering her in that direction. But then again, did it really matter? Wouldn't it be better if everyone wore the clothes they felt happiest in? 'We'll have a good look,' I relented. 'Although, I thought your favourite colour was pink?'

'It was, but then the girls in Year Six say that women shouldn't wear pink because . . .' She put a finger to her mouth while she thought about it. 'I can't remember exactly, but I think it was to do with gender stereo pipes. So now everyone likes yellow.' She leaned closer and lowered her voice, 'Don't tell anyone, but I still secretly like pink.'

'Your secret is safe with me,' I said, remembering how important it was to feel part of the club at school. 'And let's keep an open mind. Here we are.'

'Ughh,' Harley faltered as we reached the door, clocking the window display of frothy tulle, sparkling beaded bodices and acres of ivory crushed silk. He looked over his shoulder furtively. 'If any of my friends from school see me going in here, I'm dead.'

'Don't be such a baby,' said Freya, before squeaking with delight at a pair of glittery stilettos. 'Mummy says I can wear high heels now I'm nine.'

Mummy had said nothing of the sort, but I let it go. I was more interested in how worried Harley seemed at the thought of any of his mates seeing him. Was it normal to be so paranoid? I wondered.

'Wow.' I pointed at a male mannequin in a smart charcoal grey suit and tie. 'Harley, doesn't that remind you of what the England football team look like when they're all dressed up?'

Harley's eyes widened. 'Do you reckon?'

'Definitely. It's not all shorts and football boots, you know. Sportsmen – and sportswomen – have to look the part when they're representing their team.'

Harley tilted his chin, considering my words. 'Suppose so.'

'And you, Grandad and your dad,' I said casually, 'you're all on the same team: Team Robinson.'

'Do you think they'll have that suit in my size?' he wondered aloud, pushing open the door and I breathed a sigh of relief.

Once inside, I briefed the sales assistant on our requirements, and she directed us to the relevant departments and told us her name was Poppy and that she'd be on hand to fetch other sizes if needed. She couldn't have been more than twenty-five, was very pretty and had a row of piercings from her earlobe to the top of her ear. Neither Freya nor Harley could drag their eyes from her.

'What lovely colouring you both have,' said Poppy, beaming at them. 'You'd look great in charcoal grey or navy,' she addressed Harley, whose cheeks instantly turned pink, and he mumbled something unintelligible under his breath.

'What about me?' Freya asked, bouncing on the spot. 'What would suit me?'

'Pretty much anything except yellow,' noted Poppy. 'But it's usually up to the bride.'

I was going to get along with Poppy.

'Harley, are you OK to browse by yourself for a minute, while I look at dresses with Freya?' I said, steering her towards the bridesmaids' rail while she absorbed the truth about yellow not really being flattering on a redhead.

Freya paused at the jewellery display and her eyes lit up. 'We'll have to wear earrings, won't we?' she said, matter-of-factly. 'I should probably get mine done today so we've got time for them to look normal when the wedding comes. Do you think we can get them pierced after this?'

'As if Mum would let you have your ears pierced,' Harley scoffed and headed off in the opposite direction towards the men's department.

'Why don't you ask Mum and Dad about that,' I suggested, turning her shoulders away from the jewellery and towards the shoes. 'It's not my decision.'

Freya was undeterred. 'Eva had hers done and green goo came out of them for ages. I hope that doesn't happen to me. Should I get hoops or studs?'

'What about these sequinned ballet shoes?' I said, picking one up from the shelf.

'O, M, actual G!' she breathed, abandoning all thought of ear piercing. 'I love these.'

'I do too,' I agreed.

I'd have loved something like this when I was her age. Most of my clothes and shoes had come from charity shops when I was still living with Mum, and I'd had to make do with whatever was in my size. I remember being disappointed at the outfit we'd found for the school Christmas party and really wanting some new jeans and a nice sparkly top, like all the other girls had. Ironically, once Mum had passed away and I was living in a children's home, I got my wish. Every child had an allowance and we'd be taken shopping to buy school uniform and casual stuff whenever we needed it. By then, of course, I'd happily have worn second-hand clothes if it had meant I could have been with my mum. But life didn't always work out like that.

I liked buying from charity shops these days. There was a fab one in Wetherley where I bought my work shirts from; I'd stopped spending a lot of money on clothes which inevitably got splashed with melted wax. Even my wedding dress was second-hand. Or *vintage*, as the girl in the shop had explained. But I couldn't have loved it more if it had been made to measure and cost ten times as much. It was hanging in the wardrobe in Holly Cottage hidden from Cole. It was the most glamourous garment I'd ever owned and I couldn't wait to wear it.

'I don't mind wearing a shirt,' Harley shouted from the other side of the shop. 'But not a tie. Ties are a symbol of oppression.'

'Are they, why?' I asked, leaving Freya trying on shoes to join him.

'Um.' Harley looked wrong-footed. 'Control. It's just a way of control.'

'You don't have to wear a tie if you don't want to,' I said casually. 'Although your dad might be a bit disappointed.'

'Why can't I just wear something I've already got,' groaned Harley, already having forgotten my Team Robinson pep talk.

'And what have you already got, sir?' asked Poppy.

Harley shrugged. 'Nothing.'

'It's a look, I suppose,' she said, pretending to consider it and then selecting a navy suit from the rail. 'But wearing nothing on Christmas Eve might be a bit chilly.'

'Haha,' Freya piped up. 'Chilly willy.'

Harley grabbed the suit from Poppy and sloped off to the changing room.

I stifled a giggle and Poppy gave me a reassuring smile. 'You focus on the dress and leave me with the suit.'

Half an hour later, a pair of sequin party shoes, a blush-pink dress with a tulle skirt and matching velvet bolero, a sharp navy three-piece suit and co-ordinating tie, a shirt and a pair of smart shoes had been paid for and set aside for alterations and we were free to leave. Freya was happy, and although Harley pretended not to care, he'd spent an inordinately long time in the changing room, which I could only assume meant he was either admiring himself or taking selfies, both of which were fine by me.

We found a coffee shop which both the kids approved of and after polishing off cheese and ham toasties and hot chocolates, we headed back into the dark evening.

Bakewell was bigger than Wetherley and it was lovely to walk through the town centre and admire all the shop windows and Christmas decorations. I was in no rush now that the business of the day was over, especially as it had been a success, so when Freya spotted that there was virtually no queue outside Santa's Grotto, I was happy to take her over.

'I'll wait outside,' said Harley once I'd paid the entrance fee for Freya.

I shook my head. 'Sorry. I need you to come in with me. It's dark and I'm not having you hanging around on your own.'

Harley's shoulders sank. 'Merry, please don't make me go in. Anyone from school could come past and see me. It would be so embarrassing.'

Freya was confused. 'Don't you want to tell Santa that you'd like a snowboard? That's what you told me you wanted.'

'Shush,' Harley grunted. 'You're just a little kid, you don't get it.'

The family in front of us disappeared into the grotto

and we were up next.

'Is it because you've been a naughty boy?' Freya probed earnestly. 'Are you on the naughty list?'

I could see that it was on the tip of Harley's tongue to tell his little sister some home truths about Santa; I could only imagine the look on Lydia's face when I took her little girl back in tears because she'd been told that Santa didn't exist.

'It's been years since I got the chance to go and see Santa. Please. Just humour me.'

'Fine,' he grumbled. 'But don't expect me to speak to him.'

The elves waved us in, and Freya skipped ahead excitedly.

'Thank you,' I whispered, but he wasn't listening. He was too busy checking the area to make sure nobody he knew was around.

'Who is it you're worried might see you?' I asked.

Harley glanced at me defensively. 'No one.'

'Sure?'

'Just boys from school.' He studied his thumb and rubbed at a pen mark.

'What are your friends' names?' I said casually, trying a different tactic. 'You know my best friend is Nell, it's only fair I know yours. Who do you hang out with?'

I held his gaze. His deep brown eyes, so like his father's, looked away.

'Before we went to Canada, my best friends were Ollie and Alex, but they joined the rugby team and now they're always at rugby practice in the week or playing matches at weekends.' He finished with a shrug.

He'd told me who he didn't hang out with, I noticed, and not who he did.

'Harley was really sad when he didn't get picked for the

rugby team,' Freya announced. 'He cried.'

'Shut up,' Harley scowled.

'Your dad told me how much you love sport,' I said. 'Are there any other things you'd like to do?'

'Yeah, snowboarding,' he replied. 'Massive open spaces and speed and snow. Not much chance of me doing that around here.'

'No,' I agreed. 'But there might be something else you like.'

I wracked my brains to try to think what else might give him a similar buzz: cross-country running, off-road biking, go-carting? I'd personally hated cross-country running at school, but it might suit Harley. I made a mental note to have a look at the school website and see what I could come up with. I'd ask Nell if she had any bright ideas too; Max was only a year older than Harley. I felt quite maternal at the thought of doing something useful for him. It was a good feeling.

'He used to play football before Canada,' Freya told me. 'And I used to have swimming lessons. But I'm not doing that anymore.'

'Football and rugby are so lame,' he said, 'and if you don't play those, you're a nobody.'

'Well, you're definitely not a nobody,' I said, feeling fiercely protective of him. 'Perhaps you'll get the chance to go skiing again, maybe with school, or, you never know, perhaps we could try to arrange a holiday to the Alps. A family holiday.'

'I know you're trying to help,' Harley said glumly. 'But one measly week on the snow is nothing. I want to go back to Whistler. I've got friends there who like the same things as me. I liked that school better too.'

'Hello!' An elf plonked herself right in front of Freya

and started chatting. Freya fired questions at her, like where did she buy her clothes and what do elves eat and do they get presents for Christmas. I kept a watchful eye on her, but was glad of the chance to talk to Harley privately.

'Perhaps you can apply for a university place in the US or Canada, that would be something to aim for, wouldn't it?' I said brightly.

He gave me a derisory look. 'Merry, I'm thirteen. I've got five years of school to get through. I don't fit in here anymore. We had a motivation and goals day at school at the start of term. We all had to talk about something we were proud of achieving. I took in a photograph of me in the air snowboarding because I thought it was cool. Now they call me Olaf.' He noticed my blank expression. 'The snowman from *Frozen*?'

I nodded, my heart aching for him. Kids could be brutal.

'When we came back to England, Freya went back to the same primary, but I'm in secondary school now and hardly know anyone. Everyone had already made friends when I got there. Now I'm just Olaf the snow boy.'

I had this awful image of him sitting on his own in the school cafeteria at lunchtime. I hated the idea of him being lonely. I'd known loneliness, I totally empathised with how he was feeling.

'I'm really sorry, Harley,' I said, risking giving him a hug. 'Thank you for telling me.'

'Please don't tell Dad any of this,' he mumbled. 'I don't want him storming into school and telling the teachers that the boys have to stop calling me Olaf. It won't help, it'll make things much, much worse.'

'If you don't want me to, I won't, but I know your parents would want to know how you're feeling.'

Harley shook his head. 'I'm not telling them. It'll

only make Mum feel more guilty than she already docs. It's not their fault, but Mum and Dad getting divorced, and then us moving to Canada for a year, has made me grow up quicker than the boys at school. They seem like little kids to me.' He glanced sideways at me. 'If I tell you a secret, will you promise not to tell anyone? Especially Dad?'

I hesitated. I'd wanted him to confide in me, so I could hardly say no. 'Of course,' I said warily, wondering what the protocol was about not telling Cole what was happening in his son's world.

'I really want to go back to Canada. My best friend in Whistler has a massive house, he says I could live with him and go to my old school. That's the only thing that's going to solve my problem.' He sighed. 'Not going to happen, though, is it?'

There was no way his parents were going to agree to that, but I wasn't going to add even more doom and gloom to the conversation. 'Thanks for talking to me,' I said. 'I feel really honoured that you told me how you feel. I promise I won't say anything.'

Harley smiled ruefully. 'Thanks for listening. Whenever I try to tell Mum anything, she makes a thousand stupid suggestions. But there's no solution. I hate living back in England. That's just the way it is.'

Cole and Lydia would be gutted if they knew how he felt, poor lonely boy. Hopefully, this was a temporary thing and he'd find his groove amongst his old friends, or if not, find a new tribe. Despite my heart aching for him, I held onto the tiniest flicker of joy that he'd opened up to me. Slowly but surely, I was finding my place in this family and it was a wonderful feeling.

'Any time you need a chat, I'm your woman.' I squeezed

his arm in solidarity and then the elf waved us forward and it was Freya's turn to talk to Santa.

'Hello, Freya,' Santa boomed from a large armchair covered in sheepskin blankets. He was sitting in front of a fake log fire and was surrounded by hessian sacks of gifts. A small Christmas tree sat in the corner with prettily wrapped presents beneath it and Christmas music rang out from a speaker fixed to the ceiling. 'Are you looking forward to Christmas?'

Harley and I hovered by the doorway. Despite his reticence, he was taking in every detail of the room, and I noticed him trying to peer at the presents.

Freya seemed to have gone shy and simply nodded. Santa beckoned her to come closer.

'And what is on your Christmas list this year?' he asked kindly.

Freya inched forward, cupped a hand to her mouth and hissed in the loudest whisper in whispering history, 'I want my mum to get back together with my dad. That's what I want.'

Her words slammed into me like a train and a tight band formed around my chest. I had no idea that was how she felt. Beside me, I heard Harley swear under his breath. Under normal circumstances, I'd say something about his bad language, but compared to his sister's revelation, I barely acknowledged it.

Beneath his red hat with the faux-fur trim, Santa's eyes slid nervously to me. 'I see.'

'Hey, Freya, don't you want a guitar?' said Harley with a forced laugh.

Freya looked back at us, and embarrassment flashed up on her face as she realised that we might have overheard her.

'That as well,' she said to Santa. 'But mostly the first thing.'

'Hohoho, a guitar,' replied Santa, stroking his beard. 'Some of my elves play the guitar. I'll have to see if there are any in my workshop. But, for now, would you like to choose something from this sack?'

Freya delved into the bag by his feet and while she was occupied, Harley sucked in a breath.

'Sorry about that,' he said. 'She's only a kid, ignore her.'

'I know, I don't mind,' I said weakly, lying through my teeth. 'It's fine.'

Freya tucked the present under her arm and said thank you to Santa, and Harley took her hand and marched her out.

'I hope your daughter gets her wish,' said Santa, holding my gaze. 'Merry Christmas, my dear.'

'Merry Christmas to you too,' I replied, trying to keep my voice steady.

I didn't have the words to tell him that Freya wasn't my daughter, that her Christmas wish was the opposite of mine. And what was I supposed to do with this information? Ignore it, as Harley suggested, and plough on with the wedding regardless?

Then there was Harley. Clearly an unhappy boy who might possibly be being bullied at school, feeling so lonely that he'd rather go back to Canada without his family than stay here. I'd promised him I wouldn't tell anyone else, but was that the right thing to do?

'Let's go,' I said to the kids, taking Freya's hand. 'I need to get you back to your dad.'

And I needed a lie-down in a darkened room. The business of being a stepmother was turning out to be even more difficult than I'd imagined.

Chapter Fifteen

Emily

30 NOVEMBER

It was Monday evening before Emily next made it to Springwood House. She arrived at five, already later than planned, because after she'd been on bus duty and broken up no end of dramas, she'd stayed to help some sixth-formers with costumes for their annual Christmas pantomime.

'Hello, back again?' Kylie smiled at Emily after letting her into reception.

'Yes. I'm going to try to come as often as I can while this is all new to my dad. I don't want him to feel he's been forgotten.'

'Will your sister be coming?' Kylie asked. 'Or are you the only one who lives close by?'

'I don't live far away,' Emily replied. 'But Ray doesn't have any other family, so it'll be just me.'

'Oh right.' A look of confusion crossed the younger woman's face and then she giggled. 'He's in his room. Quite a character, your dad, isn't he?'

'Oh dear, please don't say he's been wandering around naked again?' Emily winced.

Just then, Maude meandered into reception, holding a

satin clutch bag, her lips painted a bright red. 'Is my taxi here, yet?' she fretted. 'At this rate, I'll miss my flight.'

'On it, Maude,' said Kylie brightly, springing up from her chair.

Emily left them to it and ran upstairs to check on Ray.

Her dad had a visitor sitting on his sofa when Emily knocked and let herself in – a woman in a smart navy dress, holding a clipboard.

'She'll tell you,' Ray said to his guest, pointing at Emily.

'Tell you what?' Emily bent to kiss his cheek and smiled at the visitor. 'Hello.'

'What I like for dinner,' he answered. 'I can't think.'

'I'm Shirley, the catering manager,' the woman said, extending a hand for her to shake. 'You must be Emily?' Emily nodded and Shirley continued, 'I've popped in for a chat with your dad, to see what his favourite meals are. So far, I've got pork chops.'

'On Mondays,' Ray clarified. 'That's when Mum does them.'

'Do you know what, Ray,' Shirley said. 'Next Monday, you'll get your pork chops, and that's a promise.'

'I'm quite envious,' said Emily, warming to Shirley instantly. 'I've already heard good things about your fish pie.'

'We do our best.' Shirley looked flattered. 'My philosophy is that there is never any excuse to serve bland, uninteresting food, no matter how little appetite someone has. In fact, the smaller the appetite, the more important good food is.'

'True.' Emily looked at her dad. He seemed to have shrunk these last few months. His neck looked thin peeking out of his jumper, his face had developed angles where before there had been roundness, and only last week, she'd had to make a new hole in his belt because the waist of his jeans had been so loose.

'Was your lunch nice, Dad, what did you have?' She pulled up a chair from the little dining table and sat beside him.

Ray chuckled. 'And you say I'm the forgetful one.'

Emily looked at Shirley, confused. 'Have I missed something?'

'When your dad didn't come down for lunch, I wanted to make sure it wasn't because he was particular about his food,' Shirley explained. 'But he says you brought him a sausage roll which filled him up.'

'That was at the weekend, before you moved in here, not today.' Emily touched his arm gently. 'I've been at work all day; I've just arrived.'

'Ah, right,' Shirley said. 'Well, that won't do.'

'I was sure that was today.' Ray's forehead furrowed and his stomach gave an almighty rumble.

'I'll make sure that doesn't happen again,' said Shirley, getting to her feet. 'How does some soup and buttered toast sound, to keep you going until dinner time?'

Ray raised an eyebrow. 'Tomato?'

'If that's your favourite, I'll make it my mission,' the catering manager promised, scribbling a note on her clipboard. 'And if you think of anything you fancy, just speak to one of the staff.'

'Thanks, Shirley.' Emily saw her to the door. 'If I bring any food in other than snacks, I'll let you know. Sorry to be a nuisance.'

'You're welcome. And don't apologise. We like people to feel as if we're all part of a big happy family, looking out for one another, you know?'

Emily nodded. She did know, although she'd never experienced it personally. Ray and Tina were the only living relatives she had left, and they weren't even a *small* happy family. The thought reminded her of the photograph and she wondered whether the mysterious tin which he seemed very attached to might contain some other memories, his own parents perhaps?

She sat down in the space on the sofa vacated by Shirley. 'You know that tin, the red and black one I fetched for you?'

He gave her a shifty look. 'What about it?'

'Can I see that photograph again, the one we looked at before?'

He muttered about being up and down like a yo-yo, but, nonetheless, disappeared into his bedroom to get it. He wrenched off the lid and slid out the photograph.

She moved beside him so they could look at it together. He stared at it for such a long time that she had to double-check that he hadn't nodded off.

'I wasn't there enough for you, love,' he said finally, heaving a sigh. 'Not when you needed me.'

'You were!' she protested, putting an arm around his bony shoulders. 'Don't be hard on yourself, Dad.'

He shook his head. 'You girls were the best things in my life. And that was my problem. Whenever anything good came along, I'd panic and run. Like I had a self-destruct button built in. I was always worried I'd mess up, so I'd leave while things were still good. Jobs, friends, even family. It all amounted to the same thing, I suppose – ruining everything. Except at least by disappearing, I didn't have to see the disappointment in other people's faces.' He looked at Emily with troubled eyes. 'I was a coward.'

Emily swallowed, not quite knowing how to answer. What good would it do now to question or contradict? It was too late to change the past. 'You did your best,' she murmured, touching her cheek to his shoulder.

'My father was the one that started it,' he continued, his voice so faint that she had to concentrate to hear him. 'He was a cold fish, smart as a whip and expected nothing less than one hundred per cent from himself and everyone around him. I could never live up to those standards. No point trying. And Mother . . . well, she kept me fed and watered, but there was no softness to her. Didn't understand me.'

Emily held her breath, not wanting to interrupt him. This was the most he'd ever told her about her paternal grandparents.

Ray shook his head sadly. 'That should have made me a better dad. But I failed you.'

'You didn't fail me,' she promised. The look on his face was breaking her heart. 'We're OK, aren't we? Still here to tell the tale.'

To her horror, tears started to drip down his cheeks. She fetched some tissue paper from the bathroom and handed it to him.

'Tell me about this little cherub then,' she said, determined to cheer him up. 'What was I like as a girl?'

'Oh, you were a happy little thing.' He smiled at the photograph, and blew his nose. 'Always dancing around the flat, singing to the radio. And you liked painting, the brighter the better.'

She laughed and held up the sleeve of her vivid purple jumper. 'I haven't changed much. It was a house though, Dad, not a flat.'

'Was it?' He looked confused. 'Oh well, whatever, you liked to dance. And I'd read to you sometimes before you went to sleep.'

She smiled at him. 'I love to hear your stories. Have you got any more pictures in the tin?'

'No,' he said gruffly, hugging it to him as if worried she was about to steal it.

'Tomato soup and toast for Mr Meadows?' came a voice from the door. It was Peter, who she'd met on Saturday. He came in carrying a tray with Ray's order.

'About bloody time,' Ray muttered, getting to his feet and sitting at the table. 'A man'd starve before he got his breakfast in here.'

'You're welcome,' said Peter, grinning at Emily.

'What Dad means is thanks very much,' she replied, returning his smile.

Ray was halfway through his soup before Peter had even left the room. Emily felt a pang of protectiveness towards him and tucked a napkin into the neck of his jumper.

'I'm going now, Dad. But can I borrow this photograph? I'd like to make a copy.'

He looked at her sharply and she could almost see his brain mulling it over.

'I'll bring it back,' she promised.

'If you must.' He bit into his toast, drawing the conversation to a halt.

She put it carefully into the inside pocket of her bag to keep it flat and kissed the top of his head. 'See you soon.'

'Be good,' he said distractedly.

As if she was twelve years old. She laughed softly to herself as she left and almost ran into Will in the corridor.

'Woah!' He skidded to a halt. 'Sorry.'

'My fault.' She smiled, pleased to see him. 'Rushing to get off.'

'Are you leaving already?' His face fell. His clothes were smarter than the ones he'd been wearing on Saturday. Still jeans, but a navy shirt which made his eyes seem even bluer. He wore a lanyard around his neck.

'I'm afraid so. This was only a flying visit. Once I leave here, I've got to drive over to my mum's house before heading home.'

'Your mum's around?' He turned and walked with her in the direction of the stairs.

'Alive and well and living not far away from here. My parents separated years ago. I mean, they were never married, and they were never really *together*, together if that makes sense . . .' Emily paused, realising that Will was getting a lot of information in return for a simple question.

'But you have your dad's surname, I noticed?' he said, ruffling his thick blonde hair. He'd made himself look windswept; it suited him. 'Not your mum's.'

'Yes, how did you know?' She blinked at him. Had he been checking her out?

'I'm not stalking you, I promise,' he reassured her. 'But I spotted it on Ray's paperwork as next of kin. I'll be doing some work with him soon; we need to make sure he keeps active, now he's here.'

'Oh, I see.' Emily brushed away the prickle of disappointment and managed a smile. 'Ah, yes, active is good.'

'Anyway.' He cleared his throat. 'Got far to go home?' They took the stairs side by side.

'A little place in the Derbyshire countryside, Wysedale?'

'Oh yeah.' He nodded; the corners of his mouth pulled down as he tried to place it. 'Never been, is it nice?'

'From what I remember of it.' Emily gave a wry smile. 'I've been so busy with Dad recently that I've hardly been home. But yes, it's very pretty. You should visit some time.'

They reached the bottom step but neither of them made a move to go any further.

Will grinned. 'Best invitation I've had all day. I might just do that.'

'Oh, I didn't mean to visit me . . .' She felt a rush of heat to her face and rummaged in her pockets for her car keys to avoid his eye. 'I just meant in general. That you should come to Wysedale because there are some nice walks. If you like walks, that is?'

'Yeah, of course, I knew that was what you meant, ignore me.' His smile remained steady, but for a fraction of a second, a look of embarrassment flashed across his face.

'I'm sorry, that sounded rude of me,' she said, cross with herself. 'You would be very welcome at my cottage any time. I'm not really with it. Long day at school, you know.'

'You look too old to be at school,' he teased.

'Rude!' Emily gasped, pretending to be offended.

'Apologies.' He slapped his forehead. 'I'm turning into my grandad, that was the sort of bad joke he used to make. And, to be honest, I'm more into waves than walking. Surfing is my passion.' He bent his knees and stretched out his arms, pretending to balance on a surfboard.

'You look like a surfer,' she said, recalling the first time she'd seen him in jeans and a hoodie.

'Is that another way of saying I look scruffy?'

'No!' she protested with a laugh. 'Just healthy and wholesome.'

'I think I prefer scruffy.' He grimaced, making her laugh.

'I keep saying the wrong things. But thank you for making me laugh; it's just what I needed.'

'Then I'm glad to be of service.' He touched her arm gently. 'Anyway, I was lying when I said yours was the best invitation I'd had.'

'Oh?' she said, feeling ridiculously disappointed.

'Yeah,' he deadpanned. 'Bernard asked me if I'd cut his toenails for him. And I've got to tell you that takes some beating, I don't think anyone had been near his feet in some time.'

'Poor Bernard.' She pursed her lips at the thought.

'What about poor me?' He mimed sawing through wood and moping his brow and she couldn't help but giggle.

'Thanks for sharing. And with that lovely image fresh in my mind, I shall bid you goodnight.'

'Goodnight.' He touched his fingers to his head in a fake salute and grinned as she walked away.

She was still laughing when she let herself into the car and drove off to her mum's. He was so lovely, she thought and then remembered she was off men. Totally off. For a while at least.

Half an hour later, she was nursing a cup of tea in Tina's workroom. She and Ian lived in a townhouse on a modern estate at the edge of Wysedale, not far from Emily. Ian was downstairs watching some golf tournament taking place on the other side of the world. The house was set over three floors and Tina had commandeered the room at the very top in the eaves for her sewing. In theory, she was retired, but her workroom was full of garments in various stages of completion. Emily was perched on a stool surrounded by tubs of zips, buttons and threads in every hue and there were piles of fabric everywhere she looked.

'So what have we been roped into then?' Tina was sitting at her sewing table, where she had no less than three types of sewing machine set up.

'Ten bear costumes.' Emily produced a piece of brown faux-fur fabric from one of several black sacks. 'It's for the sixth-form pantomime. *Goldilocks and the Ten Bears*.'

Tina cocked an eyebrow. 'Goldilocks has to contend with ten bears before she gets the right porridge?'

Emily laughed 'Oh yeah, gluten-free, made with oat milk, with or without honey . . . it's a minefield these days. Plus, they needed extra characters to pad the story out. Anyway, I've already made the costumes, but the fur is shedding everywhere. Can you finish the edges with your overlocker so they look professional?'

Her mum shook her head fondly 'I'll see what I can do.'

Emily hugged her. 'Thanks, Mum, you're a star.'

'Mug more like,' she grumbled, but she was smiling and Emily knew she didn't mean it. 'Can you stay for dinner?'

Emily finished the last of her tea and shook her head. 'Not tonight, thanks for the offer. I'm bidding on some Victorian boots on eBay, I want to get home before the auction ends to make sure I win.'

Tina chuckled. 'I don't know where you find room for it all.'

'Don't,' Emily groaned. 'But they're just so pretty. Just think of all the journeys they've been on.'

'Next stop, Emily's wardrobe, I suppose.' Tina smiled indulgently. 'Oh well, we all have our passions, I suppose.'

'We do,' she replied distractedly, thinking of what Will had said about surfing and imagining him, tanned in his swim shorts, running into a turquoise sea with a surfboard under his arm.

As she stood up to leave, she remembered the photograph and took it carefully out of her bag.

'Look what I found at Dad's. A picture of him and me. Cute baby, wasn't I? Look at my little dress!' She held the picture out and Tina took it from her. 'I'm so pleased, I don't have many pictures of the two of us. I've borrowed it to have a copy made, I might even get a frame for Dad—' She stopped, conscious that her mum wasn't cooing over the sight of baby Emily in her red Christmassy dress but had gone deathly still. 'Mum, what's wrong?

Tina shook her head. 'Where did you get this?'

'It was in an old tin of Dad's,' said Emily. 'What's the matter, you look as if you've seen a ghost? It's only an old picture.'

'Oh love.' Tina swallowed and handed the photograph back to her daughter. 'I'm sorry to be the bearer of bad news. But that's not you.'

'It must be, who else would it be?' Emily tried to remember Ray's exact words. He hadn't said it was her, but he hadn't contradicted her either.

'Well, it's your dad, all right,' Tina muttered, shaking her head. 'He's wearing the new shirt I'd bought him for Christmas. I'd told him I was pregnant with you on Christmas Day, which I thought would be a nice surprise. But, instead, he went AWOL for a week or so. At least now I know where he went. But I've never seen that child before in my life. Or the room where the picture was taken.'

Emily stared at the picture again. 'Are you sure?'

'As sure as eggs is eggs. I think I'd know my own child.'

'Then who is it?' Emily frowned. 'And why has Dad held on to a photo of him with someone else's kid all these years?'

'I don't know, love,' said Tina shakily. 'And, to be honest, I don't want to know. Just when I think your father can't spring any more surprises on me, here he goes again. I'm sorry you're disappointed.'

'I'm gutted.' Emily wrapped her arms around her mum and held her tight. 'I thought this would be a nice memory.'

'It probably would be for someone,' said Tina, returning Emily's hug. 'I don't know what Ray was thinking letting you believe it was you in this photograph.'

Nor did she, thought Emily sadly, nor did she.

Chapter Sixteen

Merry

I let out a massive yawn as I pressed my friend Cesca's doorbell. It was only eight o'clock at night, but I'd been up early to make a batch of Midnight Forest candles ready for a weekend event and after that I'd dashed up to Manchester for my slot on *The Retail Therapy Show*. My busy day, coupled with the tossing and turning I'd done last night after my shopping trip with Harley and Freya, meant that I was tired and emotional, and shaky from not having eaten properly.

The sensible thing to do would be to postpone this evening for another night. But spending a few hours with Cesca and her sister, Fliss, would be a chance to let my hair down – literally in this case, they were going to give me some ideas on hair and make-up for my wedding day – and besides, empty slots in my diary were as rare as hens' teeth.

'Ta-dah!' I dug deep for a smile and waggled a bottle of pink Prosecco as Cesca opened the door.

'My favourite fizz and my favourite bride-to-be!' she said, beaming. 'A winning combo if ever there was one. Come on in, my love.'

I stepped inside the hallway and Cesca enveloped me in a hug. She was a great hugger. I felt emotion rise inside me and my throat tightened. Tears weren't far away. Although at least I'd managed to hold it together this time while I was live on air this afternoon. I hugged her back tightly.

'I've brought you some candles too,' I said, my cheek crushed to hers. I held up the Merry and Bright gift bag in my other hand.

'No way!' she gasped and pushed back, holding me at arm's length. 'The new ones you were selling on TV today?'

It had been my last sales slot of the year and as well as completely selling out of the Christmas gift sets, we'd also taken huge orders for the Home candles. It had gone very well – too well, if that were possible. I was going to have to put in some long hours over the next couple of weeks if we were to meet all the orders before the cut-off date for pre-Christmas delivery.

'Yep. Sold out online, but I kept a few back for you and Fliss,' I confirmed, blinking away any potential tell-tale tears.

Too late; Cesca's eyes narrowed shrewdly.

She peered in the bag and inhaled the scent. 'Divine, thank you. Now, let me take your coat,' she said firmly, 'and then you can tell me why I feel I've just been hugged by a boa constrictor.'

'I like your Christmas decorations outside.' It was a feeble attempt to change the subject, but it bought me some time. I set my bag down and slipped my coat off. 'I don't think I've ever seen so many light-up reindeer on one lawn.'

'Ben's appalled.' Cesca gave a mischievous smile. 'He keeps muttering that we'll end up with a Boeing 747 in the garden, mistaking us for the airport landing strip.'

I gave a muffled snort of laughter, imagining her poor husband losing the battle over excessive Christmas ornaments.

I followed her into the warmth of the hallway and Cesca took the bottle from my hand. 'Come in and let's get set up. Fliss won't be long. The kids are in bed and Ben's out with his mates, so we won't be disturbed.'

Cesca's house was lovely. Right now, it was decorated to within an inch of its life: wreaths on doors, garlands on mirrors, lights, candles and a massive tree in the open-plan kitchen/dining room. But even stripped back, it was beautiful; all light wood, and glass and acres of granite worktop. I was biased, of course, because Cole had built it, but even so, it was a dream family home. As was Fliss's, who lived next door. They had made their gardens into one so that the cousins could easily play together, and the two families were in and out of each other's homes so much it was basically like living in their own little commune. I would have loved to have been surrounded by family like this when I was a child.

Cesca fetched three glasses and set them on the kitchen table beside a large mirror and a selection of hair paraphernalia.

'It's ages since I've had an excuse to mess about with hair,' said Cesca. 'I used to have a Girl's World styling head when I was little, until I got obsessed with G. I. Jane and shaved her poor head with Mum's razor. She went mad when she found out.'

'About the doll?'

Cesca shook her head. 'The razor. She cut her shins to ribbons on the blunt blades. So, sit yourself in the hot seat and tell me everything.'

I knew she was referring to my little wobble at the door. I'd been mired in doubt since my shopping trip with Harley and Freya. He wanted to move back to Whistler and she wanted Cole to move back to be with Lydia. Both my future stepchildren were unhappy and I was worried about them. Although I knew I wasn't to blame, I *was* part of the problem and felt that I should therefore be part of the solution. I couldn't help thinking that maybe it might be a good idea to postpone the wedding – just for a few months – to allow everyone some breathing space. It hadn't helped that Cole hadn't come home for ages when he took them back to Lydia's. My feverish mind had imagined all sorts of scenarios, mostly involving the two of them having an amorous reunion.

'Hellooo, is anyone there?' Cesca waved her hand in front of my face.

'Sorry.' I blinked and suppressed another yawn. Now I was here I'd rather put my worries aside for an hour. 'I was thinking for my wedding hair that I want to look like me, but on a good day,' I said, eyeing up all hair rollers, curling tongs, straighteners and cans of hairspray warily. There was even a pair of scissors glinting in the light. 'A natural look that I can recreate myself easily enough.'

Cesca plopped down in a chair beside me heavily. 'Oh bum,' she said sulkily. 'I knew you were going to say that.'

As she popped the cork out of the Prosecco, the front door opened, and her sister arrived.

'Just in time!' Fliss said, slipping her boots off and helping herself to a pair of her sister's slippers.

'As usual.' Cesca grinned. 'She was the same when we were kids. Mum only had to pull a tray of flapjacks out of the oven and her beaky nose would appear around the door.'

'Beaky?' Fliss punched her sister's arm playfully. 'Thanks a lot.'

'She'd hang around long enough to stuff her face, then when it was time to wash up, she'd suddenly remember some urgent homework that she'd forgotten had to be in by the next day.'

I laughed, enjoying their sisterly banter as usual.

'What can I say, it's all in the timing.' Fliss rummaged through the cupboards. 'Luckily Saint Cesca was always on hand to show me up. Got any crisps?'

She found some, tipped them into a bowl and plonked them on the table.

'Just a small one for me,' I said, holding my hand up as Cesca poured generous measures of Prosecco. I had to drive back along the dark country lanes and wanted to keep a clear head.

'So.' Fliss knocked back half of her Prosecco. 'Tell us about the dress.'

I got out my phone and showed them the pictures Nell had taken when I'd tried it on. Both gasped, just as I'd hoped they would.

'Love it,' said Cesca.

'It's beautiful,' Fliss agreed.

'Thanks.' I beamed at them both. 'I looked at loads of expensive dresses and nothing really felt right, but I spotted this one in the window of Vintage by Violet and it was love at first sight. When I tried it on, Nell and I both had a little cry and the woman in the shop had to shove tissues at us, so we didn't mark the silk. And that was that; I'd found my perfect dress. Oh, and I bought one of their vintage comb things for my hair too.'

I produced it from my bag and Cesca nodded approvingly. 'You're right about going for a natural look; we'll let your dress do the talking. Fliss, why don't we start with the face?'

'Thanks for this, girls,' I said, while Fliss tied my hair back. 'I don't know what I'd do without you.'

'No worries,' said Fliss, slopping cleanser on a cotton wool pad and rubbing at my skin. 'Can't have you looking like a panda having a bad hair day at your own wedding.'

'Absolutely not. Sorry,' I said, unable to hold back a giant yawn. 'Busy day. I've been on the go since before it got light this morning. Making candles, packing candles, selling candles. I'm ready to drop.'

Fliss snorted. 'Only you could appear on national TV and dismiss it as "selling candles".'

'I feel ungrateful for complaining,' I replied, nibbling around the edge of a crisp absent-mindedly. 'But we've been a victim of our own success. Sales have grown faster than I can cope with.'

'Excuse the pun, but aren't you in danger of burning the candle at both ends?' Cesca pushed the crisps closer to me, but I shook my head, I didn't have much of an appetite.

'Clear and present danger,' I admitted with a groan.

'So recruit.' Fliss pursed her lips in concentration as she did something to my eyebrows. 'I'm sure you'd have lots of takers.'

'You don't want a job, do you?' I asked hopefully. 'I'm desperate for staff and I want someone I can trust.'

'Sorry.' Cesca shook her head. 'My maternity leave is almost up, and I'll be going back to the office in the new year.'

'And don't look at me,' said Fliss, pulling a face. 'Call me old-fashioned, but I want to be at home with the kids until they're in full-time school.'

'And why not,' I replied. It wouldn't be my choice; I couldn't imagine not working, but it was hers and I respected her for it. I'd just have to keep looking for someone to help.

Half an hour later, I was feeling quite relaxed. It was surprisingly therapeutic to sit still and let someone else style your hair and stroke soft brushes across your skin.

Fliss applied a final layer of blush-pink lipstick, stood back, and admired the full effect. 'I give you the bride-to be,' she announced, sweeping her arm towards me.

Cesca slid the mirror forward so I could see my reflection. My skin was glowing, I had cheekbones and my eyes looked huge. My hair fell in soft waves and Cesca had done a 'half-up' thing so that the front was pinned back with my vintage comb.

'I love this!' I examined my face in the mirror. 'Exactly what I wanted. Thank you so much. My idea of an up-do is to pile it into a messy bun and hope for the best. And I never manage to put on mascara without it ending up on my cheeks. I hope I'll be able to recreate this on the day.'

'No need.' Fliss gave me a hug. 'We'll be on hand on your wedding morning to do it for you.'

I gasped. 'Really? I had visions of my shaky hands trying to do my eyeliner.'

'Well . . .' Cesca smiled. 'We know you won't have your mum with you and that you're an only child, so we're going to be there not just as your hair and make-up team but as your honorary sisters.'

'Oh girls. That's the best possible wedding present I could have,' I said, blinking away tears.

Fliss swooped in quickly with some eye make-up remover. 'Panda eyes alert!'

Cesca handed me a tissue. 'We'd better promise not to say anything too soppy on your wedding day in case we all end up blubbing.'

I blew my nose. 'My emotions are all over the place.'

'We did notice,' said Cesca gently.

'Of course they are,' Fliss soothed. 'I was the same when I got married.'

'Understatement,' Cesca snorted. 'You locked yourself in the loo and refused to come out because you claimed you'd changed your mind. My poor brother-in-law was green with worry.'

'I am having a bit of a wobble about the wedding,' I admitted.

'Oh, love.' Cesca rubbed my arm and sat down next to me.

Fliss sat down too. 'Come on. Out with it. And whatever it is, I'm sure we can sort it out.'

'It's Harley and Freya.' I took a deep breath, trying to decide how much to tell them. 'The children have only been back in the UK since August and they've had a lot of change to contend with,' I said. 'I'm wondering if we should push the wedding back for a while until I'm sure it's the right thing to do for everyone.'

'Nooo!' Fliss looked horrified. 'Kids love weddings. Well, kids love *parties*, and a wedding is basically just a really expensive party.'

'My advice is to make them feel part of it, involve them,' Cesca suggested.

'Freya is your bridesmaid, so let Harley take charge of something too,' added Fliss. 'The music maybe, and if it's not inappropriate, maybe he can help with the drinks at the reception?'

'Good tips,' I said, forcing a smile. 'But it's the marriage I'm more concerned about. Their father will be *marrying* me and I'm not sure if they're ready to accept us becoming a permanent arrangement.'

A memory of Freya's wish to Santa came to mind, but I said nothing. It felt too painful to admit, even to my friends.

'Haven't they been separated for years?'

I nodded. 'But I'm Cole's first girlfriend.'

'Perhaps they'll be glad their dad is settling down. It'll be the end of the instability in his life, and they might like the security that comes with that,' Fliss suggested.

'You know what I think?' Cesca gave me a knowing look. 'I think you're projecting your own worries onto them. This is you getting the pre-marriage jitters and overthinking every tiny detail. You love those children and they love you too, even if they don't say it.'

'So no more talk about postponing the wedding, OK?' Fliss said firmly.

'OK,' I said, trying to ignore the gnawing uneasiness in my stomach.

I felt bad for lying not just to my friends but to Cole. Because if he knew what his little girl wanted more than anything else this Christmas, would he still want to marry me? I wasn't sure, and it wasn't a risk I was prepared to take.

Chapter Seventeen

Emily

I DECEMBER

There was a convivial atmosphere in the communal room at Springwood House when Emily arrived. The afternoon light was fading, and the twinkling lights above the fireplace and on the Christmas tree lent a cosy and welcoming glow. At one end of the room, a group of people, arranged in a semicircle with Peter at the centre, were listening to music and chatting, some of them swaying to the beat. Emily recognised the song as an old duet by Elton John and Kiki Dee, it was one of Tina's favourites. Beside the Christmas tree sat Maude with a visitor, a striking-looking woman in her seventies talking loudly in a German accent, a fluffy ginger dog asleep between them.

At the opposite end to Peter and his gang, the television was on, and all the armchairs in front of it were occupied. Emily spotted Ray's tufty silver hair amongst the row of heads and stood at the doorway for a moment, getting her thoughts in order.

Since seeing her mum, she hadn't been able to stop thinking about that baby in the photograph. She'd been so sure that it was her, so pleased that Ray had hung onto it all this time. Now it turned out, it was a random baby and she couldn't help feeling disappointed. She had to ask him about it again. It was like worrying at a scab, she doubted it would make her feel better, but she couldn't help herself.

'Anyone fancy a game of dominoes?' A man stood in front of the TV and rattled a box of tiles.

'Sit down, dear,' said Lavinia, flapping her hand at him. 'You're blocking the view.'

'Bugger off, Bernard,' Ray grumbled, craning his neck to see past him. 'Not now.'

Bernard with the toenails. Emily found herself smiling, remembering her chat with Will last night. *And well done, Dad*, she thought, *for learning someone's name*.

'Go on, old chap, just one game.' The man leaned across Ray and shook the box again.

Ray half-lifted himself out of his chair and growled.

Yaz leapt up from the floor where she'd been tying someone's laces and intervened quickly. 'Will might play with you later, Bernard,' she soothed, steering him towards the musical end of the room. 'Why don't you join in the Down Memory Lane chat with Peter.' Yaz caught Emily's eye on the way past and grinned. 'Never a dull moment.'

Emily smiled back. 'Did you say Will is here?'

The music changed to a Beatles song about being sixty-four and a cheer rang out.

'He's in the staffroom working on his computer.' Yaz raised an inquisitive eyebrow. 'Want me to tell him you're after him?'

'I'm not after him,' Emily said hurriedly. 'I mean, no, no need, thanks. I just . . . He was going to see my dad sometime this week, that was all. I wondered if he'd had chance yet.'

'I see,' Yaz replied innocently, a smile playing on her lips.

Emily found herself blushing. What was that all about? She genuinely was interested to know whether Will had seen her dad, that was all.

She squeezed in between Lavinia and Ray's chair, said hello to him and kissed his cheek, but he didn't acknowledge her; his gaze was riveted to the television.

'There's a jewellery sale coming up later,' Lavinia was saying to no one in particular. 'I might treat myself to a piece. It's been years since I had anything new. I used to wear a ring on every finger.' She stared at her hands as if surprised that they were hers. The fingernails were painted a dark oxblood red, and her knuckles swollen with arthritis. 'My rings must have shrunk.' She gave a tinkling laugh. 'Because I can't get them over my knuckles now. Oh well, at least my earrings still fit me.' She touched one of her earlobes absently. Her clip-on earrings featured two interlocking letter Cs encrusted with diamonds.

'They're lovely,' Emily said, wondering if they were genuine Chanel.

Lavinia looked at her. 'Hello, dear, we've met before, haven't we? Milan, was it? Did you dress me for that Gucci after-party?'

'No, Lavinia, but I wish I had.' Emily whistled under her breath. She was beginning to see why Will was such a frequent visitor. What she wouldn't give for a peek in the old lady's wardrobe. 'I'm Emily, Ray's daughter.'

'Oh good, you're here.' She leaned forward and raised her voice. 'There we are, Ray. You can stop wittering now, your daughter's here, look.'

Emily waved a hand in front of his face. 'Yoo-hoo, Dad?'

Ray seemed agitated. He hauled himself to the edge of his chair, ignoring them both. 'No, she's on the TV!' He pointed to the screen. 'That's my daughter.'

The TV was tuned to the shopping channel again. It was clearly Lavinia's favourite. This time, two women on the screen were chatting about candles.

Emily looked at the one Ray was getting hot under the collar about. She was green-eyed and blonde and her sort of age. Emily didn't watch shopping channels, but there was something vaguely familiar about her.

'It's OK, Dad,' she said softly, laying a hand on his knee. 'Look at me. I'm Emily. I'm your daughter.'

Ray dragged his eyes from the screen to her face for a fraction of a second. 'I know that.'

'To be fair to Ray,' said Yaz, leaning on the back of his chair, 'you do look similar.'

'I suppose, so,' Emily admitted. 'But I'm a school secretary. The chances of me presenting something on TV are about a gazillion to one.'

'You and me both,' agreed Yaz and both women laughed.

Emily looked back at Ray; he had taken a handkerchief out of his trouser pocket and was mopping his eyes. Poor thing. What was going on inside that brain of his and how could she help him feel better? Keep active, wasn't that what Will had said?

She turned to Yaz. 'Do you think it would be all right to take Dad for a walk outside?'

'Er?' Yaz looked outside at the darkening sky dubiously and then back at Emily as if she was bonkers. 'Go for it.'

'Have you hurt your foot?' Emily asked, noticing her dad limp as they made their way along the path around the garden.

Ray looked down at his shoes. 'I don't remember.'

It had taken all her powers of persuasion, but eventually Emily had coaxed him away from the TV and into wrapping up warmly. Fifteen minutes later, she had led him through the front doors and out into the crisp winter air. Now they were on their second lap. The sky was almost black, but there was plenty of lighting, from lamp posts, solar lanterns along pathways and even festoon lights criss-crossed above the oak tables and chairs on the terrace. There was a lawn intersected by large heather beds; and to the far side, a row of young trees, which Ray informed her were Victoria plum trees, beyond which was a well-tended vegetable plot.

She steered him to a bench that looked like an upended wooden rowing boat, the pointed stern forming a roof above their heads. She tugged off his shoe and found a piece of gravel inside it.

'There,' she said, slipping his foot back in, and sitting beside him. 'That'll be more comfortable.'

'It's a lovely hotel, this, Tina,' Ray said, looking back at Springwood House through the twilight. 'I like it.'

Emily smiled, not bothering to correct him. He was settling in well and that was the main thing. 'Good. That makes me very happy.'

'Remember that hotel we stayed in once, Teen?' he said, chuckling. 'The lock broke off the bedroom door and it was ages until we got rescued. We used to have fun, didn't we, love? When I wasn't being an idiot.'

'I'm sure you did,' replied Emily, taking her dad's hands in hers. They were like ice because he'd refused to wear any gloves. She'd take him back inside soon, but while he was in the mood to reminisce, there was still something she wanted to talk about. And it was nice hearing him call her mum 'Teen'; she hadn't heard that for years.

'I don't blame you for showing me the door, you know,' said Ray. He slumped back on the bench and huddled down inside his coat. 'You had to put up with a lot from me. You and little Emily were better off without me anyway.'

'Let's talk about this.' She pulled the baby photograph out of her coat pocket. She was conscious of sounding like a broken record, but she needed answers.

He peered at the photograph. 'Too dark.'

Fair point. Emily turned on the torch app on her phone. 'It's you, can you see? With a baby.'

'Oh shit.' He rubbed a hand roughly over his forehead. 'I didn't want you to find that, Teen.'

'I know the baby isn't Emily.' She watched a muscle twitch below his eye.

Ray nodded and said nothing for a while. Then he sighed. 'You were good to me, Teen. Better than I deserved. When you told me that Christmas that you were expecting, you were so happy, I couldn't let you down. I couldn't tell you what I knew. I know I was useless, but I loved you, you know.' He glanced sideways at Emily.

'Tina felt the same about you.' Emily swallowed, her dad looked so sincere, there was no doubting he was telling the truth. 'You were the love of her life.'

'And I ruined everything.' He shook his head sadly.

'You've said that before, but what do you mean? I know this photograph means a lot to you, but why?'

'It's all I've got.' He leaned forward, elbows to knees and dropped his head in his hands.

'Of the baby?' she prompted.

'I didn't want you to know, Tina. I didn't want to hurt you.' Ray's shoulders began to heave.

'Know what?' Emily's entire body was rigid with tension, she turned to face him. 'Please, Ray, just tell me. I need to know.'

A second passed, and then another.

'That's my daughter.' He reached a finger to the picture and touched the baby's face.

'I'm your daughter.' She cupped his face in her hands. 'Look at me, I'm Emily. What I mean is, whose baby is this?'

But Ray didn't seem to see her, he gazed off into the distance.

'I didn't even know she'd been born until she was a few weeks old. We were friends at first, me and Sam. I fell hard for her, but she never felt the same, even said that the baby wasn't mine. It was before I met you, Tina. I didn't cheat on you. The next time I saw Sammy, it was obvious that the little girl was mine. Sam still wouldn't admit it but I knew. The thing was, I'd met you by then and you'd found out you were expecting. I felt as if I was letting everyone down.' Tears leaked from his eyes and Emily found a tissue and handed it to him. 'It was all such a bloody mess.'

'Who is the baby?' Her heart pounded; the truth was almost within reach.

'That's little Merry,' he murmured, dragging his eyes back to the photograph. 'Mine and Sam's baby. She was born the year before you had Emily. I'm so sorry, Tina, I should have told you.'

So the baby was his; that was why he'd treasured the photograph.

'You had another child? Another daughter?' Her chest felt tight as the shock of Ray's words stole her breath. She turned to him, studying his face, trying to work out if this was real or whether his poor brain was playing tricks on him, *on them*. 'Is this true?'

Ray reached across and took Emily's hand, squeezing it briefly. 'Yes, love. Emily and Merry. My two girls. I've kept it a secret so long that it's eaten me up, burned me from the inside.'

Time seemed to stand still as Emily stared at her dad, their warm breath white in the cold night air between them. Her heart thumped so loudly, she could hear the rapid beat in her ears. *My two girls.*

'Oh my God,' she gasped. 'All this time, I've had a sister.'

She pressed a hand to her mouth and gulped in air as her head began to spin. If she hadn't been sitting down, she'd have fallen. If this was true, then her dad's admission changed everything. For him, for her, and – she felt a prickle of dread creep down her spine – Tina. What would this do to her? She couldn't possibly keep this secret from her mum, could she?

Chapter Eighteen

Emily

In her haste to leave Springwood House, Emily took the stairs too fast, misjudged the last step and stumbled. She yelped, lunged forward and grabbed at thin air before landing on the floor in a heap, twisting her ankle as she fell.

'Ouch,' she moaned, glancing down at her foot. 'That hurt!'

'Oh, Emily!' Kylie squealed, flying to her side from behind the reception desk. 'What happened? Have you broken anything, shall I fetch help?'

Emily attempted to circle her foot and winced with pain. 'No thanks. I wasn't concentrating, that was all. Just twisted, I think.'

After their chilly walk, she had returned Ray to his flat but had made her excuses to leave. All she wanted to do was get home so she could process what Ray had told her, about Merry, the half-sister he claimed she had. In a perfect world, she'd have someone to go home to. Someone who'd make her a hot chocolate, pull her into a giant hug and listen to her while she poured her heart out. Instead, she was going to have to make do with calling Izzy and hoping she was free for a chat. A wave of self-pity washed over her, and she felt dangerously close to tears. Independence was all well and good, but it got a bit lonely sometimes.

With Kylie's support, Emily hobbled to a chair and sat down.

The younger woman peered into her eyes. 'You look really pale. As if you've seen a ghost.'

'I just . . .' Emily gulped in air and shook her head. 'Not a ghost, better than that. Or maybe worse, I'm not sure.' She dipped her head as a solitary tear rolled down her face. She didn't know how she felt, she had always wanted siblings, but this was so unexpected, so much to take in.

'It's shock,' Kylie said confidently. 'I'll make you a cup of tea with sugar in it. That'll help.'

'Thank you, that's very kind.' Emily smiled weakly even though she didn't take sugar. Shock was an understatement, and it was probably going to take a lot more than sweet tea to help her process what she'd learned today. Still, she appreciated the gesture.

'Don't move!' Kylie cried over her shoulder as she darted off in the direction of the staffroom.

Emily made a noise which was halfway between a sob and a laugh. She wasn't going anywhere in a hurry with this throbbing pain in her ankle.

A few seconds later, Kylie was back. 'The kettle's on, but Will is on his way, he said you need rice.'

'Rice?' Emily repeated.

Kylie gave a mystified shrug. 'Don't ask me.' Just then, the phone in reception began to ring and she darted off to answer it. 'Sorry. Back in a jiffy.'

'I'm fine. No need to bother Will,' Emily said, getting to her feet and instantly stumbling back down. 'Bloody hell, that hurts.' She squeezed her eyes shut to block out the stinging pain and when she opened them, Will was beside her.

'Sounds like there's every need,' he said firmly. 'You're coming to sit down for five minutes in the staffroom. Let someone look after you for a change.'

She nodded meekly, too overwhelmed to argue. Picking up her bag, he held her waist, taking her weight, and told her to lean on him with her arm around his shoulders. He steered her into a comfy chair in the empty staffroom and raised her ankle on a footstool before easing off her boot gently.

She grimaced, cursing herself for choosing novelty socks that morning.

He looked at her and grinned. 'Llamas wearing Santa hats. Cute.'

'As if today wasn't embarrassing enough,' she replied, and then moaned when he prodded her ankle. 'What are you doing?'

'RICE,' he said, fetching a cold compress from the fridge. 'Rest, ice, compression and elevation.'

She laughed softly, realising what Kylie had meant. The kettle, which had been building up to boiling point, clicked off.

'That's more like it. Want to talk about it?' he asked softly. 'Or can I interest you in tea and cake.'

'Definitely tea and cake please.' She gave him a watery smile.

'Coming up.' He got to his feet and took mugs down from a shelf. 'There's always tons of cake going spare, and boxes of chocolates. Visitors often bring gifts for the staff. People feel guilty for putting their relatives in here. I know I did.'

'*You* did?' She looked up sharply.

'Yep. My grandad spent his last years here. It broke my heart to have to "lock him up", as I'd thought of it at the

182

time. But the change in him was almost instantaneous. He seemed peaceful, whereas when he'd been trying to manage at home, he was like a coiled spring, full of anxiety and fear.'

'You make it sound as if it was a decision you had to make on your own,' she said, intrigued.

'That's exactly what it was. I don't have any other family. Sugar?' He held up a canister marked sugar and she shook her head. 'My dad disappeared before I was even born. My mum died in prison and Grandad brought me up.'

Emily blew out a breath. 'Families, eh?' It made her own new discovery look quite tame in comparison. 'Thank goodness for your grandad.'

He gave her a sad smile. 'He was my everything. When he got Alzheimer's disease and started forgetting who I was, I lost my entire family. I felt bad that I couldn't care for him myself after he'd looked after me, but I had to work.'

She smiled wistfully. 'It's hard to know what the right thing to do is when you're on your own.'

He set plates on the table beside her where she could reach and pulled up a chair opposite. 'Listen to me giving you my life story when I'm supposed to be looking after you. Here you go.'

He handed her a mug of tea and she sipped at it. It was strong and steaming hot and instantly reviving.

'This is perfect, thank you.'

He grinned and took a bite of his cake. 'The power of tea and cake should never be underestimated in my opinion.'

'I'm Ray's only family too,' she told him, tearing off a piece of cake and popping it in her mouth. 'So I'm the one who had to make that call to move him and it was . . . it was . . .' Except she wasn't his only family anymore was she? Her family tree had a new branch, and somewhere out there, she had a sister.

Will looked at her with his friendly smile and kind eyes. 'It's OK, you don't have to tell me if you don't want to.'

Emily held his gaze, weighing up whether to confide in him or not. It would be nice to talk about it with someone who was here in the present, rather than someone whose memory flitted backwards and forwards. They hadn't known each other long, but she felt a connection to him, he seemed like a person she could trust.

'I do want to.' She set down her mug and reached inside her bag which Will had placed on the floor beside her. 'Remember this?' She showed him the photograph and he nodded. 'We misread the writing on the back. It says *Merry's* first Christmas, not merry first Christmas. Merry is the name of the baby.'

Will took the picture from her. 'So that's not you?' he asked, confused.

'Apparently that's my sister. My half-sister.' She stared at the little blonde girl, her face lit up with happiness as she looked at her dad – *their dad*, she thought with a jolt.

'And you didn't know about her?'

'Not until today, no.'

He whistled under her breath. 'Oh man. That's wild. How do you feel?'

'Honestly?' She gave him a half-smile and shrugged. 'I don't know yet. Mindblown, I think. If I hadn't seen this photograph, would I have ever found out, I wonder?'

'I've spent a lot of time with dementia patients over the years,' said Will. 'This happens more often than you'd believe. Something will happen out of the blue to trigger a memory, or past traumas, secrets they vowed they'd never confess. Some people own up to love affairs or decide to track down children given up for adoption which other family members know nothing about.'

Emily nodded. 'Maybe Dad feels that time is running out to come clean before he loses his memory completely.' She had a sudden thought; maybe this was why he'd come back to the area. Maybe he wanted to be near his family. *Both* of his daughters. 'I wonder where she is now?' she murmured.

Will turned over the compress on Emily's ankle, easing the cold fabric gently over her skin. 'Are you going to try to find her?'

Emily blinked at him. 'I don't know, I hadn't thought . . . It's all a lot to take in.'

He passed the picture back to her and her breath hitched as his fingers brushed against hers.

'Emily,' he said steadily. 'This is a lot to get your head around. I can't begin to imagine how it would feel to suddenly discover a sibling after spending the first three decades of life as an only child. Take your time, let it sink in. And, in the meantime, try not to fling yourself down any more staircases.'

They smiled at each other, he was attempting to lighten the mood and she appreciated the gesture.

'I'll do my best. And thank you for looking after me. You're a good man. A good friend.'

'Saint Will at your service.' His eyes flicked away, and he clapped his hands together as if changing the subject. 'Now can I call someone to come and drive you home? A significant other maybe?'

'Thanks, but I can manage by myself. My ankle already feels stronger.' She brushed crumbs from her lap. 'And there isn't a significant other. Not anymore.'

'Ah.' He raised an eyebrow. 'Hence the ready meals and Netflix?'

She smiled. 'Exactly. There was someone, but he got fed up with me putting my dad first.'

'What?' Will pulled a face and Emily felt a rush of warmth towards him; she couldn't imagine him being anything less than supportive in the same situation. 'Perhaps now that your dad is settled, you'll able to start afresh.'

Emily wrinkled her nose. 'Absolutely no way, he had his chance. There's no going back there.'

He laughed in surprise. 'No, I wasn't suggesting that you go back to *him*.'

'OK, good.' Emily reached for the llama sock Will had peeled off and tugged it back on. 'Because life is simpler without him.'

'Right, right.' He nodded thoughtfully. 'Well, I don't want to *un*simplify your life, but I was thinking maybe we could go for a drink one evening? Or share a curry while watching an old episode of *Friends*? Like the party animals that we are.' He shrugged as if to say that it was no big deal either way. But the faint blush on his cheeks gave him away.

She blinked at him. 'Um, are you asking me out on a date?'

'If you'd rather not, I understand.' The corner of his mouth lifted into a smile. 'I'm sure Bernard will have some more personal hygiene chores to keep me busy, if I'm lucky.'

Nerves of excitement fluttered inside her; she could almost hear Izzy's voice yelling at her to say yes, but there was a lot going on and she needed space to process it all. 'I'm flattered, Will. But can we take a rain check on the drink? I think I need a bit of time to get my head around Dad's news.'

'Of course.' He ran a hand through his hair, looking flustered. 'I totally understand. It was insensitive of me to ask under the circumstances.'

'Not at all,' she said, anxious to reassure him. 'There's nothing wrong with asking for what you want out of life.'

He grinned. 'Motto to live by, right there.'

She got to her feet gingerly, testing out her ankle. It still ached, but she'd be able to make it home. 'Thanks again for the cake and for listening. I needed both.'

Will stood up too and collected their mugs. 'We all do. Be kind to yourself, Emily. You've got a lot on your shoulders; you don't have to do it alone.'

She quickly said goodbye and left the room before she did something stupid like cry, or worse, throw her arms around his neck and kiss his lovely mouth. He was such a nice guy and genuinely seemed to want to help. But no, she told herself firmly. It wasn't the right time to get involved with someone. Not when her family life was in such turmoil. She had a new sister to get to grips with first, and what she was going to do about that was anybody's guess.

Chapter Nineteen

Merry

4 DECEMBER

'So where do you want me?' Cole asked, joining me in the living room of Holly Cottage.

'Now there's a question,' I said saucily, putting my bag of nail polishes on the coffee table.

'Don't distract me,' he warned, his eyes flashing with mischief, 'or you'll be late to your own party.'

He slid his arms around my waist and pulled me in for a kiss. It was Friday night, the log burner was blazing merrily, I had two of my Mistletoe Kiss candles giving off an amazing smell and the lighting was low. The setting was perfect for a romantic evening, but I was going to have to hold that thought. Tonight was my hen party and in assorted homes across Wetherley, my dearest friends were, like me, getting their glad rags on for an evening of festivities.

'So how are you enjoying being engaged to me?' I asked, pressing myself closer. 'I'm not being too much of a bridezilla, I hope?'

'No complaints so far.' His eyes blazed as his hands reached further down my back. 'Although I think we're going to have to get more bathroom storage in the next house.'

I gave him a guilty look; the bathroom cabinet was bulging with new products since my evening with Cesca and Fliss. 'Sorry, blame my hair and beauty consultants. They've insisted I start a proper beauty regime before the big day.'

'*Regime?*' He looked horrified. 'You mean there's more to looking good than a shower and a shave?'

I giggled. 'I know! Apparently, my flannel and bar of carbolic soap just didn't cut it. Anyway, to answer your question, I'll sit on the sofa. And you sit here, at my feet.' I tapped the footstool.

'Yes, m'lady.' He pretended to tug his forelock and sat down.

'Here's the polish.' I handed him the dark red nail varnish. 'But first you have to separate the toes, so the paint doesn't come off and smudge on the others.'

He gave me a quizzical look as I pointed to the roll of kitchen paper.

'It's times like these when I'm glad I'm a man,' said Cole.

'Oh no, this is all part of the fun,' I protested, lifting my leg, and settling my foot on his thigh. 'The preparation, the WhatsApp chats about outfits, the tights or no tights conversation, the who's drinking and who's driving debate?'

'And is anyone driving?' He looked sceptical.

'Nope. Now grab that kitchen roll and I'll talk you through it.'

He wove tissue paper between each toe, carefully following my instructions.

When Nell had broached the subject of a hen party, I'd point-blank refused. But that day in the market a few weeks ago when a mother and daughter had come to Nell's stall had stayed with me. The daughter had said something about celebrating every moment, big or small. And so Nell had got her wish and tonight was the night. The two of them had really stuck with me, their relationship, their bond. It wasn't something I'd had myself, but maybe I would in the future, with a daughter or my own, and in the meantime, I had my work cut out, earning a place in the heart of my stepdaughter. If only I hadn't heard her make that wish to Santa, I'd feel a thousand times better about marrying her father.

Cole unscrewed the lid of the nail polish and carefully scraped off the excess inside the neck of the bottle. I felt such a huge rush of love for him that it made me feel dizzy. What was going on in Lydia's house? I wondered. Had Freya said something to her mum? Had Harley? Maybe Cole knew and didn't want to say anything? I couldn't hold back, I needed to know.

'Is everything OK with the kids? And Lydia?' I asked, keeping my voice neutral.

He looked up warily. 'As far as I know. Why?'

I shrugged. 'That day we got engaged, Freya was talking about Lydia being sad if she didn't come to the wedding. I just wondered if anything has been said.'

Cole bent over my foot, carefully applying red paint to my big toe, and chuckled. 'Lydia will not be sad, I promise.'

'Must be weird for her though,' I continued. 'Her husband marrying someone else.'

He gave me a curious look. '*Ex-husband*. And she was the one who instigated our separation. A long time ago.'

My heart thudded. I knew I was playing with fire, but I couldn't help myself. 'So if she hadn't, do you think you'd still be married? All living together, one happy family?'

Cole sat back, replaced the lid on the nail polish and took my hand. 'What's going on here?'

'Nothing, I . . . I just . . .' I felt my throat tighten and the words got stuck in my throat. 'Nothing.'

'I love you,' he said, his eyes creased with concern. 'You captured my heart from the day I met you. Nobody else comes close. Have I done anything to make you doubt me?'

I shook my head and managed a smile.

'We've both got a past, we've both been on a journey which has brought us to today. And I'm right where I want to be.'

'Me too,' I agreed.

He reached forward and brought his mouth to mine, kissing my worries away.

'Good.' He grinned at me and picked up the nail polish again. 'Now can I please get on with my job. I'm getting *Basic Instinct* vibes looking at you from this angle and it's torture knowing I can't do anything about it.'

'Keep your eyes on the job please, Mr Robinson,' I said, laughing.

I was wearing only a towel, or two towels if you counted the one wrapped turban-style around my wet hair. It was taking me a lot longer to get ready than usual. Mind you, I was making more of an effort. I'd exfoliated, used a face *and* hair mask and I'd fake-tanned. Not a lot, but after trying on all my outfits and declaring them not quite right, I'd ordered a dress online at the last minute and now didn't have the right tights to match, so bare legs it was.

'I was thinking about that wedding rhyme,' I said. 'Something old, something new, something borrowed, something blue. Does my wedding ring count as new?'

Cole pondered that. 'Maybe. I'll google it, we don't want to get it wrong.'

'I don't think axes will fall on our heads from above if we get part of an old rhyme wrong.' I shook my head fondly, secretly loving how seriously he took everything.

He gave me a sheepish smile. 'You know me. I like to get the details right.'

'My dress is old. So that's OK.'

Cole did a double take. 'Why are you wearing an *old dress* to get married in?'

I snorted. 'Ha! The look on your face. Don't worry, darling. It's vintage and absolutely beautiful. Trust me.'

'Of course I trust you.' His gaze met mine. 'You'll walk up that aisle looking like a million dollars, even if you were still wearing that towel.'

'Thanks. At least I know if I run out of time to get dressed, you'll still marry me,' I teased. 'Astrid has bought me a lovely little white beaded bag, so that's borrowed sorted. I'll have a chat with the girls tonight and get some blue ideas.'

'On a hen party?' He raised an eyebrow. 'That shouldn't be difficult.'

'Hmm. Nell is under strict instructions not to lower the tone.'

Cole grinned. 'If Nell can manage half an hour without making an innuendo about nuts, I'll foot your drinks bill.'

'I think we both know your money is safe.'

Five minutes later, he'd painted two coats of Midnight Red on my toes and was carefully putting everything away.

'There you are, Cinderella, your feet shall go to the ball.' He unwound the tissue from between my toes.

'Thank you,' I said, inspecting his handiwork. 'I don't need to get my boots on for another half-hour, so they'll have plenty of time to dry.'

'Boots?' He looked bemused. 'You mean after all that no one is going to see them anyway?'

'It's December, I was hardly going to go out in sandals.' I held my hands out to show him my fingernails. 'But they match my nails, so I feel put together. And, you never know, I might end up taking my boots off and dancing on the table.'

'Your night sounds a lot more fun than my stag do will be,' Cole said wistfully. 'Indoor crazy golf with Dad, Harley and Paul, followed by sushi, because, despite my aversion to wasabi, it's Harley's favourite.'

I snorted involuntarily, remembering the day we first met when I'd been helping Nell out on her stall last year. We'd been handing out free samples of wasabi peas that day and Cole had decided to eat a large handful and had given his sinuses a clear-out he'd never forgotten. 'It's very sweet of you to do what Harley likes, I know he'll appreciate it.'

He pulled a face. 'I'm hoping a bit of time with the men in the family will do him good. Lydia is finding him hard work: moody and sullen. Not the ray of sunshine he used to be.'

'I've noticed that too,' I said. 'Is he OK, do you think?' I knew the answer to this, but of course I couldn't tell Cole that because of my promise to Harley.

'He's thirteen,' said Cole wryly. 'I'd be more suspicious if he wasn't grumpy. It's just a phase, don't worry, and if anything is seriously bothering him, we'll winkle it out of him on the stag night.'

I couldn't push the subject any harder without raising suspicion, and anyway, it was clear that Lydia and Cole were in touch about the well-being of their kids.

'I hope so.' I stretched my arms above my head languorously. If I didn't move soon, I'd be too comfortable to go out at all. 'If I'd known you'd turn out to be such a willing beautician, I'd have done this ages ago. We should make every Friday night pamper night.'

'Oh yeah . . .' He gave me a dubious look. 'And what's in it for me?'

'This.' I tugged him towards me and fell back on the sofa, bringing him with me.

'OK.' He pretended to think about it. 'I've definitely had worse Friday nights.'

'On that note, you do remember promising to pick us up and drive us home?'

'Beautician and taxi driver.' He grinned. 'I get all the best jobs. By the way, what are you wearing under that towel?'

'Just a tan. Oh, and a couple of white bits.'

He moaned. 'Tease.'

I leaned forward and kissed him. Heaven. This man. He was sexy and fun, and I loved him with every inch of my body. 'When I'm home, I'm all yours,' I promised. 'Although I must admit, I do regret having to leave you all alone when the fire is lit, and the candles are burning.'

'Don't regret anything,' he said softly. 'You're going out to celebrate marrying me. What better reason to leave me than that? Anyway, I've got some emails to reply to from the accountant. I'm sure the time will fly by.'

I touched his face. 'You work so hard. It's late, you haven't had dinner yet. Why don't you find something good on TV and put your feet up instead?'

'Maybe I'll have the TV on in the background.'

'That's still working,' I said sternly. 'OK, your turn. Haircut.'

We changed places so that he was sitting on the sofa, and I plugged in the hair clippers.

'Not too short,' he instructed, checking the setting.

'Relax,' I said, starting at the base of his neck. 'I'm getting quite good at this.'

I caught his eye, both of us remembering my first attempt in the summer which ended up with Cole having to wear a baseball cap for a month to cover up his bald patch.

'I think the second time you allowed me to do your hair was one of the scariest times of my life,' I admitted, carefully holding his ear out of my way.

He pulled me onto his lap, his deep brown eyes suddenly serious and I switched the clippers off. 'Merry, there's something that scares me too sometimes.'

'Oh?' I held my breath. Our bodies were so close, my heart pounding so hard that it felt impossible that he couldn't feel it too. This was the moment, the perfect opportunity to tell him what Freya had said, to hint at what Harley had confessed to me without betraying his confidence. But before I could formulate the words, Cole continued.

'I stuffed my marriage last time by working too hard, losing sight of the important things. What's to stop that happening again? I'm still the same man, I haven't changed.'

I touched his face and smiled at him. 'Well, that's good because I never want you to change. You are amazing just the way you are.'

He shook his head, frowning. 'You say that now, but I'm making the same mistakes. Take this year for example. My plan was to sell the houses at Orchard Gardens and use the profits to buy a place of my own – *our own*. A proper home where the kids can have their own rooms and feel settled in. Instead, I ploughed the money back into the business, I'm building more houses for other people and Christmas has rolled around again and I'm . . . *we're* still living in a rental and when the kids come over, they're squashed in the spare room.'

'It's not any old rental,' I reminded him, brushing his lips with my own. 'The landlord of this one is really hot.'

'Yeah, yeah, I know.' He exhaled, smiling softly, and tightened his arms around me. 'It just feels like Groundhog Day, like I should have moved on.'

'That's not how it feels for me. It feels exciting and new.' I traced my fingers along the side of his jaw and he pressed his lips against my hand. 'And next year, when we look for a proper forever home, it will be as Mr and Mrs Robinson. If you'd bought a house earlier this year, it would always have felt like yours, but now I know it'll be properly ours.'

The worry lines between his brows softened. 'I don't know how you do it, but you always say exactly the right thing to make the sun come out in my world.'

'*Our world*,' I corrected him, putting my hands behind his neck and bringing his mouth to mine.

It wasn't the right moment to tell him what Freya had said after all. Why ruin a perfect moment? *Let's keep our world full of sunshine*, I thought. Just for a while longer.

Chapter Twenty

Merry

Nell tapped her fork on the side of her champagne glass to get everyone's attention. She cleared her throat and got to her feet. 'I wish to say a few words about my dearest friend, Merry.'

Hester put her fingers in her mouth and whistled and everyone else cheered.

'This should be interesting,' I said, steadying Nell's arm. Two drinks in and she was already a bit wobbly. 'Please keep it clean.'

My hen party was under way in a Thai restaurant. Apparently, we'd been given their best table, although I did wonder whether the words 'hen party' had influenced their choice of location as we were well away from the other diners. Even so, we were attracting a lot of attention. Possibly something to do with the inflatable gold crown I'd been forced to wear, and the large, framed photo of Cole dressed in a very small pair of swimming trunks in the centre of the table.

Nell mimed zipping her lips shut. 'So I should avoid telling everyone about when you stood behind the photographer at my wedding and flashed your knickers while the men were having a group shot?'

'That sort of thing, yes,' I said, shaking my head in resignation while everyone laughed.

We were on our second bottle of fizz and the starters hadn't arrived yet. I was feeling on the nice side of tipsy already. I probably should have ordered something more substantial than salad to begin with, but I wasn't hungry. Working long hours and being preoccupied with wedding stuff had led me to miss meals. On top of that, I was still carrying around that niggling worry about Freya's Christmas wish. All this had had the effect of shrinking my appetite.

I was probably worrying unnecessarily, I told myself firmly. I vowed to work harder on my party mood and took a big sip of champagne.

'And should I not mention how you upstaged the bride a second time when all us girls were having our picture taken?' Nell continued.

Cesca gasped. 'You flashed twice in one day?'

'Technically, yes,' I protested, 'but only because I'd stood on an ant's nest and they were running up my legs.'

Astrid let out a bark of laughter, 'I'd forgotten that story.'

'Hmm.' Nell pursed her lips. 'Fortunately for Merry, Olek's two male cousins offered to help, dropped to their knees and stuck their heads up her dress to slap the ants off her while she danced on the spot squealing. Best wedding they'd ever been to, they said.'

I giggled at the memory. 'The photographer did catch the whole thing on camera. But nothing could have upstaged you that day, you looked every inch the radiant bride.'

'As will you on Christmas Eve. Merry, I'm so proud to be your best friend,' Nell said, growing serious as she waved her glass in the air. 'We've been through so much together. Cole is a lucky man and I know you're going to make him a wonderful partner for life. I half expected that on your hen do I'd be secretly thinking that no man would be good enough for you, but you've found yourself a diamond in Cole.'

'Thank you. That means a lot.' I felt tears prickle.

'He's not that bad, I suppose,' said Hester grudgingly, although she had a sparkle in her eye. 'And proposing to you is probably the best thing he's done in a long time, so he gets my vote too.'

'Whoop, whoop!' Fliss chimed in.

'To the future Mrs Robinson!' Nell lifted her glass high, and the others joined in.

'Cheers!' I said, raising my own glass. 'And thank you, Nell. For organising tonight and persuading me to have a hen party, you were right of course, and you're the best friend a girl could wish for.'

'Aww.' She bent down and kissed my cheek, sloshing liquid down the front of my dress. 'Oops, sorry.'

I brushed the drips away. 'Don't worry. It's not a real hen party if you haven't had a drink poured down your cleavage.'

'Precisely,' said Hester, topping up our glasses. 'And at least champagne is classy. I was handcuffed to an ironing board on my hen night. It doesn't get less aspirational than that.'

We cackled with laughter, almost frightening off the waitstaff who'd chosen that moment to bring over our starters. Conversation was briefly postponed while the right food found the right person and we all tucked in.

'You may well laugh,' Hester continued, between mouthfuls of noodle salad. 'But flagging down a cab was an absolute nightmare.'

The image of the elegant and immaculately turned-out Hester trying to climb into a taxi while manhandling an ironing board had us in stitches.

'And the taxi driver who did eventually pick me up fancied himself as a comedian and amused himself throughout the entire journey with terrible puns, like having to charge me a flat rate, and going full steam ahead because he was pressed for time and asking if I was "bored" yet.'

'I hope someone was there to help you when you got home?' Astrid asked. She gingerly picked off flakes of red chilli from the top of her crab cakes and cut into them.

Hester nodded. 'Paul, luckily. Although after he'd watched an ironing board emerge from the back of a taxi, followed by his drunken fiancée, he was weak with laughter. And then while I waited for him to fetch bolt cutters from the garage, I began to feel sick. I only just made it to the downstairs loo.' She paused and covered her face as we all laughed. 'Imagine if you will, me on my knees bent over the loo, and Paul standing behind me, one hand keeping my hair back, the other holding the ironing board out horizontally to take the weight off my wrist.'

'I don't suppose you have any of this on camera, do you?' I asked, wiping tears of laughter from my eyes.

'No, thank goodness,' she replied with a giggle. 'But at least you know that whatever happens to you tonight won't be as bad as that.'

'What's that supposed to mean?' I looked uneasily around the circle and my friends dropped their gazes to their glasses, except Nell, who widened her eyes innocently.

'We're teasing,' said Astrid, taking pity on me. 'This is your night, to have your way.'

'So no butlers in the buff unfortunately,' Cesca sniggered and inhaled a piece of chopped peanut, causing her to cough and splutter.

Fliss slapped her back in the rough way only a sibling could get away with. 'So, are you and Cole completely loved up?'

'Completely,' I confirmed. 'He even gave me a pedicure tonight before I came out, I could get used to that.'

Nell put a hand on her chest. 'How romantic! Olek's idea of romance is to lift the duvet and stick his backside out before he breaks wind.'

'Try living with a man whose favourite food group is pulses,' said Fliss, grimacing. 'He can lift the duvet hands-free.'

'I sympathise,' said Cesca. 'I've heard your husband's *trumpet voluntary* in the morning when he's out in the garden. It's not the best way to wake up.'

'Woah!' I put my hands over my ears. 'You're supposed to be telling me the benefits of marriage, not putting me off.'

'Oh, there are lots of benefits of marriage,' said Nell. 'Um . . .'

The table fell silent while they all tried to think of something and then we all collapsed in gales of laughter again.

'You and I are the only ones who haven't been married,' I said to Astrid. 'Were you never tempted?'

I had always wanted to ask her this but had never felt like I should pry. She was such a wonderful woman, it struck me as odd that she'd been single for so long before she met Fred. But, as Astrid said, it was my night and if I couldn't get away with probing tonight, then when would I?

'Not really,' replied Astrid. She put her hand on Hester's arm. 'I'm very fond of your father, but I like my own space.'

'I get that,' said Nell, dipping a piece of chicken into her satay sauce. 'But I can't believe you've never come close.'

Astrid tilted her head to one side. 'Well . . . there was one time in Las Vegas.'

Everyone gasped and my eyes were like saucers; this was the first time I'd heard anything like this from my strait-laced friend.

'Details please!' I demanded.

'Please remember this was a long time ago.' She raised both hands. 'Before I became your teacher. I was very young.'

'You can tell us anything,' encouraged Nell. She drew a circle in the air with her index finger. 'Circle of trust. What happens on the hen, stays on the hen.'

'Hear, hear,' said Hester, drumming her hands on the table. 'Come on, Astrid, spill the beans.'

'OK, OK.' Astrid smiled, peering into her glass. It was empty and Fliss quickly topped it up. 'I was in California with some of my girlfriends travelling around.'

'Like you do,' said Fliss.

'We got to Las Vegas and couldn't believe it: the size of it, the glitz, the glamour. We were from a small town in Southern Germany, the most exciting thing we'd seen up until then was the Oktoberfest in München. After a few too many tequila sunrises one day, I met a man called Jurgos. He'd booked a chapel and was due to be married by an Elvis Presley impersonator. He was a big Elvis fan, you see.' Astrid sipped her champagne. 'But the problem was he hadn't found a wife yet.'

'Bit of a stumbling block, that, I'd have thought,' I offered, trying to imagine a young Astrid knocking back tequila.

'I told him I liked Elvis.' She shrugged. 'And he asked me to marry him. I said why not. It was all *ein bisschen Spaß*, you know, just for fun.'

I gawped at her in disbelief.

'And what happened?' Cesca asked.

'He went to buy a ring and I went back to our motel room with my friends, and we got dressed up. We were caught up in the moment, you know, just young women, fearless and carefree.'

'Did he turn up to the chapel?' Hester asked.

Astrid nodded. 'In a suit and tie. He was very handsome. I wore a long flowing dress with wide sleeves in bright colours.'

'Like tonight.' I pointed at her purple patterned dress. Astrid was as addicted to colour as I was to candles.

'Jurgos took my arm ready to go inside. But I told him I couldn't go through with it.' She smiled sadly, hitching her shoulders.

'You got cold feet?' Fliss nodded sagely.

'Oh no,' said Astrid. 'It was July.'

Cesca and Hester laughed so hard at her misunderstanding that they could hardly breathe.

'Go on, Astrid, what happened then?' I prompted.

'I said that now we're here it feels real, but at the same time it's fake. We were having fun, but I knew deep inside that a joke wedding isn't something I'd be proud of in the future. Marriage should be about commitment and honesty. I didn't know the first thing about him. And also, I had told him a lie. I did not like Elvis Presley.'

We all gasped. 'What did he say to that?' Nell asked.

'He kissed me and thanked me for making him see sense. He also said that I'd done him a favour: his mother would be sad if she missed his wedding. But mostly, he could never marry someone who didn't love Elvis as much as he did. And that, my friends, is as near as I've been to marriage,' Astrid concluded.

'Ah, well at least it ended amicably,' I consoled.

'Who says it ended there?' said Astrid with a twinkle in

her eye. 'He'd booked the honeymoon suite at his motel; we didn't let *that* go to waste.'

'Astrid! You minx!' Hester pressed a hand to her mouth.

And we all laughed again until the waitstaff arrived and cleared away our empty plates.

'Cesca and I wanted to club together to get you a wedding present,' said Fliss. 'Have you got a list yet?'

We hadn't. No gift list, no photographer, no cars to get us to the registry office, let alone invitations, presents for the bridesmaid, writing wedding vows, organising a wedding rehearsal . . . My stomach churned at the thought of all the jobs left to do.

'There isn't a gift list,' I admitted. 'But you're already doing my hair and make-up on the day. So no presents please, just your presence.'

'Risky move.' Cesca sucked in a breath. 'Because I guarantee you will get gifts and then instead of getting a complete set of stuff, nothing will match.'

'But things chosen for us,' I argued. 'So they'll be special.'

'My gift will be your wedding cake,' Astrid said. 'What sort would you like?'

'That's a great gift, thank you.' I reached across the table and squeezed her hand. 'How about Christmas cake? It's the same as wedding cake, so it kills two birds with one stone.'

'Forget about making things easier, this is your wedding,' Astrid chided. 'Have what you like.'

'Does Cole like Christmas cake?' I asked Hester. 'I feel bad that I don't know, but last Christmas I was still getting to know him.'

'He does,' she confirmed. 'But he hates marzipan and isn't bothered about icing.'

'What?' I pretended to look horrified. 'They're my favourite bits!'

'That's it then, you're made for each other.' Hester chinked her glass against mine.

'To the perfect couple!' Nell proposed another toast, and we all drank. 'I know what I'd like to give you,' Nell said. 'My services as a sales assistant for Merry and Bright. That way, you can have two weeks honeymoon without worrying about the shop.'

'That would be amazing!' My heart leapt. I'd been unsure what to do about the business. I hadn't had time to find an assistant and I didn't want to put even more work on Fred's shoulders. 'But what about your own business?'

She wrinkled her nose. 'You'd be doing me a favour, I promise. I need a break from the market. Funnily enough, one of my regulars was asking the other day if I'd ever consider selling and, if so, to let her know. I'm seriously considering it. I fancy a new challenge.'

'I salute you,' said Astrid. 'We should always be open to new ideas and adventures.'

'Thanks, Astrid.' Nell touched her glass to hers.

'But you built that stall from nothing. I thought you loved it?' I said, bewildered. 'Besides, you can sell nuts to full-cheeked squirrels, you're brilliant at it!'

She laughed. 'Let's hope that's a transferable skill. I'm not sure what I want to do next, but I do know it'll be indoors, I'm done with chilblains and a permanent nose like Rudolph. So if you hear of anything, girls, let me know. And, in the meantime, Merry, consider yourself on annual leave from the twenty-third of December, OK?'

'Deal,' I said, thrilled at the prospect. 'I can't tell you how grateful I am. This is going to be an excellent Christmas.'

I was dying to know what Cole had in mind for our honeymoon. He had missed his kids terribly when they were in Canada, and I didn't want to be the one to suggest he spend Christmas apart from them. I wouldn't mind them coming with us, but would they want to? Unlikely that Harley would want to spend a week with newly-weds. And as for Freya – my new role as Daddy's wife would mean that she hadn't got her Christmas wish.

'Oh, Merry,' said Hester. 'That's exactly the sort of thing Freya says.'

My heart skipped a beat and I stared at Hester, horror-struck. *That won't be what she says this year*, I thought, *not if her parents don't get back together*.

I felt a wave of dizziness and blinked, trying to focus, but everything had turned into a blur. Around me, I was aware that the main courses had arrived, and everyone was oohing and ahhing about the aroma and how beautiful all the food looked. I pressed a hand to my face. Perhaps it was the alcohol, or maybe I was just tired with everything that had been going on, but I had a sudden urge to close my eyes and disappear.

'Excuse me,' I mumbled, pushing myself up from my chair. My crown slipped and fell to the ground.

'Merry?' Nell's voice was full of concern. 'You OK?'

'Absolutely fine. Just going to the loo,' I replied, without meeting her eye.

Inside the ladies' toilets, I soaked a paper towel in water, locked myself in a cubicle and sat on the loo holding the cool towel to my forehead. *Breathe, Merry, just breathe*.

I couldn't stay here long; I didn't want anyone to come and find me locked in the loo on my hen night. Because they'd know I was upset about something, and I didn't want to have to explain my hazy thoughts.

I *was* having a good time with my friends and, apart from the crown, they hadn't made me do anything tacky. And Cole would collect us later. As Nell said, we were the perfect couple, I wasn't having cold feet about marrying him. I recalled Astrid's misunderstanding about cold feet and laughed under my breath, but somehow it turned into a sob.

I want my mum to get back together with my dad. That's what I want.

Oh hell. What should I do? Anything, nothing? Tell Cole? Keep quiet?

'Merry?' I heard Hester call from outside the toilet.

'In the end cubicle,' I said, through the door, quickly drying my tears.

'What's up?'

'I'm fine,' I sniffed. 'Just the alcohol making me emotional.'

'Are you sure,' she persisted, 'because you seemed a bit distracted and then I made a comment about Freya and the blood drained from your face.'

'Do you think she likes me?' I blurted out.

'Who Freya?' Hester gave a laugh of disbelief. 'I know she likes you.'

'As Cole's girlfriend maybe,' I said, 'but what about in the future, as his wife?'

There was a long pause and then the toes of her shoes appeared in the gap under the door.

'Oh, darling,' she said, her voice low. 'I think I know what this is about.'

I shook my head, even though she couldn't see me. 'I don't think you do.'

'Was it something Freya said when you took her to see Santa?'

I froze. 'How did you know about that?'

'So I'm right.' Hester sighed. 'Look, kids can be very self-absorbed sometimes. Try not to take what she said to heart.'

'Freya wants her parents back together and I don't blame her. How can I not take it to heart when I'm the one preventing that from happening?'

'That's not true and you know it.'

I dried my eyes and stood up. 'How do you know about the Santa thing. Did Freya tell you?'

'Harley called me. He was worried about you. He cares about you, they both do.'

'Harley? Bless him.' The thought of him worrying about me even though he had his own issues melted my heart. I unlocked the door and looked sheepishly at Hester. 'Sorry, I'm being an idiot.'

She pulled me into a hug. 'Lydia and Cole wouldn't get back together even if Freya really did want it to happen.'

I smiled ruefully. 'You would say that. Lydia might feel differently.'

She shook her head. 'Lydia feels terrible about what Freya said to you.'

I buried my face in my hands and groaned. 'Oh my God, she knows too? And Cole?'

'Freya told her mum. I think Harley was cross with her and Lydia intervened to find out what they were arguing about, and it all came out. I don't think Cole knows.'

Did that mean Harley had confided in Lydia too about his own struggles? I hoped so.

'Lydia was mortified apparently.' Hester got her phone out of her bag. 'Call her yourself. Then you can forget it ever happened.'

I blinked at her. 'What now? From the ladies' toilets? No, absolutely not!'

But before I knew what was happening, Hester had dialled Lydia's number, thrust the phone at me and fled from the loos, leaving me to answer when she picked up.

'Thank goodness you called,' Lydia heaved a sigh after I'd announced myself. 'If I'd thought for one second that you'd taken it seriously, then I'd have got in touch with you myself.'

'But Freya was so convincing when she told Santa what she wanted,' I blurted.

'Oh, she's always sure at the time,' Lydia reassured me. 'But last week she wanted to be an explorer and paddle down rivers in South America to discover new animals. And this week? A famous horse rider, purely, I might add, because she wants to plait horses' manes. No doubt she'll change her mind when she discovers what mucking out is.'

We both laughed, but I still wasn't convinced.

'Daydreaming about your career when you're nine is one thing, but asking for something for Christmas when it's nearly upon us is another. She sounded like she meant it.'

'Maybe trying on a bridesmaid dress brought it home to her that Daddy really is marrying someone new,' said Lydia. 'But I promise you, she has never had anything but good things to say about you.'

I swallowed, feeling dangerously close to crying again. 'That's really generous of you to say.'

Lydia was silent for a moment, and I realised that this was probably as hard for her as it was for me. 'What she really, really wants for Christmas is a kitten. She even burst into tears worried that she didn't ask Santa for one when she had the chance.'

'Bless her.' I smiled down the phone. 'And is she getting one?'

Lydia laughed. 'She is. I've found a silver tabby kitten who'll be ready to leave the litter by Christmas.'

'Oh fantastic, she'll be thrilled! I can't wait to see her face when she finds out.'

'She will. Hey, the kids are great,' said Lydia, 'but I've learned not to react to everything they come out with. I focus on the big stuff and the little stuff tends to sort itself out.'

'It does,' I agreed, thinking back to Harley's request to live with his friend in Whistler. I needn't have been worrying about either of them. Lydia had it under control. 'But you and Cole . . . I mean . . . when you heard that Freya wanted you two to get back together. How does that make you feel?'

Lydia laughed softly. 'I used to feel guilty that our marriage had broken down, but now I think differently. He's a good man, Merry, and for what it's worth, I think the two of you are a good match. I admit I was dreading Cole meeting someone else and my kids spending time with a woman I had no say over. But when I met you, I was relieved; it was obvious straight away that you make him happy, and he'd been unhappy for so long after I told him I wanted to end our marriage. You're good for Cole and you're good with the children too.'

I closed my eyes. Thank goodness. It genuinely felt like I had her blessing and the relief that gave me was liberating. 'I guess he's always had good taste in women.'

We both laughed at that.

'Actually, can I let you into a secret?' Lydia said, lowering her voice.

'Of course.'

'I've met someone. The kids don't know yet – in fact, neither does Cole. It's early days and we're taking it slow, but I like him a lot. So there, now you can really relax about Cole and me.'

Tears of gratitude sprang to my eyes. Cole and Lydia had been divorced for ages before we met, so this shouldn't have affected me at all. I wondered whether subconsciously I'd been waiting for him to wake up and realise he wanted her back. The fear of rejection ran deep with me; perhaps after growing up in care, it always would. 'I'm really happy for you and I won't say a word,' I promised. 'And thank you, Lydia. This means a lot.'

I ended the call and stared at myself in the mirror. A big smile slowly spread across my face. All that worrying for nothing. I clearly had a lot to learn about parenting. But, for now, my conscience was clear: I had Lydia's blessing and Freya didn't really want her parents to get back together, she wanted a kitten. Now there was a gift I'd have been happy to supply. I'd have loved a kitten for Christmas when I was her age.

Finally I left the ladies toilets and rejoined my friends.

'Now then,' I said, dancing back to our booth. 'Who's for another bottle of champagne? I'm ready to party!'

My friends whooped and cheered, and the waiter was summoned again.

'All OK?' Hester asked discreetly as I returned her phone.

I squeezed her hand and nodded. 'All good.'

If anyone had told me that an unexpected conversation with Cole's ex-wife during my hen party would prove to be the highlight of my night, I wouldn't have believed them. But there you go, I thought, wedging on my gold crown, life was full of surprises.

Chapter Twenty-One

Emily

4 DECEMBER

Thank goodness it was Friday, Emily had been fidgety all week at school. She couldn't stop thinking about her new relative. If there even was one, of course. All this talk of Ray having another daughter could be just that – talk. But somehow, she didn't think so. His story seemed plausible and, of course, there was photographic evidence of a blonde baby girl, about two years older than her.

She looked at the clock for the umpteenth time: still another half an hour. She returned to her computer screen, proofreading an email to parents about the change to the school bus schedule on the last day of term. She'd just pressed send when she heard a low buzzing noise coming from her handbag on the floor beside her office chair.

She picked her phone up and read the screen: it was a text from Izzy. She let out a long breath – finally! Emily had tried calling and texting ever since leaving Springwood House on Tuesday, but her calls had gone to voicemail and the texts had remained unanswered. It had been torture not being able to talk to her best friend about what had happened.

She glanced through the glass panel in the headteacher's office door and checked on the meeting. Alison was deep in conversation with her visitor and looked like she could be busy for a while

SO SO SORRY I haven't been in touch. I dropped my phone in the sea, waited in vain for it to dry out and ended up getting a new one . . . ANYWAY, what is the big news??? I know you're at school and can't make private calls, but ring me AS SOON as the bell goes. I'm free all day and will be standing by. Hope everything is OK, your voicemail was very mysterious last night. Love you xxx

Officially, Emily wasn't allowed to make private calls unless it was an emergency. And although this wasn't a life-or-death situation, how many times in your life did you find out you'd got a secret big sister? This had to warrant special dispensation, Emily thought. Sod it; if someone came out, she'd just have to cut the call, she thought, selecting Izzy's number.

'Hellooo!' Izzy's voice shouted down the line. Emily could hear wind in the background and the crashing of waves. 'Hold on, Em, I'll just find a sheltered spot.'

'Sure, hurry up though,' Emily replied as loudly as she dared. She felt a pang of longing, imagining Izzy on the beach near her home in Jersey.

'That's better!' said Izzy. The wind had receded, and her voice sounded echoey. 'Sorry about that. I was getting my ten thousand steps in on the beach. It's cold, but the fresh air is glorious.' She paused to blow her nose.

'So jealous,' Emily groaned. 'My steps are up and down school corridors and the only thing fresh about it is some of the kids' language.'

'I'm glad you rang.' Izzy's voice was laced with worry. 'I've been on tenterhooks since I got your messages. What's up?'

'Right.' Emily took a deep breath. 'Are you sitting down?'

'Er, no, I'm in a cave on the beach and it's wet.' Izzy hesitated. 'Bloody hell, Em. Hurry up and put me out of my misery.'

'You know that old baby photograph?'

'The one you sent me on WhatsApp of you and your dad? What about it?'

'That's the thing.' Emily paused. 'It's not me, it turns out I have a sister.'

Izzy squealed so loud that Emily had to hold the phone away from her ear. 'You are kidding me!'

'I'll tell you more tonight after work,' Emily said, trying to keep her voice down. 'But assuming Dad hasn't just got confused and made it all up, he told me that before I was born, he had a fling with a woman called Sam who had his child. Which means that somewhere on the planet I have a half-sister called Merry.'

'Oh my word,' Izzy gasped. 'A sister! This is epic. How do you feel?'

Emily puffed her cheeks out. 'Bamboozled, to be honest. My emotions have been up and down for the last few days. But, overall, I think I'm cautiously excited.'

'Of course you are,' Izzy cried. 'What is the one thing you have always gone on and on about all your life?'

'Um, one boob being bigger than the other?' she said, joking.

Izzy hooted with laughter. 'No, you goon! A sister, siblings, a bigger family!'

Emily chewed the inside of her cheek. 'That is true.'

'So? What's next? Ooh, I could fly over, and we could track her down together.' Izzy was getting caught up in the drama of it, as Emily knew she would.

'Thanks,' she replied with a smile, 'but I need to take it slow. Think about what to do, for example whether I tell Mum or not.'

'I would.' Izzy sounded very definite. 'She's got Ian now and your parents have been split up for years. She might not like it, but I'm sure she'll cope.'

'Hmm, maybe.' Emily recalled Tina's reaction when she saw the baby in the photograph. She'd been adamant that she didn't want to know anything about it, that she'd had enough surprises from her ex.

'Put it this way,' added Izzy, getting to the heart of the matter, 'if you want to discover more about Merry, would you be happy doing it behind Tina's back?'

Emily didn't have to think twice about that one. Ray might have done things behind Tina's back, but there was no way she was going to follow suit. 'Definitely not.'

'So when are you going to tell her?'

Just then, the bell rang signalling the end of school, swiftly followed by the shouting of teenagers released from their educational shackles.

'No point sawing your arm off slowly.' Emily's stomach dipped with nerves. 'So I guess . . . today?'

'Emily!' Tina exclaimed, as she opened the door. 'What a lovely surprise!'

Emily felt a rush of love for her mum, followed immediately by a stab of guilt. Her mum was such a kind person, she hoped what she was going to tell her this evening wouldn't upset her too much. She hated the thought of hurting her, but at the same time she didn't want to keep secrets either. Emily only hoped she'd have the courage to say what she'd come here to say.

'Hi, Mum.' Emily kissed her cheek and thrust the bunch of flowers at her that she'd picked up on the way. Guilt flowers.

'Beautiful flowers too!' Tina sniffed them and stepped aside to let her in. 'Thanks, love. If you've come for those costumes for school, I'm afraid I haven't quite finished them yet.'

'No,' said Emily softly. 'That's not why I'm here.'

Tina, attuned to the subtle tones of her daughter's voice, scanned her face. 'Darling? Has something happened?'

Emily pulled herself up tall; the sooner it was out in the open, the better. 'Have you got time for a chat?'

Tina nodded. 'Come through, and say hello to Ian while I put these in water.'

Emily followed her mum along the hallway and into the kitchen, where her stepdad was sitting at the table reading his newspaper. She gave him a hug and flicked on the kettle while Tina unwrapped her flowers. She was glad Ian was there, he'd be able to comfort her mum if she took the news badly.

'Have you seen this?' He tapped the headline on the front page. 'Petrol prices are going up again. Holy Moses,' he said, shaking his head. 'At this rate, we're going to need a mortgage just to fill up the car. Do you know how much petrol used to cost me when I learned to drive? Th—'

'Thirty-nine pence, by any chance?' she replied.

Tina caught her eye and they both laughed.

'Very funny,' said Ian amiably. 'You sit down, Em. I'll make us coffee.'

Emily did as she was told and sat down, collecting her thoughts while Ian riffled through cupboards for mugs and Tina stood at the sink, snipping the stems off her flowers.

The price of fuel was one of his favourite topics, along with trying to work out which TV programmes he'd seen an actor in before and the state of the greens at his golf club. Emily was very fond of her stepdad. Mostly because he'd never once let her mum down. He'd moved in with her and had stayed put. He went to work in the morning and came home in the evening. Or at least he used to before he retired. And he was absolutely devoted to Tina, which meant he was all right by Emily.

'Everything OK at work?' Tina arranged the flowers in a vase on the table and took a seat beside her.

'School's fine,' she said with a weak smile. 'Everyone's counting down to the end of term. Even the kids are too knackered to play up.'

'And Ray?' Tina probed. 'Settling in OK?'

'Dad is . . .' She took a deep breath. 'Definitely more relaxed than he was in his own flat. He's been talking about the past quite a bit.'

'Oh yes?' Tina looked at her warily. 'Which part of the past?'

'That's all we chuffing need,' Ian muttered, setting mugs down on the table.

Emily picked up her coffee and blew on the surface, grateful for something to do with her hands.

'It started with that photograph. The one you told me wasn't of me and . . .' Her mouth had gone dry with nerves, and she took a small sip of the hot liquid and swallowed.

'So that's what this is about.' Tina's shoulders sank. 'I was hoping I'd heard the last of it, but I suppose you've found out more.'

Emily's heart thudded against her ribs. She was about to ruin Tina's evening – probably a lot more than just one evening – and guilt flooded through her. 'I have.'

Ian joined them at the table and laid a hand over Tina's.

'Listen, Em,' he said smoothly. 'Tina told me about the photo. Ray has been vague about his life for the best part of forty years. I don't wish ill on the man, but whatever he claims, you've got to take with a pinch of salt. Especially now his mind's going. Sorry, Emily, no offence meant.'

'None taken,' she replied. 'I know this is a difficult subject. For all of us.'

'Ian, I know you're just trying to protect me. But Emily's my daughter, if there's something on her mind, I want to listen. Emily, whatever it is, just tell me.'

She sucked in a breath. 'OK. Mum. There's no easy way to say this, but Dad says that he's got another daughter. The baby in the photograph.'

'That other little girl was his?' Tina pressed a hand to her chest, her dark eyes, so different to Emily's, wide in shock.

'I haven't got any proof,' Emily added, swallowing the lump in her throat. 'Other than his word, but I think I believe him.'

She thought back to Ray's words the other night, how he'd mistaken her for Tina and how full of remorse he was for the way he'd behaved. The stories he'd told her had been too full of emotion for them to be false.

'What's her name?' Tina asked in a croaky voice. 'Did he keep in touch with her? Where is she now, and the mother?' She started to cry, and Emily leapt to her side and hugged her tightly.

'Her name is—' she began, but she was interrupted by Ian.

'Don't torture yourself, Tina,' he said, his jaw tense. 'Emily, is this necessary? Of course, you're entitled to a relationship with your dad, but he didn't make your mum happy, and it was a long time ago. Let her move on.'

Emily bit her lip; he had a point. She looked around for some tissue for her mum's tears and passed her some kitchen paper. 'I'm sorry.'

'It's all right, I want to know,' said Tina, drying her eyes. She pushed her coffee away. 'There's a bottle of wine in the fridge. Could you pour me a glass please? I'd get it myself but I'm not sure my legs will hold me up.'

Ian got to his feet with a sigh and poured Tina a generous glass of wine. 'Emily?'

Emily declined; she'd have to drive later.

'Ian, why don't you go and find some sport to watch on the television and leave us girls to chat?' Tina squeezed his hand and the two of them exchanged fond looks.

He left the bottle on the table, patted Emily's shoulder and left them to it.

'Dad didn't want you to know any of this,' Emily began once Ian had shut the door. 'Because he doesn't want to hurt you.'

Tina smiled, shaking her head. She glanced furtively at the door to make sure she wasn't being overheard. 'Your dad was my first love even if he was a hopeless case. And I think perhaps Ian has always felt like second best, that he doesn't measure up. But he does, Ian has nothing to worry about. And nothing you can say about your father will change a thing. The only person I care about in this is you.'

Emily breathed a sigh of relief. 'Thanks, Mum. Do you mind if I talk about it all?'

Tina shook her head and while she sipped her wine and listened, Emily told her what she knew. About Merry. About how Sam and Ray's relationship had been over long he'd started dating Tina and how guilty he had felt.

'Well, that's something at least,' Tina muttered. 'But he was obviously in touch with the other woman over that Christmas.'

'Sam,' Emily supplied. 'Merry's mum is called Sam.'

'Sam.' Tina's eyes narrowed as she wracked her brains. 'It must be Sam Shaw. I remember your dad mentioning her when we first got together. She was the last girlfriend he had before me.'

Emily's breath hitched; it hadn't occurred to her for a second that her mum might have heard of her. 'Dad didn't mention her surname. So I guess that would make her Merry Shaw.'

Tina huffed. 'Unless this Sam woman gave her child the surname Meadows, like I did. Although a fat lot of good it did me.'

Emily frowned. 'What do you mean?'

'I thought if you had Ray's surname, even though we weren't married, that he'd feel a deeper bond with you. I hoped it would make him stick around. Fool that I was.'

Emily took her mum's hand and squeezed it. 'You weren't a fool; you were a brilliant mum who always put me first. And maybe it's a good thing that Dad was an unreliable partner, because it meant you met Ian.'

Tina nodded. 'Life's a lot more plain sailing these days. Having your father coming in and out of our lives was like being permanently strapped into a rollercoaster.'

Emily smiled ruefully. 'That's how I've felt since finding out about having a half-sister.'

'Oh darling!' Her mum's face crumpled. 'I've made this all about me when I should have been thinking about you. How do you feel?'

'I'm not sure yet.' Emily was conscious of not upsetting her mum, but she couldn't see how discovering she had a sibling could be a bad thing. 'It's you I'm more bothered about.'

'You know, funnily enough, I think I've always known on some level that Ray was hiding something from me.'

She looked defeated. 'When I first saw that photograph, it set the cogs whirring in my brain, remembering tiny moments that had given me pause at the time. He was always restless; he couldn't even sit still for five minutes without jiggling his legs. Your dad was on the streets for a while, you know, homeless. I put it down to that.'

Emily gasped. 'I didn't know that.'

Tina nodded. 'He said he wanted to put the past behind him when you were born. But I can't imagine that sort of thing ever really goes away.'

'Poor Dad,' she murmured.

'Your gran was horrified when she met Ray for the first time,' Tina chuckled. 'She soon came round. He was a free spirit, your dad. He was a rubbish partner, but I have no regrets.' She looked up at Emily and touched her cheek. 'Because he gave me you. The best thing in my life.'

Emily leaned into her mum, and they hugged for a long time.

'I think I'd like to try to find Merry. Do you mind?' Emily pulled back and looked into her mum's eyes.

Tina blew out a shaky breath and Emily could see how much it cost her to say her next words. 'How could I mind? You've always wanted a sister.'

'Thanks, Mum.'

Emily left soon afterwards for her cottage in Wysedale, her head spinning with all this new information, her emotions all over the place. Tonight's task would be to see what she could find on the internet about Merry Shaw. Googling her own sister — if that wasn't the definition of a dysfunctional family, she didn't know what was.

Chapter Twenty-Two

Merry

'Enjoy, everyone,' said Cole, sitting down opposite his dad. 'Eat it while it's hot.'

'Don't worry, little chap, I'll save you a bit,' said Fred to Otto, who had a hopeful paw on Fred's leg.

'I've already put some in a dish for him,' I admitted, giving Astrid a guilty look. 'Is he allowed it?'

'Of course,' she replied, tickling her little dog under his chin. 'It is almost Christmas after all.'

It certainly was. A shiver ran down my spine as I put down a bowl on the floor for Otto. Two weeks and three days to go before the wedding. Time was flying by.

Otto had hoovered up his portion by the time I took my seat at the table again and he flopped contently at Astrid's feet. I topped up everyone's glasses and tucked into my own dinner.

I loved the kitchen at Holly Cottage. Cole had kitted it out last year after the room had been flooded. It wasn't huge, but it was cosy and warm and currently smelled delicious. The spotlights had been turned off and we were eating by fairy lights, which I'd wound around the curtain rail and across the tops of the cupboards, plus three Winter Wonderland candles glowed on the table, giving off their warming scent of cinnamon, cloves, nutmeg and a hint of sweetness from orange oil.

'To us,' said Cole, raising a glass. 'Thanks for joining us.'

'Dinner with two of our favourite people?' Astrid remarked, wiping a splash of gravy from Fred's chin. 'We're the ones who should be doing the thanking.'

'I'm glad I didn't eat too much at lunch.' Fred speared a chunk of beef. 'This is hitting the spot.'

We wouldn't normally have been entertaining on a weeknight when we had work in the morning, but Cole and I had had a few hours off this afternoon to sort out some wedding jobs and it seemed a good opportunity to catch up with them both.

'Thanks, it was a team effort,' said Cole, adding a second helping of slow-cooked beef casserole to his dad's plate and flashing me a smile. 'Hardly cordon bleu, but it's warm and hearty and good for a cold winter's night.'

I smiled back. The two of us were ridiculously smiley. Things between us were better than ever. We probably looked cheesy with our permanent smiles, but so what? Life could be tough, but right now, we were madly in love and enjoying planning a future together. And since I'd had that talk with Lydia, I felt far more confident about becoming Mrs Robinson on Christmas Eve.

'Team is a very generous description,' I said, laughing. 'Cole is a far better cook than I am, but I'm happy to be his assistant and learn from him.'

'Then you complement each other perfectly,' replied Astrid. 'Which has to be a good foundation for a marriage. And I agree with Fred, this is *sehr lecker.*'

'Which means delicious,' said Fred, earnestly earning himself a pat on his hand from Astrid. 'All sorted for the wedding now, are you?'

Cole and I looked at each other and nodded. We'd had a productive afternoon and had nailed most of the items on our to-do list.

'Almost,' I said. 'The theme is simply Christmas party. We want everyone to have fun, enjoy the magic of Christmas, no big formal speeches, no standing on ceremony.'

'And all our wedding music is going to be Christmassy too,' Cole added, drumming his fingers on the table. 'We've made a playlist of some of our favourite songs and we're hoping everyone is going to join in and have a sing-song.'

'Song sheets will be provided,' I said. 'So, no excuses.'

'Noted,' said Fred. He cleared his throat. 'Lalalalaaaah.'

'Thanks, Dad.' Cole pretended to block his ears. 'I won't be calling on you to do a solo if you don't mind.'

'Who's your best man?' Fred asked his son.

Cole took a sip of his wine. 'I'm not having one.'

'And I'm not having anyone to give me away either,' I added.

We'd discussed this at length. It was a bit unorthodox, but we decided that it was our wedding and therefore we should do it our own way.

'All our guests are just as important as each other, so you'll all be part of the ceremony.' I'd had an idea for making this happen using candles, but I was keeping it secret for now.

'That said, we would like both of you to be our witnesses and sign the register with us,' Cole said, looking from Astrid to Fred.

'We'd be delighted,' beamed Fred. He stood up and clapped his son's back in a manly hug and then kissed my cheek.

Astrid was on her feet too, kissing us on both cheeks.

'*Ach mein Schatz*,' she said, her eyes shining with tears.

'I am so happy to see *you* so happy. I am looking forward to this wedding very much.'

'Steady on, old girl,' Fred teased, offering her his hand-kerchief. 'What are you going to be like on the day, if you're crying just thinking about it?'

'I will be the happiest old lady in England and any tears will be joyful ones,' she declared, dabbing her eyes and then lifting her glass. 'Let us drink to the happy day. *Prost!*'

Fred raised his. 'That means—'

'Cheers!' Cole and I chorused together.

Fred chuckled, 'Sorry, I'm turning into a bore with my new language skills.'

'Never, *mein Bärchen*,' Astrid protested, stroking his cheek. 'You could never bore us.'

We all sat down again, and Cole and I exchanged furtive grins; we could never decide what we liked most: Astrid's terms of endearment for Fred or the coy and adoring expression he wore whenever she used them.

'Anyone for seconds?' I asked, peering into the casserole dish.

'Remember to leave room for a slice of my *bundt kuchen*,' Astrid warned.

Astrid never arrived empty-handed, and tonight's gift was a magnificent apple and honey bundt cake glazed with cinnamon icing and studded with pieces of walnut. We turned to marvel at it sitting majestically on the worktop.

'Pudding goes into a different part of my stomach,' Fred replied. 'But as I've got a new pair of trousers for the wedding and I want to be able to fit into them, I'll leave it at two helpings. Even though that mashed potato was delicious.'

'I added extra butter and cream into it, as it's Christmas,' I said, setting the cake on the table and handing Astrid a knife. 'Which was the least I could do, seeing as I've failed to provide my only employee with a Christmas party.'

'Oh, don't worry about that.' Fred gave an awkward laugh as Astrid shot him a meaningful look. 'Erm . . . while we're on the subject of my employment, I've got some news.'

'You've been headhunted by Yankee Candle and you're leaving me, I knew it,' I teased, pressing a hand dramatically to my forehead. Fred had been with me for a year, and although only part-time, I couldn't manage without him.

'No, dear, I wouldn't want to work for anyone else.' He coughed politely. 'But I've decided to retire.'

'You're already retired,' said Cole.

'Properly this time,' said Astrid, sliding pieces of cake towards us all.

'My second and final retirement.' He gave me an apologetic smile. 'I've loved working for Merry and Bright, but I'm getting old and tired, and you need someone with more energy and who can be there full-time.'

'Oh Fred,' I stood up and gave my future father-in-law a hug. 'I'm pleased for you and very grateful to have had you with me for the last year, but I'm devastated for myself.'

'Thank you for that.' Fred hugged me back. 'But you'll be fine without me and if you do get stuck, I won't be far away.'

Astrid coughed. 'Unless of course we *are* far away.'

'I'm sorry to tell you now, especially as you've got such a lot on your plate,' Fred said, 'but I would like to have a clear diary for the New Year.'

'Of course,' I replied, my brain spinning. This was terrible news. Fred was indispensable. Irreplaceable.

'Oh, darling,' Astrid covered my hand in hers. 'I can see the little clogs in your mind working. Don't make any fast decisions tonight.'

'*Cogs,*' Fred whispered.

I smiled, imagining tiny feet tapping furiously in my head. 'I like clogs better. And no, don't worry, I won't.'

'Seeing how quickly my friend Maude has faded away has made us both think,' said Astrid, taking Fred's hand. 'We want to seize life, make the most of our health, and each other.'

Maude had been a neighbour of Astrid's and they had become good friends over the years. But gradually her dementia had become too severe for her to continue living on her own without help and she'd moved to a specialist care home earlier this year.

'Very sensible,' said Cole. 'You never know how much time you have left.'

Fred covered his son's hand with his; I knew they were both thinking of Cole's mum, who had died from a stroke several years ago.

'We think so,' Fred agreed. 'Which is why we've decided to travel to India.'

'India?' Cole and I burst out simultaneously.

'We've seen a documentary on television about it,' said Astrid. 'We're going to cross the continent by train.'

'An adventure,' they both said together.

'One last hurrah,' added Fred.

'This is our *first* hurrah!' Astrid looked indignant.

'Bloody hell.' Cole shook his head, bemused. 'I didn't see that coming.'

Neither had I. I'd expected to hear about the latest goings-on at Rosewood retirement village, not to find out that my oldest friend and her beau were planning an adventure to the other side of the world. I swallowed hard.

'To adventure,' I said, proposing another toast. 'And many more of them.'

I held my smile for as long as I could despite feeling sick inside. The timing couldn't be worse. This afternoon, Conan at *The Retail Therapy Show* had phoned and offered me a fabulous sales slot as part of their 'Home is Where the Heart is' focus in January. The Home scented candles he'd said would be ideal and I'd agreed in an instant. I'd planned on announcing it tonight and proposing a toast to the future of Merry and Bright. Now, the thought of trying to manage the shop and deliver all the additional orders for the show without Fred was horrifying. Nell's offer of two weeks' help was very generous, but it wouldn't be anywhere near enough. This was my own fault, all of it. I should have listened to Hester; she'd warned me about relying on Fred. I should have sorted out my staffing situation months ago.

I glanced at Cole, who was listening to Astrid talking about India. He had been such a rock for me from the day we met. His love, his enthusiasm and his belief in me had given me the confidence to build my business. But how would he react if I asked him to postpone the honeymoon until, say, Easter? Would he share my enthusiasm for this opportunity for Merry and Bright, or did I risk ruining the start of our married life by putting work first?

Getting married, having a family and a home of my own had always been my dream. I didn't want to jeopardise that. But I couldn't bear to pass up this chance for Merry and Bright either.

'OK, darling?' Cole murmured. 'You look miles away.'

'It's just . . .' I swallowed, feeling dangerously close to tears. I slid my eyes in Fred's direction and Cole nodded, understanding.

He brought my hand to his lips and kissed it. 'It'll be fine. You can do this.'

I shook off my doubts and I smiled at him, my chief supporter. I'd overcome obstacles before and I could do it again, of course I could. 'You know me; I love a challenge.'

Chapter Twenty-Three

Emily

It was lunchtime, the skies were clear and bright and after a morning spent typing up reports, Emily was in desperate need of some fresh air. She wrapped up warm, picked up her mug of soup and headed out of school to the car park for some privacy while she made a phone call. She'd been like a coiled spring and if she didn't talk to someone soon, she'd probably burst. Izzy was on a spa day with her mum, who was over in Jersey for a visit, and wasn't picking up her messages, and anyway, if Emily were to be totally truthful, there was someone else she wanted to share her news with.

She wiped away the damp from one of the wooden benches with the end of her scarf, set her soup down beside her and waited for her call to be answered.

'Springwood House, Gail Honeywell speaking,' came the smooth tones of the manager.

Oh knickers, thought Emily, she'd been hoping Kylie would answer. Getting Gail to assist her would be much more difficult.

'Gail, hi, this is Emily Meadows, Ray's daughter?'

'Emily! I understand you had a fall on the premises a few days ago. Did you require medical treatment? Are you fully recovered?' Gail sounded wary, perhaps thinking that Emily was one of those litigious types who went through life looking for someone to blame.

'Fine now, thank you,' Emily replied, eager to put Gail's mind at rest. 'Luckily Will was there and administered first aid, I was well looked after.'

'Oh, what a relief. So there'll be no need to file a report then.' Gail perked up instantly. 'How can I help?'

'It's Will I need to speak to, actually. Is he there?' Annoyingly, Emily felt herself blush, which was silly, seeing as her reason for needing Will was perfectly innocent.

'He's not working at Springwood House today, I'm afraid, or for the rest of the week,' Gail replied. 'And obviously I wouldn't be able to pass on his mobile number. Data protection, et cetera.'

'Oh,' Emily said, deflated. 'No, of course not.'

'If this is related to your father's care, contact should be channelled through us,' she added pointedly.

'It's not about Dad, at least not directly,' said Emily, 'but there is a personal matter which I'd like Will's help with.'

'Ah, I understand *completely*,' replied Gail, obviously under the misconception that personal meant romantic. Emily could hear the sly smile in the other woman's voice. Poor Will, she hoped this didn't put him in an embarrassing position. 'I'll message him right now.'

'Thank you so much, I owe you one,' she said with a sigh of gratitude and gave her number to Gail.

'Just come to our Christmas Fair this weekend,' Gail said. 'That's all I ask, the more the merrier.'

Emily pulled a face as she ended the call. The event had slipped her mind, what with everything else that had been going on.

She had almost finished her soup when Alison's car pulled up and the head teacher got out and waved to her.

'I won't interrupt your lunch,' said her boss, coming to join her. 'But I just wanted to say how pleased I've been with your work recently.'

'It has been easier to concentrate at school, knowing that my dad isn't going to go walkabout,' she admitted.

'You've handled your private problems most professionally. I've also heard that you've been helping with the sixth-form pantomime. And Ivan tells me that you brought him Santa hats for the choir for their Christmas performance.'

'At the residential home?' Emily nodded. 'Yes. I'll be attending that on Saturday, give them my support.'

'That's marvellous!' Alison's eyes lit up. 'You've really thrown yourself into school life, Emily, I'm impressed. I want you to know that I'll be recommending to the governors that we offer you the permanent position as my secretary.'

'Oh thank you, that's . . .' Emily scrabbled for the right response. This was what she'd been hoping for, but instead of feeling excited, she felt a creeping sense of dread. It was a steady job, nice people, great holidays, so why wasn't she leaping up and down with joy?

Alison saved her from formulating a suitable response by pointing at the phone beside her which was vibrating with an incoming call. 'I'll leave you to get that in peace.'

Emily grabbed her phone, which showed a call from an unknown number. 'Hello?'

'Emily? It's Will. I've had an urgent message to call you, is everything OK?'

Her insides fizzed with trepidation. 'I've discovered who she is, Will, my sister I mean. At least I think I have.'

There. She had finally been able to tell someone the news she'd been keeping close to her chest for what felt like ages.

'That's great!' Will replied with enthusiasm. 'I can't wait to hear all about it.'

'I know her name and I've even—'

'This is amazing, Emily, and I hate to do this to you, but I'm in the middle of a training session in Manchester, I'm going to have to cut this short. I only called because I thought it might be an emergency.'

'Oh. Right, of course.' She gave an embarrassed laugh. 'I'm really sorry to have interrupted you.'

'Hey, this is great news, *really* great,' he said. 'And I'm glad you called me. I'm . . . Well, it's made my day if you want to know. But I genuinely need to dash.'

'I understand.'

'I'll call you the very second I'm out of work and make it up to you, I promise.'

'Or . . .' Emily bit her lip. 'You know that rain check I took on going for a drink?'

'Remember? I'm still feeling the burn.' He laughed softly and she felt the knot in her stomach begin to unfurl in the warmth of his voice.

'How about tonight?' she suggested. 'I mean, full disclosure it's to do with finding my sister.'

'That's cool, I can handle that. Any time after seven.'

'Excellent.' Emily grinned. 'You get back to work and I'll text you the details.'

'It's a date.'

She walked back into school in a daze, her spirits soaring. A job offer and a date and it was only Monday . . .

★

'I hope this place is all right?' said Emily later that evening. She put two soft drinks down on the table that Will had secured for them near the open fire. 'I've never been before, but the reviews were good.'

It was just after seven o'clock and they were in the Bristly Badger pub in the centre of Wetherley, just off the market square.

'Love it,' said Will, 'and always up for finding a new pub.'

'Me too,' agreed Emily, taking in the details of the Bristly Badger. It had a welcoming vibe, decorated up to the hilt with Christmas lights and tinsel, and all the bar staff were dressed in novelty sweaters. 'I'm far more at home in a cosy pub than a swanky restaurant where you have to navigate an entire army of cutlery, all the time worrying that you were buttering your bread with the wrong knife.'

Will grinned. 'Same here. Give me a shack on a beach where you eat with your fingers any time.'

'Heaven,' she said with a wistful sigh. For a second, Emily's imagination transported her to a white sandy beach, turquoise waters and an azure sky. A table for two under a parasol, a platter of freshly caught fish grilled on the barbecue, their fingers greasy with butter, skin sun-kissed and tingling from swimming in the sea . . .

'Not too hot by the fire?' Will asked, breaking her thoughts.

'Oh. Not at all.' She pressed a hand to her warm cheeks, which had nothing to do with the log fire and everything to do with the thought of Will wearing nothing but shorts and a suntan. 'I'm getting used to warm rooms. Springwood House is practically tropical. My cottage feels glacial by comparison.'

'Mine definitely is glacial,' he replied and told her that he lived in a house-share with two other guys, both of whom liked to keep the heating costs down. 'I have to pile on the layers, and they tease me for being too soft. I'm getting warm now though.' He pulled off his jumper over his head and his shirt came untucked, revealing a strip of toned stomach.

Me too. Butterflies danced in her stomach; he was far sexier than Gavin had been. Not just in looks – although he was very handsome – but in the way he focused on her so intently. Who knew eye contact could be such a turn-on? Another flush of heat rose to her face, and she gulped her tonic water too quickly and coughed. This was not why she'd asked him to meet up.

'OK,' she began, placing the palms of her hands on the table. 'Firstly, thanks for agreeing to meet me, and secondly, apologies for disturbing you at work today.'

Will grinned. 'I feel like we've slipped into a committee meeting and any second you're going to be reading the minutes of the last meeting.'

'Sorry,' she gave a bashful laugh. 'I am a bit nervous; I promise I don't have a full agenda to get through. It's just that I've got all this stuff to get off my chest and I can't wait to tell you.'

A look passed across his face; his expression brightening as he absorbed her words. Until this moment, it hadn't dawned on her just how important it felt to share this new information with him. But it was, and it seemed as if he felt it too.

He reached for her hand on the table, covered it with his, and she felt her heart hitch at his touch. 'I'm all ears, take your time.'

'Right.' She drew in a breath. 'These days, I never know how much of what Dad tells me is fact and how much is fiction. Sometimes it's obvious. Like the other day when he told me he'd met Charles Darwin's sister at lunch and what a charming woman she was. On the other hand, insisting he had another daughter called Merry with a woman he used to go out with was a tricky one, because although it was very specific, it came totally out of the blue.'

'Go on.' He nodded encouragement.

'So here's what we've got.' Emily put the photograph on the table in front of them, grateful that Will wasn't hurrying her or asking questions, but simply listening. 'My dad pictured with a baby girl and the words Merry's first Christmas written on the back. He has mentioned Sam and Sammy several times and my mum remembers that he had an ex-girlfriend called Sam. Sam Shaw.'

Will drew a finger through the condensation on his glass. 'So far, it looks like what Ray has told you is stacking up.'

'Agreed. In which case, I'm looking for a half-sister called Merry Shaw or Merry Meadows. Unless she now goes by her married name, of course.'

She looked at Will, her eyes dancing with secret knowledge.

He put down his glass and stared at her. 'You've found her, haven't you?'

'How can you tell?' she said, smiling.

He shook his head, laughing. 'Because you're practically buzzing with excitement.'

She let out a bubble of laughter. 'Sorry. I can't contain myself.'

'Don't apologise.' He looked at her with such warmth that she felt her heart swell. 'The first time I saw you looking around Springwood House with Gail, you were carrying the weight of the world on your shoulders. Seeing you so fired up makes me happy.'

They smiled at each other for a few seconds, their eyes locked, until Emily's pulse began to race.

Then Will gestured for her to continue. 'I interrupted you, you were saying that you may have found her?'

Emily leaned closer to him, her eyes dancing. 'There's only a Merry Shaw living right here in Wetherley. A stone's throw from where I live. I can hardly believe it!'

'No way!' His jaw dropped. 'Hence us meeting here.'

'Exactly.' She beamed, delighted with his reaction.

Will looked around them furtively, pretending to be undercover. 'Maybe she's even in the pub,' he whispered.

'Wouldn't that be amazing,' she laughed. 'I've found out lots more about her too. But the thing that was troubling me was, why now? What has sparked Dad to start talking about his secret daughter after all these years of saying nothing. And I think I've worked it out. Watch this.'

She shuffled closer to him, opened the internet browser on her phone and played a clip of the shopping channel which Lavinia was obsessed with. She hit the pause button. 'There, look. *That* is Merry Shaw presenting her company's range of candles. And I reckon this is what Dad must have seen to trigger his memory.'

Will brought the phone closer and studied the screen. 'That makes perfect sense. I'm sure he had his reasons for not telling the rest of his family about this other child. But now because of the dementia, he doesn't have the same control over his brain as he once did.'

'I feel a bit guilty,' she admitted. 'He's been saying that his daughter was on the television, but I dismissed it because I thought he meant me, and he was just getting confused. But if my research is correct, my sister is an entrepreneur with her own business called Merry and Bright. How cool is that?'

Will whistled under his breath. 'What an incredible discovery.'

'Isn't it?' She grinned at him. 'I've been watching the TV show on catch-up and what sealed it for me was the episode last month when Merry talked about her mum, Sam, who died when Merry was small. Her new candle was even inspired by the smell of her mum's perfume. It was very emotional to watch.'

A shiver ran down the length of her spine. The thought of her sibling growing up without her mother, when only a few miles away, in the same county, Emily had always had Tina looking after her made her heart break.

'Poor kid,' Will murmured. 'So she grew up without either of her parents?'

Emily nodded sadly. 'Let's hope she had a relative to take care of her like you did.'

'Yeah. Good old Grandad,' Will said, his voice full of affection. 'Merry turned out OK, though, didn't she? Her own business, a slot on television. That's impressive.'

'It is,' Emily said proudly and then pulled a face. 'I'm going to have to up my game.'

She was only half joking; Merry had made such a success of her life and what did she have to show for hers?

Will looked bemused. 'I can't believe you're getting competitive with a sibling you haven't even met yet.'

'Ah,' said Emily. 'That's where you're wrong. We *have* already met.'

He choked on his Coke. 'You're kidding me?'

'Nope.' Her eyes sparkled. 'Drink up, I've got more to show you.'

Will downed the last of his Coke straight away. 'The plot thickens.'

★

The dark night air was crisp and frosty, and Emily gasped as her foot skidded on a patch of ice as they left the pub.

'Oh no you don't,' said Will, darting an arm out to steady her and then taking her hand in his. 'Not on my watch. One twisted ankle is quite enough for now.'

She met his gaze shyly, secretly thrilled to have an excuse to touch him. 'If you insist.'

Even though she had planned this evening, had known what she was going to tell him, she hadn't expected this: this deepening chemistry between them. She felt exhilarated and giddy with it all.

As they crossed Wetherley market square, their warm breath swirled around their faces. The stalls which had been full of life and colour and noise when she'd been here with Tina were shuttered and closed, but even after hours most of them glowed with the twinkle of Christmas lights strung around every surface and along rooftops. There were still people around: couples, hand in hand, heads down against the cold, a family trailing past, the man jiggling a small jubilant child on his shoulders, the woman pushing a buggy, all of them singing 'Jingle Bells', an older couple out walking their little dog.

'Magical, isn't it?' said Emily softly as they headed towards a magnificent Norwegian fir tree, resplendent in lights and sparkling with hundreds of coloured baubles.

Will smiled at her. 'You're a fan of Christmas?'

They were almost there; her destination was already in her sights and nerves fluttered in her chest like butterflies' wings. She glanced sideways at Will to see if he'd noticed what was ahead of them, but his gaze was fixed on the Christmas tree.

'Absolutely. There are no children in my social circle,' she explained. 'I really notice it at this time of year. It's one of the best things about working in a school; kids give you an excuse to find the child inside yourself at Christmas.'

'I don't think mine was ever lost,' he said wryly, and they both laughed.

'OK, stop there,' she said, tightening her grip on his fingers and forcing him to stop in his tracks. 'Look over there.' She pointed at the row of shops opposite the marketplace. Pretty black and white half-timbered buildings housed all sorts of businesses, from a hair salon to a hardware store and there, right in front of them, with a bunch of mistletoe suspended under the entrance was Merry's shop.

'Merry and Bright!' Will exclaimed. 'You found her shop? That is so cool.'

'I know,' she said, drinking in the look of surprise on his face.

He shook his head. 'You're amazing.'

She smiled at him, aware of a tug deep inside her, an unfurling of something she couldn't quite name. The next second, she found herself wrapped in his arms, her feet on tiptoes as he pulled her in close and pressed a tender kiss to her cheek.

'It was actually really straightforward,' she replied, delighted at his response. 'Merry has got a website and an Instagram account, which is how I found the shop, and there are loads of pictures of her with her fiancé and his kids. And you won't believe this, but I've met her before. Twice, it turns out: once here in the market and once at the school gates because one of the kids is at the school where I work.'

'And now the universe has decided to put you in touch.' He tucked an arm around her waist. 'You OK with all this?'

She exhaled. 'I think so. All those years when I thought I didn't have any family other than Mum and Dad, and I did.

Merry and I have been living close to each other all along.'

In truth, Emily was absolutely thrilled, but she didn't want to get too carried away. Not until she'd worked out what to do next.

The two of them walked across the street to peer through the window. The shop was closed, and all the main lights were off, but spotlights shone down on the window display. It was only a narrow shelf on the inside, a windowsill really, but the length of it was draped with swags of eucalyptus and fir, tiny copper fairy lights were woven through them, giving off a golden glow, and dotted through the display at various heights were the candles: Mistletoe Kiss, Midnight Forest, Winter Wonderland.

'It's beautiful,' said Emily, a lump forming in her throat. 'She's a genius, I'm so proud of her.'

'As she will be of you, I'm sure.' Will squeezed her hand and for a long time neither of them said anything, they just stood side by side.

He was such easy company, she thought, allowing herself to lean against him ever so slightly, and he had a way of knowing just the right thing to say. Desire for him fluttered in her stomach, and she let out a shaky breath.

'You OK?' He looked at her with concern in his eyes.

Emily nodded, glad he couldn't see how pink her face must be. 'It's just a lot. Being here, discovering all this, seeing Merry's shop, knowing that this is her life— it's mind-blowing.'

Tears pricked at her eyes, and she tried to blink them away.

'Hey. It's OK to cry.' He peeled off his gloves and touched her cold face with his warm hand. 'It's just your body's way of letting go of stress.'

She nodded, pressing her cheek into his hand. 'I can't

241

believe I'm standing here, outside my sister's shop.'

'Thank you, Emily,' he said, drawing his hand away.

She raised an enquiring eyebrow. 'For what? Dragging you out in the cold and weeping on you?'

'For letting me share this with you. This is a big day; one you'll always remember. I'm honoured to be here.'

'I can't imagine anyone else I'd rather share it with than you.'

It was true. Somehow, over the last couple of weeks, despite being sure she wasn't looking for another relationship, he'd got under her skin. His face was the one she saw as she closed her eyes at night, his words bringing a smile to her lips when she remembered something he'd said. His positive manner, his friendly smile, those beautiful, mesmerising blue eyes sparkling in the reflection of the lights . . .

'Wow,' he said with a grin. 'Day made.'

She reached for his hand and turned to face him. All it would take was one more step and they'd be in kissing distance. She flicked her eyes upwards; they were almost underneath the mistletoe. She could feel her pulse thudding in her ears. Was he thinking what she was thinking?

'So what's next?' he asked, holding her gaze. 'Do you plan to get in touch?'

'Um. I think so,' she said briskly, brushing aside her romantic thoughts; his mind was clearly on a different path. 'I might try to speak to Dad again. Check if he has any more photographs anywhere and then . . .' She shrugged, trying to sound casual. 'I guess I'll attempt to make contact and hope she doesn't reject my advances. Merry might not be as happy about this as I am.'

'I can't imagine anyone not being happy to meet you.' He cleared his throat and took a step back. 'Will you let me know how you get on? I'm fully invested now.'

'Sure.' Emily bit back her disappointment; his words felt like a dismissal. He was obviously ready for the evening to end. 'I'd better let you go. You've had a long day and I've bombarded you with information about me and my family. You must think me very selfish: I haven't let you get a word in about your life.'

'That's easily solved,' he said with a grin. 'Our second date can be all about me.'

Her heart started to race. 'I'd like that.'

'Result!' he said, punching the air triumphantly. 'And I hope you appreciate how gentlemanly I've been tonight. The temptation to kiss you under that mistletoe is—'

He didn't get to the end of the sentence because Emily's lips were on his. And — thank heavens — he kissed her back and she was so grateful that he didn't pull away and stare at her in disgust that she kissed him again. And she would probably have kissed him for even longer if some teenagers hadn't walked past and made vomit noises at them and shouted at them to get a room.

'Oh my God,' Emily whispered. 'We just snogged outside my sister's shop. I hope she hasn't got CCTV.'

'You are a bad influence on me, Emily Meadows,' said Will, his eyes bright with mirth. 'I was going to wait until our second date to kiss you.'

'Oh well,' she said, grinning at him. 'You know what they say, life's short, so eat the cake, buy the shoes and kiss the boy.'

'Do they say that?' he asked, amused.

She laughed and shrugged. 'I don't really know, but they should.'

And checking the teenagers were no longer in view, she kissed him again.

Chapter Twenty-Four

Merry

Astrid handed me a takeaway cup of hot chocolate decorated with whipped cream and topped with a chocolate flake.

'*Danke schön*,' I said, picking out the chocolate and biting straight into it.

It was Saturday afternoon, and we were manning the Merry and Bright stall at a Christmas Fair at Springwood House where Astrid's friend Maude was a resident.

'*Bitte schön*,' Astrid replied. 'Are you hungry?'

My stomach gave a hollow rumble. 'A bit. I missed lunch.'

I'd left home this morning without having breakfast either. Nell had told me yesterday that she thought I looked thin, and I'd told her that ironically it was called the 'too much on my plate' diet, which we'd both thought hilarious. On the plus side, by starting at the crack of dawn today, I'd managed to pour four hundred candles, giving us a head start for next week, which meant that at least I could have tomorrow off.

Astrid perched on a stool and narrowed her eyes. 'You are working too hard. I worry about you. Drink up.'

'Yes, Mum,' I teased. I sipped my hot chocolate, its sugary hit giving me an instant energy boost. 'There's no need to worry. It's Christmas, we're all working too hard. But not Fred,' I added quickly. 'I'm making sure he takes a proper lunch break and leaves on time. We need to keep him fit and healthy for your big trip.'

My smiled wavered, only for a fraction of a second, but Astrid eyed me shrewdly.

'It will work out, you know, after Fred has gone,' she said, patting my arm. 'You are afraid of the unknown, that is all. You will find somebody just right to work at Merry and Bright. Put it out to the universe and see what it delivers.'

'A customer by the look of it,' I replied as an elderly lady with long silver hair clutching a sequinned handbag approached us.

'Sit,' Astrid ordered. 'I can serve this lady.'

I didn't argue.

I'd agreed to attend the fair when Astrid had mentioned it back in the autumn before I knew I was getting married. She'd seen a poster advertising for stallholders during one of her visits to Maude. It had crossed my mind to cancel as I was so busy. But the proceeds of today's event were going to a dementia charity, and I knew it meant a lot to Astrid. So here I was.

I was having a nice time with lots of random chats with people, including the bubbly receptionist who'd bought some candles for her mum. All the staff here were lovely and the event was very organised.

'It's actually quite nice to do something other than wedding planning,' I said when our customer had gone. 'Christmas has got lost a bit this year since the wedding took over.'

'Unlike last year, when Christmas took *all* your attention,' replied Astrid. 'Well, nearly all – I think Cole featured quite heavily in your conversations too.'

We exchanged smiles. I'd only just come out of a relationship and hadn't wanted to meet anyone new. But Cole and I had found more and more reasons to spend time together and by Christmas Eve, I'd fallen in love with him.

'He still does,' I admitted. 'I'm even more head over heels now.'

And now that I knew Freya wasn't really against her dad marrying me, the wedding couldn't come soon enough, nothing was going to keep us apart.

I put down my empty cup and quickly stood up as a man approached the stall and picked up a candle to smell.

'I can manage now, Astrid,' I said. 'Why don't you spend some time with Maude?'

'If you're sure?' she said, getting to her feet. 'She has some Christmas presents to wrap in her room and asked for my help. See you later, *Liebling*.'

Once Astrid had gone, I turned my attention to my customer and for the next twenty minutes, I was busy selling and chatting to the people who visited my stall.

'These smell lovely!' Gail, Springwood House's manager, wafted her hand over the lit flame of my new Home candle and inhaled. 'The aroma has filled the whole room. I'm going to have to take one. This is what I want my house to smell of.'

'Thank you,' I said, slipping one into a gift bag.

Gail handed over the money. 'I love these Christmas events, but it's disastrous for my bank balance.'

'They do make nice gifts,' I agreed.

She pulled a guilty face. 'They *would*, but the things I've bought today won't end up under the Christmas tree. They're treats for me.'

'Same here!' I showed her the chocolate reindeer which I had bought to put in Cole's stocking but had already nibbled off the antlers. 'So far I've managed to restrain myself from biting into the marshmallows I've bought for the children, but the afternoon isn't over yet.'

We were laughing when a man approached the stall. He was carrying a record sleeve and it looked like he had missed most of his chin with the razor; patches of silver stubble stood out on his pale skin.

'Hello, Ray,' said Gail warmly. 'Are you having a good time?'

He frowned and scratched his head as if not sure of the answer. 'Yes, I think so. I met Charles Darwin's sister.'

I'd been warned that the residents could get confused and that I should just go along with them and enter their world.

'I bet that was interesting. What was she like?' I smiled at him.

'Snooty,' replied Ray. 'Told me I couldn't play my music today because it isn't a Christmas—' He stopped mid-sentence and sniffed. 'What's that smell?'

'It's this candle, Ray,' said Gail. 'It's lovely isn't it? I've just bought one for my house.'

'I like that smell,' he mumbled and bent right over the candle, sniffing again. Then he picked it up and lifted it up to his nose.

'Please be careful of the hot wax!' I'd had enough accidents with candles to know that melted wax was dangerous.

'I'll buy one.' He set it down, much to my relief. 'A new one, though, not a burned one.'

'Is it for a present, Ray?' asked Gail, linking her arm in his. 'Because we don't have candles in our rooms.'

Ray ignored her.

'She always smelled nice,' he said, with a faraway look on his face. 'Always. That's hard you know, when you're on the streets.'

'Ray? Why not buy one for your lovely daughter?' Gail said brightly, in an attempt to bring his focus back.

'I will,' he replied, digging into his pocket. He produced a ten-pound note and handed it over, looking at me directly for the first time. 'You look a bit like my girl.'

Gail studied my face. 'You're right, Ray, she does a bit. Similar colouring. Is Emily coming today?'

He shrugged. 'She came this morning. Brought me a hot sausage roll.'

'She sounds like my sort of woman.' I smiled brightly. 'And you've bought my favourite candle, so I'm sure your daughter will love it too.'

I popped the candle into a gift bag, thanked him for his purchase and Gail took him off to get a drink. I might get Fred to investigate branded gift bags, I thought, before remembering that his days at Merry and Bright were numbered. Maybe I needed two part-time staff, to give us more flexibility around holidays, perhaps someone who was marketing-savvy? And perhaps a Saturday worker too, I'd quite like not to have to work at weekends, especially when Harley and Freya were staying over.

I was still musing over where I should place a job advertisement when Astrid returned.

'Maude has dropped off to sleep and I've just seen a children's choir arrive in a minibus, so I thought I'd come back to watch.'

'Oh fabulous! Is there anything more Christmassy than children singing carols?'

I got a tissue out of my bag and tucked it into my pocket in preparation for the tears which were bound to appear. I was always the same: I'd be a blubbering wreck before the kids reached the end of the first verse of 'Silent Night'.

'Here they come!' Astrid tugged my arm, and we watched as a crowd of secondary-school-age boys and girls all wearing identical red and white Santa hats burst noisily into the room. A teacher, wearing a fleece jacket with 'Darley Academy' emblazoned in huge letters across the back, herded them towards the Christmas tree in front of the window.

'That's Harley's school!' I said, pointing out the school logo to Astrid.

There was an enthusiastic burst of applause from various corners of the room as the kids filed past and you could almost see their mood change as their bravado gradually seeped away to be replaced by nerves.

I'd been scanning the children half-heartedly, not expecting to see anyone I knew when a tall boy with hunched shoulders and his hat pulled right down over his eyebrows caught my eye. It was Harley! He was walking beside a girl, their bodies close and their little fingers hooked together. That was adorable. Freya had mentioned something about a girl; it looked like things were going well in that department. I was so happy for him.

'That's Harley!' I hissed, grabbing hold of Astrid's arm.

At that moment, Harley spotted us, and a look of sheer horror came over his face. He released the girl's hand as if it had burned him and muttered to her under this breath. The kids behind him pushed forward and he began moving again, hands shoved in his pockets, while the girl scanned the room looking for what, or who, had upset him.

Astrid chuckled. 'I don't think he is as pleased to see us as we are him.'

'Bless him,' I said anxiously. 'I might go and say hello, put his mind at rest.'

I squeezed past Astrid and away from my stall and headed

to the Christmas tree where the teacher was trying to get the kids organised.

'OK, spread out, into your positions,' the teacher was saying, flapping his arms about like an angry bird. 'Semicircle, chop-chop. No, Henry, you can't have any mulled wine. Where's Lizzie? Toilet? Again? For heaven's sake. Who's got the Bluetooth speaker?'

'Hey, Harley!' I said quietly, sidling up beside him and tapping his arm. 'This is a surprise! I didn't know you were in the choir?'

'What are you doing here?' he mumbled. His cheeks were pink with embarrassment, and it dawned on me that far from reassuring him, approaching him had made things much worse.

'I've got a stall, selling candles,' I said, feeling my face grow as hot as his. I did a ridiculous wave to the row of kids all staring at me. 'Um, I just wanted to say good luck.'

The boy behind him whistled and said, 'She's well fit, Robbo, is that your mum?' causing several others to snigger under their breath.

Harley gritted his teeth. 'It's my dad's girlfriend. She's just going. Aren't you?'

I nodded meekly, annoyed with myself for misjudging the situation. I should have known better, given the drama when I'd picked him up from school.

'Absolutely. See you later. Good luck, everyone.'

I was going to take a photo of the choir without him noticing. Lydia would love it. The fact that he was here, with the choir, was such a good sign; he might not have made the rugby or football team, but he'd found another group to be a part of and my heart swelled with pride for him.

'Since when has he been in the school choir?' Astrid said, bemused. 'He has certainly never mentioned it to Fred or me.'

'No idea,' I replied with a shrug, watching as Harley pulled his Santa hat further down over his eyebrows. The girl he'd been holding hands with pushed it back up and Harley grinned at her. But, unfortunately, he caught me watching him and scowled, slumping down as if trying to make himself invisible. 'I always had him down as a sportsman not a musician. I don't think Cole knows, otherwise he'd have wanted to be here to see him perform.'

'Hmm, maybe that's why he hasn't told anyone,' Astrid mused. 'So that he wouldn't have an audience.'

'Let's sit down,' I suggested. 'Then at least we'll be less conspicuous.'

We sat on our stools just as Gail bustled towards the children and conferred with the teacher.

I raised my eyes to Harley again and risked giving him a thumbs up. To my delight, he nodded his head, and his mouth curved into the most unenthusiastic of smiles, but it was a smile, nonetheless. I hoped that meant he'd forgiven me for approaching him in front of his mates.

'Ladies and gentlemen!' Gail clapped her hands and the noise level in the room fell instantly. 'Thank you for joining us this afternoon for our festive fair in aid of the charity Dementia UK. I hope you've found plenty to enjoy and stocked up with gifts for the big day. And now to really get us in the Christmas spirit, it gives me great pleasure to introduce the Darley Academy choir, singing a medley of some of your festive favourites. Let's give them a round of applause.'

Everyone clapped, although none perhaps as wholeheartedly as me. When I finally stopped clapping, I crossed my fingers, sending Harley luck and love.

'I need the loo,' I whispered to Astrid. 'I feel so nervous for him.'

She smiled fondly at me and squeezed my arm. 'That's your maternal instincts kicking in, *mein Schatz.*'

But there was no time to go anywhere, because the next second, the teacher raised his hands in front of the choir and pointed at the student in control of the music and a few cheers rang out as the audience recognised the first few bars of 'White Christmas'.

As the music rose in volume and the children began to sing, every single person was mesmerised. Teaspoons stopped rattling on saucers, feet stopped shuffling across the carpet and conversations all around the room came to an abrupt halt.

Gradually, the audience started to join in, their older voices uniting with the young ones to produce such a joyous sound that within seconds the tissue I'd had at the ready was damp. There was a booming tenor somewhere behind me and a tremulous soprano from a glamourous silver-haired lady on the sofa. Even Astrid was humming softly under her breath.

'They are amazing,' I whispered, brushing tears from my face.

'*Wunderbar,*' Astrid agreed, blowing her nose.

It wasn't just their voices, it was the way some of the kids were performing, as if they were on stage at Wembley singing to an adoring crowd. A couple of the smaller ones had bells, which they shook with great enthusiasm. There were even a couple of lads who grabbed their crotch and pointed a finger out to the audience, which was all kinds of inappropriate but hilarious too.

The stallholders, the visitors, the residents, even the staff had stopped to listen. The music had brought everyone together.

And then the next verse began.

The choir fell silent all except one person: Harley.

Astrid and I gasped in unison and glanced at each other.

A solo?

'*Meine Gute*,' Astrid muttered.

'Oh my goodness,' I said at the same time.

I held my breath, one hand pressed to my chest and the other gripping Astrid's arm as I willed him on.

The audience stopped singing so as not to drown out this young voice as it rang out across the room, so clear and pure, with just the occasional wobble when he hit the high notes. The girl beside him slipped her hand into his, her face glowing with pride.

When Harley got to the line about your day being merry and bright, he looked my way and smiled, and I tried to smile back, but it was virtually impossible because I was trying so hard not to sob. I only managed a grimace, but it didn't matter; he could see I was proud of him. Probably the proudest I'd ever been of anyone.

Harley's solo ended, and everyone came together again to belt out the chorus and I finally let out the breath I'd been holding and blinked away the tears. Harley exhaled and pulled off his hat to rake a hand through his hair and the sight of his dark red hair, just like Cole's, brought a warm smile to my face. I quickly pulled my phone out of my pocket and took a photo, sending it in a WhatsApp message to Cole to share the moment with him. Out of the corner of my eye, another woman raised her phone to do the same. Another emotional mum presumably. Or stepmum, I thought with a grin.

It had been worth coming to this fair just to witness this moment. I didn't care if I didn't sell another candle; seeing that Harley had found his tribe and was finally fitting in at school was all the reward I needed for today.

'He is a black horse,' said Astrid, shaking her head. 'He kept that talent hidden.'

'A dark horse indeed,' I replied, correcting her. 'I can't wait to tell Cole how magnificent he was. And Lydia too.'

The song came to an end, and I jumped to my feet, my arms raised above my head, and shouted for more, until Astrid tugged my sleeve and made me sit down.

The next song began and the choir, buoyed by the success of their first number, linked arms and began swaying side to side, belting out that it was beginning to look a lot like Christmas. A male member of staff asked one of the residents to dance and then other staff followed suit. Before long, there were quite a few up on their feet, moving in time with the music, and a new party atmosphere took over the room.

My cheeks were still wet with tears, and I was so wrapped up with finding a dry tissue to mop them up that it took me a while to notice that I had a new customer.

'Hello,' I said, quickly blowing my nose. 'Sorry, I didn't see you there, children singing gets me every time.'

'Hello, again.' The blonde woman in front of me smiled shyly. 'I don't know if you remember, but we've met before. My name's Emily.'

Chapter Twenty-Five

Emily

Emily's heart was racing, and her stomach was in knots; she'd done it, she'd introduced herself to her sister.

She'd given herself until the end of 'White Christmas' to decide whether to approach her or not. Her head had told her to stay sitting by her dad, to do nothing and say nothing. Because if she walked up and started to talk without having prepared first, it could go terribly wrong. Unfortunately, as soon as the music stopped, Emily's heart took over.

Because there in front of her, despite being the last person she'd expected to see, was the big sister she'd always fantasised about having. It had to be fate.

And now the words were out of her mouth; there was no going back. The conversation she'd been playing over and over in her head since finding out about Merry had begun.

Merry's eyes lit up in recognition and she smiled. 'Yes, I remember you! We met outside school when I came to collect Harley. You were the teacher who came to our rescue.'

'School secretary,' she corrected. 'But yes, that was me.' So far, so good.

255

'I'm Merry Shaw, Harley's stepmum.' Merry held up her hands. 'Well, almost his stepmum.'

'Yes, I know,' Emily replied without thinking.

'You do?' Merry looked surprised.

'I mean, I guessed who you were,' she said, fanning her glowing face with her hand. 'It's getting very warm in here.'

There was someone else behind the Merry and Bright stall, Emily noticed now. An older lady wearing a magnificent patchwork kimono and an armful of jingly bangles. She stood up and touched Merry's shoulder.

'I'm going now, *Schatz.*'

'And this is my friend Astrid,' Merry said, standing aside to bring her into the conversation. 'Astrid, this is one of the staff from Harley's school.'

Emily and Astrid smiled their hellos.

'I will now say goodbye to Maude if she's awake, and then go home to Otto. Tell Harley how proud I am of him. *Bis später.*'

'I will.' Merry kissed the woman on both cheeks and thanked her for her help.

As soon as Astrid mentioned Maude, Emily realised that she'd seen her here before with a little dog when she'd been visiting her dad. Emily's head span: so Maude was friends with Astrid and Astrid was friends with Merry. Talk about it being a small world! How many other tiny connections had there been over the years between the two of them? she wondered.

'Harley has taken us by surprise today,' Merry confided once Astrid had gone. 'We didn't even know he was in the choir, let alone that he had such a beautiful voice. I took a photo to show his parents, but I wish I'd videoed his solo.'

'Kids hide all sorts of things from their parents at that age,' said Emily. 'Mostly because they don't think it's important. And he probably wouldn't have thanked you for preserving the moment on video.'

'True.' Merry sighed, gazing over at the choir, which was nearing the end of the song.

They still had an attentive audience, but some people had started moving about and there was a queue building at the mulled wine stall. Emily turned back to the row of armchairs to check on her dad; he was still next to Lavinia in a world of his own. He'd insisted on calling her Tina today and hadn't wanted to chat; it broke her heart when he was like this. She knew it wasn't his fault, but she felt shut out.

Will was here too somewhere; she hadn't seen him yet, but Kylie had told her that his old friend Bernard was bedbound with flu, so Will had offered to play Scrabble with him in his room. Hopefully, she'd catch up with him before she left.

Emily cleared her throat. 'You and I also met before that day at school. In Wetherley market, at Nell's Nuts.'

Merry shook herself out of her reverie and gasped. 'Yes! That's it! I knew I'd seen you somewhere before, but I couldn't place you. You were with your mum, right?'

Emily nodded. 'And your friend, Nell, was trying to persuade you to have a hen party.'

'She managed it.' Merry rolled her eyes amiably. 'As usual. Although you said something about celebrating every moment big or small and it really stuck with me.'

'Really?' Emily smiled. 'And was it a success?'

'We had a great time, and you were right: I would have regretted not doing it. So thanks for the nudge. Mind you, I think we all regretted it next morning.' She winced comically, pressing a hand to her temple. 'Don't tell Harley though, I like him to think I'm a paragon of virtue.'

'I won't breathe a word,' Emily promised with a grin. A wave of happiness washed over her, and she was glad she'd plucked up the courage to come over. Merry was so easy to talk to; she felt as if she knew her already. Her imagination had already leapt ahead, envisaging shopping trips and family holidays and long text conversations full of in-jokes and the gentle teasing she'd seen go on between Izzy and her sisters. *Please let this happen*, she thought.

The choir's next song was 'Jingle Bells'. This was clearly one of their favourites; the kids' voices grew louder, over-powering the music, causing them to speed up. Emily could see that Ivan's conducting was getting a little bit frantic.

'Oh dear, and it was all going so well.' She caught Merry's eye, and they both laughed

'I've just remembered,' said Merry suddenly. 'You were worried about your dad that day in the market. You said he has dementia. How is he? Is this the care home you were talking about? Is that why you're here?'

'Um . . .' Emily's mouth went dry. *Funny story, he's 'our dad', as it turns out . . .*

This was the perfect opening. She'd read stories on the internet about long-lost siblings reuniting, but now it was her in the hot seat, she wasn't sure what to say. Or how to say it. Or even whether she should say it at all.

'Yes, his name's Ray,' Emily said deliberately, watching Merry's face for a flicker of recognition. She could hear the tremor in her own voice. 'I moved him in not long after I met you. It's such a relief to know he's being cared for.'

'I can imagine,' Merry replied warmly. 'I'm no expert at residential homes, but this one seems nice. Does your dad like it?'

Merry hadn't reacted to Ray's name at all, Emily noticed. What was her story? Who did *she* think her father was?

'He seems happy.' Emily gave a brittle laugh. 'Actually, it turns out he has been keeping one or two secrets, which I've only just found out about.'

'Nothing too shocking, I hope? Gosh, please forget I said that, it was intrusive, I'm sorry.' Merry looked appalled at her own question.

'No need to apologise.' Emily swallowed, meeting Merry's gaze. This was it. This was her chance. Perspiration prickled under her arms, and she could scarcely peel her tongue from the roof of her mouth. 'I don't mind talking about him because . . . well, the thing is when I moved him in, I found a tin—'

'Emily! There you are!' said a voice from behind.

She almost jumped out of her skin when Will appeared beside her.

'Will!' she gasped. 'You nearly gave me a heart attack.'

'Whoops.' He pulled a face. 'Not quite the effect I was going for.'

She couldn't help smiling at him. His timing was terrible, but she couldn't deny how good it was to be near him again. He had occupied her thoughts almost as much as Merry this week; between the two of them, she'd hardly slept a wink.

'You do look a bit hot and bothered,' Merry said, sounding concerned. 'Can I get you some water?'

Emily took a deep breath. 'No thank you, I'm fine. Just caught off guard.'

'Hello again,' Will said to Merry. 'Having fun?'

'You two have met?' Emily gave Will a challenging look. *And yet he hadn't given her the heads-up?*

'Your boyfriend kindly helped me unload my car,' Merry explained.

'Oh, he's not my . . .' She coughed. 'We're just friends.'

'That's not what you said last night,' he remarked suggestively, arching an eyebrow.

Emily looked at Merry and shook her head, laughing.
'Sorry about him, he suffers from delusions.'

Merry grinned and folded her arms, clearly enjoying the
banter. 'Now I don't know who to believe.'

'Me definitely.' Will picked up one of the candles and
inhaled. 'Nice. Merry, if you need help loading up at the
end of the afternoon, I'm your man.'

'You're very sweet,' said Merry, laughing. 'But don't let
me monopolise you, you were looking for Emily?'

'Yes, I was, can I borrow you, Em?' His blue eyes bore
into hers, suddenly serious.

Her heart skipped at the shortening of her name. It
implied an intimacy that they didn't share. At least not yet.

'Um. Can it wait?' she asked, she flicked her eyes
discreetly towards Merry, trying to convey she was in the
middle of something.

He pulled a face. 'Not really, there's no time to lose. And
you won't want to miss this, I promise.' He took her hand,
holding it firmly in his. 'Excuse us, I'll bring her back.'

Merry looked at Emily and smirked. 'Now there's an
offer.'

'Will! I'm talking!' Emily protested. His enthusiasm was
endearing, but seriously, could the man not take a hint?

Will shook his head. 'I know, but Kylie has just spotted
a tiny muntjac deer in the grounds. If we don't hurry,
we'll miss it.'

Emily opened her mouth to argue, but Merry clasped
her hands together.

'Oh, you must go! I get deer in my garden and the baby
ones are adorable. Go, go, go! If you manage to take a
photo, bring it back and show me.' She waved them off

so excitedly that Emily had no choice but to let Will lead her outside.

Once they were out of the room and in the corridor, she ground to a halt, refusing to take a single step more.

'What was all that about?' Emily said, throwing her hands up. 'I was in the middle of something far more important than looking at a deer. As I think you well know.'

'I apologise,' he said, taking hold of her hands. 'But I promise this is important too.'

'Will!' Emily groaned. 'It has taken me ages to work up to telling Merry who I really am, and I'd just got to the perfect point in the conversation. My body is so full of adrenalin, I'm surprised my feet are still on the ground. And then in waltzes you with some ridiculous story about baby muntjacs.'

'It was Merry who mentioned the babies, not me. But I take your point,' said Will swiftly, sensing Emily's mounting exasperation. 'This is tough for you, I get that.'

'Made a lot tougher by you,' Emily muttered, shaking her hands loose from his. She felt tired and angry and unbearably frustrated; she'd been so close to telling her sister the truth. 'I can't restart that conversation with Merry now, the moment has gone.'

'That's why I interrupted you,' he said softly. 'There isn't any deer outside, as far as I know.'

'What?' She stared at him, open-mouthed.

'I could see from your body language that you were on the verge of telling Merry what you found out about your dad. I had to do something.'

'No, you didn't,' she said incredulously. 'You didn't have to do anything.'

She liked Will, he made her laugh, she liked his energy and his enthusiasm, but this was a step too far.

A group of people chose that moment to exit the lounge and start a loud conversation nearby.

'Shall we take this outside?' Will suggested. 'Where we can talk in private?'

'Fine.' Emily stomped off along the corridor, through reception and out into the wintry afternoon with Will beside her. The light was already fading from the day and the air was damp and cold. She bitterly regretted not having collected her coat, but she was too cross to go back inside. Besides, she'd probably bump into Merry again and she couldn't face her now.

They walked along the path that ran past the communal lounge in silence. Through the windows, misted with condensation, she could see the stalls, the Christmas tree and the choir. Emily shivered in the cold as her breath formed clouds in front of her face.

'I know you're annoyed with me,' Will began.

'Yes, well, you have no idea how hard that was for me, standing there in front of Merry, trying to introduce the subject of us being related.'

He caught hold of her arm, forcing her to standstill. 'I know I barged in on your conversation, but I just couldn't stand by and—'

'And what? Let me speak to my own sister?'

'Emily.' His blue eyes held hers so intensely that she felt herself weakening. 'Please hear me out.'

'This had better be good.' Emily stared at him, doing her best to give him a mutinous look. 'You've got two minutes.'

Any longer than that and she wouldn't be able to keep a stiff upper lip. Her emotions were all over the place. She'd been so close, *so close*, to opening up to Merry and now instead she was standing in the cold looking at her sister through a window. Without her coat on. Her teeth chattered and she clenched her jaw.

Will tugged his hoodie over his head and handed it to her. 'Here take this. No arguments.'

'Wasn't going to argue,' she said, diving into the warmth. *Bliss*. She tried to ignore the delicious scent of him which enveloped her. 'Thank you.'

'Well, that's a step in the right direction.' He risked a smile.

She tried giving him an icy glare, but her face wouldn't behave.

'Don't make me smile,' she muttered, pulling the neck of his hoodie up to keep her chin warm. 'Not when I'm trying so hard to be cross.'

He really was a beautiful guy, those gorgeous blue eyes, that hair which was just on the sexy side of scruffy. And there was an irresistible vitality about him, almost as if his body was struggling to contain all his energy.

'Understood,' he said with mock severity.

'One minute left,' she warned. But, in truth, the anger had left her and more than anything she wanted him to open his arms and pull her in for a hug, preferably inside in the warm.

'OK. When you first found out about having a sister, how did you feel?'

'Um, well I found out in stages, like little pieces of a jigsaw puzzle, and slowly put them together,' she said. 'So I guess it dawned on me gradually.'

He nodded. 'Now imagine if you'd found out all in one go and someone had presented the unequivocal facts to you.'

'I'd have been shocked,' she said. 'And I probably wouldn't have believed it.'

'And who'd have blamed you,' said Will softly.

Emily met his gaze and slowly she nodded, realising what he was telling her. 'And that was precisely what I was about to do to her, wasn't I? I was so wrapped up in telling Merry our story that I wasn't thinking about her reaction. How she'd feel finding out something so life-changing in a public place.'

'And Ray is here too,' Will reminded her. 'We don't know how he'll respond.'

Emily groaned. 'That could have been a disaster.'

'Could have been,' he repeated. 'But crisis averted.'

'Thanks to you. I owe you an apology.'

He grinned and lifted his hand to the back of his head, ruffling his hair. He was only wearing a long-sleeved T-shirt. It was tight-fitting, and she could see every detail of his muscular frame. She felt a dart of desire shoot through her and forced herself to meet his eyes.

'Tell you what.' He took another step towards her until their bodies were almost touching and slid his hands up her arms. 'Let's call it quits for telling fibs about deer in the bushes.'

'Deal.' She held out her hand and he shook it, amused. 'And maybe giving it a bit more time isn't a bad thing. She already has a family; she might decide that she doesn't want any more complications in her life. I need to prepare myself for the fact that she might not be as pleased to find me as I am to find her.'

He gave her a lopsided smile. 'I can't imagine she wouldn't. You're both lovely.'

'Oh yes, I'd forgotten that; you helped her when she arrived,' Emily said pointedly. 'Thanks for warning me that she was here.'

He pulled a face. 'Sorry, I did intend to. I offered to go and sit with Bernard for a while because he's ill. But while I was there, he had a seizure, and I couldn't leave him. As soon as the doctor arrived, I came down and found you already talking to Merry.'

'Oh poor Bernard. Of course you couldn't leave him.' Emily shivered and threaded her arm through his. He really was a good guy and he had been looking out for her. They turned back the way they had come. 'It's bloody freezing, remind me whose bright idea it was to come outside?'

Will laughed. 'In my defence, you looked so angry that I thought you might actually punch me. I didn't want any witnesses to my humiliation. But if you're cold, I know a great way to warm up, but it involves skin-to-skin contact. A little trick I learned surfing.'

A dart of desire pinged through her and she raised her eyebrows. 'If you think you're getting your cold hands on my warm skin, you can think again, mister.'

'Maybe save that for another time.' He slipped an arm around her shoulders, and pulled her close, and she leaned into him, revelling in the feel of him, the delicious smell of his cologne.

'Maybe,' she said coyly. 'But now can we please go inside in the warm and decide the best way to approach Merry, so she gets chance to process all this in private.'

'How about a letter?' Will suggested.

'A letter! That's brilliant, Will. I can tell her everything, I can enclose the photo of her with Dad as a baby and she can take her time to absorb it all. It's perfect!'

She stood up on her tiptoes and pressed a kiss to his lips.

'Hey, I thought we were just friends,' he teased.

'When did I say that?

'Er . . .' He narrowed his eyes, pretending to think about it. 'Literally five minutes ago in front of Merry.'

Emily giggled and kissed him again. 'Well, if it's OK with you, I'd like us to be more than friends.'

'Yes!' He punched the air.

She felt elated as they headed back inside and it was in no small part down to him. The contrast between Will and Gavin couldn't be greater, she mused. With Gavin, everything had seemed such a struggle, he'd constantly made her choose between her love life and her family, that she couldn't have both. Will made her feel as if she could achieve anything; life felt easy.

Maybe, just maybe, she thought, sneaking a look at his handsome face, this could be her chance to have it all.

Chapter Twenty-Six

Dear Merry,

It was lovely to bump into you again on Saturday at the Christmas Fair. We seem to be making a habit of it, don't we!

Sorry I didn't come back to show you pictures of tiny deer, but it turned out there weren't any. It was just a ruse on Will's part. He wanted to stop me from talking to you before I said something that I might regret. He was right: it was the wrong time and place. But I still want to tell you, so I've decided to put it down in a letter instead so that you can read it in your own time and decide what to do without me breathing down your neck.

OK, here goes.

I've lost count of the number of times I've tried to put pen to paper. I have so much I want to tell you and I hope that this will come as good news and not bad. Each time I've met you, I've come away feeling like you're the sort of person I could be friends with. Which is great, but it ups the stakes too.

I'm being mysterious and it's not intentional, but it's hard to know which bit to write first.

I'll start with me. I grew up in Bakewell with my mum, Tina. Ever since I was small, I have wanted to be part of a bigger family. My best friend Izzy has two sisters and I've always been envious of the fun she has with them and the *way they rally round each other like a private cheerleading club. My parents had a rocky on-off relationship. I was an accident, and although (as you've seen) Mum and I have a great bond, she didn't want any more kids — certainly not with my dad at any rate, who was in and out of my life when I was younger.*

When I moved my dad, Ray, into Springwood House, I found out that he'd been keeping a tin with various mementoes from his life. There was a photograph of him holding a baby at Christmastime, and I've enclosed a copy of it inside this envelope. I assumed the baby was me — she looks like me and why else would my dad be holding a baby and sharing such a happy moment?

When I showed my mum, she got upset. You see, the baby isn't me and she didn't have a clue who it was, but she knew the picture must have been taken around the time that she found out she was pregnant.

Dad's dementia is getting worse and half the time I don't know whether to believe the things he says. But recently he told me that his ex-girlfriend, Sam, had a baby and that he was the father. He also told me that he had loved Sam very much. I've told my mum about this, and she remembers the name of the girlfriend Dad had before her — Sam Shaw.

The day I realised that somewhere in the world I have a half-sister was one of the best days of my entire life. And a bit of digging on the internet has brought me to you. I couldn't believe that you were someone I had already met and liked.

Merry, I think there's a good chance that the baby in this photograph might be you. If it isn't, then I'm sorry to have troubled you. But if it, is I can't tell you how happy I am to have found you.

I completely understand that this might not be what you want in your life right now, or maybe ever. And I apologise if this letter has caused you any upset, it truly is not what I intend.

I'm putting my mobile number at the bottom of this letter. If you'd like to get in touch to talk, then please do. If you'd rather not contact me, I won't bother you again, and either way, I wish you a very happy Christmas and the best of luck with your wedding.

Warmest wishes,

Emily Meadows x

Chapter Twenty-Seven

Emily

It was Sunday night and Wetherley town centre was deserted. Emily slowly walked past Merry and Bright to double-check that there was no one in.

Her hand closed around the letter in her pocket as she reached the end of the row of shops. She turned and retraced her steps, peering in again. Definitely, one hundred per cent empty.

She took a deep breath, and headed directly for the shop door. She checked left and right to make sure nobody was watching and carefully opened the letter flap and pushed the letter through.

And then she walked away as fast as she could. She rounded the corner, raced along the side street and opened the passenger door of Will's car.

'Mission complete,' she said, exhaling with relief.

'Did it go OK?' he asked.

She nodded. 'So now we wait.'

He reached across the divide between them and gave her a hug. 'How do you feel?'

'Excited. Scared. Wondering what she's going to think,' she said with a wry smile. 'And if I'll get a wink of sleep tonight.'

Will let her go and smiled at her. 'I'm really proud of you, you've done a brave thing. And now I've met Merry, I think you've done the right thing. She's nice and whatever happens next, however she reacts, I don't think she'll be unkind.'

Emily returned his smile. 'Thank you for being here and boosting me. I need a friend right now.'

For a fleeting moment, a look of disappointment flashed across Will's face. 'Any time.'

'Will.' She took his hand and laced her fingers through his. She'd just been brave posting that letter, she could be brave again. 'When I say friend, I mean someone special, by my side. It wasn't a relegation to friend zone. Just in case that was what you were thinking.'

A smile lit up his face and he laughed. 'Busted. You can read me like a book. In which case, can you tell what I'm thinking now?'

Emily had no idea, but she was thinking that she'd quite like to kiss him, so she decided to go with that. She tugged him closer until their faces were almost touching.

'This?' she murmured before kissing him full on the lips.

'Amazing. You're a mind-reader.' He returned her kiss, his arms reaching around her to bring her closer still.

By the time they came up for air, giggling and delighted with each other, the windows had steamed up and Emily was getting increasingly hot under all her layers.

'Wow,' she said, grinning at him. 'You are a very good kisser.'

'So are you,' replied Will, sitting back in his seat. 'I think we'd better stop there or we might be in danger of doing something illegal in a public place.'

'And we can't have that.' Emily's cheeks were flushed, and she was glad of the darkness to conceal them. 'I feel like a teenager, snogging in a car.'

His eyes glittered. 'What would you like to do now?'

'I think I'd like to go home and let you take my mind off that letter.'

'That sounds like a plan.' He started the engine.

She grabbed his face and kissed him again before he could put the car into gear. 'You are turning out to be one of my very favourite occupational therapists.'

'*One of*?' He pretended to look insulted.

'The night is young.'

There was a tingling sensation in her stomach as the car began to move, although whether it was because of delivering that letter to Merry, or the prospect of an evening with Will, she couldn't be sure. Either way, she felt more alive in that moment than she had in a very long time.

Tomorrow, she thought, taking a last look at Merry and Bright as they went by, she could be waking up to a very different life.

Chapter Twenty-Eight

Merry

14 DECEMBER

'Bye, darling, have a lovely day!' I shouted.

Freya gave me one last wave before disappearing into a crowd of girls as they made their way inside, the shrill ring of the school bell cutting across all the playground noise.

I drove away slowly, careful to avoid the other parents or carers who'd arrived even later than us, and began to prepare myself for the day. It was Monday morning. The children rarely stayed over on a weekday because Lydia's house was much closer to their schools than Holly Cottage. But Lydia had had an early meeting in London to get to, so Cole had offered to drop them off at their respective schools this morning. But then an hour ago, he'd received an urgent call from Josh, his foreman, about an emergency on the building site. I wasn't sure what had happened, but I'd caught the words 'Portaloo' and 'blockage' and frankly that was enough.

I ran through a mental list of what I had to do today as I headed towards Wetherley and had got as far as the ring road when Harley rang.

'I'm really sorry, but I think I've left my rugby boots in your car, and I need them today.'

A quick look over my shoulder into the footwell behind confirmed it.

'Yes, you have. Can you borrow some?' I asked, hopefully.

'No, because they all need them at the same time as me. If I don't have my own, I'll have to wear the massive pair from lost property, and everyone will take the pi—'

'Harley,' I warned. Cole had had a word with him for swearing last night in front of Freya. Harley had argued back, saying that everyone at school swore and that it was no big deal, at which point Cole had marched him out of the room. I didn't get to hear the rest of the conversation, but neither of them spoke for a while when they came back in.

'Sorry. Please could you bring them for me, Merry, I'll get teased otherwise and I can't handle that today,' he pleaded.

I sighed. Fred had a doctor's appointment first thing and there was no one to open the shop.

'Please,' he said again. He did sound desperate. 'I owe you one.'

'Does that mean you'll sing at our wedding?' I asked.

I'd told Cole how brilliant his son's solo had been on Saturday and both of us had asked him if we could have a repeat performance during the marriage ceremony. Our request had been met with a resounding no.

Harley sighed in exasperation. 'OK. Forget it.'

'No, no, Harley, it's fine,' I said, taking pity on him. 'I'm turning the car around now.'

I parked in my space near the back of the shop, unlocked the door and went inside. The detour had added another forty-five minutes to my journey, but it had been worth it.

I'd left his kitbag with the school receptionist and Harley had sent me a text to thank me, adding a kiss at the end of it for the first time.

I quickly switched on the coffee machine before walking through the shop, turning the lights on and flipping the sign on the door from 'closed' to 'open'.

Five minutes later, I was ready for business. Gentle Christmas music played in the background and the smell of cinnamon and cloves from the candles I'd lit mixed with the aroma of my coffee to create a delicious layer of scents throughout the shop. I opened my emails to tackle the orders which would have come in over the weekend and almost fell off my chair when the door flew open, and Nell burst in.

'Guess what!' she cried breathlessly. She looked like she had just run all the way across the market from her stall.

'You've just sold a bag of almonds to Tom Hardy?' I said, laughing. There weren't many men who could tempt Nell away from Olek, but Tom was top of the list.

'No, no,' she replied, bending down to pick up all the post by the door which I hadn't got around to sorting yet. 'I've agreed the sale on my stall. Nell's Nuts will live on, but without Nell.'

'Congratulations!' I hugged her and we danced around in a circle in excitement. 'When did this happen?'

'It was all so easy,' she said, beaming. 'Those customers I told you about made me an offer. Olek and I discussed it and we've accepted.'

We went into the workroom and while I poured her some coffee, she gave me the details.

'And how do you feel?' I asked, leaning against the workbench.

'Excited,' she said, her brown eyes sparkling at me. She put the post down between us and picked up her mug.

'And I haven't felt that for a long time. The market stall was fun, but I'm ready for a new challenge. Seeing you build up Merry and Bright has inspired me.'

I looked at my friend, surprised. 'Really?'

Nell nodded. 'You've grabbed every opportunity with both hands, taken risks, you've been brave and daring. I'm going to be channelling your energy for my next venture.'

'You're a good friend,' I said, touched. 'And I know that whatever you do you'll be brilliant at it.'

I flicked through the letters. The usual suspects were there – flyers, junk mail, a letter from a supplier and . . . I paused, my hand hovering over an envelope with my name handwritten on the front of it and PERSONAL underlined underneath. No address or stamp. How odd.

'I'm in no rush,' Nell was saying. 'I've got my honeymoon cover to do here first anyway. What's that, a Christmas card?'

'I don't think so, it feels too flimsy.' I tore open the envelope and removed a single sheet of paper. 'Oh! It's a letter.'

Dear Merry,
It was lovely to bump into you . . .

My eyes skimmed the words, scarcely believing what I was reading.

'Oh my . . .' I gasped, staring at Nell.

Her eyes widened. 'What is it?'

'It's from Emily.' I swallowed; my mouth had gone dry. 'That girl who came to the stall with her mum a few weeks ago.'

Nell looked nonplussed. 'Who?'

I moved closer so that we could read it together, my heart thumping so hard that I could hardly catch my breath. I had to read it twice before it started to sink in. When I got to the end a second time, I delved back into the envelope and pulled out a photograph.

'Oh my God, Nell, look!' My hands were shaking so much that she had to hold it still for me. 'It's me. That baby – that is me!'

'You're kidding!' Her mouth opened, looking from the picture to me and back again.

I'd seen pictures of me in that dress before. It was our flat too, I recognised it straight away, my mum must have taken the photograph. And the man . . . Memories stirred inside me, snatches of his voice, the roughness of his cheek against mine, the lemony smell of his skin . . . I knew him. I remembered him. I knew him only as Mum's friend.

I read the letter again, tears running down my face.

'I don't understand what all this means.' Nell frowned.

'I think it means . . .' I sobbed; my throat so tight I had to fight to find the words. 'I think it means that I might have found my family.'

Chapter Twenty-Nine

Merry

Delilah's Café doorbell tinkled as I entered, and a girl hurried out from the kitchen to serve me. I quickly cast my eye over the clientele, looking for Emily, but I was the first to arrive.

This place was the closest café to Harley's school, where Emily worked, and meeting here had been her suggestion; neutral territory, she'd said on the phone this morning.

I'd only dropped Harley off and collected him from school a handful of times, but on how many of those occasions had Emily been there? Or in Wetherley market, or out shopping in Bakewell? How many times over the years had we had sliding doors moments? According to her dad, he was *my* dad too. Which meant I had a sister. A dad and a sister in the space of a few hours. This whole thing was surreal. It felt like I was living in a dream.

I wanted it to be true. I wanted it so badly that my body was in pain: my stomach was in knots, my shoulders tight and every so often my heartbeat would treble . . . even my jaw ached from being tensed ever since opening Emily's letter this morning.

'What would you like?' the girl asked. Her black hair was tied up in a red and white polka-dot scarf and she wore a matching apron. She waved her hand elegantly over the display of cakes like a conductor summoning her orchestra. 'I can recommend the boozy puff pastry mince pies.'

'They do look delicious,' I replied. My body wasn't in the mood for food; it was far too busy trying to keep my heart from taking the elevator from my feet to my throat. 'But just a gingerbread latte please.'

'I wish I had your willpower,' she said wistfully. 'My name is Delilah and I'm a pastry-aholic. Take a seat wherever you like. I'll bring it over.'

'Thanks. I'll open a tab if that's OK? I'm expecting someone.' I turned to glance at the door in case she'd arrived while my back was turned. But there was no one behind me.

'Of course.' Delilah smiled. 'And if you change your mind about cakes or pastries, let me know.'

The café was warm and cosy and smelled of vanilla and coffee and caramelised sugar. The counter was at the front, the centre was taken up with three squishy leather sofas and the rest of the space was filled with random tables and mismatched velvet chairs. A pink Christmas tree, decorated in delightfully kitsch decorations, was squeezed between a coat stand and a small table piled haphazardly with newspapers, and fairy lights were strung around the windows and across a chalkboard announcing the day's menu.

Delilah had gone to a lot of effort to make her customers relax, I thought, choosing a window table where I could see someone arriving from any direction. Any other time and it would have worked for me, but now I perched stiffly on a chair and set my phone on the table just in case Emily cancelled at the last minute. I checked the time; still ten minutes before we were due to meet.

I ran over the phone call she and I had had earlier after

exchanging a few texts. It was all a bit blurry, like when you went to the doctor's and they gave you precise instructions and you nodded, thinking you were taking it all in, and then, as soon as you got home, realised you hadn't understood a word. She thanked me over and over for getting in touch and I said that I should be the one doing the thanking and then we'd both cried for the rest of the conversation. I had so many questions and so did she. At which point, it was obvious we had to meet and share what we knew as soon as possible. And as we'd met before, I didn't see any reason to be worried that she might turn out to be a psycho.

We'd met before. I shook my head in wonder at that; it was too incredible to comprehend.

I looked up and down the street through the window. It was late afternoon and already dark outside, and the café had probably already waved goodbye to most of today's customers. There weren't many of us here. A couple of men were sipping hot chocolates and whispering together. A woman with a pair of glasses perched in her hair tapped at her laptop and two young people in hoodies and joggers were playing cards.

'Here you are.' Delilah perched a tray on the edge of my table and lifted off a tall glass of frothy coffee with a foil-wrapped mint chocolate. 'For while you're waiting.'

'That's very kind, thank you.'

As I tipped a packet of sugar into my latte, the bell over the door chimed softly and in walked Emily. Her eyes were bright, the tip of her nose red from the cold. She was wearing an emerald-green velvet coat and a thick teal scarf wound several times around her neck.

Emotion welled in my chest at the sight of her and I got to my feet, tears already filling my eyes.

'Hey. You came.' Emily did a self-conscious jazz-hands greeting, which was exactly the sort of thing I'd do.

'I came.' My smile was so big, I worried I might look manic instead of just happy to see her. 'How could I not? Your letter is probably the most exciting letter I've received in my entire life.'

'Probably the weirdest too.' She gave a nervous laugh.

'Well . . .' Outwardly, I'm sure it looked as if I was considering her words; inside, my heart was banging, every nerve ending sparking, my pulse blazing. 'Weird in an amazing way.'

'Phew.' Emily puffed out her cheeks. 'I was really hoping you'd feel that way.'

'So,' I said, slowly just to be sure that this was really happening. 'Your dad thinks I'm his daughter too?'

I was on the edge of my nerves, elated but scared. I didn't want to get my hopes up only for them to come crashing down. Emily's dad had dementia. What if this was just his memory playing tricks with him? What if this led to nothing?

'Yep.' A flush rose to her face. 'But he never mentioned it before he got dementia, so he might not be telling the truth!'

'But if it is true, we—' I felt my voice wobble, realising how much I wanted it to be true. 'We are sisters.'

We stood facing one another. Both wearing cautious smiles, both unsure what to do next. But as I stood there, I felt an overwhelming bond with this woman, as if at cellular level, my DNA was recognising hers. *Yes!* my cells were saying. *We have a match. Bingo!* I didn't know her, not really, but somewhere deep within me *I did*. It had only been two days since I'd seen her at Springwood House, but on another level, I'd been waiting a lifetime for this.

And then I opened my arms, and she flew into them, and we hugged each other tightly, like we never wanted to let go, and we laughed until tears streamed down our faces. The other people in the café watched us, bemused smiles on their faces as if they too knew something special was happening and they were glad they'd been witnesses to it.

'Thank you,' I said, through my tears. 'Thank you for getting in touch and sending that photograph.'

I pulled back from her so I could see her face.

'Thank *you*,' she replied. 'You know, it's funny, but I liked you instantly when we met. I mean, I liked Nell too. But it was your words that I kept thinking about afterwards. And at that point I had no clue about Dad's secrets.'

'That's strange, because I feel the same.' I led her back to my table and she slipped into the chair opposite mine, her eyes never leaving my face. 'Like I said on Saturday, your words really stuck with me about my hen do. If the universe sends you an opportunity to celebrate, take it. That's what you said.'

'You remembered it word for word!' Emily looked delighted. 'Little did I know then that the universe was going to deliver us both such a curveball.'

'And then some!' I said. 'It felt like you understood me. I loved watching your relationship with your mum too. I lost my mum when I was eleven, but, just recently, organising my wedding has highlighted the gap she left in my life more than ever.'

'I'm so sorry.' Emily reached for my hand across the table and squeezed it and we just sat there smiling until I got a packet of tissues out and we both mopped our eyes and checked each other's faces for mascara streaks.

Delilah chose that moment to come over, a hand pressed to her chest. 'You guys! I don't know what you're celebrating, but you've got me tearing up behind the counter.'

'Oh, you know,' said Emily casually. 'Just family stuff.'

'Yeah,' I joined in. 'You know what sisters are like when they get going.'

'Sisters,' remarked Delilah, shaking her head. 'I thought you looked alike. What can I get you, lovely?'

'You think we look alike?' I asked, pleased she noticed a similarity.

'Er, yeah?' Delilah looked at me as if I was bonkers.

Nell had spotted it too, but it had completely passed me by. Emily was fresh-faced and pretty, she had a blunt fringe cut into her blonde hair, whereas mine was all one length – a low-maintenance look, which suited my last-minute approach to hair and make-up.

Emily shrugged off her scarf and coat as she ordered. 'Gingerbread latte, please, with extra sugar.'

'Snap!' I said, pleased to find something in common.

'Got it.' Delilah wrote it down. 'Anything to eat?'

'One of your mince pies please,' said Emily.

Delilah looked at me and jerked her head towards Emily. 'See. Obviously, the brains of the family.'

'Uh-huh.' Emily shook her head. 'She's the brains, runs her own successful company.'

'Me?' I protested. 'You're the smart one, Miss Marple, working out the clues. You're the reason we're both sitting here.'

'Now, now, girls.' Delilah laughed and went to fetch Emily's order.

'Remember meeting Astrid on Saturday?' I asked. 'She's German and makes the most amazing *lebkuchen*, you'll have to try some.'

Emily's chest rose and fell, and for a second, she said nothing. 'I'd like that.'

I gazed at her, realising that in the space of two minutes, I'd already decided that whatever the outcome of this meeting, I wanted Emily in my life. Even if this turned out to be a big mistake and we weren't related at all.

'So.'

'So.'

We both spoke at the same time and laughed easily.

'You go first,' I said and sipped my latte.

'I was just going to say that I hope I've done the right thing by contacting you now.' Emily shifted in her seat. 'It's almost Christmas and you're getting married, and you must be busy with Merry and Bright, but once I'd started putting it all together, I needed to know whether it really was you in that photograph, whether I really do have a sister.'

'You did the right thing,' I said, understanding completely. 'And I'd have done the same. My fiancé Cole thought I was rushing into meeting you so quickly. But how could I not? It would have been like suspecting you had all six numbers on the lottery and not scrabbling to check your ticket immediately.'

Her eyes shone. 'It does feel a bit like a lottery win.'

'Cole says hi, by the way. He offered to come along too for support.' I looked at my engagement ring and smiled to myself. He'd driven over this morning and held me while I'd cried, overwhelmed with the shock of seeing a photograph of myself as a baby, in my old home. I had almost nothing from my early childhood, no photographs of me and Mum. And all this time, a man who claimed to be my dad hadn't been far away with his other daughter. A family I could have been part of instead of growing up alone. But today wasn't about dwelling on the might-have-beens it was about finding out what I might have now.

She smiled. 'So did Will. But he and I are very new, it's too soon to be putting all this family stuff on him. And my best friend—'

'Lives in Jersey?' I said.

'Well remembered!' Emily looked impressed. 'But I've told her about you. And Will and I FaceTimed her last night after delivering my letter.'

'One latte and one mince pie,' said Delilah, gently setting everything down on the table between us and gliding away after Emily smiled her thanks.

'I haven't been able to eat all day,' Emily admitted.

'Me neither.' At that moment, my stomach kicked into action and gave an almighty rumble. 'Whoops.'

We both laughed and Emily cut the mince pie in half and pushed the plate between us so we could share it. We bit into our respective halves, and I savoured the sweetness of the fruit, the kick of whatever alcohol Delilah had mixed into it and the lightness of the pastry. It tasted like heaven.

'So. Let's get the facts straight.' I got out the photograph that Emily had sent and looked at it. 'Like I said on the phone, the photo was definitely taken in our flat, and I'm as sure as I can be that the baby is me.'

She nodded. 'And Ray, my dad? You recognise him?'

'I only remembered his name after you told me. He was a friend of Mum's, as far as I knew.' I frowned; my memories were hazy from that part of my life. I had very clear ones of me and Mum, and I had vague recollections of various friends dropping into the flat and he was one of them. 'He was obviously there at some point over my first Christmas, but I only saw him a handful of times when I was little. I think the last time I'd have seen him was when I was about five or six. I read my schoolbook to him, and I got fed up with it, so he read me a story instead. And he liked music,' I said, with a sudden recollection. 'He'd always put our little radio on. We didn't have CDs or records or anything like that. But he'd sing or hum and whistle if he didn't know the words.'

Emily stared at her. 'Oh my gosh! I asked him what I was like when I was little, and he said something about me dancing in the flat. But Mum and I never lived in a flat. So that must have been you.'

My heart gave a leap. 'I wonder what else he remembers. I'd love to hear about my mum.'

'Do you mind me asking what happened to her?' Emily asked softly. 'It's OK if you'd rather not.'

I drank the last of my latte and pushed the cup away. 'I don't know anything about her early life, but I do know that she was living rough when she got pregnant with me at seventeen.'

Emily's face crumpled. 'That must have been awful, poor girl.'

I nodded. 'My earliest memories are of the two of us in our little flat, never any other family. She and I were very close. She was a fun mum, but she had regular bouts of illness. I was too little to understand at the time, but now I realise she must have been suffering from depression. I'd be sent to live with foster parents while she got well again. I had a long spell of being fostered when I was eleven and I remember being excited to go home for Christmas. But one day my social worker came to school to tell me that she'd died. She'd killed herself. I never went home again, and I spent the rest of my childhood in care.'

'Oh Merry, I'm so sorry.' Emily had tears in her eyes. She reached across the table and took my hands and I tried to smile. 'Dad was often away,' said Emily. 'He got restless staying in the same place and would disappear off somewhere for weeks and sometimes months on end. Mum used to despair. That was what broke them in the end – the not knowing when he'd be back. I hated him being away, but at least I always had Mum. I didn't realise how lucky I was.'

'I never knew who my dad was,' I told her. 'There's no one listed on my birth certificate. Until I started school, I didn't know that that was unusual. But then I noticed most of the other kids had two parents and I began asking questions. Mum used to tell me stories of a lovely man who'd been her best friend and had given her money so she could pay for a night in a shelter. She never used his name, she just called him Daddy. I asked her why he didn't live with us, and she said . . .' I paused, reaching back through time to remember how she'd worded it. 'She said he couldn't stay with us because he needed to keep moving.'

'That sounds like him.' Emily swallowed and her eyes shone with tears.

We sat in silence for a while, lost in thought, until she spoke again.

'I have always wanted a sister.'

'Same here,' I said with a grin. 'I mean, I'd have settled for a brother, but having a sister has always seemed like a double bonus: a best friend and a sibling all rolled into one.'

'I've always envied people with big families,' she said.

I laughed softly. 'I envy people with *any* size family.'

'Maybe our family has just got bigger.' She fiddled with a napkin and then raised her eyes to mine.

I wanted that, so much. It would be the icing on the most amazing Christmas cake. But equally I didn't want to set myself up for a fall either.

'Do you think your dad is really telling the truth. About me, I mean?' I asked, holding my breath.

'Honestly? I don't know. Sometimes he thinks I'm Tina, my mum, sometimes he's convinced he's just met random people from the nineteenth century. But he does seem very sure that you're his daughter and he was worried about my mum finding out. She knows now, because I couldn't keep this from her, it's too important.'

'You believe that we're related, don't you?' I said, meeting her gaze.

'I do,' she replied, her green eyes wide. 'I think we're half-sisters.'

'In which case, we've got some catching up to do,' I replied, dotting the last few flakes of pastry with my fingertip and putting them in my mouth. 'Tell me a bit about yourself.'

'OK.' She sat up taller in her chair. 'I'm thirty-five, my favourite drink is Guinness, but when on a first date, I drink wine so men don't think I'm too laddish.'

'To hell with what they think,' I declared. 'Drink the dark stuff if it makes you happy. I would.'

'Maybe I will.' She grinned. 'What do you drink?'

'Er, rosé,' I said sheepishly. 'Moving swiftly on.'

We both laughed.

I sat and listened, and I learned all the things I would already have known about my sister if things had been different. That she lived in a rented cottage by herself, and she'd painted the walls shades of pink and there was a roll-top bath of dreams in the bathroom. How she took the job at the school just so she could look out for her dad, how her first love is fashion and she can't resist a thrift-shop bargain (her velvet coat was only fifteen pounds and still had the tag in) and how her ex-boyfriend dumped her last month, but now she was glad because she'd met Will, although it was early days, and she didn't want to get too excited.

'OK. So, I'm Merry Shaw,' I began when it was my turn. 'Thirty-six. Likes a snap decision. Loves the scent of citrus fruit, especially bergamot – yes, it's a thing – creative, romantic. I like dresses, but rarely have the right shoes, or tights for that matter. My best friends are Nell, who I met at college when I was about sixteen, and Astrid, who used to be my art teacher but is now my friend and mentor and is also the love interest of Fred, my soon-to-be father-in-law. Totally in love with my fiancé and can't wait to marry him on Christmas Eve.'

Emily sighed wistfully. 'That is very romantic. How did you meet?'

And I was off again; telling her far more than I would normally to someone I'd only just met. But it felt right. There was a trust there which I'd never experienced with anyone else before. I even ended up telling her all about Harley and Freya and the drama we'd had wedding-outfit shopping. I told her how Freya had made me want to postpone the wedding and that Harley had told me stuff he didn't want his father to know.

'So not the bond-building experience I'd imagined,' I concluded wryly.

'Sorry, ladies.' Delilah's voice startled us both. I looked up to see her hovering by the counter. 'I need to lock up soon, five-minute warning?'

'Oh, my Lord!' Emily laughed, looking around. 'We're the last ones here.'

'Everyone must have left without us even noticing,' I said in surprise.

We stood up and got our things together and bickered over paying the bill.

'I'm the oldest,' I said, enjoying the sound of that for the first time. 'My treat.'

We thanked Delilah, leaving her a tip and promising to come back soon, and left together. The ice-cold air swirled around my face, and I pulled my scarf up and put my gloves on.

'So, what next?' I asked. 'Where do we go from here?'

Emily grinned. 'How do you fancy meeting Dad?'

'Would that be OK?' My stomach pinged with trepidation. 'When?'

Her eyes sparkled in the reflection of the café fairy lights. 'Is tonight too soon?'

My heart swooped with joy and I gave a burst of laughter. 'Seriously? Tonight would be amazing.'

We quickly sorted out the details and hugged our goodbyes. The decades of being an only child were over and I felt like my heart might just break with happiness.

Chapter Thirty

Emily

Emily could hear her dad humming in his bathroom. He always took ages. Sometimes he was so long that she had to knock on the door to check on him. Usually, he'd forgotten what he'd gone in there for, and he'd be reading the back of a shampoo bottle or something random. But at least he was humming, which was a good sign. He could be very curmudgeonly when he wanted to be. And she wanted this first meeting with Merry to be a success.

She pulled back the curtains a little bit and opened a window. Dad had eaten his dinner in his room and there was an eggy pong in the air. She didn't want Merry sitting there holding her nose.

Her phone buzzed with a text message from Izzy asking for an update and her heart skipped. She pressed call and Izzy answered on the first ring.

'Emily!' Izzy breathed a sigh of relief. 'I've been going out of my head wanting to know how it was all going. And I didn't want to call in case you were still with her and it was obvious I was after the gossip.'

'God, I miss you at times like this.' Emily sighed wistfully.

'I miss you too, but cheer up, you've got a sister now.'

'We *think*,' Emily reminded her. 'There's no actual proof; Merry didn't ever know who her dad was. But whether we are related or not, I've definitely gained a new friend. Not that she'll ever replace you.'

Izzy laughed. 'Glad to hear it. Sounds like your coffee date went well then?'

'Really well. I'm in Dad's flat now and she's on her way over.'

'You are kidding me!' Izzy gasped. 'Wow, you sisters don't hang around.'

'We've hung around long enough,' Emily replied. 'I can't wait for you to meet her. She is lovely and funny. And she's made a real success of her life after a tricky start. I'm really proud of her.'

'Oh, Em, I'm so pleased it's gone well so far,' Izzy said softly. 'And a new man on the scene too. I couldn't be happier for you. You deserve all the good things.'

'I can't wait you for to meet Will in person either.' Emily felt a thrill at the sound of his name. She'd phoned Izzy back after Will had left last night and told her all about him. Izzy approved.

'New Year's Eve party at ours?' Izzy suggested. 'Bring him with you. Just think about it.'

Izzy had the best parties and where she lived meant that she and Andrew could have a fire on the beach and see in the New Year under the stars with the sound of the sea as their soundtrack. Will would love that. Emily had said no when Izzy had first asked her because she was still looking after Dad. But now . . . her head whirled, wondering. Maybe there was a chance . . .

The sound of the toilet flushing signalled that her time was almost up.

'I will think about it,' Emily promised. 'Although, for all I know, Will already has his own plans. We're not even officially a thing yet. Listen, I'd better go, I think Dad is coming out of the bathroom.'

'OK. Good luck,' said Izzy with a squeak of excitement. 'And go slowly with your dad. I know you want this to work, but don't force it.'

'Roger that,' Emily said and blew a kiss down the phone just as the bathroom door opened and Dad emerged wearing only his underpants. Her heart sank. 'Everything OK, Dad?'

'I'm very tired.' He yawned and headed towards his bed. 'Goodnight.'

Emily leapt to her feet in a panic. It was seven-thirty; Merry was going to be here any moment.

'Here are your pyjamas.' She pulled them out from under his pillow and took his arm. 'You go back in the bathroom and put them on. And I'll make you some hot chocolate to have before bed, it'll help you sleep.'

He probably didn't need help, but it gave her an excuse to stay.

'Don't need help,' Ray replied, for once making perfect sense. His fingertips rasped against his stubble. 'You can go now.'

'I am going,' she said firmly. 'After you've put your pyjamas on.'

Dad muttered something under his breath about being as bossy as her mother and dropped his pants to the floor. Emily turned away quickly; some things were better not seen.

The phone rang in the flat and Emily hurried to pick it up.

'I have clean pyjamas on Sundays,' he said, kicking the ones Emily gave him to one side.

'Luckily, it's Monday today,' Emily replied and answered the call, already knowing who it would be. 'Hello, Ray Meadow's room.'

'Hey, it's Kylie on reception. There's a lady called Merry Shaw here.'

'Thank you, send her up.' A surge of nerves overtook her as she ended the call.

Ray was still struggling with his pyjamas. Emily braced herself and tried not to look as she bent down and held the bottoms out for him to step into, grateful that he'd given up his battle for clean ones, and by the time there was a knock at the door, he was at least clothed.

Dad looked at the door sharply. 'That's all we bloody need.'

'Coming,' Emily called out.

'No, she's not,' Dad shouted.

'You've got a visitor, Dad.' Emily looked him in the eye to make sure he was listening. She smoothed his hair down tenderly as if he was a little boy about to leave for school. His eyes had a faraway look in them, and she wondered where he was, what he was thinking about.

'Hot chocolate and bed,' he noted grumpily. 'That's what you said.'

'You remember that then,' she said dryly. 'This is a special visitor; I think you're going to want to see her.'

He made a big show of his displeasure, but Emily opened the door anyway.

There was Merry, holding a big bunch of flowers in one hand and a small bag in the other.

'Shut the door,' Dad yelled. 'Don't let her in, she's after my money!'

Emily shot a look of apology at Merry before turning to comfort him. 'It's OK, Dad, this is a friend. We can let her in, it's safe.'

He pushed past her and slammed the door in Merry's face. 'They're always here. Banging on my door. They pretend they just want to talk and then they try to steal from me. They're from one of those cults, wanting to brainwash me.'

'Good luck trying to brainwash you,' Emily replied. Her heart was pounding, this was not the tear-jerking family reunion she'd envisaged. She gently pulled her dad into a hug. 'My friend is here to see you. My friend. OK?'

He nodded sceptically.

Emily took a deep breath. 'I'm going to open the door now, Dad.'

With one final glance at her dad, she walked calmly to the door and opened it.

Merry was still there, thank goodness, looking understandably apprehensive.

'Let's start again.' Emily cringed with embarrassment. 'Would you like to come in?'

Chapter Thirty-One

Merry

I flinched as the door slammed in my face and lowered the flowers. Behind the door, I could hear Emily calming him down. Her tone was kind but confident. She was so good with him; she knew just what to say and he obviously felt safe with her. I worried that I wouldn't know what to do.

I set my shoulders back and stood up tall. If Emily could do this, so could I. I wasn't scared. Well, maybe a bit, but there was no way I was backing out now. If there was even the remotest chance of learning more about my mum, I was going to take it.

My phone buzzed in my bag with a message. It was Cole. He'd driven me here, but we'd agreed that he'd wait downstairs.

Good luck, my darling, I hope it goes well. Remember this is just the first meeting. It might come as a shock to this guy. Don't be disappointed if it doesn't turn out as you planned. xx

I sent a quick reply.

So far, it's not turning out to be the tear-jerking father-daughter reunion I envisaged. He thinks I'm from a cult.

His response came instantly.

It's his illness talking, try not to take it personally. I love you xx

I managed to text him back that I loved him too when the door opened.

Emily looked harassed and apologetic.

'Let's start again,' she said, blowing a sharp breath out of the side of her mouth which ruffled her fringe. 'Would you like to come in? Although I wouldn't have blamed you if you'd left after that welcome.'

'Of course, I wouldn't leave.' I gave her a hug. Her shape already felt familiar to me. 'It'll take more than being accused of being from a cult to get rid of me.'

Emily grinned. 'OK. No brainwashing though.'

'Brainwashing is off the agenda. Understood.'

Emily set her shoulders back and exhaled. 'Come and meet Dad.'

I followed Emily into the flat, apprehensive about what Ray might accuse me of next.

'Bloody hell,' she tutted. 'He's fallen asleep.'

I looked at the man sitting at the far end of the room in an armchair, his legs resting on a footstool, and my breath caught. It was the man who'd bought a candle from me on Saturday. We'd met each other, had a conversation, and yet there had not been a flicker of recognition on either side.

I felt Emily's arm go around me.

'You're trembling,' she said, concerned. 'Are you OK?'

I nodded. I couldn't find the words to say that this was something I'd dreamed about all my life, that I'd convinced myself would never happen in a million years. Of course I knew I had a father, but without anything to go on, no name, no clues, I'd trained myself not to hope. And here before me was a man claiming to be my parent. Family. A blood connection to another human being. Every cell of my body tingled and hummed.

I walked slowly towards him, taking in his features, the shock of wiry silver hair, the roughly shaven chin. He looked thin and slight, wrapped up in a huge dressing gown. The man in my memory had been big, with strong arms which had swung me around. A sandy-coloured beard, shoulder-length blonde hair and bright green eyes. A man who crackled with energy. There was little left of the man I remembered; no wonder I hadn't recognised him.

I shivered and Emily, mistaking my reaction, rushed to close the window. 'Sorry. It gets a bit fruity in here.'

'We met on Saturday.' I looked from him to Emily in disbelief. 'He came to my stall at the fair. If you hadn't put us in touch, I'd never have known who he was – who he *is*.'

His words came back to me. *She always smelled nice. Not easy when you're on the streets.* It had been the aroma of Home he'd been referring to. The candle inspired by Mum.

I told Emily the story, missing out the part about him buying a candle for her.

'He has to be talking about your mum,' Emily said, gesturing for me to sit down on a small sofa.

I nodded. 'I hope he remembers some more. That's been one of the worst things about growing up without her. I've had no one to tell me stories about her, I'd like to know what sort of a person she was.'

I put the flowers on the table and asked Emily for a vase. She found a pottery one under the sink and some scissors and I arranged them while she made a cup of hot chocolate for her dad.

'He'll wake up again soon, don't worry,' she said. 'This is standard behaviour for Dad. Full of bluster one minute, zonked out the next. It's like having a puppy.'

'I'm partial to a nap myself,' I said, watching his chest rise and fall, his lips puffing out tiny breaths.

'Me too. I think the world would be a nicer place if we all took a nap after lunch.'

'And possibly mid-morning, after elevenses.'

We both laughed.

Emily offered me a drink and while she poured me a glass of water, I took in the room from my spot in the kitchenette. There were two doors off this main living area, and I could see into his bedroom from here. There were some framed photographs beside his bed.

'It's very homely in here,' I said, turning the vase to check my arrangement.

'It's the reason I chose it,' replied Emily, setting a mug on the coffee table for Ray and a glass for me. 'I was aware that this was probably going to be his last house move. I wanted him to feel at home. And I'm so glad I did. Because if he hadn't moved to Springwood House none of this might have happened.'

'Really?' I put the little bits of stem I'd trimmed off into the bin. 'What makes you so sure?'

'The TV in his old flat didn't show Freeview channels so he would never have seen you on *The Retail Therapy Show*. The TV in the lounge downstairs was tuned to it the very first afternoon he was here. And there you were, on screen, a young woman called Merry, telling the presenter about your mum, Sam. He began talking about you immediately.'

I swallowed a lump in my throat. 'That's incredible. I think that's what they call serendipity.'

'*I* think he's never forgotten you and perhaps on some level he realised that time was running out to find you.'

I looked at him asleep in the chair. An old man with a fading memory. So much time wasted. 'And now I'm here,' I said, smiling at Emily. 'And if he'll let me, I'll be here again.'

'That would be great,' she replied with a heavy sigh. 'I felt so guilty, moving him from his own home. But I couldn't look after him by myself. The responsibility was too much. But it has worked out well for all of us. I know he shouted just then, but as a rule, he's more relaxed. He's eating properly now they've worked out his tricks, and he's got company all day long to keep him safe and occupied. I'm his only visitor, so if you come too, that's a one hundred per cent increase.'

'He's lucky to have you,' I said warmly.

'He's family,' Emily said simply. 'And I love him. He might not have been the best dad, but you don't turn your back on family, do you?'

'No,' I replied softly.

I'd always been curious about who my father was and it had been one of my biggest regrets that I hadn't had chance to quiz Mum about it when I was older. I'd always assumed that whoever my father was didn't know I existed. But Ray had known. He had met me when I was a child and he had told Emily that he had another daughter. I didn't know the circumstances and now, given his dementia, I might never know, but there was a twinge of sadness that he hadn't come for me, like a small stone in my shoe that might never go away.

The smile must have dropped from my face because Emily groaned. 'I'm sorry, Merry, that was insensitive of me when you grew up without any family around you.

Please forgive me, I'm still new to being a sister, I could do with a siblings manual.'

'Don't give it another thought. I'm new too, remember?' I said, waving away her apology. 'And yes, to the manual, for all sorts of things. Prime example, when I marry Cole, I'll become a stepmum to his two children and, like I said this afternoon, I don't have clue what I'm doing.'

'I have every confidence in you,' she said briskly. 'And having children means you'll have a proper Christmassy Christmas! Oh I'm so jealous!'

'You could join us over Christmas some time if you're free?' I said instinctively.

Emily looked genuinely touched. 'I'd love that!'

I told her I'd send her the details and then all talk ended because Ray opened his eyes. I wondered what he was going to say when he noticed I was there.

'Welcome back, Dad,' said Emily, squatting beside him and taking his hand. 'Your hot chocolate is ready.'

He rubbed his eyes and stared at her, frowning 'Have I missed breakfast? What day is it?'

'It's Monday and you've got ages until breakfast,' she replied, standing up. 'And we've got a visitor, remember, my friend Merry?'

'Hello, Ray, nice to meet you.' I perched on the edge of the sofa, my stomach in knots.

'Likewise,' he said politely. 'Staying at this hotel, are you?'

'Um.' I looked to Emily for help, and she grinned back. 'Welcome to Dad's world, Merry.'

'Just passing through this time,' I said, playing along. I pushed the gift bag across the coffee table until it was within his reach. 'I came to bring you some chocolates. Would you like one?'

'Not for me.' He peered into the bag and shook his head. 'We always have chops on Mondays.'

'Dad has very clear memories of certain things in the past,' Emily explained.

I nodded thoughtfully, trying to think of a way to tap into his history.

'My mum used to like *lamb* chops,' I said.

He shook his head. 'Too fiddly. All bone and gristle. Like me.'

Emily opened the truffles, peeled the red foil wrapper off one and held it out to him. He ate it straight away; clearly changing his mind about chocolate.

'My mum's name was Sam Shaw,' I persisted.

Ray frowned but said nothing.

'And do you know what we used to have instead of gravy?' I don't know where this memory had come from, but suddenly it was there as clear as glass. Mum opening a can of oxtail soup and heating half of it on the tiny electric hob we had in the flat. The other half would have been put in the fridge to have the next day with bread and butter.

Ray lifted his eyes to mine and stared at me for a long moment as if his brain was trying to put together pieces of a puzzle.

'Soup,' he said finally. 'She always poured soup on her dinner.'

'Is that right, Merry?' Emily asked, her eyes wide.

I swallowed the lump in my throat and nodded. 'Oxtail soup. Sam and Merry had soup on their dinner, remember?'

The tension from Ray's face seemed to melt away and his head bobbed. 'Funny girl, she was.'

My heart began to race; he remembered her. He remembered my mum.

'Mum loved to dance,' I continued, tears pricking at my eyes. 'Our flat was only small, but we used to put the radio on and dance. I get my music taste from her. I remember us singing 'Let's Dance' by David Bowie so loud that the neighbours banged on the wall.'

'Dad loves music, don't you, Dad?' Emily prompted him. 'You brought some of your old records with you.'

'Fleetwood Mac,' he said. 'I've got it here somewhere.'

He rose to his feet, his slippers scuffing across the carpet to the dresser, and pulled out an old vinyl record. It was 'Tango in the Night'.

'Oh my word!' My heart skipped. 'She loved Fleetwood Mac too.'

'Dad, do you remember us singing together?' Emily asked. ''Everywhere' is one of my favourite songs. We used to play it all the time.'

'I love it too.' My eyes filled with tears, and I felt Emily catch hold of my hand and squeeze it.

He started to sing 'Everywhere', the record clutched to his chest. He moved his feet to the music and Emily and I sat and stared. The man who couldn't remember what day it was knew every word, every note.

And then suddenly Emily and I were singing along and dancing together and Ray smiled and sang louder. Emily grabbed his hands and danced with him and after a few seconds he let go of her and twirled me around. It was a moment that felt so spontaneous and precious and utterly joyful that I knew it was a memory that I'd treasure for the rest of my life.

Eventually, breathless and weak with laughter, we dropped back down into chairs.

'That was good fun,' I said, panting. 'I haven't danced for ages.'

'Not even on your hen night?' Emily gave me a mischievous look.

'What happens on the hen, stays on the hen,' I laughed, tapping the side of my nose.

'Merry is getting married, Dad,' she said, handing Ray his hot chocolate before it got cold.

'Sam's girl?' Ray's voice was sharp. He stared at Emily and then at me.

Emily gasped softly and I felt my chest tighten with hope.

'I'm Merry, Ray,' I said in a wobbly voice, 'Sam was my mum.'

'I loved Sam,' he mumbled, before swallowing a mouthful of his drink. 'Hated seeing her living rough. Some of us can hack it, but not Sam. I used to give her money, so she had enough for a hostel. You could have a shower, get a meal and a bed for the night. I wanted us to be together. Properly. But she wouldn't let me. Said she couldn't do love. She was wrong though, because when the baby came, she loved her. No doubt about it.'

'You mean me?' I seized on his words, wanting to hear him say it.

'Course I do.' He set down his mug. There was a brief spark of recognition in his expression and my eyes filled with tears. 'You're Merry, aren't you?'

I nodded, momentarily speechless. I quickly got the photograph out of my bag and pushed it across the table to him. 'This was me as a baby, with you at Christmas. Thirty-five years ago.'

He picked it up and looked at it. 'Handsome bugger then.'

'What was I like, as I baby?' I probed gently, eager to hear about my childhood, something I'd been deprived of for so long.

He chuckled, his eyes not leaving the picture. 'Like a little monkey. You had no fear, climbing up onto chairs, sliding down off them again. Your mum said she woke up once and you were sitting in the kitchen sink playing with the cups. You weren't even two.'

'I've always been a bit of a risk-taker,' I said to Emily, smiling through my tears.

Each snippet of information was like a drop of water on the lips of someone who'd been lost in the desert forever. I wanted to hear more, I wanted to raid his memory banks and record it all so that one day I could pass stories of my childhood to my own children.

'You told Emily that Merry is your daughter. Ray?' I swallowed. 'Is that true? Are you my father?'

Ray didn't react, he looked lost in a world of his own.

I held my breath and Emily reached for my hand. I was on the verge of repeating the question in case he hadn't heard me when he nodded his head slowly.

'One day I went to meet her at our usual place in the park. She didn't come. I asked around, but no one had seen her. I looked everywhere. I even went to the hostel she used when she had the cash, and they checked the hospitals for me. She'd just vanished. I kept waiting, but she didn't come back, not for over a year. Worried to death, I was. By then I was applying for jobs and housing and doing my best to get off the streets. Then she turned up one day pushing a pram.'

'Sam had had a baby?' Emily drew in a breath.

Ray nodded sadly. 'That's why she disappeared. She told me she had a flat, she'd got her life sorted and she didn't want to be hanging out with tramps. She meant me; she was right. My hair was long and dirty, my shoes were two sizes too big for me and I probably stank. She looked beautiful and her hair was shiny, her fingernails were clean. The baby girl was only a couple of months old, tiny with a little wrinkled face. All wrapped up in blankets. The two of them were perfect. I felt ashamed.'

'Oh Dad,' Emily murmured, 'I'm so sorry.'

Ray looked so downtrodden as he was speaking that I wanted to hug him, but I didn't dare, not just yet.

'I asked her if I was the father, but she said no. I didn't believe her; Sam wouldn't have been with anyone else, she wasn't like that. She just said it to keep me away. Her own father had knocked her and her mum about. She didn't trust men, didn't want a man near her baby. I could understand that.'

'Did she have anyone looking after her when she'd had the baby, Ray?' I asked.

Ray shrugged helplessly. 'Doubt it.'

I closed my eyes. She'd been eighteen by then and alone in the world except for a newborn, scared to trust other people. My heart broke for her all over again.

'It was seeing Sam with that baby that made me sort my life out. It took me a few months, but I did it. I cleaned myself up, got a job, got a room in a house-share and went to see her and the baby. Christmastime it was. I'd met Tina by then and she was pregnant with Emily. I didn't cheat on Tina, I just wanted Sam to see that I wasn't a dirty tramp anymore.'

Emily smiled at me with sympathy in her eyes. 'I think this is the most Dad has said for months; you picked a good day.'

I nodded. 'A brilliant day.'

She tapped the photograph. 'Dad, was this photo taken that day you went to see Sam and Merry?'

He nodded. 'Sam took it on my camera. There are more somewhere, I had a tin.' He looked around the room vaguely.

'In the wardrobe?' Emily suggested. 'Shall I get it?'

Ray yawned and nodded.

Emily went to the wardrobe and reached up to the top shelf.

He was getting tired, but there was so much more I wanted to know. About Mum, about her mental illness. I wanted to find out if he'd been in touch with her before she died.

Emily passed an old tartan biscuit tin to him, and he prised open the lid. His fingers fumbled through the contents until he found an old yellow envelope with Kodak printed on it. He put the tin on the floor and tipped the contents of the envelope out on the table. There were about twenty photographs, most of which had rainbow streaks of light across them.

'Sam opened the back of the camera by accident,' Ray muttered. 'Ruined most of the pictures.'

My hands were itching to sift through them. 'May I?' I asked.

Ray nodded and then stood up. 'I'll clean my teeth, then I'm going to bed.'

'Now?' Emily asked. 'Don't you want to look through the pictures with us?'

'No.' His reply was so abrupt that it was almost comical.

'Thank you for letting me see these, Ray,' I said, my eyes sweeping the tumble of pictures.

He shut himself in the bathroom without a reply.

Emily picked up a photograph and handed it to me. 'Oh, Merry, look!'

I gasped. It was of Mum and me. She was standing, with me on her hip, my head snuggled into her neck, her cheek pressed against the top of my head. Her eyes were closed but there was a huge smile on her face. It was a picture of pure joy, of love, of motherhood. Looking at what we'd had, what we should have continued to have, tore at my heart. I pressed a shaking hand to my mouth and tears started to fall; I felt Emily's arm wrap around me.

'This,' I said, joy and sorrow and yearning in my voice. 'This is the best thing you could possibly have given me. I don't know what magic brought you to me, Emily, but I'll be grateful to you for the rest of my life. Thank you.'

'You don't need to thank me,' she said, brushing away her own tears. 'I know I don't look it, but you've made me so happy.'

We hugged each other for a long time and then went back to the photographs. We found another lovely one of Mum on her own. She wore dungarees with a wide belt around her waist, her brown hair crimped and her eyes ringed with black eyeliner.

'She was stunning,' said Emily.

'And just a child herself,' I breathed.

The toilet flushed and Emily handed the photographs to me. 'Put them in your bag, make copies.'

I nodded. 'I'll bring the originals back, I promise.'

She put the others back in the envelope and the bathroom door opened.

'I've lost my pyjamas.'

We turned to see Ray stark naked and scratching his head in confusion.

Emily winced and jumped up. 'Sorry, Merry, I'll just—'

'*We*,' I said, standing up too. 'Sisters. You're not on your own in this now.'

Emily blinked hard. 'Do you mean that?'

'Come on, Dad,' I said, beating her to the bathroom. My heart was beating so hard I could hardly hear my own words. I'd just called someone Dad for the first time, and it felt amazing. I picked up his pyjama bottoms. 'Let's get you sorted. Lift one leg up and lean on me.'

'And slip your arms in.' Emily held up his top. 'One, two, that's it.'

Two minutes later, he was tucked up in bed and Emily and I washed the mugs and glasses and put them away.

'Is it OK if I call him Dad, do you think?' I whispered. Emily beamed. 'It's all right with me.'

'Merry?' Ray's muffled voice called from under his duvet. 'There's a pot of money on the bookcase, can you fetch it?'

I gave Emily a puzzled look and fetched what looked like the lid of a jam jar with several coins in it.

'Is this it, Dad?' I passed it to him, unable to resist trying out my new name for him again.

He took two pound coins and handed them to me. 'One for you and one for your sister. Now bugger off and let me get some bloody sleep.'

'Oh thanks, Dad.' I looked at Emily and we exchanged secret grins.

We gathered up our bags quickly, stifling our giggles and headed for the door and let ourselves out.

'Don't spend it all at once,' said Emily sternly, once we'd shut the door.

'Sod that, sis,' I retorted. 'I'm blowing the lot on sweets.'

We collapsed with fits of laughter and staggered towards the lift, clutching each other for support. I held my sister's hand and my heart felt full. She had filled a space that no man, no best friend, no career could ever fill. She had brought me home.

Chapter Thirty-Two

Emily

'Your face when Dad came out naked,' Emily snorted, as they exited the lift.

'I was expecting a few revelations tonight,' Merry replied with a giggle. 'But that one took me by surprise. You're brilliant with him, though. I was in awe, especially when I first arrived.'

Emily wrinkled her nose. 'You have to find the funny side, otherwise your heart would break. It's been exhausting, looking after him by myself this year since his health deteriorated.'

Merry hugged her. 'You're not on your own anymore. I'm happy to do my share of visiting and looking after him. But you're the boss, you might have to help me understand his needs.'

Emily's heart swelled. 'You have no idea what that means.'

Merry took a breath in as if she was about to say something and then her mouth shut abruptly.

'What is it?' Emily probed.

'It's just, we don't know for certain, do we?' Merry frowned. 'About being sisters, I mean.'

'Look at us.' Emily turned Merry's shoulders until they were both facing a mirror, generously decorated with swags of faux evergreen and silver ribbon. 'Our colouring is identical.'

'Could be coincidence?' said Merry dubiously.

'We know Sam and Ray were lovers. The timing fits,' Emily continued. 'And Dad seems convinced you're his daughter.'

'If only Mum hadn't denied it,' Merry said with a sigh.

'From what Dad says, it sounds as if she was protecting you, she'd got a home for you both, and sorted her life out and she wanted to keep you safe. Perhaps inviting Dad into your lives was a risk too far.'

'I want it to be true, I want to be his daughter.' Merry turned to face her. 'Mostly because I want to be your sister.'

'I want that too.' Emily saw her own wishes reflected in Merry's eyes.

'Then maybe that's enough,' said Merry, shrugging a shoulder. 'If in the future we need definitive proof for medical reasons or whatever, so be it.'

Emily nodded. 'But for now—'

'We're sisters.' Merry grinned.

They hugged again and then the sound of male laughter made them both glance towards the foyer. On the far side of the Christmas tree, the rest of their bodies hidden from view, were two sets of stretched-out legs.

Emily's heart pinged. She recognised one of the voices straight away. 'Will's here!'

'Sounds like he and Cole have hit if off already,' said Merry.

Both men stood up as the two women came into view.

'How did it go?' Cole asked.

'Brilliantly!' Merry was triumphant and brimming with energy. She threw herself at Cole, who laughed and caught her. 'Today has been one of the best days of my life. Hey,

Will, good to see you again! And Emily, this is Cole, my betrothed.'

'Great to meet you, Emily.' He leaned forward and kissed her cheek.

He was handsome and charming, just as Emily knew he would be. 'You too. And congratulations on marrying my . . . sister.'

She and Merry laughed with delight. It was probably going to take a long time for either of them to get used to saying that.

Emily gave Will a hug. 'This is a lovely surprise,' she said.

'Good surprise?' He mirrored her body language, pulling her close. From behind the reception desk, Kylie gave a little gasp of surprise, making them both smile conspiratorially.

'The best,' she confirmed. 'What happened at your work do, did it finish early?'

A bashful smile twitched at his lips. 'As far as I know, they're all still playing beer pong and drinking themselves under the table.'

Emily looked askance at him. 'So you're here because . . .?'

He picked up a strand of her hair and twirled it through his fingers. 'Because I couldn't stop thinking about you and Ray and how it was going with Merry, and it felt too important not to be here.'

Emily's heart leapt. She thought back to how Gavin had rolled his eyes whenever she needed to change her plans to be with her dad. How he'd seen Dad as an inconvenience standing in the way of his fun. She gave herself a shake; there was no need to keep comparing the two men. Gavin was history. Will, on the other hand, was her present – in more ways than one.

'Thank you,' she said simply. 'I'm so glad you came.'

'Basically,' he admitted, 'I'm kinda nosy.'

They both looked at Merry, who was telling Cole in animated detail about the things Ray had revealed to them, the photograph of her and her mum in her hand.

'We got off to a rocky start when Dad wouldn't let her in,' Emily told him. 'But I think Merry got what she needed.'

'And did you?' he asked gently.

'Yeah, definitely.' Emily slid her hands to his chest. 'And finding you here is the perfect ending.'

'Ending?' He raised an eyebrow.

'To that particular chapter,' she corrected. 'And now I'm all yours for the next one.'

His eyes flared and a flame of longing flickered inside her. This man stirred emotions in her she hadn't felt for . . . possibly ever before.

'Emily?' The two of them broke apart as Merry's voice interrupted their moment. 'I'd like to come back and chat to him again. Would that be OK?'

Emily beamed. 'Of course! You don't have to ask my permission. You're family.'

Merry reached for her hand and squeezed it. 'Thank you.'

'Is that definite then?' Cole asked, looking between the two women. 'You've confirmed that Ray's your father?'

Emily and Merry exchanged glances and nodded.

'We're definitely family,' Emily confirmed.

'*Family.*' Merry's eyes shone with tears. 'I never thought I'd hear anyone say that about me.' She looked up at Cole apologetically. 'Blood relatives, I mean, as opposed to by marriage.'

Cole wiped away a tear from her cheek. 'I know what you mean.'

'Awww,' Kylie sang out from behind the reception desk.

The four of them looked at her and she blushed. 'Sorry, I can't help listening. I've been WhatsApping my friends with updates. No names, obviously. But this long-lost family story is everything.'

'It is everything.' Emily's eyes glittered as Will slipped his hand into hers and gave it a squeeze.

'Hey, you two should come to our pre-wedding dinner party on Friday,' said Merry, her eyes dancing. 'So you can meet Cole's family. Nell will be there, who you've met.'

'Thank you, I'd love to come,' said Emily. She looked at Will nervously. She'd feel braver if he was there, but it was a bit early in their relationship to be thrusting a big family event on him, especially when it was family she hadn't even met herself. 'Um, Will?'

'I'd like that, if you're sure? I wouldn't want to intrude.' Will looked at her for approval and she could have kissed him.

'We'll both be there,' Emily confirmed, feeling giddy with happiness. 'Will Harley and Freya be there?'

Cole shook his head. 'Unfortunately not, they're with their mum.'

Merry pulled a face. 'Surely Lydia wouldn't mind as it's a special occasion?'

'They've already got plans, darling.' Cole looked awkwardly at Emily and Will, clearly not comfortable discussing this in front of them.

Emily took the hint. 'Not to worry, another time.'

He smiled gratefully. 'They'll be at the wedding; you'll meet them then.'

Emily felt her cheeks get hot and didn't know where to look; this was the first she'd heard of an invitation.

Merry gasped and smacked a hand to her forehead. 'YES! Oh heavens, I haven't invited you to the wedding.' She grabbed Emily's hands. 'Can you come? Do you already have plans? I mean, it's Christmas Eve, I wouldn't expect you to change them for us. But it would mean a lot to have you there.'

Emily was laughing by the time Merry took a breath.

'There's nothing I can't shuffle around,' said Emily. The only things she'd got in her diary over Christmas was to clear Dad's flat and Julia didn't mind when she did that. 'I wouldn't miss my sister's wedding for the world. But I can't answer for Will, we've actually only been on one date.'

'And that was to stand outside Merry and Bright,' Will butted in.

'Can you come?' Emily bit her lip, feeling terribly guilty about putting him on the spot in front of the happy couple. 'Are you free on Christmas Eve? I mean, it's a big ask, I'll understand if you—'

'Hell yes!' Will said with a grin and held Emily's gaze. 'I'd love to. Thanks for the invite.'

Merry's eyes shone, and she shook her head in disbelief. 'I'm going to have my family at the wedding, somebody pinch me!'

Just then, her stomach gave a massive rumble, even bigger than the one in the café, and they all laughed.

'Someone needs dinner,' said Cole, putting his arm around her. 'We should head off.'

Emily turned to Will. 'Fancy getting a takeaway and heading to mine?'

Will's eyes lit up. 'Sounds great.'

'She can pay,' Merry piped up. 'With her pocket money.'

'As long it doesn't cost more than a pound,' replied Emily.

And to the amusement of the men, the sisters started to laugh again. Because already they had a shared private joke, and it was never not going to warm their hearts.

Chapter Thirty-Three

Emily

18 DECEMBER

'One tiny twist clockwise, I think.' Emily tilted her head to one side as she studied the Christmas tree, trying to work out its best side.

'OK,' Will said with a grunt from beneath the tree, his hands around the base. He gave it a slight turn and looked back at her over his shoulder. 'Like that?'

'Perfect,' she declared, clasping her hands together. 'I love it, I think it's the best tree I've ever had! Oh, I'm so happy.'

Will emerged commando-style from underneath the branches. 'If only everyone in the world was as easily pleased.'

The school term was officially over, and Emily was feeling euphoric. Darley Academy had finished at lunchtime today after the sixth form's well-received pantomime, with the best-dressed bears Goldilocks would ever have seen.

Now it was Friday night, she had had a new job offer to consider, no more work for two and a half weeks and so much to look forward to: Merry and Cole's dinner party later; their wedding next week and plenty of time to get to know Will better too. Bliss.

She was still going to have to clear out Ray's flat and it was unlikely that she'd make it to Izzy's New Year's Eve party because Merry would be away on her honeymoon and she didn't want to leave her dad. But those things weren't the end of the world and, on balance, she was more excited about this Christmas than she could ever remember.

'I can't help it.' She held her hand out to Will and he laced his fingers through hers. 'Only two months ago, I'd been dreading the Christmas holidays because I was so worried about Dad and now everything seems to be falling into place.'

'You deserve it,' he said, squeezing her hand. 'And I agree with you, that is one good-looking tree.'

'That's when it's naked,' she replied, smiling up at him. 'Imagine how beautiful it will look by the time we've decorated it.'

'Oh, I don't know,' he said, with a twinkle in his eye. 'Some of the best things are better when they're naked.'

'Is that right?' She turned and kissed him.

'It is.' He grinned and pulled her close.

'Maybe that's a theory we can put to the test later,' she said, looping her arms around his neck.

Things were heating up between them; he was tactile and tender, and his kisses set her on fire. And tonight, after the party, he was staying over for the first time, the thought gave her a delicious thrill. She was excited but nervous too. She wasn't the sort of girl to rush into things; one-night stands held no appeal for her. She wasn't interested in a no-strings good time. It was strings or nothing for Emily.

'Unless . . .?' He waggled his eyebrows as his hands slid lower down her back.

She laughed and wriggled away from him. 'I know your game, mister. But you promised to help me trim the tree before we go out.'

'I just can't keep my hands off your baubles.' He dodged out of the way as Emily swiped at him playfully.

'You're a bad influence,' she said, grinning at him. 'Come on, let's get decorating.'

Emily made them both mugs of tea while Will retrieved a large wooden crate from under the stairs and set it on the coffee table.

She knelt in front of the table and sipped her tea as Will slid off the lid. Inside, nestled in packing straw and individually wrapped in tissue paper, were her prized vintage glass ornaments bought at a car-boot sale.

Will took out a star carefully. 'Oh surprise, it's pink.' He gave a sideways look at the walls of the cottage, 'You do like pink.'

'Very girly, I know, but it's a happy colour to live with,' she insisted. She took the star from him and hung it on the tree. 'Which makes it very welcoming to come home to.'

He liberated another bauble from its tissue paper and placed it near the top. 'That might be where we're going wrong; I think our landlord painted ours raincloud grey. It couldn't be any less feminine.'

'That's largely down to the tenants, not the walls.' Emily laughed, delving into the crate for more baubles. 'Your house is the testosterone capital of Derbyshire.'

She'd been to Will's house earlier in the week and met his two housemates, who were perfectly welcoming and great fun, but there was no doubting that the house lacked a feminine touch.

She could feel his gaze on her as they continued their task. 'What are you thinking?'

'That your last boyfriend must have been an idiot,' he answered, 'but that I'm glad because it meant you were single when we met.'

Her heart thumped. 'I could say the same about you. I'm glad *you* were single.'

He rubbed a hand through his hair. 'Have been for two years. Although that relationship wasn't ever serious. My last proper relationship ended *six* years ago.'

'What? A good-looking guy like you?' she said, surprised.

'Hard to believe, I know,' he said with a grin. 'But it took me a long time to get over her.'

Emily felt a stab of hurt on his behalf and reached for his hand. 'Oh Will, I'm sorry. What happened?'

'Her name was Kaia. She was a professional surfer – she travelled all over the world and so did I when we were together.' He pulled a face. 'But when my grandad became ill, I moved back to care for him, and she didn't want to come. Not many opportunities for surfing in Derbyshire, so we broke up.'

Emily saw the sadness in his eyes and her heart melted for him. He had given up a life he had loved and lost his girlfriend at the same time. And then to lose his only relative to Alzheimer's.

'What a tough time that must have been for you.'

'*C'est la vie.*' He shrugged amiably. 'You see someone's real personality come out when the chips are down, and the truth was that she loved surfing more than she loved me. I'm over it now.'

'Good,' Emily said firmly. 'Because it was her loss. So how did you earn a living when you were travelling?'

'I've always been an occupational therapist, but back then I worked for an agency rather than directly for the health service, so I could pick my hours. I'd work a ridiculous number of shifts and once I'd saved up enough, off I'd go until the money ran out.'

'Wow.' Emily was impressed. 'That sounds amazing.'

He looked at her enquiringly. 'Do you think?'

She nodded. 'I love that ethos of working just enough to fund your passion. It's the best of both worlds.'

Will looked thoughtful. 'I've been thinking about it more and more recently. About how to get more surfing into my life. I get a lot of job satisfaction from working with clients, but surfing is my first love; I miss the sea when I'm here.'

'I've been thinking too,' she said. 'Meeting Merry and learning how she started her own business has inspired me. She just went for it; turned a hobby into a business. I've never felt brave enough to do anything like that.'

'And now you do?'

Emily wrinkled her nose. 'I've been offered a permanent contract at the school and I'm really grateful for that, but it doesn't set my world on fire, you know?'

'I get it,' he said, nodding. 'And what does?'

'Vintage clothes,' she replied instantly, surprising herself. But it was obvious now she thought about it. Finding something pre-loved and beautiful was what gave her a buzz. So far, she'd only bought – for herself. But maybe she could buy *and* sell? 'But there are a million people already doing that with more experience.'

He shrugged. 'So get experience. There you go, your first New Year's resolution.'

She laughed. 'You make it sound so easy. What about you? Go surfing more, I guess?'

'It's probably a crazy idea,' said Will tentatively. 'But I'd love to set up a charity for kids to teach them to surf. Focusing on kids who've had a tough start in life, maybe young carers. I don't know. It might not work, but it's what I'd like to do.'

Emily felt a fluttering in her stomach; this man had such a big heart, such generosity of spirit. 'You'd be brilliant at that.'

'Surfing changed my life.' Will's eyes softened as if he was there in the water, the taste of salt on his lips. 'When you surf, you're in the moment, your focus has to be right there in your body. If you let your mind wander even for a second, whoosh, you're down. It builds strength and confidence and self-belief. It's great for your mental health. What kid can't use a bit of that?'

She shook her head. 'Wow.'

'I know. Fantasy, right?' He pulled a face.

'Not at all. You're a very special man, Will. And because of that' – she handed him the last decoration reverently – 'you get to put the star on the tree.'

'I am honoured,' he said with a bow.

He lifted the star in both hands as if he was holding a trophy and placed it on top of the tree

Will turned off all the lamps in the room and Emily bent down to the switch beside the tree and flicked on the Christmas lights.

'Merry Christmas,' she said, holding out a hand to him.

'To you too.'

Wordlessly, they moved into each other's arms and kissed. She'd known this beautiful man for only a month, things were moving fast, faster than she would normally be comfortable with, but it felt right, and he felt right in her arms. It was far too soon to tell him how she felt. So she wouldn't, not just yet.

'It's with the greatest regret,' she said, tearing herself away from him, 'that I'm going to have to stop you there. And ask you a serious question.'

'OK.' He gave her a bemused look.

She grabbed the gift she'd bought to take to Merry and Cole's, a wooden carving of two lovebirds, and grinned at him. 'Are you ready to party? Because I am.'

Chapter Thirty Four

Merry

I slithered into my sparkly dress, the satin cool against my skin. I'd only just arrived home after getting caught up at work, and Cole, understandably, had been unimpressed at having to do all the party preparations by himself.

In my defence, I was late because I might have found someone to work at Merry and Bright. A girl called Bella had responded to the advertisement I'd placed in the window. She was studying for her master's degree in marketing and needed to earn some money to make her student loan go further. The downside was that she was only interested in part-time hours, and I was fixed on wanting someone full-time. But she'd had some great ideas, which meant I lost track of the time and was late getting home.

There was a zip at the back of the dress and buttons which I couldn't do up without Cole's help. I left them open, then added some big silver hoop earrings, a spritz of perfume, and put my feet into my shoes. I was ready in the nick of time, the party was due to start in a few minutes. I'd even beat Cole for once, who was in the bathroom downstairs.

Music was playing softly in the living room and the smell of warming mulled wine permeated the whole house. Neither of us liked the taste, but everyone else I knew did and for the aroma alone it was a Christmas must-have. The kitchen table was groaning with food and rows of glasses stood to attention on the side. We'd decided against a formal dinner in the end; it was going to be a buffet and mingle party instead. There wasn't enough room to seat everyone in the kitchen for one thing, and the more people I invited, the less I wanted to cook a proper meal. Besides, tonight had always been about spending time with my favourite people before the wedding and not about food, and now it had a new and exciting purpose – to introduce my sister to everyone.

I shivered with delight and made my way downstairs, admiring our home-made garland, consisting of tinsel (Freya) and faux eucalyptus (me). Holly Cottage looked gorgeous. I'd gone to town on Christmas decorations this year, assisted by Freya whose enthusiasm for all things sparkly knew no bounds, and Holly Cottage bristled with our festive flair.

I was checking myself in the hall mirror for smudged mascara when I heard a car pull up.

'Cole, there's someone here already!' I called, tottering through the kitchen to the bathroom as fast as I could. 'I need your help.'

It was probably Nell, who liked to arrive early. And if it was Nell, it shouldn't matter, I should just open the door and let her do me up, but . . .

Tonight felt different. This was our first party, mine and Cole's. Holly Cottage might only have been rented, but it was the first place I'd ever felt truly at home. And now I thought about it, I'd never hosted a proper adult party before.

And that was why I didn't want to answer the door with my underwear on display.

Cole opened the bathroom door wearing his boxer shorts. 'Our next house has to have an upstairs bathroom. I left my trousers upstairs again.'

'Um, yes, so you did.' I tried not to look at his thighs. He had lovely thighs, they were one of my favourite parts of him, second only to his arms. I did like muscular arms, I especially liked trailing my fingers down them.

'You wanted help?' He waved a hand in front of my face, grinning at me.

'Yes, quick! My zip.' I yelped as Cole unzipped it all the way down to my bottom and pressed a languid kiss to my spine. 'Wrong direction!'

'That's a matter of opinion,' he said huskily. 'You look sensational by the way.'

'Hello?' Fred's voice came from the hallway. 'We let ourselves in.'

'We are the only ones here, I think,' I heard Astrid say.

'Quick.' I shimmied on the spot. I loved Fred and Astrid dearly, but greeting them with my dress undone to my knickers was not how I planned to start the evening. 'Do me up, it's your dad, we need to get dressed.'

Cole grinned. 'It's a long time since I heard a girl say that.'

I thumped him playfully. 'This is not the time to regale me with tales of your misspent youth.'

'It pains me to do this, but here goes.' He zipped me up and pressed another kiss to my neck. 'You do the coats, I'll do drinks.'

I watched him walk out to greet our first guests wearing a soft green shirt which set off his russet hair and deep brown eyes and . . . his boxer shorts.

'Cole!' I gasped. 'You've forgotten your trousers.'

And just like that our pre-wedding party had started.

An hour later and the house was buzzing with Christmas spirit. All my favourite people were here: Cesca, Fliss and their husbands and kids, Nell and Olek, Hester and Paul and, of course, Emily and Will. Hester and Nell were self-appointed waitresses, circling with plates of warm pastry nibbles (straight from Marks and Spencer, but anyone who had time to make their own pastry at Christmas, days before their wedding, needed to take a long hard look at their priorities, in my opinion), leaving Cole and me to chat to everyone.

'I'm having such a lovely time!' Emily cried as she danced past me holding hands with Cesca's children. 'Thank you for inviting me!'

'Believe me,' I yelled back, 'the pleasure is all mine.'

My beautiful sister, I thought. How easily our lives were gelling together despite the late start. I already loved her. We had got into the habit of speaking and texting every day. Just small trivial things, but we were finding out new things about each other and developing the bond between us. And I'd been in to see Ray again too. I hadn't found out anything more about Mum yet, but I was learning to cope with his jumbled-up mind, and in quieter moments when he relaxed, I recognised aspects of myself in him.

Emily pulled a face as the kids dived behind the sofa, dragging her with them, and I laughed as she tried to fold herself up small. Kids knew, I thought. They had in-built radars for nice people.

I glanced around to find Will and spotted him chatting to Paul. But every so often his eyes sought out Emily and a besotted smile spread across his face. Another good egg; he was a keeper.

'Hey, beautiful,' said a soft low voice in my ear. I shivered with pleasure and turned to find Cole with a fresh glass of fizz for me. I took it and swapped it for a kiss.

'Having fun?' I had to raise my voice to make myself heard over the Christmas playlist I'd asked Harley and Freya to put together for us.

'Very much,' he replied, touching his glass against mine. 'Everyone seems to be in high spirits. Dad and Astrid have just told me they've booked flights to India in March.'

My eyebrows shot up. 'Wow. They're serious about it then?'

He nodded. 'And Hester has been offered a new role as a drive-time radio presenter.'

I shook my head in disbelief. 'Then there's Nell, looking for a new challenge now she's sold her market stall.'

'And us getting married.' He pulled me into his arms. 'New starts for everyone.'

'Hey, you two!' Hester shoved a plate of smoked salmon blinis between us. 'Any last-minute requests for your wedding reception? Are we wedding-ready?'

'We should be,' I said, helping myself to a blini, I'd barely eaten again all day. 'Cole's been clutching his clipboard like Santa adding naughty boys and girls to his list for weeks.'

'No surprises which list you'd be on,' he retorted. 'And someone needs to keep track of the details because my fiancée just taps her head vaguely when I ask her anything and informs me that it's all in her brain.'

'And it is,' I said airily. 'It will be a lovely Christmassy day with my favourite people. And, therefore, it will be perfect. The details will take care of themselves, as the saying goes.'

Paul appeared and wrapped an arm around his wife. 'I thought the phrase is that the devil is in the detail.'

'The devil is definitely not invited,' I replied. 'It'll be a host of heavenly angels all the way.'

'Providing they know what time the wedding is.' Cole waggled an eyebrow.

'Oh shush. You know I get mixed up where noon is concerned.' I elbowed him playfully in the ribs. I'd sent the text invitations out with twelve-thirty a.m. on them instead of p.m. 'Easy mistake.'

'I know I'm pernickety,' Cole said, 'but I'm not planning on doing this again. And the kids will be there this time. I want it to be a special day for all of us.'

'It'll be wonderful,' Hester agreed.

'And the reception should be a jolly occasion if the crates of wine in our utility room are anything to go by,' Paul added.

'At the end of the day, it's a bit like a really good party where we just tell each other in front of our loved ones that we want to be together forever with a form to sign at the end,' I remarked.

'Just?' said Cole in mock horror. 'The day marks the start of our marriage.'

'Ooh, are we talking wedding plans?' Fliss and her husband joined us, widening our circle and diving into the blinis.

'Precisely my point!' I said, replying to Cole. 'The wedding is day one. In my admittedly limited experience of marriage, there seems to be a big emphasis on every detail of the wedding and not enough preparation for what comes after.'

'You mean the wedding night?' He smirked. 'Because you don't need to worry about that.'

'No,' I laughed. 'I'm talking about the life we make together after the wedding. That's far more important to me than the actual ceremony. That's the real celebration.'

His eyes softened. 'You're right of course.'

'That is a good point.' Nell sidled up and stuck out her plate of mini spring rolls. We all took one and munched. 'From the moment you decide to get married, all the focus is on that one day and not making the relationship work.'

'It's like when you have a baby,' Fliss put in. 'Half the sessions at my antenatal group were about writing the birth plan, which goes straight out of the window as soon as you hit the delivery suite anyway. We'd have been much better doing some practical sessions on what happens when you bring the baby home, and you have to live with it.'

'Exactly,' I agreed, making a mental note to quiz her about this separately after Christmas. My broodiness was hitting peak levels watching her little ones running around with Cesca's kids. 'I miss Harley and Freya,' I murmured to Cole.

'Me too,' he said, 'and I love that you're thinking of them. But we'll get them all day on Christmas Eve. I didn't want to push Lydia about tonight. She said she had plans; it wasn't fair to ask her to change them.'

I nodded. He had a point, but what if the kids had wanted to be here? Didn't they have rights too?

Our little gang had grown larger now; Olek had joined us, and Emily and Will were hovering nearby.

I reached an arm out to bring them closer. 'Emily, Will, come and taste these blinis before Paul hoovers them up.'

I caught Nell's eye, who pressed a hand to her chest and pulled a swoony face. *I love that you have a sister*, her expression said. I smiled back and nodded. *Me too.*

'Thanks for inviting us,' said Will.

'Yes, it's the perfect start to my Christmas holidays,' added Emily, her cheeks pink, either from the mulled wine or all the racing about with the children, I couldn't tell. 'And I'm so excited for the wedding now I've met everyone.'

'Have you done a DNA test yet?' Olek asked.

'Not yet,' said Emily, wrinkling her nose. She looked at me. 'I'd be devastated if the result came back that we aren't related.'

'Same here.' I put my arms around her shoulders. 'We've decided we're sisters, come what may. We don't need a test to confirm it. What is certain is that Emily's Dad had a relationship with my mum. He is the only living person I know who remembers her, which means whether he is my dad or not, he's the only link I have to her.'

'His memory might be sketchy, but he definitely loved Sam and he's convinced you're his daughter,' Emily reminded me.

Nell found a space to put down her canapés and held up her glass. 'I propose a toast: to sisters, including sisters from another mister!'

'And not forgetting sisters-in-law!' Hester piped up.

'To all sisters!' we cried and then all the women hugged each other.

'Would you like to see my wedding dress?' I whispered to Emily.

Emily gasped. 'Really?'

'Hester? Are you in?' I asked.

Hester sucked in a breath. 'Part of me would love to see it, but the other part wants it to be a surprise on the day. You go ahead.'

'Come on up if you change your mind,' I said, giving her a squeeze. 'OK, girls, upstairs.'

'What are you up to?' Cole narrowed his eyes, amused.

'Just wedding stuff,' I said sweetly. 'You know, nailing down that detail.'

Chapter Thirty-Five

Emily

Merry herded Emily and Nell into her bedroom, shut the door and turned around. 'Can someone undo me please?'

While Nell undid her button and pulled down the zip, Emily perched on the bed and gazed around the room. Merry's style was similar to her own: a mix of vintage and shabby chic. She had an old-fashioned dressing table, which had a triple mirror attached to it, the glass silvered with age. The dressing table had a glass top, although between the candles, perfume bottles and jewellery stands draped with chains and beads, there wasn't much to see of it.

'Sorry, it's a bit messy,' Merry said, catching her looking.

Emily shook her head and laughed. 'No more than mine. I think we share a magpie gene.'

'No prizes for guessing which is Cole's side of the bed.' Nell grinned, nodding to the nightstand nearest the window. On it was a biography of a famous drummer. 'He was telling me earlier that when he was little, he asked for a set of drums for Christmas every year. Never got them. Clearly the dream still lives on.'

Merry clasped a hand to her chest. 'Ah, sweet. I didn't know that! I was the same with the Care Bears. I wanted them all and only ever got one.'

'Me too!' Emily exclaimed.

Merry gave her a high five and the sisters laughed.

'I wish I'd brought my dress,' Nell said, flopping back on the bed beside Emily. 'We could do a dress rehearsal.'

'I wish I'd *got* a dress,' said Emily. She mentally rummaged through her wardrobe for a wedding outfit but came up empty-handed. She wanted to look her best; she was the sister of the bride after all.

'Emily, every time I've seen you, you look amazing, whatever you wear, I'm sure you'll look gorgeous.' Merry laughed before slipping behind the wardrobe door where the others couldn't see her.

'Thank you.' Emily took a deep breath in and felt her shoulders sink from somewhere up around her ears. She hadn't realised how nervous she'd been about coming to Merry's house tonight, meeting all the people who meant the most to her, being introduced as the sister Merry had never known. But now the tension was beginning to leave her. Cole, Nell, Hester, even the adorable elderly couple, Fred and Astrid, had made her feel welcome, had gathered her to them and, without question, accepted her connection to Merry. It felt as if the universe was singling her out for special treatment. She didn't know what she'd done to deserve it, but she was making the most of it.

'What colour is Freya's dress?' she asked. If there was a colour theme, would it look bad if she joined in? She didn't want Merry to think she was pushing for a part in the main event.

'Blush pink,' Merry said. 'And silver sequin shoes. She'll look gorgeous. Harley and his dad are in navy.'

'Old rose for me,' Nell said, explaining, 'I'm the best woman.'

'Hester is also in pink.' Merry's head appeared from behind the wardrobe. 'You can too, Ems, wear whatever makes you feel happy. Except a wedding dress obviously, I draw the line there.'

Ems. Her sister's nickname for her; Emily felt a swell of pride. And she was allowed to wear the bride's chosen colour, which, by chance, was her personal favourite. *Thanks again, universe.*

Emily grinned. 'Understood.'

Behind the wardrobe door, she saw Merry's dress slither to the floor and her foot push it to one side, still with her heels on.

'OK,' Merry blew out a breath. 'Are you ready for the grand reveal?'

'Whoop-whoop!' Nell cried.

'Ta-dah!' Merry closed the door of the wardrobe so they could all see her, and she slowly did a twirl.

Emily gasped. 'It's the dress from Vintage by Violet! It was you! I saw you both looking in the window. And I've since wondered but . . .'

'No way!' Nell cried.

Merry nodded slowly. 'Outside the shop, you were carrying a big box.'

Emily beamed. 'That's right. The Santa hats that the choir wore to the Christmas Fair.'

'You were there when I found my dress. So I did have a member of my family there after all.' Merry's gaze softened. 'How many other times have our worlds collided?'

'You know, girls,' said Nell, her eyes glinting, 'you should tell your story to a newspaper, it would make a great feature.'

Emily faltered. 'Um, I'm not sure how my mum would feel about that.'

Merry gave her a hug. 'Let's not think about that now. Can someone say my dress looks amazing please? Nervous bride here?'

'Oh, mate,' said Nell in a low voice.

Emily swallowed, not sure whether to tell the truth. Merry looked beautiful, but the dress hung off her, it would look a hundred times better if it was taken in down the sides and the darts which ran from the waist across her ribs to her bust.

'The style is perfect for you,' said Emily. 'It really shows off your figure. You're so slim.'

'Shit.' The smile on Merry's face slipped as she stared at her reflection in the mirror. 'It's too big, isn't it?'

Emily bit her lip and nodded. Honesty, she decided, was the best policy. It's what she would want if the boot were on the other foot. 'It might look better if it was taken in.'

'It fit you when you bought it,' Nell said, frowning, 'I was there.'

She pinched the fabric at the back of Merry's dress to make it fit. 'At least you'll be able to stuff your face on your wedding day and it won't get too tight.'

Merry flattened her hands against her chest and groaned. 'Who stole my boobs?'

'Not just your boobs,' said Nell, poking her in the ribs. 'I can't even pinch an inch.'

'Maybe it's a nervous energy thing,' Emily suggested, wondering if she was partly to blame. 'You've been working really hard, and you've just found out about me and Dad.'

Merry nodded. 'I have. Which has been the absolute best thing. But it's all been such a lot to cope with, trying to do stuff for the wedding and work out how to keep the business going without putting too much pressure on Fred. With one thing and another, I haven't had much appetite.'

Poor Merry, Emily thought, she'd gone from top of the world to rock bottom in two minutes flat.

'Why does this never happen to me?' said Emily, trying to raise the mood. 'When I'm tense, I can hoover up an entire bar of milk chocolate without even noticing.'

Nell snorted. 'That's me with a jar of peanut butter.'

'Guys,' said Merry, a hint of panic in her voice as she plucked at the loose fabric. 'Seriously. What am I going to do?'

'Stick a pair of socks in your bra?' Nell suggested.

'You need to get the dress altered,' said Emily.

She felt a stirring inside her. Could she do it? She was a fairly confident seamstress, but she'd never tackled anything as important as a wedding dress before. To make a good job of it, she'd have to unpick the bodice panels and the lining and realign them perfectly. What if she messed it up, or pricked her finger and bled on it?

Merry dropped her head, her chin starting to wobble. 'There isn't time, I get married in five days and I'm going to look like I'm wearing a sack.'

'I'll do it,' said Emily, feeling a bit sweaty as soon as the words had left her mouth. 'I can sew.'

Merry's jaw dropped. 'Do you mean it?'

Emily nodded. 'I'd need to start tomorrow though, to give myself enough time.'

Merry fired herself across the room and threw her arms around her sister. 'Thank you! Oh my Lord, the relief.'

'Well played, Emily,' said Nell, grinning at her. 'Have you made a wedding dress?'

Emily's stomach swirled with doubt mixed with pride and she laughed nervously. 'Not exactly.' She pulled a face. 'The last thing I made was a bear costume – in fact, make that ten bear costumes for the school panto.'

There was a beat of silence and then the three of them burst into laughter, which was on the verge of turning hysterical in Merry's case when there was a frantic knock at the door.

'Merry? Can I come in?'

'Cole, no!' Merry yelped and dived back behind the wardrobe door and started peeling off the dress. 'Absolutely not.'

Nell ran to the door and opened it a tiny crack. 'You can't come in, she's got her wedding dress on, it's bad luck.'

'Lydia's here,' said Cole darkly. 'She can't find Harley. He's gone missing.'

'Harley?' Merry slammed the wardrobe door shut and appeared wearing just her underwear. 'Oh no!'

'Bloody hell!' Nell flung open the bedroom door. 'Oh my God, Lydia! What's happened?'

'I'm so sorry to barge in.' A woman in a thick coat, breathless with panic, her face as pale as snow, appeared beside Cole. Downstairs, the music had been switched off and everyone had gone silent.

'Lydia thought he might be here,' said Cole grimly.

Nell threw Merry the dressing gown which had been balled up on the end of the bed and she pulled it on, shaking her head. 'I wish he was. Oh Lydia, I'm so sorry.'

'He's never done anything like this before, never,' Lydia said, rubbing her arms to stop herself from shivering.

'I'm calling the police,' Cole muttered, taking his phone out of his pocket.

'My stepson is fourteen,' Nell intervened, 'he didn't come home straight after school once and his mother called the police. Max was mortified and it made the situation far worse.'

'Cole, didn't you and Hester run away because your parents wouldn't let you stay up late at Hallowe'en?' Merry said softly. 'You must have been around the same age as Harley then.'

A frown creased Cole's brow. 'But we only went as far as McDonald's and changed our minds. We can't have been gone for more than half an hour. How long has Harley been missing?'

Lydia went bright red. 'An hour? Maybe a bit more?'

'Teenagers often act in haste,' said Emily. 'Perhaps something upset him, and he needed to let off steam. Maybe give him a bit longer?'

'He's only thirteen!' Lydia wailed. 'He's out on a winter's night. It's freezing and he didn't take a coat and he's not answering his phone.'

'Where's Freya?' Merry asked.

'I left her at home with . . . with . . .' Lydia stuttered. 'I left her with Ady. Just in case he comes back and doesn't have a key.'

'Ady?' Cole stared at her.

'My new boyfriend.' Lydia cast her eyes down to the floor. 'I introduced him to the kids for the first time tonight. Freya liked him, but I'm not sure about Harley.'

Just then, Cole's phone rang. He looked at the screen. 'Unknown number. Hello? Cole Robinson?'

Everyone held their breath, hoping for good news.

'Is it him?' Lydia said impatiently. Cole shook his head grimly.

'Right. Yeah, of course. Sorry about that. I'll sort it in the morning.' Cole hung up and looked at Merry. 'That was the wedding photographer.'

Merry groaned and covered her face with her hands. 'The deposit. Oh God, I was supposed to pay it today and I was so busy, I—'

'For Christ's sake, Merry, you had one job. Anyway, it doesn't matter now,' said Cole, and he turned away from her. 'Let's focus on Harley.'

'I'm sorry,' Merry swiped at her eyes as tears began to fall. 'This is a nightmare.'

Emily went to her, wishing there was something she could do, and put an arm on her sister's shoulders. 'You said he was unhappy, Merry,' she said softly. 'You were right to be worried.'

The room fell deathly silent, and everyone stared at Emily and then at Merry.

'What do you mean?' Lydia demanded, her eyes narrowing. 'Unhappy about what?'

Merry closed her eyes. 'Oh shit.'

Emily went cold. Had she spoken out of turn? 'I'm sorry if I—'

Lydia turned to Cole; her face stricken. 'Harley told Merry he was unhappy?'

'Did he?' Cole's brow furrowed.

Merry nodded. 'When we went shopping for wedding outfits. He said he wished he was back in Whistler.'

Cole shook his head in disbelief. 'That was weeks ago, and you didn't think to say?'

Merry gulped. 'He asked me not to say anything. I'm sorry, I didn't know what to do.'

'Well, clearly not this!' Lydia spluttered.

'And Emily seems quite well informed, considering you were supposed to be keeping it a secret.' Cole glared at Merry, and Emily could have wept; she was horrified at what she had done.

'I thought he was OK now,' Merry pleaded. 'After seeing him in the choir, I thought things had settled down.'

'Except now our son has gone missing,' stated Lydia. 'So clearly he's not OK.'

'Enough, everyone!' Nell held her arms out. 'This isn't helping.'

'No,' said Cole in a steely voice. 'It certainly isn't. Right, Lydia, we'll go out and look for him. The shops, his friends, anywhere we can think of where he might go. I can't drive because I'll be over the limit. Paul hasn't been drinking so he could possibly help too.'

'What about me?' Merry asked, tears shimmering in her eyes. 'What can I do to help?'

'You've done quite enough,' Cole muttered, turning towards the stairs.

Merry gasped in shock.

Cole swore under his breath and turned back to her. 'Forgive me, that was uncalled for, sorry.'

'Yes, it was,' Nell's voice was icy. 'We'll stay here in case Harley turns up. You go.'

Cole nodded, shot a last apologetic look at Merry and left.

Nell wrapped her arms around Merry as she dissolved into tears. Emily watched them for a moment, feeling sick with remorse and not knowing how to make it right. Neither of them seemed aware that she was still there, so she slipped downstairs and found Will.

He took one look at her and drew her into her arms. 'I've heard what's happened, but I'm sure he'll be OK.'

'I hope so. I tried to help, but I made things much worse.' She was shivering and her teeth were starting to chatter. 'Merry must hate me.'

Will frowned. 'That doesn't seem very likely.'

She felt as if her insides had been hollowed out with a spoon. 'I'm not wanted here. Not now. I've messed it up, Will. It's all ruined. Let's go home.'

Chapter Thirty-Six

Merry

The party was over. Cesca and Fliss and their families left straight away, leaving me with Astrid, Fred, Nell and Olek. As soon as I could, I slipped out through the back door, cutting myself off from the activity inside Holly Cottage: the speculation, the pacing and the cups of tea being poured and abandoned. I stepped out into the freezing velvet night, grateful for the hit of icy air. Pools of light from the windows cast a glow on the lawn, but the trees that encircled the garden on all sides felt eerily threatening in the dark.

I was frantic with worry and sick with guilt. I couldn't even sit down without wanting to jump up again immediately. Goodness only knew how poor Lydia must be feeling.

At one point earlier, I had thought that the party could become an annual pre-Christmas event. But no one was going to want to repeat this experience; it was going to be memorable for all the wrong reasons.

Poor Harley. He must have felt desperate, to do something like this. I knew I was partly to blame for this disaster, and I could have kicked myself for not sharing my concerns about Harley's state of mind with Cole. If I hadn't kept quiet, perhaps this nightmare might have been avoided.

I wrapped my arms around myself, regretting not bringing a coat, and looked up to the stars, breathing in and out, grounding myself, forcing myself to keep calm, not to panic.

The frosty grass crunched under my feet, my breath crystallised in front of my face and I felt the chilled air against my hot cheeks. Tonight was not the night to be outside for long without warm clothing. I hoped Harley was all right; Lydia had said he hadn't taken a coat, he must be freezing.

Where are you, Harley? Where did you run to?

I wished there was something more useful I could be doing. I knew it was sensible for me to stay in case Harley turned up. But it felt as if Cole and Lydia were on one team, and I was on the other. I supposed that was what step-parenting was. It wasn't a popularity contest, Cole and Lydia had every right to deal with this together. Nevertheless, it stung. I'd always be a third wheel where the children were concerned.

I squeezed my eyes shut; annoyed with myself for letting in such negative thoughts. I could hardly blame Cole for his actions, I hadn't exactly covered myself with glory. I'd let everyone down, mostly Harley. That day when he'd opened up to me, I'd listened, but I hadn't tried to help. I thought back to last weekend, when he'd sung his heart out at the Springwood House Christmas Fair. That perfect, pure voice. He'd sung with such warmth and charm. I was sure he'd found his niche, his way back into the social side of school. Which just went to prove that I knew nothing; happy kids didn't run away, did they?

And Cole. My face burned as I remembered the look of disappointment on his face. Now he thought I was the sort of woman to keep secrets from her partner. How could I repair the damage I'd done? I wanted to make a success of my relationship with his children. I loved them, but loving them wasn't enough, I needed to find a balance between being their friend and being the responsible adult. And I needed Cole's help for that.

Poor Freya, I imagined her brown eyes wide with worry, alone in the house with only Ady for company, she'd be finding this terrifying. Lydia must really like this new guy to have left Freya in his care, either that or she'd felt she had no choice.

And, then there was Emily. I groaned at the memory of Emily's devastated face when I'd muttered 'Thanks, Emily' under my breath. I should have reassured her, told her that if anyone was at fault, it was me. But in all the drama, by the time I tried to find her, she'd gone home.

My phone, which hadn't left my hand since Cole left, buzzed into life and my heart leapt into my throat. A text from Emily:

Merry, I am mortified for causing trouble for you. I am so so sorry. If there's anything I can do to put this right, I will. I'm sending you my love and am keeping Harley in my thoughts. Please let me know if you hear anything, no matter how late it is. For what it's worth, I think you did the right thing, keeping Harley's secret. I am on your side. I will always be on your side. Your sister Emily xx

My sister. I swallowed a sob; it was such a generous message after the way I had treated her. And that vote of support meant the world to me.

Thank you. It is me who should be apologising; none of this is your fault. I'll keep you posted, I promise. Thank you for being on my side, it was a bit lonely over here. Lots of love xxx

I pressed send and then checked my messages from Cole just in case I'd missed an update, but the screen remained reproachfully blank.

Then I scrolled to Harley's name and chewed the inside of my cheek. I knew he wouldn't reply if I sent him a text, but at least he'd know I cared.

Hey, dude. I know you want to be on your own right now, but everyone's worried about you. Just send me an emoji – any will do – so I know you're OK. Merry xx

I pressed send and then I refolded my arms to retain as much body heat as possible and took a step off the cold grass onto the path.

A noise reached me from the bottom of the garden: a muffled buzz like the sound of a phone receiving a message. No! Could it be...? I looked up and a flicker of light caught my eye. A small, hunched shape on the bench came into focus.

'Harley?' I gasped, stumbling towards him. 'Oh my God, Harley! There you are.'

And then I was beside him, the damp wood of the bench scraping my legs. I threw my arms around his thin body and held him tight, rocking him from side to side as he sobbed and sobbed into my neck.

'Thank you, thank you, thank you,' I whispered. 'I'm so glad you're safe.'

'I'm sorry,' he wept. 'I'm sorry to ruin your party.'

'Don't worry about that,' I said, half sobbing, half laughing. 'You have no idea how pleased I am to see you.' I fumbled at my phone, my hands shaking so much I could hardly input my code to unlock the screen. 'I need to tell your dad.'

'No.' He gripped my arms, his eyes wide. 'Not just yet.'

'Harley, I have to,' I said, kind but firm. 'Your mum is out of her mind and if they don't find you soon, they're going to call the police.'

He pressed his palms into his eyes and groaned. 'I'm going to be in such trouble.'

I didn't reply, I just kept one arm tight around him while I called Cole, who answered on the first ring.

'Still no sign of him,' Cole said grimly. 'We've driven all around school and up to the park.'

'He's here,' I blurted out. 'I've got him, he's safe.'

Cole gave an anguished moan. 'Oh, thank God.'

'Is he home? Is he OK?' Lydia demanded in the background.

'Come back to Holly Cottage, Cole,' I said. 'Your boy is safe.'

I could already hear the car screeching to a halt before we ended the call.

I set the phone on the bench and wrapped my arms around Harley again. Despite Lydia's worries, he was wrapped up in a thick down gilet over the top of his hoodie. I'd take him inside soon, but instinct told me he needed to talk before being bombarded with questions from his worried-sick relatives.

'Your grandad is in the house, pacing up and down imagining the worst, you know.'

Harley hung his head. 'I didn't think anyone would even notice I'd gone. Mum was too busy flirting with Ady.'

'Of course she noticed. You're precious to her.'

'You mean her boyfriend is,' he grunted darkly.

'Give him a chance,' I said, although I felt for Harley too; there had been so much upheaval in his life, as if being a teenager wasn't tough enough. 'It's scary meeting someone's kids. I've been in his shoes. You know that you need to pass the "kid test" if you've got any chance of ever being invited back. I was petrified when I first met you and Freya.'

He frowned. 'You didn't act scared. You were happy and smiley.'

I snorted. 'Maybe, but I'd been to the loo about ten times before your dad brought you to our hotel.'

It had been Easter time. Cole and I had flown out to Canada for a few days so we could all get to know each other. I lost about half a stone that week with nerves. I hadn't eaten much then either, I remembered, thinking back to the loose fit of my wedding dress.

'I didn't mind him at first,' Harley muttered. 'But after dinner I went into the kitchen to get a drink and they were all over each other, kissing. He had his hands on her . . . Ugh, gross.' He pulled a face and shuddered. 'I don't even want to think about it.'

I suppressed a smile, knowing he wouldn't appreciate me finding it funny. 'Adults do kiss sometimes, you know. And I bet they were embarrassed when you caught them.'

He shook his head slowly. 'They didn't even notice me.'

'Ah.' I winced. They must have been quite caught up with each other to have not noticed Harley glaring at them.

'I wanted to come to the party tonight, but Mum said no. I could have done the music or been the barman. I'd even have looked after the little kids.'

I blinked at him. 'I'd have loved you to come, you're always welcome, but it's your mum's weekend to have you.'

'Mum didn't care whether I was there or not,' he said, his face defiant and angry. 'It's Mum's turn, it's Dad's turn . . . When is it ever my turn? It's like being part of a game where everyone else gets a turn except me.

345

I'm sick of being ignored and not listened to. No one is interested in me.'

'Oh Harley.' I pushed my hand into his thick hair and brushed it off his face. 'I hear what you're saying and I'm sorry you feel that way. I know my opinion probably doesn't count for much, but I'm very interested in everything you do. You impress me a bit more every time I see you. The way you look out for Freya, the mature way you handle your problems.'

'Like running off, you mean.' He gave a bark of harsh laughter. 'Very mature.'

'I'll let you into a secret,' I said, leaning closer to his ear. 'Ask your dad and Auntie Hester about running away when they were your age.'

His eyes lit up with mischief. 'Seriously?'

'And I really do think you're mature, I was even thinking of offering you a Saturday job at Merry and Bright, just a few hours. But I'd have to clear it with your parents first.'

His brown eyes, so like his father's, widened. 'So then, I'd probably see Dad every Saturday. And you'd pay me?'

'If they agree,' I said. 'And I also need your help with something else. Your dad and I aren't supposed to be doing Christmas presents this year, but there's something I really want to get him, but I'm running out of time. Will you help? I'd have to give you my credit card.'

Harley looked sceptical. 'You trust me with your card?'

'Of course.' I scrolled on my phone until I found a picture. 'Something like this.'

A bubble of laughter escaped from him. 'No way.'

It was lovely to hear him laugh. 'Harley, it might not seem like it just now, but you are loved by so many people. But especially by your mum and dad.'

'They think I'm a kid,' he said, the smile falling from his face,

'We-ll.' I raised my eyebrows. 'You know being a kid isn't such a bad thing. Because although you might feel like you don't have much control over stuff, you also have your parents and other people in your family to lean on and learn from. And even when you're an adult and you leave home, we'll still be there cheering you on.'

He looked at me for a long moment. 'I guess you didn't have that, did you?'

I shook my head. 'I had to grow up quite quickly. I don't recommend it.'

'But you've found your dad now. That's cool.'

'Very cool,' I agreed. 'A bit like my bare legs out here in the freezing cold.'

'Oh sorry.' He unzipped his gilet and put it over my knees.

'Thanks.' I grinned. 'But I was sort of hoping we could go in.'

'In a minute.' He bit his lip. 'I just want to say I'm sorry I said no to performing at the wedding.'

'You've changed your mind?' My mind rushed ahead, imagining everyone clutching tissues and singing Harley's praises. It would add even more emotion to the day.

He shook his head. 'I'd be too nervous.'

'But you sang a solo in front of everyone at the Christmas Fair,' I said, disappointed. 'And you were brilliant at it.'

He shrugged. 'I know. But that was OK because they were strangers. Well, they were supposed to be strangers. If I'd known you were going to be there, I wouldn't have done it. Singing is a new thing, I'm not ready to share it yet.'

'I understand,' I said, giving him a hug. 'But maybe you could be in charge of the music in the registry office for us? We're taking our own speaker.'

'Cool,' said Harley with a grin.

'Harley Robinson!' Cole's voice reached us from the top of the garden, startling us both.

'Dad!' Harley sprung up, his voice breathy with nerves.

'Come here.' Cole opened his arms and Harley bounded into them. He grabbed his son's head and pressed loud kisses to his forehead. Normally, Harley would wriggle away, but tonight he buried his head in his dad's chest.

'Sorry for worrying everyone.'

'That's OK, son.' Cole ruffled his hair. 'And will you accept my apology too? I should have listened more, noticed more and I'm going to try to do better. But running away is never the answer.'

'And you should know,' Harley said, looking at me with a conspiratorial smile.

Cole frowned. 'I don't—'

'Apology accepted,' Harley interrupted.

Cole blew out a breath. 'I've got to the age of thirty-eight without a single grey hair and now I could well have gone totally white in the space of an hour.'

Harley scoffed. 'Sorry to break it to you, old man, but you've got loads of grey ones at the back.'

'What?' Cole's hand flew to the back of his head in absolute horror. 'You're kidding.'

'Don't worry, darling, it's distinguished,' I said, my eyes dancing with humour.

'Ah, well, goodbye youth. Listen, mate, your mum and I have been talking. We don't know all the answers, but we want to get it right. You're growing up and we need to start giving you more independence.'

'So can I get a Saturday job?' Harley jumped in quickly. 'With Merry, she's offered me one?'

'On the condition that you and Lydia agree,' I said, shrinking back into the bench. *Nice one, Merry, interfering again.*

'Er.' Cole scratched his head. 'Let's talk about that tomorrow; there are other things to sort out tonight.'

Harley's shoulders slumped. 'Here we go.'

'I just want you to know how much I love you, son,' Cole said, tilting Harley's chin up so he could look him in the eye. 'You've been through a lot of changes over the last few years and I'm very proud of you. But if there is anything, *anything* at all, that's bothering you, please trust me with it, OK? Because you and Freya and Merry' – he looked at me over Harley's shoulder – 'are the most important people in my world. If you're not happy, then neither am I, OK?'

Harley didn't say a word, he just leaned into his dad and wept, his thin shoulders heaving with sobs.

'OK?' Cole repeated, his own voice breaking.

'OK.'

'Good.' Cole held him at arm's length. 'And now that's out of the way, I think there's someone you need to say sorry to.'

'Mum?' Harley asked, looking nervously over his shoulder to the house. 'Is she here?'

Lydia stepped from the shadows and raised her hand. 'I am. Thank you, Merry, thanks for doing what you did and I'm sorry for what I said earlier. I was out of order.'

'Already forgotten,' I said with relief. 'And I'm sorry too. I've still got a lot to learn about kids.'

Lydia and I smiled at each other across the garden and then she extended her arms. 'And now I need a big hug from my son.'

349

Harley was across the garden in seconds and in his mum's arms and together they went into the house.

Cole and I looked at each other, both of us brimming with emotion.

'I should have told you,' I said. I got up from the damp bench, quickly putting on Harley's gilet that I'd had across my knees. 'But he made me promise. I didn't want to break his trust.'

'Darling, I'm so sorry,' he said, sweeping me into his arms. 'The way I spoke to you earlier was unforgivable.'

I shook my head. 'Under the circumstances, I—'

'No,' he said firmly. 'No. You deserve my trust and my faith. Lydia and I are grateful that he felt he could confide in you. She's feeling wretched about what happened; she thinks he might have seen her kissing this new bloke.'

I winced. 'He did.'

He nodded. 'That's what was behind this whole escapade. Nothing else. So whatever he told you didn't cause this.' He waited a beat and I knew what he was asking.

'He's missing Canada,' I said, wrapping my arms around his neck. 'And the old life he's come back to has moved on without him and he feels like he doesn't fit in. Although I think singing might be helping. But tonight he told me something else and I think you should know about it.'

'OK.'

Cole listened intently while I told him what Harley had said about his parents taking turns and how that made him feel.

'Poor kid.' Cole tutted sadly. 'It's obvious when he puts it like that. How can I have been a parent for over thirteen years and still be making mistakes?'

I shrugged. 'Because that's how we grow. Because failure is part of success. And, I guess, kids change all the time, which means their problems change too.'

'That is profound.' He nodded thoughtfully before lowering his lips to mine.

'Apparently exposing your brain to extreme cold makes you say clever things,' I said, pulling his shirt out of his trousers and slipping my freezing fingers into the warmth. 'Which might explain it.'

Cole sucked in a breath as my fingers found his skin.

'You're incredible, Merry Shaw. From now on, I'm going to be involving you in decisions about the kids more. You're more perceptive than me, and I know you love them too.' His breath was warm against my lips. 'And I love you, more than I could ever have imagined.'

'You see,' I said, my breath catching, as he snuggled in as close as he could, closing the space between us. 'You're getting smarter by the second.'

Chapter Thirty-Seven

Emily

'I love your cottage,' said Merry the following afternoon, after Emily had given her a tour of the downstairs of her cottage. 'I knew I would.'

'Thank you,' Emily beamed.

It was a 'pinch me' moment. A sister to share secrets with and hang out with. Also . . . she gulped . . . unpick the seams of her wedding dress and mess about with it days before the big day.

'Come on, you can get changed in my room,' she said, leading Merry up the staircase.

'What a pretty room.' Merry made straight for the dressing table and examined Emily's collection of perfumes. 'It's very you.'

'Pink, you mean.' Emily smiled. 'So, tell me everything. How are things with Harley now?'

Merry sat down on Emily's bed and unzipped her boots while she filled her in on the chat she and Cole had had with Harley and Lydia late last night.

'We've agreed that he's going to work for me on Saturday mornings from January for a few hours,' said Merry, 'and from now on, his parents are going to be more flexible with weekend arrangements and check that he and Freya are happy to go where they are sent.'

'So it sounds like you did the right thing after all, by not betraying Harley's secret.' Emily removed the wedding dress from Merry's bag and shook it out to get rid of the creases. 'I told you so.'

'You did,' said Merry, tugging at her boot. 'Knowing you were on my side really cheered me up.'

'Of course I am,' said Emily staunchly. 'I spend every day with young people. I know how demoralised and powerless they feel when they're not being listened to. You were there for Harley when he needed you. If you'd gone running to Cole, he'd never have trusted you again. Your instincts were spot on, you're a great parent.'

Merry's face lit up. 'That's the nicest thing you could have said, thank you. I've struggled to find my role in the family, but now I feel more confident about being a stepmum. Anyway, all's well that ends well. And apologies to you, again. I can only imagine how you must have felt after the party last night.' Merry winced. 'I felt awful about it.'

Devastated, thought Emily. She had barely said a word as Will drove them home. Then they had sat on her sofa, in front of the log fire with only the glow of the flames and the twinkle of the Christmas tree lights to see by. It should have been romantic, but Emily had been too distraught to take advantage of the mood. When Merry had texted her late last night with an update about Harley, Emily had wept with relief into Will's shirt.

'Nothing to apologise for,' Emily insisted. 'It was a horrible situation, everyone was tense, and I should have kept my mouth shut. Here, let me help.'

She took hold of the heel of Merry's boot, tugged a bit too hard and toppled backwards onto her bottom.

'You OK?' Merry pressed her lips together trying not to laugh.

'Aren't you glad you've got such a cool sister,' she said, pulling a face.

'Aren't *you*?' Merry replied with a snort, wiggling her toes in Emily's face to display her fluffy socks which had sloths all over them.

Emily's heart soared; she adored this woman so much.

'It wasn't your fault,' Merry continued. 'I should have told you that Harley didn't want his parents to know. If I'd thought for one second that it would have come up in conversation, I would have.'

'Listen,' Emily said, pulling off the other boot, using less force this time. 'We're new to this. From what I know of sibling relationships, they are rarely a smooth ride. We've just had our first bump, that's all.'

'You're right.' Merry nodded. 'Let's put it behind us.'

'Agreed,' said Emily. 'Like the new bruise on my bum.'

The two sisters laughed, and Emily was overjoyed that they were back on track again. 'The most important thing now is to get you to the registry office on time, and in a dress that clings in all the right places.'

'I've brought my wedding underwear too,' said Merry, unfolding some white tissue paper and lifting out a lace body. 'So we can get the fit right.'

Emily touched the delicate fabric. 'Good idea, the boning in this will probably make you look even slimmer.'

Merry started to slip her bra straps over her shoulders. 'Could you, er . . . turn away?'

'Oh gosh, of course.' Emily darted out of the room and closed the bedroom door to give Merry some privacy. She should probably have done that right from the start, she thought, cringing at herself. What sort of weirdo hung around when someone was trying to get changed?

'Ems?' Merry called. 'Can you help do me up?'

'Sure!' she said, opening the door again, relieved to be useful after all, and making quick work of the row of mother-of-pearl buttons at the back of the dress. 'OK, you're ready.'

As the two of them made their way downstairs, there was a knock at the door.

'I bet that's Will, he must have forgotten something,' Emily said, running down the rest of the stairs.

The front door opened straight into the living room, where she'd set up her sewing equipment. She opened the door and gasped. 'Mum!'

Emily held her breath for a few seconds, time seemed to stand still. Tina was the last person she'd expected to see. She'd kept her mum updated, telling her as much as she thought she ought to know, always conscious that discovering Merry's existence hadn't been the joyful event for Tina that it had been for her. She felt a rush of panic and she glanced from Tina to Merry, unsure how this was going to go.

'Hello, love.' Tina stood on the doorstep, her sewing box in one hand and a cake tin in the other, her eyes bright with nerves. 'I thought you might need a spare pair of hands.'

'Oh, um, thank you.' Emily let out the breath she'd been holding with a shaky smile.

'Tina!' Merry hurried down the rest of the stairs and threw her arms around the older woman's neck. 'Emily has told me so much about you, I am so thrilled to meet you, and yes to an extra pair of hands, the more, the merrier. No pun intended.'

Emily breathed a sigh of relief as Tina returned Merry's hug. 'You've met before remember, in the market.'

'Of course I remember,' Tina said, stepping into the room. She handed Emily the cake tin and unwound her scarf. 'And I made a silly comment about your mum being at your hen party. I've been cursing myself ever since Emily told me that she'd passed away. I'm sorry, Merry.'

'You weren't to know,' said Merry kindly, a big smile on her face. 'And thank you for coming, I'm really touched.'

'Me too.' Emily puffed her cheeks out and exhaled. 'I think yours is the first wedding dress I've even touched, let alone tried to alter. What do you think of the dress, Mum?'

'Give me a minute,' Tina replied softly, her eyes still on Merry. 'I want a proper look at the bride first.'

Emily gazed at her mum, knowing how much it would have cost her to come today. How meeting Merry would rewrite the memories Tina had of her and Ray's relationship. And yet here she was, lending her support, building bridges, and Emily knew it was all for her.

Merry obliged good-naturedly, holding her arms out and doing a twirl.

'Well.' Tina shook her head, her eyes glistening with tears. 'If you two aren't just peas in a pod. There's no mistaking that you're sisters. I'll say something for Ray Meadows, he makes beautiful children. Now come on, ladies, let's crack on. Emily, you start pinning, I'll get the kettle on.'

Tina marched off to the kitchen with her cake tin, leaving Emily and Merry staring at each other open-mouthed.

'I called her this morning to ask her advice on what sort of thread to use with vintage silk,' Emily whispered. 'I had no idea she'd turn up. I hope it's not going to make it awkward for you?'

Merry shook her head. 'Things are only awkward if you make them so. I love you, so it stands to reason that I'll love your mum too.'

'That's probably the nicest thing anyone's ever said to me.'

Five minutes later, Merry was standing as still as a statue while Emily examined all the darts around the bodice of the dress, wondering how best to tackle the alterations.

Tina came in with a loaded tray. 'I must say, that really is a beautiful dress.'

'Isn't it just,' said Emily, making space on the little table for the tray. 'And it'll be even more gorgeous when we've finished with it. I think we might be able to get away with just taking in each of the darts.'

'I'm so grateful to the two of you.' Merry plucked at the spare fabric around her torso. 'There's no way I could have got it altered in time if Emily hadn't offered. You're lifesavers.'

'Oh goodness.' Tina flapped a hand, embarrassed by the compliment. 'Let's save the thanks until we've done a good job, shall we? Right. Emily, you pour the coffee, while I look at what's going on around this bodice. If you could stand with your arms slightly away from your body, love.'

While Merry did as she was told, Emily glanced at the tray her mum had prepared: her best mugs, a cafetière of fresh coffee, despite Tina preferring instant, and a plate of home-made chocolate cookies, fanned out in a perfect circle.

'Wow, Merry!' Emily grinned. 'You're getting the star treatment today. Nice coffee and Mum's legendary cookies. You are honoured.'

'Oh shush, you madam,' Tina said, going a bit pink. 'This is a pre-wedding celebration. You can't drink coffee

357

out of any old mug while you're wearing a beautiful gown like this.'

'Think of it as a practice run for your wedding,' said Merry, taking a biscuit from Emily. She bit into it daintily, taking care not to let any crumbs fall on her dress. 'Maybe Tina will be making your dress from scratch.'

Emily gave a snort. 'Mum's sewing scissors will be blunt by the time I get around to marriage.'

Merry smirked. 'Oh, I don't know, you and Will seemed very cosy at the party.'

'Did they?' Tina looked up from pinning darts at the back of Merry's dress. 'I think I need to meet this young man.'

'Maybe.' Emily gave her mum a stern look. 'But only if you promise not to grill him about his job prospects.'

Tina chuckled. 'Deal. Although I can't speak for Ian, he'll be asking him about his golf handicap before the poor boy has even sat down.'

'You'll adore him, Tina,' said Merry. 'I can't imagine anyone not liking him.'

'There's lots to like,' Emily admitted, thinking of how wonderful he'd been last night, so supportive and kind. 'But I'm not sure it will last. Will's a free spirit. His first love is surfing, and he plans to spend as much of next year living by the sea as he can. Having a girlfriend in landlocked Derbyshire won't really fit into that lifestyle. And I'm too much of a home bird to do that.'

'Home doesn't have to be a place,' said Merry. 'It can be a person. When I met Cole, it felt like coming home. Now my home is wherever we are.'

Tina sighed dreamily. 'How romantic.'

Emily processed that; Merry was right. Perhaps she was putting up unnecessary barriers. 'I suppose if you both want something enough, you work to make it happen.'

'It's early days. He might decide that you're more important than a surfboard,' said Tina soothingly, but her smile didn't quite reach her eyes.

'Is that what you hoped for you and Dad?' asked Emily with a flash of perception. 'That he'd change for you?'

Tina chewed her lip and shot a nervous look at Merry as if she wasn't sure how much she should say. 'I suppose I did, but your father was never one for settling in one place for long. But I'm sure Will is a very different man. He's got a steady job for one thing. I lost track of the number of jobs Ray had.'

'Do you mind me asking about him?' Merry enquired. 'I've got so much to learn. What sort of person is he?'

Tina handed the box of dress pins to Emily and picked up her coffee cup.

'Ray's a good man, handsome, funny, never a dull moment when he was around,' she began. 'But troubled. I didn't meet his parents, but I think that was where a lot of his problems stemmed from.'

'You said once that they'd kicked him out when he was a teenager,' said Emily, through a mouthful of pins.

'They rejected him.' Tina sipped her coffee. 'He'd had mental health problems from childhood and they had no patience with what they termed his "anger issues". Consequently, your dad never felt good enough for anyone. When I first told him I loved him, he disappeared, and I didn't see him for two days. I thought it was over. I thought I'd ruined it by telling him how I felt. When he came back, he was full of apologies but told me he didn't deserve me, didn't deserve good people in his life.'

'He still says that now,' said Emily sadly.

'And my mum had rejected him too.' Merry sighed. 'Poor man.'

'As I say, he's a good man deep down, but he won't let people get close to him. As soon as people started to care about him, he'd run away.' Tina reached her hand out to Emily and squeezed it. 'But at least he's let you in now.'

'Finally,' said Emily. 'And maybe only because he knew it was now or never, with his memory starting to let him down.'

'I'm hoping he'll let me in too,' said Merry. 'I mean, he hasn't slammed the door in my face since that first meeting, so I must be doing something right.'

Emily and Merry swapped smiles at the memory.

'And how is your dad?' Tina asked, finishing her coffee and picking up her pins again.

Before Emily had a chance to formulate a response, Merry jumped in.

'Grumpy this morning,' she mused fondly. 'Said he'd been down to breakfast and was surrounded by women, blathering on at him.'

Tina huffed. 'That sounds like him. Even with his memory giving him gyp, he's still a hit with the ladies. Always was.'

'You were there today?' Emily asked, unable to keep the surprise out of her voice. She didn't know why, but she felt put out, as if Merry was somehow usurping her position as her dad's main visitor.

Merry nodded. 'I've been every day this week. But only briefly this morning. I took him a few sausage rolls left over from the party. You said he likes them. Did you hear about him getting in trouble?'

'No?' Emily said, feeling wrong-footed. 'Nobody told me.'

'It's nothing serious,' Merry reassured her. 'In fact, it's quite funny. The home has had a skip delivered round the back to get rid of some garden waste. Apparently, Dad was caught throwing cushions from the communal lounge into it. Every time he was on his own, he'd open the window and throw one out. Then he's being going out in the garden, collecting them up and sticking them in the skip. Gail asked him why he'd done it and he said they smelled of wee.'

'Cheeky old rascal,' Tina laughed, shaking her head.

'He never did!' Emily exclaimed.

She looked at Merry's face and saw the amusement in her eyes and the warmth in her smile and her heart squeezed with love. A bubble of laughter rose inside her, and she brushed away her silly jealous thoughts. Emily had wanted someone to share Ray's care with, she wasn't going to be territorial about him now that it had finally happened. Ray would enjoy seeing a new face, Merry was getting to know the father she had only just been reunited with and Emily, well, she had someone to talk to, to bounce thoughts and feelings off. Everyone was a winner.

'I think it's incredible that you've managed to visit him every day this week,' remarked Tina, shaking her head.

'Excuse me, so have I,' Emily said mock-pointedly. 'And I've been doing so for months, even before he moved into Springwood House.'

'Yes, but Merry's running a business and in the throes of wedding planning.'

'Merry's running a business, blah blah blah,' Emily mimicked, rolling her eyes and making Merry laugh.

'Oh give over,' said Tina, passing the tape measure over the dress to check Emily had made both back bodice panels equal. 'It must be bittersweet for you, Merry love, I guess, making contact with your father, only to find his memory fading.'

'I prefer to think of it as just sweet,' Merry replied, lifting her arm up so that Emily could get at the seam of her sleeve. 'I feel blessed to have this time with my dad. I can't do anything about the past, but I can be here now, getting to know him and Emily. I want to find out as much about my mum from him as I can. I've got family of my own now, rather than just marrying into Cole's family. Actual blood relatives. I can't tell you how much that has changed my life.'

'Mine too,' said Emily, gazing at her sister with love.

'That's a healthy way of looking at it,' noted Tina, placing her hands softly on both women. 'And I know I'm not a blood relative, but sometimes a girl needs a mother figure. And if you and my Emily are going to be close, then it stands to reason that that mother figure could be me. If you like, that is?'

Emily held her breath, waiting for Merry's reaction; she couldn't imagine what her life must have been like without a loving mother to guide her, inspire her and show her what love looked like. Tina had tears in her eyes and, in that moment, Emily had never loved her mum more.

'Really?' Merry's voice was faint as she looked from Tina to Emily. 'I'm . . . Gosh . . . I don't know what to say.'

'You don't need to say anything.' Tina hugged her tenderly, pressing her cheek against Merry's. 'Just remember where I am if you need me.'

Merry blinked at Emily unsurely. 'Would that be OK with you?'

Emily swallowed the lump in her throat and nodded. 'Of course, as the saying goes: a candle loses nothing by lighting another candle.'

Merry's eyes brimmed with tears. 'I'm so happy. Thank you.'

'Oh dear,' Tina sniffed. 'There's something in my eye.'

'Me too,' Emily said, laughing even as tears fell onto her cheeks. She handed round the tissues. 'But we haven't got time for all this sentimentality, we've got a dress to finish.'

'And we will,' said Tina. 'But, Emily, do me a favour, when it to comes to your wedding, do not leave alterations until the eleventh hour like your sister. I'm getting too old for this stress.'

'Come off it, Mum,' Emily teased. 'You're loving the drama.'

Tina giggled. 'It is exciting, I must admit.'

'It already feels a lot better,' Merry acknowledged.

'Can't have you looking like a waif and stray on your wedding day, can we,' said Emily, taking a step back to examine the dress.

Merry laughed. 'To be honest, I've had a lifetime of perfecting that look.'

'Oh, love,' sighed Tina, her brow furrowed in sympathy. 'That breaks my heart. I'm so sorry.'

'Me too,' added Emily, feeling her sister's pain.

Merry blinked at them both in surprise. 'But it wasn't your fault, either of you.'

'This isn't about blame,' said Tina briskly. 'This is about a little girl growing up alone without anyone to call her own.'

'You've got us now. Whether you like it or not,' remarked Emily, handing round more tissues.

'Absolutely,' Tina agreed. 'Family should be your safety net, especially when you're still growing up. This family failed you and I'm going to do everything I can to put it right. Starting with this.' She reached for her handbag, pulled out a small box and handed it to Merry. 'For your something borrowed.'

Emily peered over Merry's shoulder as she opened the lid to reveal a pair of pearl and gold earrings.

'Oh my goodness!' Merry's eyes widened.

'Mum, they're gorgeous!' Emily gasped, amazed that she hadn't seen them before.

'They belonged to my grandmother and then to my mother and eventually they'll belong to you, love,' said Tina, smiling at her daughter. 'I didn't think you'd mind Merry wearing them in between.'

'I love them.' Merry gave Tina a hug. 'And I'd be honoured to wear them.'

'OK, I think we're done,' noted Emily, replacing the lid on her pin tin.

'Why don't you go back upstairs and take off the dress,' said Tina to Merry. 'Emily can help you get out of it. Then I can get straight to work on unpicking the seams.'

'Work, don't remind me,' said Emily with a shudder as they left the room. 'Oh, I've just remembered, I'm on holiday, no work for two whole weeks! Yippee!'

Upstairs, Merry stood completely still with her arms out to the side so as not to catch herself on the pins, while Emily carefully unbuttoned her dress.

'That sounded like a bad case of the blues,' said Merry. 'Don't you like working at the school?'

'It's fine,' Emily sighed. 'It's a nice place to work, I've got a good boss and it's been the perfect job while I've had to juggle caring for Dad.'

'But?' Merry prompted.

'I'd like to do something more creative like you. But I haven't had the headspace to give it any thought. Dad has needed all of that.'

'You've got me to help with him now,' Merry reminded her. 'Besides, it's not selfish to put yourself on the agenda occasionally. Self-care means you *as well*, not you *instead*. What are you laughing at?'

Emily grinned. 'You. Giving me big-sister advice. I love it.'

'I am, aren't I!' Merry laughed. Her eyes lit up. 'Ooh, I've just had a brilliant idea. I need someone full-time to work with me at Merry and Bright. We could make it a family business. Imagine how cool that would be!'

'You're offering me a job?' Emily stared at her in surprise. 'That is really kind of you. But Merry and Bright is your dream and it's about time I started thinking about doing something for myself. Besides, you've got the ideal candidate right under your nose.'

Merry frowned. 'Have I?'

'Yes, Nell!' Emily said, laughing. 'I've never seen someone drop so many hints! Last night she was telling me how much she was looking forward to taking over the business while you're on honeymoon. I'm not sure I should tell you this, but she's got some great ideas on marketing and sales and even how to use the flat upstairs as part of the candle business.'

Merry looked bewildered. 'But . . . Nell has run her own show for years, I thought she'd be insulted if I offered her a job.'

Emily just smiled smugly and said nothing.

'Well. Thanks for the tip, I'm flabbergasted.' Merry gave herself a shake in surprise. 'But back to you, what's your dream job?'

Emily laughed. 'Will asked me that yesterday and I haven't been able to stop thinking about it. Something to do with vintage clothes, I think. It's just a hobby now, but that's my passion.'

'Merry and Bright started out as a hobby, remember,' said Merry, holding her hands. 'There's a saying about finding a job you love and then never having to work a day in your life.'

'That was Mark Twain,' said Emily absently. 'But I'm not sure if I could make a profit.'

'You definitely won't make a profit if you don't try. Do it,' urged Merry firmly. 'I mean it, just do it. What's the worst that can happen?'

'I make a total mess of it, make no money and have to go back to being a secretary feeling like a failure?'

'But it won't have been a failure because you'll have learned stuff along the way,' Merry argued. 'Look, next year is going to happen anyway, so you might as well spend it doing something you love. And if this time next year, you end up being a secretary again, at least you've had a stab at living the dream.'

Emily stared at her. 'I can't decide if that's the worst or the best career advice I've ever had in my life.'

Merry grinned. 'You're going to take it though, aren't you?'

'You know what?' said Emily, her mind whirring with possibilities. 'I think I might.'

Chapter Thirty-Eight

Emily

'You keep staring at me.' Emily gave Will a sideways look. 'I can feel your eyes on me.'

It was Christmas Eve, the day of the wedding, and she and Will were walking along the corridor towards her dad's room, hand in hand.

'Do I?' He smiled, all wide blue-eyed innocence. 'I can't help it. You look so beautiful.'

It was on the tip of her tongue to brush off the compliment, say something derogatory, like how her outfit hid a multitude of sins, but instead, she smiled, her heart bouncing with joy. 'Thank you, I feel beautiful.'

She'd found the vintage navy dress, tipped with pink and matching jacket (very Jackie O, the shop assistant had whispered) only yesterday. It had been a last-minute shopping trip with her mum, who Merry had invited to the wedding along with Emily's stepdad. Tina and Ian were busy this afternoon but would be joining them at Hester's house for the reception later. The wedding dress now fitted like a satin glove and Merry had cried when she'd seen her reflection. In fact, they all had. And although not completely pink, Emily thought her outfit would fit in perfectly with the bridesmaids' dresses.

'You scrub up nicely yourself.' Emily brushed a tiny piece of fluff from his borrowed suit jacket.

Will tugged at his shirt collar. 'I've only ever been to one wedding and it was on a beach in Cape Verde. We all wore shorts, including the bride and groom.'

They stopped outside her dad's room and faced each other. Emily ran her hands down his lapels, smoothing the fabric, which, she acknowledged to herself, was just another excuse to touch him.

'Right now,' she said, already worrying about the state of undress they were going to find her dad in, 'that sounds like the dream.'

Will's eyes flashed. 'I'll bear that in mind for future reference.'

Emily's hands curled around the back of his neck, and he stepped closer. 'So, do you think we have a future then?'

He held her gaze. 'For as long as you'll have me.'

Her heart swelled. The truth was that she was falling in love with this man. And yes, she'd only known him less than two months. But she couldn't imagine a future without him.

'I . . .' Emily interrupted herself with a gasp and laughed. 'I almost said I love you then. But it's too soon, isn't it?'

'Oh yes,' he said with mock seriousness. 'Far too soon. Wait until tomorrow morning at least. It can be my Christmas present.'

'Deal.' Happiness bubbled up inside her. And he was hers. Along with finding Merry, he was the best present she could wish for. 'Now all we need to do is get Dad to the church on time.'

Will kissed her. 'It'll be fine, I love a challenge.'

'It's only us,' she called, opening the door. 'Emily and Will.'

Her dad was in the bathroom drying his hands, dressed in trousers and a shirt. Good start.

'Don't let *him* in,' Ray grumbled, jerking his head towards Will. 'Always making me do daft stuff.'

Emily smiled, bemused, but pleased he knew who they both were today without prompting. 'What stuff?'

'We've been working on his balance,' Will explained. 'Walking in a straight line, standing on one leg, heel lifts. Have you been doing those exercises I told you about?' he asked Ray.

'What for? Not planning on entering the Olympics, am I?' Ray picked up the handset of his phone, sat down and pointed it at the TV like a remote control. 'Sit down, the pair of you, standing around like guests at a funeral.'

Will sat, but Emily grabbed a tie from the wardrobe and crouched in front of him. She tied it in a knot and smoothed down his shirt collar. His jaw, she noticed with a tut, was covered in patches of stubble.

'Dad! You promised you'd have a shave.'

Ray rubbed a hand over his chin. 'Had half a shave.'

Emily sighed and led him back to the bathroom. 'Today is a full-shave day.'

'Why?' He folded his arms across his chest.

'Because Merry is getting married.' Emily filled the sink with water, blobbed some shaving foam on his face and picked up his razor.

Ray peered at her. 'Little Merry? Getting married?'

She shook her head fondly. 'Yes, Dad. Only she's thirty-six now. And not so little.'

'I don't think so, love, I'm only thirty-five.'

'You're sixty-five. And very handsome with it.' Emily chewed her lip in concentration as she shaved the rest of her dad's face, grateful that he wasn't arguing.

'I was a handsome bugger,' he said absently. 'Who's she getting married to?'

'Cole. A nice man called Cole.'

Ray sniggered. 'His father a miner, was he, with a name like that?'

From the other room, Emily heard Will laugh.

'Not sure what he did. He makes candles now with Merry.'

'Old King Cole was a merry arsehole . . .' Ray sang loudly and then broke into a wheezy laugh.

'Dad, please do not sing that at the wedding!'

Will was guffawing now.

Emily had a lot of reservations about taking her dad to Merry's wedding. His behaviour was so unpredictable that she wouldn't be able to relax for a minute. But at the end of the day, Merry wanted him there, and so if Emily could make that happen, she would. Maybe by tomorrow Ray would have forgotten that he'd been to his daughter's wedding, but Merry wouldn't, and that was far more important. Mind you, she thought, if he shouted arsehole at any point in the service, nobody else would forget he'd been there either.

'You're done.' She handed her dad a towel to pat his face dry and ushered him out of the bathroom.

Will was ready with Ray's jacket and held it out to him, helping him with the sleeves.

'Let's go,' said Emily, 'before he tries to sit down again.'

Will nodded his head to Ray's feet. 'You're still wearing your slippers.'

Ray scratched his head. 'Now where did I put my shoes after I polished them?'

Emily scanned around the room. 'There, under the coffee table.'

Will knelt and retrieved a pair of black dress shoes covered in a thick layer of dried-on cream. 'Oh dear. What colour polish did you use?'

Ray shrugged. 'That one.' He pointed to a tube of something poking out from under the sofa.

Will reached down and picked it up and his shoulders started to shake with laughter as he showed Emily.

'Haemorrhoid cream?' she groaned. 'Dad! How are we going to get that off?'

Will was helpless with laughter, and it took him several attempts to get his words out. 'I should think that's the least of his worries. Where do you think he's put the shoe polish?'

Emily closed her eyes, trying to block out that particular image.

It only took a couple of minutes to clean the shoes with a damp cloth; Emily and Will decided not to look for the shoe polish.

'You look really smart, Dad.' Emily kissed his cheek. 'You're going to do Merry proud.'

'Little Merry?' He frowned.

Emily looped her arm through his and suppressed a sigh. 'That's the one. Let's go.'

Ray wouldn't budge. 'Where's my tin? I need my tin.'

'We need to go, Ray, or we'll end up missing the wedding altogether,' Will tried to cajole him.

Ray marched to his wardrobe and flung open the doors. 'It was in here, unless someone's stolen it. Taken all my money,' he chuntered.

They let him get on with it. They'd built in contingency time, and they'd still get there before the start of the service.

'I'm exhausted already,' Emily murmured, reaching for Will's hand.

He laced his fingers through hers and brought her hand to his lips. 'You're doing great.'

She'd never get bored of this, she thought. They didn't seem to be able to exist in the same room as each other without some sort of connection, a look, a brushing of fingers as they passed, sitting with legs entwined. She thought of this morning, waking beside him in the semi-darkness, watching him breathe, his golden lashes resting on his beautiful face. How she'd curled her body into him, sliding her leg over his, tracing circles on his lean stomach with her fingers, her cheek soft against his chest. If only every morning could start like that.

Merry's words had come back to her about home being a person rather than a place, about following her passion. And as she lay there, she'd come to a decision, and her heart had started to beat faster. It was time to start doing something for herself, making her own life a priority. She'd slipped out of bed, careful not to disturb Will, and before she had time to change her mind, typed an email to her boss. Subject line: resignation. She was going to leave her safe and steady job and do something which excited her. She'd still have to go back to school in the New Year and work her notice period until the end of January. But then . . . who knew? She'd give herself some time, to work out what she really wanted to do with her life. Because, as Merry had said, she'd never fulfil her dreams if she didn't even try.

There was a crash and clatter as Ray tipped the contents of the tin on the floor and sifted.

'Jackpot,' he said and then got to his feet, seemingly perfectly at ease with the chaos he'd left on the carpet behind him. He looked at them both and scowled. 'Come on then, what are we waiting for? We've got a wedding to get to.'

Emily bit her tongue and opened the door. 'And who's getting married, Dad, can you remember?'

'Your sister,' he said, stopping in front of her to pat her cheek. 'Thank you, love. For making this happen.'

Will took his arm and the two of them headed for the lift.

'No, Dad,' she whispered to herself, blinking back a tear. 'Thank you, for making it happen.'

Chapter Thirty-Nine

Merry

24 DECEMBER

'Woohoo! Let's get this wedding started!' Nell popped the cork on the chilled bottle of German Sekt that Astrid had brought with her, and we all held out our champagne flutes in anticipation.

Foam spilled out of the top and Cesca stepped in quickly with her glass to catch it.

'Merry, may the sun shine in your heart today and forever. Cherish the day, *meine Liebe*, you deserve it.' Astrid raised her glass. 'To our beautiful bride.'

Fliss, Nell and Cesca joined Astrid in toasting me and I did my best to hold back the tears.

So far, I was having a perfect day, and it looked as if Cole and I were to have a white wedding. Snow had been falling since first light, delicate gentle flakes as if the sky had judged it just right: enough to be pretty and dust the frozen ground with layer of sparkle, but not too heavy to make travelling to the registry office too treacherous. I could only imagine the excitement at Hester's house, where Cole and the kids had stayed last night.

'Thank you,' I said with a sniff. 'You're all lovely and I'm so lucky to have you here with me. I've always wondered what it would be like, getting ready on my wedding day without my mum. But I needn't have worried. I feel surrounded by love today.'

Fliss handed me a tissue from a box on the table. 'OK, everyone, no more making Merry cry, she doesn't want to greet Cole looking like a panda.'

I'd expected to wake up a bag of nerves. But I was oddly relaxed sitting at my kitchen table, in my dressing gown, soaking up the laughter and the happiness, the teasing and the little acts of kindness, and being warmed by the presence and love of my dearest friends. And now, with only a couple of hours until I'd be walking up the aisle towards Cole, I couldn't imagine a more joyful start to the day.

Nell wasn't dressed yet either. She had stayed with me last night. We'd watched a Christmas romcom, face masks on, with mugs of hot chocolate and a box of cherry liqueurs. We'd intended to have an early night, but neither of us could get to sleep and she ended up getting into bed with me and we'd lain in the dark reminiscing about the best and funniest memories we'd shared until eventually we'd drifted off to sleep.

Our dresses hung in the living room, where the fire had been lit and the Christmas tree shimmered and sparkled.

Astrid had been the first to arrive to get ready with us. She looked glamourous and striking in an evergreen satin dress with Swarovski crystals around the neckline. Her matching cape set her outfit off beautifully.

Finally, Cesca and Fliss had joined us with their magic bag of tricks. Astrid only wanted a natural look and I'd already had a practice run, so they knew what I wanted. Nell was happy to give them free rein.

'And I'd better go easy on the bubbles,' said Fliss, refusing a top-up. 'I want to get Merry's eyeliner straight before I have any more booze.'

She placed a mirror on the table in front of me and slipped a band around my hair to keep it off my face.

'Oh my God,' I said, seeing my pale face and wide eyes staring back at me in the mirror. 'I'm getting married. I can't believe it.'

'I can't believe how glowing your skin is,' said Fliss, dotting moisturiser onto my face. 'You're making my life very easy.'

'The only thing I can't believe is that no man has snapped you up before now,' remarked Nell, touching her glass to mine. 'Happy wedding day, Merry. Love you lots.'

'Ditto, best woman.' We smiled at each other, my best friend and I, connected by threads of friendship and laughter, ups and downs, weaving our lives into a patchwork of memories. 'Thank you for choosing to sit next to me on that first day in college and for every day since. And especially today.'

'Well, Nell is making *my* job very hard, with her thick wodge of auburn waves,' said Cesca, grappling to twist all her hair into a chignon. 'I'm going to need scaffolding to hold this lot up.'

'No offence taken,' said Nell dryly, which made us all laugh.

'Some sugar to keep up our energy levels,' Astrid prompted, producing a dish of fresh strawberries and some tiny sugar cookies from a container.

'Perfection,' I sighed, savouring the sweetness on my tongue while Fliss was rubbing blusher into the apples of my cheeks. 'Thank you, Fairy Godmother, providing just what I need before I even realise it.'

'*Bitte schön, mein Schatz.* Do you know, I am in my eighth decade, and I have never been a part of a bride's preparations? So thank *you*.' Astrid pressed a hand to my arm. 'Thank you for including me, this is a day I shall treasure forever.'

'You've been my cheerleader since I was a lost little teenager, fighting for my place in the world, and you were my inspiration,' I replied. 'I couldn't imagine doing this without you.'

'You guys.' Cesca pulled a tissue from her sleeve. 'All this mutual appreciation. I'm already in bits and Merry hasn't even got her dress on yet. OK, Nell, you're done. Do not make any sudden movements or the whole lot will come crashing down.'

'And you keep still too,' Fliss murmured, her tongue between her teeth. 'I'm doing your eyeliner.'

I closed my eyes and let the conversation wash over me.

'Wow, that looks amazing, sorry, Merry, but I think I'll be upstaging the bride,' Nell exclaimed.

'Don't worry,' Fliss whispered loudly into my ear. 'I'll cake her face with fake tan, there'll be no contest.'

'I might do my own make-up,' said Astrid. 'Just to be on the safe side.'

'I think we should do this again,' said Nell. 'A girls' weekend. Lounging around in robes, drinking champagne, being pampered.'

'Ooh yes!' Fliss gave a little moan of pleasure. 'A weekend of being able to go to the loo without being followed. Or have a bath and not have to get out because someone's demanding snacks.'

'I can't guarantee that,' Cesca sniggered.

'Yes!' I agreed once Fliss's hand had moved away. 'Let's do it. How about in January? And maybe Hester and Emily could come too.'

Nell grinned. 'Listen to you, Kim Kardashian, with your big entourage.'

I laughed. Cole had said the same yesterday. He'd reminded me that I'd wanted a small wedding because I only had a few people to invite. Now my guests equalled his.

'If you're sure an old lady won't cramp your style,' Astrid said. 'I'd love to come.'

Fliss pressed a hand to her chest. 'Are you kidding me, Astrid? If you were any more stylish, you'd be on the cover of *Vogue*.'

'Seconded,' Nell said, raising her glass. 'Move over, Helen Mirren, Astrid is coming for you.'

Cesca took out her phone and tapped in a note for herself. 'I'll send some possible venues and a list of dates ASAP.'

I shook my head in wonder. 'I wish I could be like you. So organised.'

'I don't,' countered Fliss, with a giggle. 'One person in my life who marches into my kitchen and lines up all the mugs so the handles face the same direction is quite enough, thank you.'

'We should all celebrate who we are and not try to be someone else,' said Astrid, topping up everyone's glass.

'Hear, hear,' said Nell, swapping seats with me so Fliss could do her face and Cesca could tame my wayward frizz into something befitting a bride.

'A toast,' Astrid proposed. 'To all of us, to our uniqueness, our differences and the love and friendship which brings us together.'

We drank to that, although I was being very careful not to drink too much. I wanted to remember every moment of today, not lose it in a fuzzy-headed haze.

The doorbell rang and Astrid went to answer it, returning a minute later carrying a large box containing the wedding flowers.

Everyone oohed and ahhed.

'Oh my word,' I gasped, taking my bouquet from the box. 'These are even more incredible than I imagined.'

I'd gone for a circular arrangement with cream Snow Ballet and silvery pink Earl Grey roses, sprays of mistletoe and hypericum berries interwoven with sprigs of fragrant spruce and eucalyptus. The effect was romantic and wintry and had a vintage softness to it which complemented my wedding dress perfectly.

There was a second knock on the door and this time Fliss went. She returned seconds later looking puzzled. 'There's a man outside who says he's got a drum kit to deliver.'

'Excellent! Just in time.' I grinned at her. 'Ask him if he'd mind carrying it upstairs as a special favour seeing as it's my wedding day. It's Cole's Christmas present,' I added, noticing the look on everyone's faces. 'He's always wanted one, ever since he was a little boy.'

'Oh,' Nell laughed. 'Now I know why you wanted noise-cancelling headphones for Christmas.'

I tapped my head. 'I've thought it all through.'

Astrid laughed in disbelief. '*Mein Gott*, he will be banging all Christmas.'

No one had an answer for that, and I didn't dare look Nell in the eye.

'I can't wait to see you in your dress again,' Nell said, changing the subject. 'It's getting very real now, isn't it?'

I nodded. 'Very.'

'Five minutes and then you can,' said Cesca. 'I'm almost done. Just need to pin the pearl hair comb in place.'

Just as she picked up the vintage hair comb, my mobile rang, and Astrid passed it to me.

'Sorry!' I mouthed to Cesca, my heart skipping when I read the name on the screen. 'Cole! Happy wedding day.'

'Happy wedding day, darling,' he replied, his voice low and husky enough to set my stomach in a spin. 'My second Christmas Eve spent loving you.'

I smiled, remembering last Christmas Eve, the day we finally admitted how much we meant to each other. 'Ditto. Is everything OK there?'

'Fine, fine. Everything's under control,' he said, a little too fast.

'Cole?' I waited.

'OK, there was a slight moment of panic when Harley forgot the safe place he'd put the box containing the wedding rings. But, luckily, he remembered just before Paul was about to fly off into town and buy some replacements.'

I laughed, picturing the scene, Cole ransacking the entire house with Paul, while Hester sipped her coffee and told them all to stop flapping.

'Anyway, we're just about to set off for the registry office, but before that, I called for two things,' he continued. 'First. If I forget to say this later, I want you to know that I've never been as certain of anything in my life as I am about marrying you today. I love you with every beat of my heart. I can't wait to start the rest of my life with you as my wife.'

'Oh Cole.' I blinked hard, and Fliss passed me a tissue quickly. 'I love you too and I can't wait either.'

The flickers of self-doubt which had been flashing in my head ever since Cole had proposed had vanished. There would be no more thinking that I wasn't deserving of taking my place in his family – *our family*. I knew it wasn't true now. I'd proved my affection for his children, and, in turn, they were embracing me into their lives too. And look at my unexpected relationship with Emily. I hadn't had any problems accommodating my new affection for her, or Dad.

I might not have had a typical upbringing, but I knew how to love unconditionally and through Cole and my family I'd learned how to receive unconditional love too.

'And the second?' I asked, my face already aching from smiling down the phone at him.

He laughed. 'The second is a quiz.'

'Excuse me a minute,' Nell said, darting out of the kitchen and out through the front door.

I looked askance at the others, who shrugged, evidently as in the dark as me.

'How intriguing,' I said, sitting back in my seat. 'OK, fire away.'

'Question one. What is your favourite Christmas song?'

"Last Christmas' by Wham!' I said without hesitation.

'Correct.' I could hear the smile in his voice. 'Question two. Where is your fantasy Christmas holiday destination?'

I smiled, wondering where this was leading. 'The chalet in the 'Last Christmas' music video, with open fires, and the snowball fight. I'd leave out the big hairspray quiffs though.'

'OK, note to self,' Cole pretended to mutter. 'Unpack hairspray.'

'You've lost me!' I said, laughing. 'Cole, what are you talking about?'

'Is Nell there?' he asked.

'No, she . . .' I turned to see her return, her face beaming with secrets she was obviously desperate to spill. 'Yes, she is.'

Nell handed me a large silver envelope and nodded for me to open it. Inside was a brochure for a Swiss ski resort, a ski pass and a day pass for a spa. I stared at the contents; the ski pass was dated from Boxing Day. The spa day was for the day after that.

'I don't understand.'

'I've booked it. Five nights in the ski lodge in Switzerland from the Wham! video.' His voice was bubbling with excitement, I could hear how pleased he was. 'I took a risk and booked your dream Christmas without telling you. Spur of the moment, I know. Not like me, you're a bad influence. Actually, scratch that; a good influence.'

Cesca, Fliss and Nell linked arms and started singing the chorus to 'Last Christmas'; they were clearly all in on the secret.

'Wait?' I gasped in wonder. 'The *actual* chalet from the video?'

'Yes!' Cole cried. 'We leave tomorrow, back in time for New Year, before Will whisks Emily off to Jersey. We conferred on dates, so no need to start worrying about your dad. All timed with expert precision.'

'You researched all this? For me?' A sudden thought struck me. 'But the children, we can't leave them at Christmas?'

'Exactly what I thought you'd say, which is why they're coming too. Not the most orthodox honeymoon.'

'But the best,' I finished for him.

'Now I need to go and get ready,' he said. 'I've got a very important appointment coming up.'

After we ended the call, I sat there for a moment in a daze.

'Just when I thought today couldn't get any better!' I said, astounded. 'The honeymoon of my dreams.'

At last, our hair and make-up was done, and we moved into the cosy living room so that Nell and I could get into our dresses. Nell was dressed in a flash, but my hands were shaking. I slipped off my dressing gown, Astrid took my wedding dress off its hanger and she and Nell held it out for me as I stepped into it. Nell did up the buttons and then stood back.

The silk felt liquid against my skin, the fabric rustling and swishing as I moved. The fluted lace sleeves fell to just above my wrist, showing off the pearl bracelet Nell had given me last night, so like Tina's earrings that they could have been a matching set. Emotion welled inside me as Nell handed me my bouquet; I felt beautiful.

You could have heard a pin drop in the room; the four women stared at me, open-mouthed, completely silent.

'That bad, huh?' I said with a nervous laugh, breaking the tension.

The next second, my friends crowded around me, all talking at once.

'That dress is out of this world.'

'Give us a twirl!'

'Wait until Cole sees you.'

'And not just Cole, everyone is going to fall in love with you.'

'You look radiant!'

Astrid, her face soft with love, pressed a hand to her mouth and whispered something in German, which for once I didn't understand, but I was fairly sure was a compliment.

We all took photos on our phones, doing selfies in front of the Christmas tree, until my phone buzzed with a message from Emily to say that they were on their way, and we realised what the time was.

Cesca and Fliss packed up their hair and make-up stuff and got into the car and Astrid made a last trip to the bathroom, leaving Nell and me looking at our reflections in the hall mirror, arms around each other's waists.

Nell swallowed and I could see she was struggling to get her words out. 'You look . . . incredible.'

'So do you,' I said. 'We are going to turn some heads walking down that aisle.'

'I'm so proud of you, you know,' she said. 'You've made such a success of your life.'

'I couldn't have done it without you.' I leaned my head against hers. 'I *can't* do it without you, which is why I've got a proposition for you.'

Nell quirked an eyebrow. 'Go on.'

I took her hands in mine. 'I'd like you to become a partner in Merry and Bright.'

I'd been planning on saying that after Christmas, but now just felt like the right time.

Her jaw fell open. 'What did you say?'

'I'd really like you to join me, grow the business together, see how far we can take it,' I explained. 'I thought I wanted more staff, but actually, I want someone to share my dream with me and I can't think of anyone I'd rather do that with than you.'

She shook her head, completely stunned. 'I didn't see that coming. At. All.'

I shrugged nonchalantly. 'You know me, full of ideas. Although, full disclosure, it was Emily who pointed out how perfect we'd be together. Clever girl. What do you say?'

'Oh my God.' She hugged me tight. 'Yes! Absolutely yes!'

My heart swelled with love for my friend. We'd be perfect partners; next year was going to be so exciting, so full of possibilities.

'OK,' I laughed, peeling her off me. 'Mind the dress.'

'Sorry, sorry,' she said, smoothing my shoulders and

384

patting my hair back into position. 'Remember last Christmas when you were grumpy and adamant that you wanted to veto Christmas Day altogether?'

I gave a snort. 'And instead, I fell in love and woke up in an airport hotel with the man of my dreams.'

'Twelve months later and you're marrying him.' Nell lifted her hand. 'High five.'

We touched our hands together and ended up in another hug.

'So' – Astrid appeared beside us, wrapping her arms around both of us – 'I think you're ready.'

I looked at my two friends and felt my heart race. This was it. The day I'd dreamed about for so long. I thought about all the times in the past when I had longed to be loved, when I had wanted, more than anything, to belong. And I thought about the wonderful man who'd be waiting for me at the registry office, offering me all that and more.

'I *know* I'm ready,' I replied and together we stepped out into the snowy day and into Cesca's waiting car.

Chapter Forty

Emily

The snow had all but stopped by the time Will pulled into the car park of Wetherley's registry office. Snow covered the ground, but the flakes were now so tiny that they were no more than diamond specks in the air.

Emily looked at the covered porch of the registry office. The pillars had been decorated with Christmas lights, bunches of mistletoe tied with pale pink ribbon hung from the underside of the roof and a forest of Christmas trees of varying heights were trimmed with silver, white and pink baubles. It was beautiful. Her sister was a creative genius.

A crowd had already gathered, dressed in their wedding finery, and Emily's stomach pitched with nerves.

'Look at all those people,' she murmured.

'It'll all be good,' Will reassured her, giving her that smile that already felt like home.

She took a calming breath. He was right. Today was shaping up to be a day she'd remember forever. Everything was going to plan, and they were on time. Ray had dropped off to sleep as soon as they'd got in Will's car and the drive through the snow had been surprisingly stress-free and beautiful. They'd chatted, telling each other random facts that the other didn't yet know. At times, Emily felt as if she'd known Will forever, and it came as a surprise when he told her something new about himself: like how he'd got the scar on the back of his hand, about the band he'd been in with his mates when he was sixteen and how he'd once turned up his jeans while he was still in them using superglue and managed to stick the denim to his ankles. Each new story felt like a jewel for her to store away to treasure when they were apart.

'Thanks for doing this with me,' she said, turning to Will. 'I mean, not just any old "meet the family" gig, but a wedding. A lot of men would have found this too intense.'

'Not me.' He grinned at her. 'I'm just a little orphan kid, remember. Days like this are the stuff of dreams.'

'Even so,' she said, 'it *is* Christmas Eve and I'm monopolising you. I hope your friends don't mind.'

'My friends are happy for me. And probably pleased that I'm not crashing their family Christmases for once.'

'Not as pleased as I am.' She looked at her father asleep in the back of the car, at peace. 'I'm so glad I've got you to help me.'

Will turned the engine off and took the keys from the ignition. In the back of the car, Ray shifted position but didn't wake up. 'There's nothing else I'd rather be doing.' He reached for her hand. It was cold and he rubbed it between his warm ones. 'That day we met, I saw you crossing the car park with your dad, I knew just how it felt to be in your shoes, to be moving a loved one into residential care. And then when I offered to help you unload the car . . .' He shrugged. 'I looked at you and it felt as if I was waking up from a long sleep. And I know it's not cool to admit it, because we haven't known each other very long, but I care about you, Emily.'

Emily's stomach did a loop the loop. 'I don't care whether it's cool or not, because I feel the same,' she said softly.

'I hoped you'd say something like that.' He pretended to wipe his brow. 'Because I've got a surprise booked for you for New Year. A trip.'

'Really?' She touched his face, he'd been growing a beard, it defined his jaw, and her skin tingled with the rough sensation of the stubble against her fingertips. She might not be brave enough to say it yet, but she loved this man. 'I love surprises.'

He grinned nervously. 'I hope you like this one, I mean, you should, you did promise you'd show me round one day.'

Emily gave him a quizzical look. 'Wysedale?'

He laughed. 'No, Jersey. I organised it with Izzy.'

She laughed in disbelief. 'No way!'

'Yep.' He looked proud of himself. 'And I checked with Cole too, to make sure there'd be someone around to pop in and see your dad.'

Emily shook her head and let out a sigh of happiness. 'New Year in Jersey. I can't believe it. Just you and me and . . .'

'Don't include me,' came a voice from the back. 'I'm off on a cruise soon. Down the Nile with Arthur.'

Emily and Will grinned at each other.

'Right you are, Dad, I'll bear that in mind,' said Emily brightly. 'Are you ready for the wedding?'

'In this weather? Who's getting married, a flippin' Eskimo?'

Emily giggled. 'Merry's getting married, Dad.'

'Little Merry? Last time I saw her she must only have been six.'

Just then, a Range Rover pulled up in front of the entrance and the crowd started to cheer.

'She's here, she's here, she's here!' Emily said, suddenly all panicky. She quickly pinned on the corsage Merry had sent her made from Earl Grey roses, gypsophila and soft fern, and pressed a kiss to Will's mouth. 'It's time. Come on, Dad.'

Will helped Ray climb out from the back of the car and Emily tucked her dad's scarf into the neck of his coat and pinned on his buttonhole. Together they made their way to the entrance, Ray in the middle and Will and Emily either side, partly so he didn't slip in the snow, but mostly so they could keep an eye on him.

Emily recognised Fred, Cole's father, looking resplendent in a navy suit, a little girl who must have been Freya twirling around in circles, making her bridesmaid's dress fly, and beaming faces on the people she'd met at the party at the weekend. She got her phone out of her bag to take pictures just in time to see Merry alight from the car.

She wore a long empire-line coat over her dress, in off-white velvet, and ivory leather buttoned boots peeped from under her hem. They were the Victorian pair Emily had won on eBay and they finished off her dress beautifully. Her bouquet was perfect, her hair shone in golden waves, half pinned up with a pearl comb. But it wasn't only her outfit which caught Emily's attention, it was the look of pure joy on her face.

'Oh, Merry! You look stunning!' Emily said.

Merry pressed her cheek to hers. 'Thank you, little sis. And thanks so much for bringing Dad, it means the world. How's he doing?'

'Fine' said Emily, deciding to keep his imminent trip up the Nile to herself. 'Looking forward to the service.'

They both looked at Ray. He was under the mistletoe, pointing up at it with his lips puckered ready for a kiss from anyone who caught his eye. Will stood by stifling a laugh. Emily and Merry exchanged fond smiles and then, without needing to speak, they dashed across, one either side of him and each kissed his cheek.

'One for the album,' said one of Merry's friends, catching the moment on her camera.

'Doesn't Merry make a beautiful bride?' said Emily to Ray.

'Merry?' Their father stared at the bride in bewilderment.

Merry did a twirl for him. 'Ta-dah! I'm getting married!'

Ray frowned and dug into his pocket, muttering something under his breath about having lost something.

'If everyone would please make their way inside please,' said an authoritative voice from inside the foyer.

'We'd better go,' Emily said, giving her sister a hug. 'I'm so proud to be here, as your sister.'

'And I'm so proud to have you here, it's a dream come true.' Merry's eyes shone.

'Good luck,' Emily said, pressing a kiss to her cheek.

And then the crowd was swept inside, taking Emily with them, leaving just the wedding party standing on the steps outside.

Chapter Forty One

Cole

Inside the registry office, Hester and Paul were stationed at the entrance handing out small Merry and Bright candles to everyone as they filed in and Cole was sitting in the first row trying to get his nerves under control. He was starting to perspire, and his left leg wouldn't stop jiggling. He watched Harley out of the corner of his eye race to the front of the room and change the music to something he recognised as one of Freya's favourites. Harley winced at his dad, making him smile; Gwen Stefani was not Harley's cup of tea, but he wouldn't complain today. In fact, ever since the party, he'd seemed to have perked up a lot. According to Lydia he'd even made an effort to be nice to Ady.

'Merry's here,' said Harley, sliding into the row at speed and landing next to his dad.

Cole let out a breath. 'Thank goodness for that. And on time too.'

Merry, true to form, had miraculously organised everything beautifully right at the last minute, as he'd known she would. They were always going to have a different approach to getting things done. And that was OK. They were good for each other; they had a great life to look forward to.

Mrs Merry Robinson, his eyes misted over, he could hardly believe his luck.

'Dad?' Harley's voice brought him back to the present. 'I just want to say how happy I am for you, marrying Merry. She's a great person and I think you're going to make a brilliant team.'

Cole looked at his boy in wonder. 'Thanks, son. I really appreciate that. Come here.'

He lifted his arm and Harley slid underneath and allowed himself to be hugged.

'I love you, Dad, and I'm really proud of you.'

'I feel the same about you, mate.' Cole was filled with admiration for his son, his precious boy, on the verge of becoming a man, far wiser than Cole had been at his age. He kissed Harley's head and felt a sudden urge to have him at his side for the service. 'Can I ask you a favour,' he said, pulling back to look Harley in the eye.

Harley nodded willingly. 'Sure.'

'Would you be my best man?'

'Me?' His voice went up an octave and he looked at his dad warily. 'Are you sure?'

'Positive.' Cole swallowed, his voice breaking. 'A best man should be someone I love and respect. Who better than my own son?'

Harley nodded wordlessly, leaned into his dad and hugged him tight.

'I'd better let Merry know,' said Cole, pulling his phone from inside his jacket and sending her a text. He smiled to himself, imagining her gasping with pleasure. He'd done a good thing and Harley would remember this for the rest of his life.

Chapter Forty-Two

Merry

From outside the room, we could hear Gwen Stefani and Blake Shelton belting out their Christmas hit. Barbara, our registrar, who sported a strong cranberry lip and the sharpest chin-length bob I'd ever seen, closed the double doors as the last guests entered.

'They're all in.' Barbara beamed, tucking her hair behind her ears. Quite large ears, I noticed absently. 'Although quite a few of them are dancing in their seats to the music.'

'I chose this song,' Freya piped up. She looked adorable in her pink dress. Her sequin shoes might not live to see another day, but I didn't think she minded.

'And Cole's definitely there?'

Barbara twinkled her eyes. 'He certainly is, looking absolutely dashing. His best man is there too, showing his grandad how to moon-walk.'

We all laughed and my heart flipped with joy. Cole had sent me a text only moments ago with the surprise announcement that Harley was going to be his best man. It was the perfect addition to the ceremony and I could just imagine how proud Harley would be right now.

Freya tapped Barbara's arm. 'I'm getting a kitten for Christmas, but it's not my main present because I already know about it and I've got to share her with my brother, although Harley says he'd rather have a snake, but Mum said no way. And I can't get her for another week because she's too small to leave her mummy. But I'm not too small to leave mine; I'm going skiing tomorrow with Dad and Merry, for our family honeymoon and . . .' She paused briefly for breath before giving Barbara a twirl. 'Do you like my dress?'

'I *love* your dress!' Barbara caught hold of one of Freya's hands and spun her around. 'And that all sounds very exciting. Now, are you ready to walk down the aisle?'

Freya nodded. 'I've been ready since before breakfast.'

There was no hesitation on Freya's part now, no sign that she was not happy about this wedding and it was wonderful to see the little girl's excitement.

Nell handed Freya the posy of winter flowers which matched hers. 'Did you have ketchup on your breakfast by any chance?' Her eyes slid to mine in amusement and then down to a small orangey pink mark on her chest where it looked as if someone had done their best to sponge it off.

The little girl looked amazed. 'How did you know?'

'And are you ready?' Barbara asked me.

I nodded. 'Oh, I should warn you that my dad has dementia, just in case, you know, he says something unexpected.'

Barbara smiled. 'Don't give it a moment's thought. This is your wedding, with your loved ones around you to celebrate with you, and that's all that matters. Besides, I've been doing this job for fifteen years, nothing surprises me anymore. I've seen every last-minute alteration, every surprise appearance you could imagine. All right then.'

As Barbara opened the double doors, a sudden emotion hit me with such strength that I let out a gasp. Because I had a last-minute alteration of my own and I couldn't go down the aisle just yet.

Barbara paused and immediately closed the doors again. Nell looked at me sharply. 'What's up?'

'I want Astrid,' I said shakily.

'Shall I fetch her?' Nell offered.

'Can I?' Freya said excitedly.

'Yes please, darling,' I said, smiling at the little girl.

Barbara opened the door wide enough for her to slip in and Freya skipped up the aisle to where Astrid was sitting beside Fred.

'What's going on?' Nell murmured.

'Nothing to worry about, you'll see.' I gave her a mischievous grin and she shook her head bemused.

Seconds later, Freya reappeared holding Astrid's hand.

'*Was ist los, mein Schatz?*' Astrid's eyes scanned mine, her face pinched with concern.

'There's something I need to ask you,' I said, catching her hand. 'Astrid, you've been in my life, guiding me and caring for me, longer than anyone else I know.'

My dear old friend cupped a hand to my cheek. 'And it has been my pleasure, *Liebling*.'

'Which is why I'd really love you to be by my side as I walk down the aisle to Cole.'

Astrid's mouth fell open. 'What? I don't . . . What are you saying?'

'I'm saying,' I began, my eyes sparkling, 'that I'd be honoured if you would give me away? I'm sorry it's such short notice.'

Astrid's eyes blinked away tears. '*Mein liebes Kind*. Don't apologise for paying me the greatest compliment of my life. But your father is here, and your sister?'

We smiled at each other, my old art teacher and I, and I thought about the teenage girl I'd been, desperate for love, for connection with someone, for someone to call mine. There had been hundreds of kids in my school, but she had seen me and cared for me.

I shook my head. 'I want us to have this moment together, you've been a special part of my life for more than twenty years and I hope you always will be. There's no one else I'd rather have at my side today as I start a new life with Cole.'

'Merry, I think this might be the happiest and proudest day of my life,' she replied.

Barbara handed her a tissue and cleared her throat softly. 'If everyone's ready, let's get this show on the road. Give me two ticks to get in position and in you come.'

The registry office sparkled with Christmas joy, from the twinkling trees we'd arranged at the front, to the festive flowers hung at the end of every other row, bunches of holly, trailing ivy and sprays of white roses tied with pink ribbon. And on the table where we'd be signing the register was a trio of candles, only one of which was currently lit.

Everyone's heads turned as the doors opened. I took Astrid's arm and we walked to the threshold of the room, Nell and Freya falling into position behind me. Cameras flashed and my friends waved. My dad stood up to see what the fuss was about, and Emily mouthed 'HELP' and persuaded him back to his seat. And there standing at the top of the aisle waiting for me, with his back turned, was Cole. I took in a sharp breath, light-headed with joy.

'Good luck, my angel,' Astrid murmured.

She pressed a hand to my cheek, and I leaned against it, and then the time for talking was over as 'Somewhere in My Memories', the beautiful piece of music John Williams wrote for *Home Alone*, filled the room. Chosen by me, not only because that was my favourite Christmas film, but because of its message of love and hope and family.

Everyone stood up and before I knew it, we were walking forward. And as the choir sang about precious moments and special people and magic and home, Cole turned to look at me, his chocolate-brown eyes widening as they found mine, and he flashed me that devastating smile which could lift my spirits in a heartbeat. Barbara was right: he was dashing and, somehow, this wonderful man was waiting for me. It was all I could do not to sprint up the aisle and leap into his arms.

'Hello, beautiful,' Cole murmured when I reached his side.

'Hello,' I whispered back. 'Fancy meeting you here.'

'Someone told me if I hung around for a while, the most wonderful woman in the world would appear,' he said with a casual shrug.

I looked over my shoulder. 'Is it OK if I wait here until she shows up?'

He touched my face, his thumb rough against my skin. 'She showed up. Thank goodness.'

I leaned around him to grin at Harley, who flashed the ring box at me from out of his trouser pocket. My almost stepson, already turning into a man. And next to me, smiling from ear to ear was Freya, my almost stepdaughter. My heart was bursting with love for this little family. *My family*. I couldn't be prouder of them.

Barbara coughed lightly and Astrid and Freya melted away to sit by Fred, Nell took my bouquet from me, and the service began.

The registrar spoke about the precious gift of marriage and the love which had brought us all here today, and in between gazing lovingly at Cole and trying not to cry,

I noticed the candles weren't the ones I'd selected for today, the scent was different, the perfume intoxicating and romantic, of orange blossom and white jasmine. I frowned, wondering how the mix-up could have happened. I'd packed the candles myself. Cole looked at me, his eyes questioning, and I smiled back to reassure him, pushing the candles out of my mind. In the grand scheme of things, it was irrelevant.

'Now, ladies and gentlemen, we come to my favourite part in the service: the wedding vows.' Barbara beamed at her audience. 'I'm going to invite . . . Oh, hello there.'

I felt a hand on my arm and turned to see my dad standing beside me.

'Hi, Dad,' I said softly, covering his hand with mine. 'I think you're supposed to be sitting down for this bit.'

'Yes but—' Dad scratched his head. 'I've got something for you. But I've lost it.'

'Thank goodness for that, Ray,' said Cole, his lips twitching. 'I thought you were about to object.'

'Dad, please sit down.' Emily's face was scarlet. She put her hand to his elbow. 'I'm so sorry, everyone. He was up and out of his chair before I could stop him.'

'Take your time, Ray,' said Barbara kindly. 'What is it that you've got?'

Dad stared at her curiously; the tips of her ears were poking out from her hair, and I prayed he didn't say anything rude.

'It's fine, Emily,' I said, trying to put my poor sister at ease. 'Honestly. Having a parent at my wedding is something I never thought possible.'

'A wedding?' Dad gave a laugh of surprise, looking from Cole to me and then to Barbara. 'Oh yes!' He remembered suddenly.

'Oh God,' Emily muttered under her breath.

'I asked Sammy to marry me once,' Dad said, rubbing his fingers along his jaw. He'd had a proper shave, he looked quite different without his silver chin tufts.

'Did you?' My heart thudded.

'At first, she said yes, but then she changed her mind. Don't blame her.' His eyes misted over.

Imagine if she'd said yes. An entirely different life flashed in cinematic detail through my brain. If Mum hadn't been alone, if she'd had someone to support her when she felt low, maybe she would still have been here now . . .

I squeezed my eyes shut for a fraction of a second and felt the comfort of Cole's arm around me. And then I stood up tall and took a deep breath.

The past had gone and there was nothing we could do about it now. But we had today, I thought, looking at the people I loved gathered around me, and we had tomorrow and really that was all that mattered.

'Bought her a ring and everything,' Dad said, reaching into his pocket. He pulled out a silver wishbone ring.

I stared at the small band nestled in the palm of his hand as if it might disappear if I stopped looking at it for even a second. Her fingers must have been tiny. I had nothing of my mother's, not one single item. 'That was Mum's?'

Dad nodded. 'It was until she gave it back to me. I hung on to it just in case. It's yours now.'

'I . . .' I tried to speak, but the words wouldn't come.

Cole took the ring from Dad for me and slipped it on to my little finger.

'Thank you, Dad. I'll treasure it.'

Dad gave a firm nod and shuffled back to his seat, Emily beside him.

'She's here,' I whispered to Cole, looking down at my little finger. 'My mum's here with me.'

Cole peeled back the cuff of his shirt to reveal a fine gold bracelet. 'I wasn't going to tell anyone about this, but my mum is here too.'

Barbara dabbed her eyes with a handkerchief. 'So it seems I can still be surprised. Now where was I . . .?'

There were no further interruptions; and the first part of the formal stuff was over in a flash.

Harley stepped up officiously with the rings and handed them over, and Cole took hold of my hand.

'Merry, I give you this ring as a sign of my love.' His voice was clear and strong, and although I knew that everyone around us could hear, it felt as if there was just two of us in the room. 'From the moment I met you, my life has been an adventure and I never want that to change. I love you with all my heart and I apologise now, because I'm never leaving your side. I'll be there when your feet are cold at night and you need to warm them on me, I'll be there to fetch milk when we've run out before you've had your first caffeine hit of the day. I'll be there when you're feeling sad and need a hug. I'll be there to order a dessert with two spoons in a restaurant so you can eat most of it, and I'll be there to paint your toenails when you're too old and creaky to reach them. But mostly I'll be there to remind you each day how much you are loved.'

'Thank you,' I mouthed softly. My heart swelled with joy as Cole slid my wedding ring onto my left hand. We held each other's gaze, incredulous, happy and so in love I thought my heart would burst.

I picked up Cole's wedding ring and slipped it onto the tip of his finger.

'My darling, Cole. I give you this ring as a sign of our love and our marriage. Loving you is the easiest job in the world, and I am the lucky woman who gets to do it for the rest of her life. I promise to do my best to make you happy and to let you sometimes win arguments. I promise to love you in good times and in bad, and I promise to love you even when you are too old to paint my toenails without getting the polish everywhere. Cole, thank you for welcoming me into your family, thank you for allowing me to know and love your amazing children. Thank you for believing in me and encouraging me and not minding when I'm still pouring candles long after I said I would be. My love for you will last a lifetime; thank you for bringing me home.'

I wiggled the ring onto his finger and blew out a breath of relief.

'Merry and Cole will now perform the candle ceremony,' said Barbara, moving to the side of the table. 'I am going to invite Hester and Emily, Cole and Merry's sisters, to light the slim candles on this table.'

The two sisters followed instructions. Will, I noticed, kept a firm eye on Dad while Emily was busy.

'Now, Merry and Cole will take these lit candles. Together they will light the tall unity candle in the centre. This symbolises their two lives, their two families and their two sets of friends becoming one.'

Cole picked up his candle and I did the same, and together we lit the central candle. The wick fizzed and glowed as both flames touched it. The label on the glass jar caught my eye. Instead of the Merry and Bright logo, there was a line of familiar handwriting. I looked at Fred quizzically, who gave me a wink, and then Cole led me back around the table to finish the ceremony.

'This unity candle,' Barbara intoned, 'has been handmade with love by Fred, in honour of his son and daughter-in-law's wedding. The scent is a blend of orange blossom and white jasmine symbolising love, beauty and purity, and Fred has named this candle "Together".'

'Oh Fred!' I gasped in surprise. 'Thank you.'

Fred got to his feet and blew us a kiss and sat back down again.

'Every guest has been given one of these candles on the way in, in order that you can take them home as a symbol of the love you have witnessed here today.' Barbara produced her handkerchief again and dabbed her eyes. 'And that, ladies and gentlemen, is another first for me.'

My eyes swam with tears: so many surprises, so many gestures of love, I felt it all around me.

Cole squeezed my hand and gave me a look of reassurance as Barbara came to the bit we'd all been waiting for.

'. . . It therefore gives me the greatest honour and privilege to announce that you are now husband and wife. Congratulations to you both.'

'Can I kiss my wife now?' Cole jumped in, making everyone laugh, except Harley, who covered his face in horror.

'You may,' said Barbara, inclining her head.

For a second, I just looked at my husband, drinking him in, the shine in my eyes showing him the depth of my love. He took my hands and drew me towards him and his kiss, when it came, felt like sunshine, lighting my world. Cheers and applause and a wolf whistle I'd recognise anywhere as Nell's echoed around the room.

'Merry Christmas, Mrs Robinson,' he murmured, finally pulling away when Harley's noises of protest were getting louder.

'Merry Christmas, Mr Robinson,' I echoed.

Signing the register took only a matter of minutes and then Harley scooted over to the music system again to play the song we'd chosen to leave the ceremony to. It was Mariah Carey, 'All I want for Christmas is you'. Cheesy, but the lyrics were perfect.

Cole and I turned around to face the doors, ready to begin our procession past friends and family as soon as the music kicked in. But a few seconds later and we were still waiting in anticipation.

'It's not working,' said Harley, rubbing a hand through his hair. 'The speaker won't connect to the Bluetooth.'

'Bear with us, everyone!' Barbara cried. 'Slight technical hitch.'

'I said we should have booked an organist,' Cole whispered.

'You did no such thing,' I giggled, leaning into him.

'I don't want a lot for Christmas!'

Everyone gasped and cheered as Harley's voice rang out across the room.

Cole and I whirled around to see him standing on the table.

'I don't believe it!' I gasped and blew my stepson a kiss, making him grin.

'There is just one thing I need.' He waved his hands, to get everyone up. 'Come on, you all know the words . . .'

He was right, everyone did. And so with all our friends and family singing at the tops of their voices that they didn't care about the presents, Cole and I walked back down the aisle hand in hand, stopping to kiss our friends and families on the way.

'Happy?' Cole asked.

'Very,' I said, nodding.

'Good,' he said, 'happy wife, happy life.'

'Now that's a motto I can get behind.' I smiled, swinging his hand in mine. 'Have I told you recently how much I love you?'

'Not once since we got married, no,' he said, feigning indignation. 'Very remiss.'

Together we pushed open the doors to the porch and a rush of cold air made us gasp. New snow lay on the ground, a soft white blanket sparkling in the low afternoon sun.

'I love you!' I cried, reaching my arms around my husband, my heart, my future.

Cole picked me up and swung me around, and we kissed again and again, our kisses mixing with our laughter.

And then the air was filled with confetti and camera flashes and hugs from Hester and Nell, a wave from Dad and cries of congratulations and, above all, love.

Will had his arm around Emily and I caught her eye and we blew each other kisses.

'You two next,' I mouthed, making her laugh.

I gazed around me, looking at all the faces, old and new, I saw my own joy and happiness reflected back at me, and my heart could not have been fuller.

As Cole drew me to his side for another photograph, I remembered last Christmas Eve, when I'd dared to give him my heart. My life had changed beyond recognition since then. I didn't know what the next year would bring – of course, I didn't, who did? But I was sure about one thing; that it would be full of love. And if we put love at the heart of everything we did, then how could we possibly fail?

Epilogue

Christmas Eve 2000

Hilary Burgess's favourite thing was order; her collection of alphabetised books, VHS cassettes and CDs gave her life. And it was this trait which made her the perfect person to oversee the computerisation of Derbyshire County Council's social services archive. She couldn't abide mess, or loose ends, or clutter. She gave a shudder as she passed her colleague Bernard's desk. Honestly, she thought, shaking her head, who in their right mind could finish work for the Christmas break and leave Scrabble tiles all over his workstation? Bernard, that was who.

She set down a heavy cardboard box full of correspondence and lifted off the lid. She'd sort through this last one and then she'd call it a day.

It was 4 p.m. and everyone had already left. It was disgraceful, if you asked Hilary; she was a stickler for the rules. She was paid until half past five and she would leave then and not a minute sooner. Besides, an empty office with no ringing phones, no constant chatter about the Christmas party was heavenly. She hadn't gone to the party. She'd been at rehearsal with her rock choir. Not that she'd told anyone about that. Her colleagues only knew Hilary the buttoned-up, obsessive neat freak. They'd do their nut if they could see her belting out 'We are the Champions' by

Queen, in her leather trousers, her long black hair swinging loosely around her shoulders.

Hilary settled herself at her desk with a cup of tea and a mince pie and began to work methodically through the files inside the box. Some of it could be thrown away, but most of it would be sent off to be scanned, digitised forever.

As she took out yet another folder, three sheets of paper, their corners pinched together, fluttered onto her desk. The paper had been torn from one of those reporter's notebooks, the sort with a spiral of wire at the top.

She looked back in the box to see if there was an envelope for it, but she couldn't see anything. She tutted, shaking her head. Whoever had filed it had done a poor job. She sipped her tea and began to read the letter. It took her a. while because the writing was smudged and hard to read.

December 1996

Dear M,

I don't know whether you'll see this when I'm gone or not. I hope so. Maybe you'll get it when you're eighteen. I don't know how these things work. That's me all over — I never know the answers.

And that's how I feel now — that I've run out of answers. I don't know how to be your mum; I only know that I love you and want the best for you. I've decided that the best is not with me.

My own mother hardly ever looked at me, did you know that? She had no interest in me at all, I'm not even sure if she loved me. I had four nannies at one point, each of them competing with me for her attention. I know I'll never be able to steer you safely through life. I haven't even managed to do that for myself. I'd have no chance doing it for someone else.

But I do love you, you must believe that. I'm not like my mum, I can hardly take my eyes off you. I look at you and my heart wants to burst, knowing that you're mine. Against all the odds, I made the most beautiful child and, whatever happens next for you, know that I loved you with every cell of my body.

I'm sorry for everything. I am so sorry you ended up with me as your mother. You deserve better. Without me around to mess things up, I hope that's what you'll get. I hope you remember me with love, even though I've let you down. But I wouldn't blame you if you don't. Will you miss me? I wonder. The selfish part of me hopes you will, but I know that's not fair. Above all else, I want your life to be full of light and happiness.

I've hurt everyone who ever loved me, including your father, Ray. Remember Ray? He used to visit sometimes when you were little. But not anymore. I sent him away when I found out he had another family, another daughter. I hope he manages to make a go of it with them. He's a nice man. A bit flaky, but then who am I to talk?

My darling girl, I spoke to you on the phone last night. You were full of stories about the foster carers you're with. The snake and feeding it the frozen chicks. The massive Christmas tree in the living room. It sounds so much better than here with me. You're having fun, part of a big family, living with a woman who is so good at being a mum that she looks after other people's kids too. I envy her. But I'm grateful to her too.

I'm getting sleepy now, M, so I'll say goodnight. Always remember how much I loved you, you'll carry a piece of my heart with you wherever you go.

Your loving mum xxxx

Hilary set the letter down on her desk, opened her drawer to extract a packet of tissues and blew her nose. She read all sorts of stuff; you got hardened to it in this job, but there was something about that one which reached deep into Hilary's heart and squeezed it tight. That poor mother, did she get help? And what about M? Did she get her life full of light and happiness? Hilary hoped so. She rummaged around in the box for something that might give her a clue as to the writer's identity, but there was nothing. She ate another mince pie while she decided what to do with the letter.

Technically, she should dispose of it. There was no way of filing it accurately, there was no name, no address, nothing. But she couldn't do it. She couldn't consign those words of love to the bin. So, instead, she tucked it deep inside another file and left it for someone else to deal with. Maybe one day the letter might be reunited with the daughter – who knows, stranger things had happened.

She brushed the crumbs off her bosom and sighed, feeling quite emotional after all that.

She looked at the clock: half past four. Oh, what the hell. She slipped her arms into her coat and shovelled her pens haphazardly back into her drawer. She was going to finish early for once. She turned off the lights on the office Christmas tree as she walked out of the office. *Merry Christmas, everyone*, she thought with a smile, *even you, Bernard*.

The Thank Yous

This Christmassy book has been an absolute joy to write. I've never written a follow-on novel before, and it was a real treat to be back in Wetherley with the gang. So thank you to you lovely readers for asking what happens next for Merry and Cole.

A heartfelt thank you to my agent, Sheila Crowley. This is the first book we have worked on together and I'm very blessed to be benefitting from your energy, your eye for detail and your ambition for my publishing. Thank you for championing me.

A huge thank you to my incredibly dedicated publishing team at Orion. I know you've got your own page at the back, but I can't not mention two absolute diamonds: Sam Eades, who has worked editorial wonders with this novel in order to make it shine, and Victoria Laws, who conjures up such sparkling sales figures. Thank you, ladies.

Talking of sales, many thanks to all the wonderful book-sellers who make space on their shelves for my books. I'm truly grateful for your support.

Writers need other writers and I'm very lucky to have the talented Isabelle Broom in my life. You have swept me away (see what I did there) on numerous writing trips, made me laugh for hours and hours and got up super early for weeks on end to do word races with me as we neared the end of our respective books. Thank you, Broom!

The other special writer I must thank is Kirsty Greenwood, who held my hand all the way through the edits and gave me some really good ideas too. You are such a talented writer and I'm so proud to call you a friend. Thank you, Kirsty for all the fun and laughs and especially the truffle salt.

Thank you to Cesca Major and Debbie Flint for your insight into the world of TV shopping channels and bringing the studios to life for me. Any mistakes are all mine! Also thanks to Chris Hanbury for answering my questions about surfing.

Thank you to Henry Butcher for always answering my weird questions without batting an eyelid. This book's random queries included bowling in cricket, using clippers to cut hair and trying to sing when your voice is breaking. Thanks, Henners!

I sometimes ask my readers for their input, and I am always inundated with help. For this book, I asked my Facebook followers for funny stories from their weddings or hen parties, and I had a hilarious time reading through them all. Particular thanks to Helen Handy for sharing that she was handcuffed to an ironing board at her hen party! And thank you to poor Zoe Allen Thiedeman, who managed to stand on an ants' nest while having her wedding photographs taken!

Thank you as always to my wonderful family, Tony, Isabel and Phoebe, for your love and support and help with everything from cover design to plot holes, and sometimes for just listening to me moan about how hard writing is. I love you all very much.

And finally, I could not have written this book without the help of a dear friend, Sue Haswell, and her sister Catherine Scarlett, whose father, John, lived with dementia for the last few years of his life. Sue and Catherine very kindly shared John's story and several of the incidents described in this book were inspired by things that John did or said. I am indebted to you ladies for letting me borrow your father's experiences and for demonstrating that even at tough moments, we can find a lighter side of life.

Much love,
Cathy xxx

Credits

Cathy Bramley and Orion Fiction would like to thank everyone at Orion who worked on the publication of *Merrily Ever After* in the UK.

Editorial
Sam Eades
Lucy Brem
Rhea Kurien

Copy editor
Jade Craddock

Proofreader
Jane Howard

Audio
Paul Stark
Jake Alderson

Contracts
Anne Goddard
Ellie Bowker

Design
Rachael Lancaster
Joanna Ridley
Nick May

Editorial Management
Charlie Panayiotou
Jane Hughes
Bartley Shaw

Finance
Jasdip Nandra
Sue Baker

Production
Ruth Sharvell

Marketing
Katie Moss

Brittany Sankey
Yadira Da Trindade

Publicity
Alainna Hadjigeorgiou

Sales
Jen Wilson
Esther Waters
Victoria Laws
Rachael Hum
Ellie Kyrke-Smith
Frances Doyle
Georgina Cutler

Operations
Jo Jacobs
Sharon Willis

Can two complete strangers save Christmas?

Christmas has always meant something special to Merry - even without a family of her own. This year, her heart might be broken but her new candle business is booming. The last thing she needs is another project - but when her hometown's annual event needs some fresh festive inspiration, Merry can't resist.

Cole loves a project too - though it's usually of the bricks and mortar variety. As a single dad, his Christmas wish is to see his kids again, so getting the new house finished for when they're all together is the perfect distraction.

But this Christmas, magic is in the air for these two strangers. Will it bring them all the joy they planned for . . . and take their hearts by surprise too?

After all, anything can happen at Christmas. . .

Praise for *THE MERRY CHRISTMAS PROJECT*:

'Stuffed with Cathy's sparkling wit and warmth'

Milly Johnson

Three women. Three secrets.
One unforgettable summer.

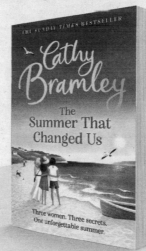

The sparkling seaside village of Merle Bay, with its beautiful beach scattered with seaglass, is a place where anyone can have a fresh start.

For Katie, it is the perfect hideout after a childhood trauma left her feeling exposed. For Robyn, the fresh sea air is helping to heal her scars, but maybe not her marriage. For Grace, a new start could help her move on from a heartbreaking loss. When they meet on Seaglass Beach one day, they form an instant bond and soon they're sharing prosecco, laughter - and even their biggest secrets...

Together, the women feel stronger than ever before. So can their friendship help them face old fears and find happy endings - as well as new beginnings?

Praise for Cathy Bramley:
'Filled with warmth and laughter'
Carole Matthews

It started with a wish list.
Now can she make it happen?

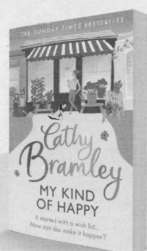

'Flowers are sunshine for the soul.'

Flowers have always made Fearne smile. She treasures the memories of her beloved grandmother's floristry and helping her to arrange beautiful blooms that brought such joy to their recipients.

But ever since a family tragedy a year ago, Fearne has been searching for her own contentment. When Fearne makes a chance discovery she decides to start a happiness wish list, and an exciting new seed of hope is planted...

As Fearne steps out of her comfort zone and into the unknown, she starts to remember that happiness is a life lived in full bloom. Because isn't there always a chance your wishes might come true?

Praise for Cathy Bramley:
'A warm hug of a book'
Phillipa Ashley

Can she find her perfect fit?

Gina Moss is single and proud. She's focused on her thriving childminding business, which she runs from her cottage at the edge of The Evergreens: a charming Victorian home to three elderly residents who adore playing with the kids Gina minds. To Gina, they all feel like family. Then a run-in (literally) with a tall, handsome American stranger gives her the tummy-flutters...

But then a tragedy puts her older friends at risk of eviction — and Gina in charge of the battle to save them. The house sale brings her closer to Dexter, one of the owners — and the stranger who set her heart alight. As the sparks fly between them, Gina carries on fighting for her friends, her home and her business.

But can she fight for her chance at love — and win it all, too?

'A book full of warmth and kindness'

Sarah Morgan

Also By

Ivy Lane

Tilly Parker needs a fresh start, fresh air and a fresh attitude if she is ever to leave the past behind and move on. Seeking out peace and quiet in a new town, will Tilly learn to stop hiding amongst the sweetpeas and let people back into her life – and her heart?

Appleby Farm

Freya Moorcroft is happy with her life, but she still misses the beautiful Appleby Farm of her childhood. Discovering the farm is in serious financial trouble, Freya is determined to turn things around. But will saving Appleby Farm and following her heart come at a price?

Conditional Love

Sophie Stone's life is safe and predictable, just the way she likes it. But then a mysterious benefactor leaves her an inheritance, with one big catch: meet the father she has never seen. Will Sophie be able to build a future on her own terms – and maybe even find love along the way?

Wickham Hall

Holly Swift has landed her dream job: events co-ordinator at Wickham Hall. She gets to organize for a living, and it helps distract from her problems at home. But life isn't quite as easily organized as a Wickham Hall event. Can Holly learn to let go and live in the moment?

The Plumberry School Of Comfort Food

Verity Bloom hasn't been interested in cooking ever since she lost her best friend and baking companion two years ago. But when tragedy strikes at her friend's cookery school, can Verity find the magic ingredient to help, while still writing her own recipe for happiness?

White Lies And Wishes

When unlikely trio Jo, Sarah and Carrie meet by chance, they embark on a mission to make their wishes come true. But with hidden issues, hidden talents, and hidden demons, the new friends must admit what they really want if they are ever to get their happy endings...

The Lemon Tree Café

Finding herself unexpectedly jobless, Rosie Featherstone begins helping her beloved grandmother at the Lemon Tree Café. But when disaster looms for the café's fortunes, can Rosie find a way to save the Lemon Tree Café and help both herself and Nonna achieve the happy ending they deserve?

Hetty's Farmhouse Bakery

Hetty Greengrass holds her family together, but lately she's full of self-doubt. Taking part in a competition to find the very best produce might be just the thing she needs. But with cracks appearing and shocking secrets coming to light, Hetty must decide where her priorities really lie...

A Match Made In Devon

Nina has always dreamed of being a star, but after a series of very public blunders, she's forced to lay low in Devon. But soon Nina learns that even more drama can be found in a small village, and when a gorgeous man catches her eye, will Nina still want to return to the bright lights?

A Vintage Summer

Fed up with London, Lottie Allbright takes up the offer of a live-in job managing a local vineyard, Butterworth Wines, where a tragic death has left everyone at a loss. Lottie's determined to save the vineyard, but then she discovers something that will turn her summer – and her world – upside down...